Praise for *New York Times* bestselling author Diana Palmer

"Palmer proves that love and passion can be found even in the most dangerous situations."
—*Publishers Weekly* on *Untamed*

"You just can't do better than a Diana Palmer story to make your heart lighter and smile brighter."
—*Fresh Fiction* on *Wyoming Rugged*

"Diana Palmer is a mesmerizing storyteller who captures the essence of what a romance should be."
—*Affaire de Coeur*

"The popular Palmer has penned another winning novel, a perfect blend of romance and suspense."
—*Booklist* on *Lawman*

"Diana Palmer's characters leap off the page. She captures their emotions and scars beautifully and makes them come alive for readers."
—*RT Book Reviews* on *Lawless*

D0250085

Dear Reader,

I can't believe that it has been thirty years since my first Long, Tall Texan book, *Calhoun*, debuted! The series was suggested by my former editor, Tara Gavin, who asked if I might like to set stories in a fictional town of my own design. Would I! And the rest is history.

As the years went by, I found more and more sexy ranchers and cowboys to add to the collection. My readers (especially Amy!) found time to gift me with a notebook listing every single one of them, wives and kids and connections to other families in my own Texas town of Jacobsville. Eventually the town got a little too big for me, so I added another smaller town called Comanche Wells and began to fill it up, too.

You can't imagine how much pleasure this series has given me. I continue to add to the population of Jacobs County, Texas, and I have no plans to stop. Ever.

I hope all of you enjoy reading the Long, Tall Texans as much as I enjoy writing them. Thank you all for your kindness and loyalty and friendship. I am your biggest fan!

Love,

Diana Palmer

NEW YORK TIMES BESTSELLING AUTHOR

DIANA PALMER

WRANGLING THE RANCHER

2 Heartfelt Stories
Justin
and
Quinn (Previously published as *Sutton's Way*)

HARLEQUIN SPECIAL RELEASE

If you purchased this book without a cover you should be aware
that this book is stolen property. It was reported as "unsold and
destroyed" to the publisher, and neither the author nor the
publisher has received any payment for this "stripped book."

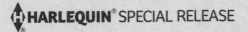 HARLEQUIN® SPECIAL RELEASE

Recycling programs
for this product may
not exist in your area.

ISBN-13: 978-1-335-49855-7

Wrangling the Rancher

Copyright © 2023 by Harlequin Enterprises ULC

Justin
First published in 1988.
This edition published in 2023.
Copyright © 1988 by Diana Palmer

Quinn
First published as Sutton's Way in 1989.
This edition published in 2023.
Copyright © 1989 by Diana Palmer

All rights reserved. No part of this book may be used or reproduced in
any manner whatsoever without written permission except in the case of
brief quotations embodied in critical articles and reviews.

This is a work of fiction. Names, characters, places and incidents
are either the product of the author's imagination or are used fictitiously.
Any resemblance to actual persons, living or dead, businesses,
companies, events or locales is entirely coincidental.

For questions and comments about the quality of this book,
please contact us at CustomerService@Harlequin.com.

Harlequin Enterprises ULC
22 Adelaide St. West, 41st Floor
Toronto, Ontario M5H 4E3, Canada
www.Harlequin.com

Printed in U.S.A.

CONTENTS

A prolific author of more than one hundred books, **Diana Palmer** got her start as a newspaper reporter. A *New York Times* bestselling author and voted one of the top ten romance writers in America, she has a gift for telling the most sensual tales with charm and humor. Diana lives with her family in Cornelia, Georgia. Visit her website at dianapalmer.com.

Books by Diana Palmer

Long, Tall Texans

Fearless
Heartless
Dangerous
Merciless
Courageous
Protector
Invincible
Untamed
Defender
Undaunted

The Wyoming Men

Wyoming Tough
Wyoming Fierce
Wyoming Bold
Wyoming Strong
Wyoming Rugged
Wyoming Brave

Morcai Battalion

The Morcai Battalion
The Morcai Battalion: The Recruit
The Morcai Battalion: Invictus
The Morcai Battalion: The Rescue

Visit the Author Profile page
at Harlequin.com for more titles.

JUSTIN

To the editors at Silhouette Books,
with love.

CHAPTER ONE

IT WAS A warm morning, and the weatherman had already promised temperatures into the eighties for the afternoon. But the weather didn't seem to slow down the bidders, and the auctioneer standing on the elegant porch of the tall white mansion kept his monotone steady even though he had to periodically wipe streams of sweat from his heavily jowled face.

As he watched the estate auction, Justin Ballenger's black eyes narrowed under the brim of his expensive creamy Stetson. He wasn't buying. Not today. But he had a personal interest in this particular auction. The Jacobs's home was being sold, lock, stock and barrel, and he should have felt a sense of triumph at seeing old Bass Jacobs's legacy go down the drain. Oddly enough, he didn't. He felt vaguely disturbed by the whole proceeding. It was like watching predators pick a helpless victim to the bone.

He kept searching the crowd for Shelby Jacobs, but she was nowhere in sight. Possibly she and her brother, Tyler, were in the house, helping to sort the furniture and other antique offerings.

A movement to his left caught his eye. Abby Ballenger, his sister-in-law of six weeks, stood beside him.

"I didn't expect to see you here," she remarked, smiling up at him. She'd lived with him and Calhoun, her almost-stepbrothers, since the tragic deaths of their father and her mother. Their parents were to have been married, so the brothers took Abby in and looked after her. And just weeks before, she and Calhoun had married.

"I never miss an auction," he replied. He looked toward the auctioneer. "I haven't seen the Jacobses."

"Ty's in Arizona." Abby sighed, and she didn't miss the sudden glare of Justin's dark eyes. "He didn't go without a fight, either, but there was some kind of emergency on that ranch he's helping to manage."

"Shelby's alone?" The words were almost wrenched from him.

"Afraid so." Abby glanced up at him and away, barely suppressing a smile. "She's at the apartment she's rented in town." Abby smoothed a fold of her gray skirt. "It's above the law office where she works…"

Justin's hard, dark face went even tauter. The smoking cigarette in his hand was forgotten as he turned to Abby, his whipcord-lean body towering over her. "That isn't an apartment, for God's sake, it's an old storeroom!"

"Barry Holman is letting her convert it," Abby said, her guileless pale eyes the picture of innocence under her dark hair. "She doesn't have much choice, Justin. With the house being sold, where else can she afford to live on what she makes? Everything had to go, you know. Tyler and Shelby thought they could at least hold onto the house and property, but it took every last dime to meet their father's debts."

Justin muttered something under his breath, glaring toward the big, elegant house that somehow embodied everything he'd hated about the Jacobs family for the past six years, since Shelby had broken their engagement and betrayed him.

"Aren't you glad?" Abby baited him gently. "You hate her, after all. It should please you to see her brought to her knees in public."

He didn't say another word. He turned abruptly, his expression as uncompromising as stone, and strode to where his black Thunderbird was parked. Abby smiled secretively. She'd thought that he'd react, if she could make him see how badly this was going to hurt Shelby. All these long years he'd avoided any contact with the Jacobs family, any mention of them at home. But in recent months, the strain was beginning to tell on him. Abby knew almost certainly that he still felt something for the woman who'd jilted him, and she knew Shelby felt something for Justin, too. Abby, deliriously happy in her own marriage, wanted the rest of the world to be as happy as she was. Perhaps by nudging Justin in the right direction, she might make two miserable people happy.

Justin had only found out about the estate sale that morning, when Calhoun mentioned it at the office at their joint feedlot operation. It had been in the papers, but Justin had been out of town looking at cattle and he hadn't seen the notice.

He wasn't surprised that Shelby was staying away from the auction. She'd been born in that house. She'd lived in it all her life. Shelby's grandfather, in fact, had founded the small Texas town of Jacobsville. They were old money, and the ragged little Ballenger boys from the run-down cattle ranch down the road weren't the kind of friends Mrs. Bass Jacobs had wanted for her children, Tyler and Shelby. But she'd died, and Mr. Jacobs had been friendly toward the Ballengers, especially when Justin and Calhoun had opened their feedlot. And when the old man found out that Shelby intended to marry Justin Ballenger, he'd told Justin he couldn't be more pleased.

Justin tried never to think about the night Bass Jacobs and young Tom Wheelor had come to see him. Now it all came back. Bass Jacobs had been upset. He told Justin outright that Shelby was in love with Tom and not only in love, the couple had been sleeping together all through the farce of Shelby's "engagement" to Justin. He was ashamed of her, Bass lamented. The engagement was Shelby's way of bringing her reluctant suitor into line, and now that Justin had served his purpose, Shelby didn't need him anymore. Sadly, he handed Justin Shelby's engagement ring and Tom Wheelor had mumbled a red-faced apology. Bass had even cried. Perhaps his shame had prompted his next move, because he'd promised on the spot to give Justin the financial backing he needed to make the new feedlot a success. There was only one condition—that Shelby never know where the money came from. Then he'd left.

Never one to believe ill of anyone without hard evidence, Justin phoned Shelby while Bass was still starting his car. But she didn't deny what Justin had been told. In fact, she confirmed all of it, even the part about having slept with Wheelor. She'd only wanted to make Tom jealous so he'd propose, she told Justin. She hoped he hadn't been too upset with her, but then, she'd always had everything she wanted, and Justin wasn't rich enough to cater to her tastes just yet. But Tom was...

Justin had believed her. And because she'd pushed him away the one time he'd tried to make love to her, her confession rang with the truth. He'd gone on a legendary bender afterward. And for the past six years, no other woman had ever gotten close enough to make a dent in his heart. He'd been impervious to all the offers, and there had been some. He wasn't a handsome man. His dark face was too craggy, his features too irregular, his unsmiling countenance too forbidding. But he had wealth and power, and that drew women to him. He was too bitter, though, to accept that kind of attention. Shelby had hurt him as no one else in his life ever had, and for years all he'd lived for was the thought of vengeance.

But now that he saw her brought to her knees financially, it was unsatisfying. All he could think of was that she was going to be hurt and she had no family, no friends to comfort her.

The apartment above the law office where she worked was tiny, and it didn't sit well with him that it was in such proximity to her bachelor boss. He knew Holman by reputation, and rumor had it that he liked pretty women. Shelby, with her long black hair, slender figure and green, sparkling eyes, would more than qualify. She was twenty-seven now, hardly a girl, but she didn't look much older than she had when she and Justin became engaged. She had an innocence about her, still, that made Justin grind his teeth. It was false; she'd even admitted it.

He paused at the door to the apartment, his hand raised to knock. There was a muffled noise from inside. Not laughter. Tears?

His jaw tautened and he knocked roughly.

The noise ceased abruptly. There was a scraping sound, like a chair being moved, and soft footsteps that echoed the quick, hard beat of his heart.

The door opened. Shelby stood there, in clinging faded jeans and a blue checked shirt, her long dark hair disheveled and curling down her back, her green eyes red-rimmed and wet.

"Did you come to gloat, Justin?" she asked with quiet bitterness.

"It gives me no pleasure to see you humbled," he replied, his chin lifted, his black eyes narrow. "Abby said you were alone."

She sighed, dropping her eyes to his dusty, worn boots. "I've been alone for a long time. I've learned to live with it." She shifted restlessly. "Are there a lot of people at the auction?"

"The yard's full," he said. He took off his hat and held it in one hand while the other raked his thick, straight black hair.

She looked up, her eyes lingering helplessly on the hard lines of his craggy face, on the chiseled mouth she'd kissed so hungrily six years ago. She'd been so desperately in love with him then. But he'd become something out of her slight experience the night they became engaged, and his ardor had frightened her. She'd fought away from him, and the memory of how it had been with him, just before the fear became tangible, was formidable. She'd wanted so much more than they'd shared, but she had more reason than most women to fear intimacy. But Justin didn't know that and she'd been too shy to explain her actions.

She turned away with a groan of anguish. "If you can bear my company, I'll fix you a glass of iced tea."

He hesitated, but only for an instant. "I could use that," he said quietly. "It's hot as hell out there."

He followed her inside, absently closing the door behind him. But he stopped dead when he saw what she was having to contend with. He stiffened and almost cursed out loud.

There were only two rooms in the makeshift apartment. They were bare except for a worn sofa and chair, a scratched coffee table and a small television set. Her clothes were apparently being kept in a closet, because there was no evidence of a dresser. The kitchen boasted a toaster oven and a hot plate and a tiny refrigerator. This, when she was used to servants and silk robes, silver services and Chippendale furniture.

"My God," he breathed.

Her back stiffened, but she didn't turn when she heard the pity in his deep voice. "I don't need sympathy, thank you," she said tightly. "It wasn't my fault that we lost the place, it was my father's. It was his to lose. I can make my own way in the world."

"Not like this, damn it!" He slammed his hat down on the coffee table and took the pitcher of tea out of her hands, moving it aside. His lean, work-roughened hands held her wrists and he stared down at her with determination. "I won't stand by and watch you try to survive in a rattrap like this. Barry Holman and his charity be damned!"

Shelby was shocked, not only by what he was saying, but by the way he looked. "It's not a rattrap," she faltered.

"Compared to what you were used to, it is," he returned doggedly. His chest rose and fell on an angry sigh. "You can stay with me for the time being."

She blushed beet-red. "In your house, alone with you?"

He lifted his chin. "In my house," he agreed. "*Not* in my bed. You won't have to pay me for a roof over your head. I do remember with vivid clarity that you don't like my hands on you."

She could have gone through the floor at the bitter mockery in the words. She couldn't meet those black eyes or challenge the flat statement without embarrassing them both. Anyway, it was so long ago. It didn't matter now.

She looked at his shirt instead, at the thick mat of black hair under the white silk. He'd let her touch him there, once. The night of their engagement, he'd unbuttoned it and given her hands free license to do what they liked. He'd kissed her as if he'd die to kiss her, but he'd frightened her half out of her mind when the kisses went a little too far.

Until that night, he'd never tried to touch her, or gone further than brief, light kisses. His holding back had first disturbed her and then made her curious. Surely Justin was as experienced as his brother, Calhoun. But perhaps he'd had hang-ups about the distance between their social standing. Justin had been barely middle class at the time, and Shelby's family was wealthy. It hadn't mattered to her, but she could see that it might have bothered Justin. And especially after she jilted him, because of her father's treacherous insistence.

She'd gotten even with her father, though. He'd planned for her to marry Tom Wheelor, in a cold-blooded merger of property, and Justin had gotten in the way. But Shelby had refused Tom Wheelor's advances and she'd never let him touch her. She'd told Bass Jacobs she wouldn't marry his wealthy young friend. The old man hadn't capitulated then, but just before his death, when he realized how desperately Shelby loved Justin, he'd felt bad about what he'd done. He hadn't told her that his guilt had driven him to stake Justin's feedlot, but he'd apologized.

She looked up then, searching Justin's dark eyes quietly, remembering. It had been hard, going on without him. Her dreams of loving him and bearing his sons had died long ago, but it was still a pleasure beyond bearing just to look at him. And his hands on her wrists made her body glow, tingle with forbidden longings, like the warm threat of his powerful, cologne-scented body. If only her father hadn't interfered. Inevitably, she'd have been able to explain her fears to Justin, to ask him to be gentle, to go slow. But it was too late now.

"I know you don't want me anymore, Justin," she said gently. "I even understand why. You don't need to feel responsible for me. I'll be all right. I can take care of myself."

He breathed slowly, trying to keep himself under control. The feel of her silky skin was giving him some problems. Unwillingly, his thumbs began to caress her wrists.

"I know that," he said. "But you don't belong here."

"I can't afford a better apartment just yet," she said. "But I'll get a raise when I've been working for two months, and then maybe I can get the room that Abby had at Mrs. Simpson's."

"You can get it now," he said tersely. "I'll loan you the money."

She lowered her eyes. "No. It wouldn't look right."

"Only you and I would know."

She bit her lower lip. She couldn't tell him that she hated the thought of being in this place, so near Barry Holman, who was a nice boss but a hopeless womanizer. She hesitated.

Before she could say yes or no, there was a knock on the door. Justin let her go reluctantly and watched her move toward the door.

Barry Holman stood there, in jeans and a sweat-shirt, blond and blue-eyed and hopeful. "Hi, Shelby," he said pleasantly. "I thought you might need some help moving…in." His voice trailed away and he saw Justin standing behind her.

"Not really," Justin said with a cold smile. "She's on her way over to Mrs. Simpson's to take on Abby's old room. I'm helping her move, although I knew she appre-ciated the offer of this—" he looked around distastefully "—apartment."

Barry Holman swallowed. He'd known Justin for a long time, and he was just about convinced that the rumors he'd heard were true. Justin might not want Shelby himself, but he was damned visible if anybody else made a pass at her.

"Well," he said, still smiling, "I'd better get back downstairs then. I had some calls to make. Good to see you again, Justin. See you early Monday morn-ing, Shelby."

"Thanks anyway, Mr. Holman," she said. "I don't want to seem ungrateful, but Mrs. Simpson offers meals as well, and it's peaceful there." She smiled. "I'm not used to town living, and Mrs. Simpson has the room free right now…"

"No hard feelings, you go right ahead." Barry grinned. "So long."

Justin glared after him. "Lover boy," he muttered. "Just what you need."

She turned, her eyes soft on his face. "I'm twenty-seven," she said. "I want to marry and have children eventually. Mr. Holman is very nice, and he doesn't have any bad habits."

"Except that he'll sleep with anything that wears skirts," he replied tersely. He didn't like thinking about Shelby having another man's children. His black eyes searched over her body. Yes, she was getting older, not that she looked it. In eight or ten years, children might be a risk for her. His expression hardened.

"He's never said anything improper to me." She faltered, confused by the way he was looking at her.

"Give him time." He drew in a slow breath. "I said I'll loan you enough to get the room at Mrs. Simpson's. If you're hell-bent on independence, you can pay me back at your convenience."

She had to swallow her pride, and it hurt to let him help her when she knew how bitter he was about the past. But he was a caring man, and she was a stray person in the world. Justin's heart was too big to allow him to turn his back on her, even after what he thought she'd done to him. Quick, hot tears sprang to her green eyes as she remembered what she'd been forced to say to him, the way she'd hurt him.

"I'm so sorry," she said unexpectedly, biting her lip as she turned away.

The words, and the emotion behind them, surprised him. Surely she didn't have any regrets this late. Or was she just putting on an act to get his sympathy? He couldn't trust her.

She got herself back together and brushed at the loose hair at her neck as she poured the tea into two glasses filled with ice. "I'll let you lend me the money, if you really don't mind," she said, handing him his glass without looking up. "I don't like the idea of living alone."

"Neither do I, Shelby, but it's something you get used

to after a while," he said quietly. He sipped his tea, but he couldn't pry his eyes away from her soft oval face. "What is it like, having to work for a living?"

She didn't react to the mockery in the words. She smiled. "I like it," she said surprisingly, and lifted her eyes to his. "I had things to do, you know, when we had money. I belonged to a lot of volunteer groups and charities. But law offices cater to unhappy people. When I can help them feel a little better, it makes me forget my own problems."

His black brows drew together as he sipped the cool, sweet amber liquid. The glass was cold under his lean fingers.

She searched his black eyes. "You don't believe me, do you, Justin?" she asked perceptively. "You saw me as a socialite, a reasonably attractive woman with money and a cultured background. But that was an illusion. You never really knew me."

"I wanted you, though," he replied, watching her. "But you never wanted me, honey. Not physically, at any rate."

"You rushed me!" she burst out, coloring as she remembered that night.

"Rushed you! Up until that night, I hadn't even kissed you intimately, for God's sake!" His black eyes glittered at her as he remembered her rejection and his own sick certainty that she didn't love him. "I'd kept you on a pedestal until then. And all the time, you were sleeping with that boy millionaire!"

She threw up her hands. "I never slept with Tom Wheelor!"

"You said you did," he reminded her with a cold smile. "You swore it, in fact."

She closed her eyes on a wave of bitter regret. "Yes, I said it," she agreed wearily, and turned away. "I'd almost forgotten."

"And all the postmortems accomplish nothing, do they?" he asked. He put down the glass and pulled out a cigarette, lighting it without removing his eyes from her stiff expression. "It doesn't matter anymore. Let's go. I'll run over to Mrs. Simpson's and you can see about the room."

Shelby knew that he'd never give an inch. He hadn't forgotten anything and he still despised her. She felt as if the world was sitting on her thin shoulders as she got her purse and followed him to the door. She didn't look at him as they left.

CHAPTER TWO

JUSTIN TUCKED A wad of bills into Shelby's purse when he stopped the Thunderbird on the side of the road near Mrs. Simpson's house. She tried to protest, but he simply smoked his cigarette and ignored her.

"I told you earlier that the money was between you and me," he said quietly, his dark eyes challenging as he cut the engine. He turned in the bucket seat, his long legs stretched out as he touched the power-window switch on the console panel. It was a rural road, and sparsely traveled. He had stopped under a spreading oak tree. He hooked his elbow on the open window to study Shelby narrowly. "I meant it. If you want to look on it as a loan, that's up to you."

She chewed on her lower lip. "I'll be able to pay you back one day," she said doggedly, even though she knew better. With what she made, it was going to be a struggle to eat and pay the rent. New clothes might become impossible.

"I'm not worried about it."

"Yes, but I am." She looked up, all her misgivings in her green eyes. "Oh, Justin, what am I going to do?" she moaned. "I'm alone for the first time in my life. Ty's in Arizona, I have no family..." She got a grip on herself, averting her eyes. "It's just panic," she said tightly. "Just fear. I'll get used to it. I'm sorry I said that."

He didn't speak. He'd never seen Shelby helpless. She'd always been poised and calm. It was new and faintly disturbing to see her frightened.

"If things get too rough," he replied quietly, "you can move in with me."

She laughed hollowly. "That would do our reputations a world of good."

He blew out a cloud of smoke. "If gossip bothers you all that much, we can get married." He said it carelessly, but his eyes were sharp on her face.

She knew she wasn't breathing. She looked at him as the old wounds opened with a vengeance. "Why?" she asked.

He didn't want to answer her. He didn't want to admit, even to himself, that he was still vulnerable. He shrugged. "You need a place to stay. I'm tired of living alone. Since Abby and Calhoun moved out, the damned house is like a mausoleum."

"You feel sorry for me," she accused.

He took another draw from the cigarette. "Maybe I do. So what? Right now you don't have many options. Either you borrow from me to afford Mrs. Simpson's boarding house, or you marry me." He studied the tip of the cigarette. "Of course, you can always go back to that converted storeroom over Barry Holman's office and show him that you're available—"

"You stop that," she muttered. She shifted restlessly. "Mr. Holman isn't that kind of man. And you have no reason to feel possessive about me."

"Haven't I?" His black eyes searched hers. "But I am, just the same. And I remember your saying the same thing about me. We were engaged once, Shelby. That kind of involvement doesn't go away."

"Some involvement," she said with a tired sigh. "I never could decide why you wanted to marry me."

"You were a feather in my cap," he said coldly, lying through his teeth. "A rich sophisticate. I was just a country boy with stars in my eyes, and you took me for a hell of a ride, lady. Now it's my turn. I've got money and you haven't." His dark eyes narrowed. "And don't think I want to marry you out of some lingering passion."

He hadn't forgotten. It was in his eyes, his whole look. He'd marry her and make her hunger for a love he'd never felt, couldn't feel for her. He held her in contempt because he thought she'd slept with Tom Wheelor, and that was the biggest joke of all. She was still a virgin, and wouldn't it throw a stick into his spokes to find that out the hard way?

"No." She sighed, belatedly answering his question. "I'm not stupid enough to think you still want me, after what I did to your pride." She lifted her eyes to study the proud, arrogant set of his dark head, his eyes shadowed by the Stetson he always wore. "I used to think you cared for me a little, even though you never said you did."

That was the truth. She'd never really been sure why he wanted to marry her. Except for that one night, he hadn't been wild to try to get her into bed, and he'd never seemed emotionally involved, either. But she'd been so in love with him that she had not realized how relatively uninvolved he'd seemed until after their engagement had been broken.

He ignored her remarks. "If you want security, I can give it to you," he said quietly. "I've got money now, although I'll never be in the same class as your father was. He had millions."

She closed her eyes on a wave of shame. She had her father and her own naïveté to thank for Justin's bitterness. But Justin wanted revenge and she'd be a fool to deliver herself on a silver platter to him. "No, Justin. I can't marry you," she said after a minute. Her hand reached for the door handle. "It was a crazy idea!" She averted her face so that all he could see of it was her profile.

He put his hand over hers briefly, holding it, and then withdrew his fingers almost as quickly. His expression hardened. "It's a big house," he said. "With Calhoun and Abby living down the road, there's only Lopez and Maria living with me. You wouldn't need to work if you didn't want to, and you'd have security."

He was offering her heaven, except that it was impersonal on his part. More than anything else, he felt sorry for her. But under the pity was a darker need; she could feel it. Something in him wanted revenge for her rejection six years ago. His pride wanted restitution. Well, didn't she owe him that, she wondered bitterly, after what her father had cost him? And she'd be near him. She'd have meals with him. She could sit with him in the evenings while he watched television. She could sleep under the same roof. Her hungry heart wanted that, so badly. Too badly.

"I don't guess you'd… I don't suppose you'd ever want a…" She couldn't even say it. *A child,* she was thinking, although God only knew how she'd manage to deal with what had to happen to produce one.

"I won't want a divorce," he said, misunderstanding her thoughts. His eyes narrowed. "I'm not exactly Mr. America, in case you haven't noticed. And I don't want a woman I have to buy, unless it's on my terms."

That sounded suspiciously like a dig at her, because she'd refused him for what he thought was a lack of money. Her eyes lifted to his. "Do you still hate me, Justin?" she asked; she needed to know.

He stared at her without speaking for a long moment, quietly smoking his cigarette. "I'm not sure what I feel."

That reply was honest enough, even if it wasn't a declaration of undying love. There were so many wounds between them, so much bitterness. It was probably an insane thing to do, but she couldn't resist the temptation.

She stared at his cigarette instead of at him. "I'll marry you, then, if you mean it."

He didn't move, but something inside him went wild at the words. She couldn't know how many nights he'd spent aching for just the sight of her, how desperately he wanted her near him. But he could never trust her again, and that was the hell of it. She was just a stray person, he told himself. Just someone who needed help. He had to think of her that way, and not want the moon. She might even play up to him out of gratitude, so he'd have to be on his guard every minute. But, oh, God, he wanted her so!

"Then we don't need to see Mrs. Simpson until we've had time to make plans." He started the car, pulled out onto the road and turned the Thunderbird toward the feedlot and his house. His hands had a perceptible tremor. He gripped the steering wheel hard to keep Shelby from seeing how her answer affected him.

If Maria and Lopez were shocked to see Shelby with Justin, they didn't say anything. Lopez vanished into the kitchen while Maria fussed over Shelby, bringing coffee and pastries into the living room where Justin sprawled in his armchair and Shelby perched nervously on the edge of the sofa.

"Thank you, Maria," Shelby said with a warm smile.

The Mexican woman smiled back. "It is my pleasure, *señorita*. I will be in the kitchen if you need me, *señor,*" she added to Justin before she went out, discreetly closing the door behind her.

Shelby noticed that Justin didn't comment on Maria's obvious conclusions. Perhaps Maria thought he might want to wrestle her down onto the sofa, but Shelby knew better. Justin had done that once, and only once. And she'd been so frightened that she'd reacted stupidly. She'd never forgiven herself for that. Justin had probably thought she found his ardor distasteful, and that was the last thing it had been.

She sighed, lowering her eyes to his black boots. They weren't working boots; they were the ones he wore when he dressed up. He had such big feet and hands. She smiled, remembering how it had been when they'd first started dating. They'd been like children, fascinated with each other's company, both of them a little shy and reserved. It had never gone beyond kisses except the night they got engaged.

"I said, do you want some coffee?" Justin repeated pointedly, holding the silver coffeepot over a cup he'd just filled.

"Oh. Yes, thank you." She took it black, and apparently he remembered her preference, because he didn't offer her any cream or sugar. He poured his own cup full, put a dash of cream in it and sat back with the china cup and saucer balanced on his crossed knee.

Shelby glanced at him and wondered how she could contemplate living under the same roof with him. He was so unapproachable. Obviously he wanted revenge. She'd be a fool to give him that much rope to hang her with.

On the other hand, if she was living with him, she had a better chance than ever of changing his mind about her. All she really had to do to prove her innocence was to get him into bed. But that was the whole problem. She was scared to death of intimacy.

"Why the blush?" he asked, watching her.

She cleared her throat. "It's warm in here," she said.

"Is it?" He laughed mirthlessly and sipped his coffee. "In case you wondered, you'll have your own room. I won't expect any repayment for giving you a home."

The blush went scarlet. She had to fight not to fling her cup at him. "You're making me sound like a charity case."

"I'll bet that rankles," he agreed. "But Tyler can't help you and hold down a job at the same time. And you'll never make it on what Holman pays you, with all due respect to him. Secretaries in small towns don't make much."

"I'm not mercenary," she said defensively.

"Sure," he replied. He sipped his coffee without another word.

"Listen, Justin, it was all my father's idea, that fake engagement to Tom Wheelor—"

"Your father would never have done that to me," he interrupted coldly, and his eyes went black, threatening as he leaned forward. "Don't try to use him for a scapegoat just because he's dead. He was one of the best friends I had."

That's what you think, she mused bitterly. Obviously it wasn't going to do any good to talk to him. Just because her father had put on a show of liking him was no reason to put the man on a pedestal. God only knew why Justin had such respect for a man who'd caused him years of bitter humiliation.

"You'll never trust me again, will you?" she asked softly.

He studied her lovely face, her pale green eyes staring at him, her gaze burning into his soul. "No," he replied with the honesty that was as much a part of him as his craggy face and thick black hair. "There's too much water under the bridge. But if you think I'm nursing a broken heart, don't. I found you out just a little too soon. My pride suffered, but you never touched my heart."

"I don't imagine any woman ever got close enough to do that," she said, her voice soft. She traced the rim of the china cup. "Abby told me once that you haven't dated anyone for a long time."

"I'm thirty-seven years old," he reminded her. "I sowed my wild oats years ago, even before I started going with you." He finished his coffee and put the cup down. His black eyes met hers in a direct gaze. "And we both know that you've sown yours, and who with."

"You don't know me at all, Justin," she said. "You never did. You said I was a status symbol to you, and looking back, I guess I was, at that." She laughed bitterly. "You used to take me around to your friends to show me off, and I felt like one of those purebred horses Ty used to take to the steeplechase."

He stared at her over his smoking cigarette. "I took you around because you were pretty and sweet, and I liked being with you," he said heavily. "That was a lot of garbage about wanting you for a status symbol."

She leaned back wearily. "Thank you for telling me," she said. "But I guess it doesn't matter now, does it?" She finished her coffee and put the cup down. "Are we going to have a church wedding?" she asked.

"Aren't we a little old for that kind of ceremony?" he asked.

"I can see you're still eating live rattlesnakes to keep your venom potent," she said without flinching. "I want a church wedding."

He dusted the long ash from his cigarette into an ashtray. "It would be quicker to go to a justice of the peace."

"I'm not pregnant," she reminded him, averting her self-conscious face. "There's no great rush, is there?"

She was tying him up in knots. He glared at her. "All right, have your church wedding. You can stay at Mrs. Simpson's until we're married, just to keep everything discreet." His dark eyes narrowed as he got up and crushed out his cigarette. "There's just one thing. Don't you come down that aisle in a white dress. If you dare, I'll walk out the front door of the church and keep going."

She lifted her chin. "Don't you know what every woman in the congregation will think?"

The soft accusation in her green eyes made him feel guilty. He was still hurt by Shelby's affair with Tom Wheelor. He'd wanted to sting her, but he hadn't counted on the wounded look in her eyes.

"You can wear something cream-colored," he muttered reluctantly.

Her lower lip trembled. "Take me to bed." Her eyes dared him, even though she went scarlet and shuddered at her own boldness. "If you think I'm lying about being innocent, I can prove I'm telling the truth!"

His black eyes cut back to hers, unblinking. "You know as well as I do that it takes a doctor to establish virginity. Even an experienced man can't tell."

Her face colored. She could have told him that in her case, it would be more than normally evident, and that her doctor could so easily settle all his doubts. She started to, despite her embarrassment at discussing such an intimate subject, but before she could open her mouth, there was a quick knock at the door and Lopez came in with a message for Justin.

"I've got some cattle out in the road," he told Shelby. "Come on. I'll run you over to Mrs. Simpson's first. You can call Abby and make plans for the wedding. She'll be glad to help with the invitations and such."

She didn't even argue. She was too drained. They were going to be married, but he was going to see to it that she was publicly disgraced, like an adultress being paraded through the streets.

Her teeth ground together as they went out to the car. Well, she'd get around him somehow. She wasn't going to wear anything except a white gown to walk down that aisle. And if he left her standing there, all right. Maybe he didn't even mean what he'd said. She had to keep believing that, for the sake of her pride. He didn't know, and she'd hurt him badly. But, oh, how different things had been six years ago.

Shelby had known the Ballengers all her life. Ty, her brother, and Calhoun, Justin's brother, were friends. That meant that she naturally saw Justin from time to time. At first he'd been cold and very standoffish, but Shelby had thought of him as a challenge. She'd started teasing him gently, flirting shyly. And the change in him had been devastating.

They'd gone to a Halloween party at a mutual friend's, and someone had handed Shelby a guitar. To Justin's amazement, she'd played it easily, trying to slow down enough to adjust to the rather inept efforts of their host, who was learning to play lead guitar.

Without a word, Justin had perched himself on a chair beside her and held out his hand. Their host, with a grin that Shelby hadn't understood at the time, gave the instrument to Justin. He nodded to Shelby, tapped out the meter with his booted foot and launched into a rendition of *San Antonio Rose* that brought the house down.

After the first shock wore off, Shelby's long, graceful fingers caught up the rhythm and seconded him to perfection. He looked into her eyes as they wound to a finish, and he smiled. And at that moment, Shelby gave him her heart.

It wasn't a sudden thing, really. She'd known for years how kind he was. He'd just taken Abby in and given her a home when the girl's mother and Mr. Ballenger had died in a tragic car wreck. Justin was always around when someone needed a helping hand, and there wasn't a more generous or harder working man in Jacobsville. He had a temper, too, but he controlled it most of the time, and his men respected him because he didn't ask them to do anything he wasn't willing to do himself. He was the boss, along with Calhoun, but Justin was always the first to arrive and the last to leave when there was a job to be done. He had many admirable qualities, and Shelby was young and impressionable, and just at the right age to fall hopelessly in love with an older man.

After that night, she seemed to see Justin everywhere. At the restaurant where she had lunch with a friend on Tuesdays and Thursdays, at social events, at charity bazaars, where she went riding on trails that wound near the Ballenger property. It didn't occur to her to wonder why such a reclusive, hard-working man suddenly had so much free time and spent it at places she was known to frequent. She was in love, and every second spent with Justin fed her hungry heart.

She hadn't thought he was interested in her at first. They had a lot in common, despite their very different backgrounds, and he seemed to enjoy talking to her.

Then, very suddenly, everything changed. They were walking down the trail, near where they'd tied their horses, and Justin had suddenly stopped walking to lean against a tree. He didn't say a word, but the expression in his eyes spoke volumes. He had a smoking cigarette in one hand, but he held out the other one to Shelby.

Shelby didn't know what to expect when she took it. Her heart was hammering and she looked at his mouth and wanted it obsessively. Perhaps he knew that, but he didn't take advantage of it.

He pulled her closer. Only their hands were touching. Then, his black eyes searching her soft green ones, he bent slowly, giving her all the time in the world to pull back, to hesitate, to show him that she didn't want him.

But she did. She stood very still as his hard lips brushed hers, her eyes open, watching him. He lifted his head and searched her eyes.

He dropped the cigarette and ground it out under his boot while her heart went crazy. His arms slid around her, bringing her against him but not intimately. He bent again and kissed her with tenderness and respect, with soft wonder. She kissed him back the same way, her arms around his shoulders, her mind sinking into layers of pleasure.

He drew back a minute later and let her go without a word. He took her hand in his and they started walking.

"Do you want a big wedding, or will a civil service

do?" he asked as easily as if they were discussing the weather.

And just that quickly they were engaged. That night they went back to her house and told her father. Although his first expression was explosive, they didn't see it. He turned away long enough to compose himself, and then he made happy conversation and welcomed Justin into the family. Justin took Shelby home to share the news with Calhoun and Abby, but Abby was spending the night with a girlfriend and Calhoun had flown to Oklahoma to see a man on business.

They'd had the house to themselves. Shelby remembered so vividly how they'd laughed and toasted their future happiness. Then he'd drawn her to him and kissed her in a very different way, and she'd blushed at the intimacy of his tongue probing delicately inside her lips.

"We're going to be married," he'd whispered with open delight at her innocence. "I won't hurt you."

"I know." She buried her face in his white silk shirt. "But it's so new, being like this with you."

"It's new for me, too," he breathed. His chest rose and fell heavily. He moved her hands a little to the side of the buttons on his shirt and pressed them hard against him while he flipped buttons out of buttonholes and then guided her fingers to the thick mat of hair that covered his muscular, suntanned chest.

"Now," he breathed. "Touch me, Shelby."

She was shocked at this new intimacy, but when he bent and took her mouth under his, she forgot the shock and relaxed against him. Her fingers curled, liking the feel of him, the smell of him that lingered like spice in her nostrils.

"Harder," he whispered roughly. He pressed her hands closer and when she looked up, there was an expression in his eyes that she'd never seen in the weeks they'd been going together. Something wild and out of control was visible there. She trembled a little at that glimpse of desire she hadn't expected to find in such a controlled man.

Then his hand went under her nape, lifting her up to his mouth, and he took her lips in brief, biting kisses that had an unexpected, unbelievable effect on her. She moaned helplessly, frightened at the new sensations.

But to Justin, a moan had a totally different meaning. He thought she was as immersed in pleasure as he was, and his mouth grew suddenly invasive, insistent. His hands dropped to Shelby's slender hips and suddenly lifted her against him into an embrace that shocked her senseless.

She knew very little about men and intimacy, but the changed contours of Justin's hard body told her graphically what he was feeling. He groaned into her mouth as he moved against her in blatant arousal.

She struggled, but he was strong and half out of his mind with unbridled passion. He didn't realize that she was trying to get away until she dragged her mouth away from his and pushed at him, begging him to stop.

He lifted his head, breathing roughly, his eyes black with frustration.

"Shelby..." he ground out in agony.

"Let me go!" she moaned. "Please... Justin, don't!"

"I'll stop before we go all the way," he whispered against her mouth, and bent to kiss her again. Her protests muffled under his warm, drugging mouth, he lifted her off the floor and carried her to the sofa, putting her down gently, full-length, on its soft cushions.

He shuddered with unbearable need, his mouth rough as it pressed against hers. His body slid over her, pushing her into the cushions, heavy and hard and intimate. She felt his sudden loss of control with real fear. She knew what could happen, and that they were engaged. He might not try very hard to stop.

"Justin!"

"I'm not going to take your chastity, Shelby," he breathed into her mouth. His brows drew together in agonized pleasure as his hands slid over her hips. "Oh, God, honey, don't hold back with me. Let me love you. Kiss me back…"

The words died against her soft mouth. He kissed her with growing hunger, his loss of control evident in the urgent movement of his hips against hers, his hands suddenly searching as they moved over her soft breasts. Then his knee moved between her legs and she panicked.

She began to fight him, afraid of the unfamiliar intimacy that was beyond her experience. She pushed at him. All at once, he seemed to feel her resistance. He lifted his head, his eyes blazing with black hunger, and just stared at her for an instant, disoriented. Then when he saw the rejection, felt it in the stiffness of her body, he suddenly tore away from her and got to his feet. By the time she was able to breathe again, he was standing several feet away smoking a cigarette. Several tense minutes passed before he turned around again to pour brandy into two snifters. He gave her one and smiled mockingly at the way she avoided touching him.

He turned away from her to stare out the window

while he sipped his brandy. His back was ramrod stiff. "We'll sleep together when we're married," he said. "I hope you know that I don't plan on separate rooms."

"I know." She sipped her own drink with shaking hands, wanting to explain, but his attitude was hardly welcoming. "Justin... I'm a virgin."

"Don't you think I knew that?" he asked tersely. He looked at her and his expression was a cold and totally unreadable mask, hiding emotions she couldn't even guess at. "My God, we're going to be married. Do I have to stop touching you altogether until the ring's on your finger?"

She started to speak and lowered her eyes to her glass. She stiffened. "Perhaps...it might be wiser."

"Considering my lack of control, I suppose you mean." He said it icily, in a tone she'd never heard him use. He drank his brandy and after a while, the anger seemed to go out of him, to Shelby's relief. He didn't apologize, but he went to her and took her hand gently, smiling at her as if nothing at all had happened. They drank brandy, and he taught her a Mexican drinking song as the aftereffects of the evening and the potency of the aged brandy began to work on them. Maria and Lopez had chanced to come home then from a party and Justin had taken Shelby home. Maria had been raging at him in Spanish, and Shelby only found out later that the song he'd been teaching her wasn't one she could ever sing in public.

She'd looked forward to the wedding with joy and also with apprehension. Justin's passion had unsettled her and made her doubt her ability to match him. He was experienced and she wasn't, and she was more afraid than ever of having him make love to her when he was totally out of control.

But there was no cause for alarm, because there was no more heated lovemaking. The most ardent move he made for days afterward was to kiss her cheek or hold hands with her, and all the while, those black eyes wandered over her with the strangest searching expression. She relaxed and began to enjoy his company again, losing her nervousness since he wasn't making any more demands on her.

Then, suddenly, her father had put an end to it. Give up Justin, he'd demanded, or watch him lose everything he had. Justin would end up hating her, her father had said. He'd blame her for making him poor and their marriage wouldn't stand a chance. His pride alone would kill it.

She'd been very young and unworldly, and her father was an old hand at getting what he wanted. He'd enlisted aid from Tom Wheelor, who was motivated by the thought of a beneficial merger. And she'd done what her father asked and lied to Justin, admitted to having an affair with Tom, to wanting wealth and position, things that Justin couldn't give her.

So long ago, she thought. So much pain. She'd only been protecting Justin, trying to spare him the agony of losing everything he and his family had worked so long and so hard to achieve. But in the process, she'd sacrificed her own happiness. She had only herself to blame for Justin's cold attitude. And not only did she blame herself for her betrayal, but she also hadn't been honest with him about the reasons she'd been afraid to let him touch her.

Now he was going to marry her out of pity, not out of

love. And, too, there was always his wish for revenge. She didn't know how she was going to live with him, but only proximity was going to change his mind about her. And living with him would be so sweet. Even though she couldn't be the kind of woman he needed, it was all of heaven to be near him. Maybe one day she'd find the courage to tell him the truth about herself, to make him understand.

All her doubts were back. But she'd given her word to go through with the wedding, and she couldn't back down now. She was going to have to make the best of it, and hope that Justin's thirst for revenge wasn't prompting his decision to marry her.

CHAPTER THREE

ABBY WAS ENLISTED to help Shelby with the wedding preparations. Shelby had always liked the Ballenger brothers' ward. Abby seemed to understand so well what was going on between Justin and his ex-fiancée.

"I don't imagine Justin is making it easy for you," Abby said while they addressed envelopes for the invitations that they'd just picked up from the printer.

Shelby brushed back a strand of dark hair, sighing gently. "He feels sorry for me," she said with a faint smile. "And maybe he's bent on revenge. But I'm afraid that's all he's got to give me."

"He seemed to be coming around pretty well the night we all went to that square dance and Calhoun spent most of it dancing with you," Abby recalled, tongue in cheek. It was easy to laugh about the past now, although she and Justin had been devastated at the time.

Shelby cleared her throat. "Justin had enough to say to me when we danced. Afterward, I guess he gave Calhoun the devil, if his expression was anything to go by. He was mad."

"Mad!" Abby laughed. Her blue-gray eyes searched Shelby's. "He went home and got drunk. Worse," she confessed ruefully, "he got me drunk, too. When Calhoun got back from taking you home, we were sprawled on the sofa together trying to figure out a way to get up and lock him out of the house."

Shelby's eyes glistened with amused light. "Abby!"

"Oh, it gets even better," she added. "Justin taught me this horribly obscene Spanish drinking song…"

Shelby blushed, remembering the first time she'd heard that song. "He taught it to me, too, the night we got engaged, and we were just starting to sing it when Maria came in and was furious."

Abby finished one of the envelopes and put an invitation in it, sealing it absently while she studied Shelby's reflective expression. "Justin never got over you, you know."

Shelby's eyes lifted. "He never got over what I did, you mean. He's so unbending, Abby. And I can't blame him for the way he feels. At the time, I lacerated his pride."

"Why?"

The other woman only smiled. "I thought I was saving him, you see," she said quietly. "My father didn't want a cowboy for a son-in-law. He had a rich man all earmarked for me, a financially advantageous marriage. But I wouldn't play along, and when he found out I'd agreed to marry Justin, he set out to destroy the relationship." She turned a sealed envelope in her hands. "I never realized how ruthless my father could be until then. He threatened to ruin Justin if I didn't go along." She smoothed the envelope as she remembered the bitterness. "I didn't believe him, so I called his bluff. The bank foreclosed on the feedlot and the Ballenger boys almost lost everything."

"It was a long time ago," Abby said, touching her hand gently. "The feedlot is prosperous now. In fact, it was then. Wasn't it?"

"My father promised that if I went along with his proposition, he'd pull a few strings and talk the bank out of putting the place on public auction. Justin told me about the bankruptcy proceedings," she added. "He was devastated. He even talked about calling off the engagement, so I figured I was going to lose him anyway and it might as well be to his advantage. At the time," she added, remembering how distant Justin had been, how standoffish, "I remember thinking that he'd changed his mind about marrying me. I was pretty reserved." She didn't enlarge on that, but she remembered clearly the way Justin had reacted when she'd struggled away from him on the sofa. But surely that hadn't hurt his pride. He must have been pretty experienced.

Abby leaned forward. "What did your father do?"

"He produced Tom Wheelor, my new fiancé, and took him to meet Justin. He told Justin," she continued dully, "that I'd only been dating him to make Tom propose, because Tom was rich and Justin wasn't. He made out that it was all my fault, that I was the culprit. Justin believed him. He believed that I'd deliberately led him on, just to get Tom jealous enough to marry me. And then Dad told Justin that Tom and I were lovers, and Tom confirmed it."

Abby lifted her eyes. "You weren't," she said with certainty.

Shelby smiled. "Bless you for seeing the truth. Of course we weren't. But in order to save Justin's fledgling business, I had to go along with my father's lie. So when Justin called me and asked me for the truth, I told him what I'd been coached to say." She lowered her gaze to the carpet. "I told him that I wanted money, that I'd never wanted him, that it was all a game I'd been playing to amuse myself while I brought Tom in line." Her eyes closed. "I don't think I'll ever be able to forget the silence on the line, or the way he hung up, so quietly. A few weeks later, all the talk of bankruptcy died down, so I guess Dad convinced the bank that the Ballengers were a good risk. Tom Wheelor and I went around together for a while, to convince Justin, and then I went to Europe for six months and did my best to get myself killed on ski jumps all over Switzerland. Eventually I came back, but something in me died because of what my father did. He realized it at last, just before I lost him. He even apologized. But it was much too late."

"If you could just make Justin listen..." Abby sighed.

"He won't. He can't forgive me, Abby. It was like a public execution. Everybody knew that I'd jilted him for a richer man. You know how he hates gossip. That destroyed his pride."

Abby grimaced. "He must have realized that your father didn't approve of him."

"Oh, that was the beauty of it. My father welcomed Justin into the family with open arms and made a production about how proud he was going to be of his new son." She laughed bitterly. "Even when he went to Justin with Tom, my father played his part to perfection. He was almost in tears at the callous way I'd treated poor Justin."

"But why? Just for a merger? Didn't he care about your happiness?"

"My father was an empire builder," she said simply. "He let nothing get in the way of business, especially not the children. Ty never knew," she added. "He'd have been furious if he'd had any inkling, but it was part of the bargain that I couldn't tell Ty, either."

"Haven't you ever told Ty the truth?"

"It didn't seem necessary," Shelby replied. "Ty is a loner. It's hard even for me to talk to him, to get close to him. I think that may be why he's never married. He can't open up to people. Dad was hard on him. Even harder than he was on me. He ridiculed Ty and browbeat him most of our childhood. He grew up tough because he had to be, to survive his home life."

"I never knew. I like Ty," Abby said with a smile. "He's a very special man."

Shelby smiled back. She didn't tell Abby that Ty had been infatuated with her. And on top of losing his entire heritage and having to go to work for someone else, losing his chance with Abby was just the last straw. Ty had left for Arizona and his new job without a voiced regret. Perhaps the change would do him good.

Mrs. Simpson brought in a tray of cake and coffee and the three women sat and talked about the wedding until Abby had to leave. Shelby hadn't told anyone what Justin had said about her dress. But the next day she went into Jacobsville to the small boutique that one of her childhood playmates now owned, and the smart linen suit she bought to be married in was white.

That didn't worry her, because she knew she could prove to Justin that she was more than entitled to the symbolic white dress. Then she went for her premarital examination.

Dr. Sims had been her family doctor for half her life, and the tall, graying man was like family to all his patients. His quiet explanation after the examination, after the blood test was done by his lab, made her feel sick all over. And even though she protested, he was quietly firm about the necessity.

"It's only a very minor bit of surgery," he said. "You'll hardly feel it. And frankly, Shelby, if it isn't done, your wedding night is going to be a nightmare." He explained it in detail, and when he finished, she realized that she didn't have a choice. Justin might swear that he was never going to touch her in bed, but she knew it was unrealistic to assume that they could live together without going too far. And with the minor surgery, some pain could be avoided.

She finally agreed, but she insisted that he do only a partial job, so that there was no doubt she was a virgin. Doctor Sims muttered something about old-fashioned idiocy, but he did as she asked. He murmured something about the difficulty she might still encounter because of her stubbornness and that she might need to come back and see him. She hadn't wanted to argue about it, but it was important for Justin to believe her. This was the only proof she had left. The thing was, she hadn't counted on the prospect of such discomfort, and it began to wear on her mind. Had she done the right thing? She wanted Justin to know, without having to be told, that she was innocent. But that prospect of being hurt was just as frightening as it had been in the past—more so.

The wedding was the social event of the season. Shelby hadn't expected so many people to congregate in the Jacobsville Methodist church to see her get married. Certainly there were more spectators than she'd included on her list.

Abby and Calhoun were sitting in the family pew, holding hands, the tall blond man and the dark-haired woman so much in love that they radiated it all around. Beside them was Shelby's green-eyed, black-haired brother, Tyler, towering above everyone except Calhoun. There were neighbors and friends, and Misty Davies, Abby's friend, on the other side of the church. Justin was nowhere in sight, and Shelby almost panicked as she remembered his threat to leave if she wore a white dress.

But when the wedding march struck up, the minister and Justin were waiting for her at the altar. She had to bite her lower lip hard and grip her bouquet of daisies to keep from shaking as she walked down the aisle.

She and Justin had decided not to have a best man or a matron of honor, or much ceremony except for the actual service. There were plenty of flowers around the altar, and a candelabra with three unlit white candles. The minister was in his robes, and Justin was in a formal black suit, very elegant as he waited for his bride to join him.

When she reached him, and took her place at his side, she looked up. Her green eyes caught his black ones and her expression invited him to do what he'd threatened, to walk out of the church.

It was a tense moment and for one horrible second, he looked as if he were thinking about it. But the moment passed. He lifted his cold eyes to the minister and he repeated what he was told to say without a trace of expression in his deep voice.

He placed a thin gold band on her hand. There had been no engagement ring, and he hadn't mentioned buying one. He'd bought her ring himself, on a trip to town, and he hadn't asked if she wanted him to wear one. Probably he didn't want to.

They replied to the final questions and lit two candles, each holding a flame to the third candle, signifying the unity of two people into one. The minister pronounced them man and wife. He invited Justin to kiss his bride.

Justin turned to Shelby with an expression she couldn't read. He looked down at her for a long moment before he bent his head and brushed a light, cool kiss across her lips. Then he took her arm and propelled her down the aisle and outside into the hall, where they were surrounded seconds later by well-wishers.

There was no time to talk. The reception was held in the fellowship hall of the church, and punch, cake and canapés were consumed while Shelby and Justin were each occupied with guests.

Someone had a camera and asked them to pose for a photograph. They hadn't hired anyone to take pictures of the wedding, an oversight that Shelby was secretly disappointed at. She'd hoped for at least a photograph of them together, but perhaps this one would do.

She stood beside Justin and smiled, feeling his arm draw her to his side. Her eyes lifted to his, but it was hard to hold the smile as those black eyes cut into hers.

The instant the camera was gone, he glared at her. "I said any color except white."

"Yes, Justin, I know you did," she said calmly. "And think how you'd have felt if I'd insisted that you wear a blue dress instead of a black suit to be married in."

He blinked, as if he wasn't quite sure he'd heard right. "A white dress means—" he began indignantly.

"—a first wedding," she finished for him. "This is mine."

His eyes kindled. "You and I both know there's an implied second reason for wearing white, and you aren't entitled to it." He noticed something darken her eyes and his own narrowed. "You told me you could prove it, though, didn't you, Shelby?" He smiled coldly. "I just might let you do that before we're through."

She blushed and averted her eyes. For an instant, she felt cowardly, thinking about how difficult it was going to be if he wasn't gentle, if he treated her like the scarlet woman he thought she was. It didn't bear consideration, and she shivered. "I don't have to prove anything to you."

He laughed, the sound of it like ice shattering. "You can't, can you? It was all bravado, to keep me guessing until we were married."

Her eyes lifted to his. "Justin…"

"Never mind." He pulled out a cigarette and lit it. "I told you, we won't be sharing a bed. I don't care about your chastity."

She felt an aching sadness for what might have been between them and she looked at him, her eyes soft and quietly adoring on his craggy features. He was so beautiful. Not handsome, but beautifully made, for a man, from his lithe, powerful build to his black eyes and thick black hair and olive complexion. He looked exactly the way a man should, she decided.

He glanced down at her, caught in that warm appraisal. His cigarette hovered in midair while he searched her eyes, holding them for so long that her heart went wild in her chest. She let her eyes fall to his chiseled mouth, and she wanted it suddenly with barely contained passion. If only she could be the uninhibited woman she wanted to be, and not such a frightened innocent. Justin intimidated her. He had to be at least as worldly as Calhoun. She'd disappoint him, anyway, but if only she could tell him the truth and ask him to be gentle. She shivered at the thought of telling him something so intimate.

It was a blessing that Ty chose that moment to say his goodbyes, sparing Shelby the embarrassment of having Justin mock her for her weakness.

"I've got to catch a plane back to Arizona," he told his sister as he bent his head to brush her cheek with his lips. "My temporary lady boss is scared stiff of men."

Shelby's eyes brightened. "She's what?"

Ty looked frankly uncomfortable. "She's nervous around men," he said reluctantly. "Damn it, she hides behind me at dances, at meetings…it's embarrassing."

Shelby had to fight down laughter. Her very independent brother didn't like clinging women, but this one seemed to be affecting him very strangely. His temporary boss was the niece of his permanent boss. She lived in Arizona, where she was trying to cope with an indebted dude ranch. Ty's boss in Jacobsville had sent him out to help. He'd hated it at the beginning, and he still seemed to, but maybe the mysterious Arizona lady was getting to him.

"Maybe she feels safe with you?" Shelby asked.

He glowered at her. "Well, it's got to stop. It's like having poison ivy wrap itself around you."

"Is she ugly?" Shelby persisted.

"Kind of plain and unsophisticated," he murmured. "Not too bad, I guess, if you like tomboys. I don't," he added doggedly.

"Why don't you quit?" Justin asked. "You can work for Calhoun and me, we've already offered you a job."

"Yes, I know. I appreciated it, too, considering how strained things were between our families," Ty said honestly. "But this job is kind of a challenge and that part I like."

Justin smiled. "Come and stay when you get homesick."

Ty shook his outstretched hand. "I might, one day.

I like kids," he added. "A few nieces and nephews wouldn't bother me."

Justin looked murderous and Shelby went scarlet. Ty frowned, and Justin thanked God that Calhoun and Abby joined them in time to ward off trouble. He didn't want to think about kids. Shelby sure wouldn't want his, not if the way she'd reacted to him the one time he'd been ardent with her was any indication. She was repulsed by him.

"Isn't this a nice wedding?" Calhoun asked Ty, joining the small group with his arm around a laughing Abby. "Doesn't it give you any ideas?"

Ty smiled at Abby. "It does that, all right. It makes me want to get an inoculation, quick," he murmured drily.

"You'll outgrow that attitude one day," Calhoun assured him. "We all get chopped down at the ankles eventually," he added, and ducked when Abby hit his chest. "Sorry, honey." He chuckled, brushing a lazy kiss against her forehead. "You know I didn't mean it."

"Can we give you a lift to the airport, or did you rent a car?" Abby asked Ty.

"I rented a car, but thanks all the same. Why don't you two walk me out to it?" He kissed Shelby again. "Be happy," he said gently.

"I expect to," she said, and smiled in Justin's direction.

Ty nodded, but he didn't look convinced. When he followed Abby and Calhoun out of the fellowship hall, he was preoccupied and frowning thoughtfully.

The reception seemed to go on forever, and Shelby was grateful when it was finally time to go home. Justin had sent Lopez to fetch Shelby's things from Mrs. Simpson's house early that morning. The guest room had been prepared for Shelby. Maria had questioned that, but only once, because Justin's cold eyes had silenced her. Maria understood more than he realized, anyway. She, like everyone else on the property, knew that despite his bitterness, Justin still had a soft spot for Shelby. She was alone and impoverished, and it didn't surprise anybody that Justin had married her. If he felt the need for a little vengeance in the process, that wasn't unexpected, either.

"Thank God that's over," Justin said wearily when they were alone in the house. He'd tugged off his tie and jacket and unbuttoned the neck of his shirt and rolled up the sleeves. He looked ten years older than he was.

Shelby put her purse on the hall table and took off her high heels, smoothing her stockinged feet on the soft pile of the carpet. It felt good not to be two inches taller.

Justin glanced at her and smiled to himself, but he turned away before she could see it. "Do you want to go out for supper or have it here?"

"I don't care."

"I suppose it would look odd if we went to a restaurant on our wedding night, wouldn't it?" he added, turning to give her a mocking smile.

She glared at him. "Go ahead," she invited. "Spoil the rest of it, too. God forbid that I should enjoy my own wedding day."

He frowned as she turned and started up the staircase. "What the hell are you talking about?"

She didn't look at him. She held onto the railing and stared up at the landing. "You couldn't have made your feelings plainer if you'd worn a sign with all your grievances painted on it in blood. I know you hate me, Justin. You married me out of pity, but part of you still wants to make me pay for what I did to you."

He'd lit a cigarette and he was smoking it, propped against the doorjamb, his face quiet, his black eyes curious. "Dreams die hard, honey, didn't you know?" he asked coldly.

She turned around, her green eyes steady on his. "You weren't the only one who dreamed, Justin," she said. "I cared about you!"

His jaw tautened. "Sure you did. That's why you sold me out for that boy millionaire."

She stroked the banister absently. "Odd that I didn't marry him, isn't it?" she asked casually. "Very odd, wouldn't you say, when I wanted his money badly enough to jilt you."

He lifted the cigarette to his mouth. "He threw you over, I guess, when he found out you wanted the money more than you wanted him."

"I never wanted him, or his money," she said honestly. "I had enough of my own."

He smiled at her. "Did you?" Surely she didn't expect him to believe she was unaware of how much financial trouble her father had been in.

"You won't listen," she muttered. "You never would. I tried to tell you why I broke off the engagement—"

"You told me, all right! You couldn't stand for me to touch you, but I knew that already." His eyes glittered dangerously. "You pushed me away the night we got engaged," he added huskily. "You were shaking like a leaf and your eyes were as big as saucers. You couldn't get away from me quick enough."

Her lips parted on a slow breath. "And you thought it was revulsion, of course?" she asked miserably.

"What else could it have been?" he shot back, his eyes glaring. "I didn't come down in the last rain shower." He turned. "Change your clothes and we'll have supper. I don't know about you, but I'm hungry."

She wished she could tell him the truth. She wanted to, but he was so remote and his detached attitude intimidated her. With a sigh, she turned and went up the staircase numbly, wondering how she was going to live with a man she couldn't even talk to about intimacy.

They had a quiet wedding supper. Maria put everything on the table and she and Lopez went out for the evening, offering quiet congratulations before they left.

Justin leaned back in his chair when he'd finished his steak and salad, watching Shelby pick at hers.

He felt vaguely guilty about their wedding day. But in a way, he was hiding from her. Hiding his real feelings, hiding his apprehension about losing her a second time. It had wrung him out emotionally six years before. He didn't think he could bear it a second time, so he was trying to protect himself from becoming too vulnerable. But her sad little face was getting to him.

"Damn it, Shelby," he ground out, "don't look like that."

She lifted her eyes. There was no life in them anymore. "I'm tired," she said softly. "Do you mind if I go to bed after we eat?"

"Yes, I mind." He threw down his napkin and lit a cigarette. "It's our wedding night."

She laughed bitterly. "So it is. What did you have in mind, some more comments on my scarlet past?"

He frowned slightly. She didn't sound like Shelby. That edge to her voice was disturbing. His eyes narrowed. She'd lost her father, her home, her entire way of life, even her brother. She'd lost everything in recent weeks, and married him because she needed a little security. He'd given her hell, and now she looked as if today was the last straw on the camel's back. He hadn't meant for it to be that way. He didn't want to hurt her. But he couldn't seem to keep quiet; there were so many wounds.

He sighed heavily. His black eyes searched her wan face, remembering better times, happier times, when he could look at her and get drunk on just the sight of her smile.

"Are you sure you want to keep on working?" he asked quietly, just to change the subject, to get the conversation on an easier level.

She stared down at her plate. "Yes, I'd like to," she said. "I've never really done any work before, except society functions and volunteer work. I like my job."

"And Barry Holman?" he asked, his smile a challenge.

She got up. She was still wearing her white skirt with a pale pink blouse, and she looked feminine and elegant and very desirable. Her long hair waved down to her shoulders, and Justin wanted to get up and catch two handfuls of it and kiss her until she couldn't stand up.

"Mr. Holman is my boss," she said. "Not my lover. I don't have a lover."

He got up, too, moving closer, his eyes narrow and calculating, his body tense with years of frustrated desire. "You're going to have one," he said curtly.

She wouldn't back away. She wouldn't give him the satisfaction of watching her run. She lifted her face proudly, even though her knees felt weak and her heart was racing madly. She was afraid of him because of their past, because he wanted revenge. She was afraid because he thought she was experienced, and even with that minor surgery, she knew that it wasn't going to be the easiest time of her life. Justin was deceptively strong. She knew the power in that lean, hard body, and to be overwhelmed by it in passion was a little scary.

He watched the fear flicker in her eyes, and understood it instantly. "You're off base, honey," he said quietly. "Way off base. I'd never hurt you in bed, not for revenge or any other reason."

Her lower lip trembled on a stifled sob and tears welled in her eyes. She lowered her gaze to his broad chest, missing the faint shock in his face at her reaction. "Maybe you wouldn't be able to help it," she whispered.

"Shelby, are you really afraid of me?" he asked huskily.

Her thin shoulders shifted. "Yes. I'm sorry."

"Were you afraid with him?" he asked. "With Wheelor?"

She opened her mouth to speak and just gave up. What was the use? He wasn't going to listen. She turned away and went toward the staircase.

"Running won't solve anything," he said shortly, watching her go with mingled feelings, the foremost of which was anger.

"Neither will trying to talk to you," she replied. She turned at the bottom of the staircase, her green eyes bright with unshed tears and returning spirit. "Do your worst. Make me pay. I'm fresh out of things I care about. I've got absolutely nothing left to lose, so look out, Justin. I'm not going to live up to your idea of a society wife. I'm going to be myself, and I'm sorry if it destroys any of your old illusions."

He eyed her quietly. "Meaning what?"

"No affairs," she replied, picking the thought out of his mind. "Despite what you think of me, I'm not starved for a man."

"That much I'd believe," he said shortly. "My God,
I get more warmth out of an ice cube than I ever got
from you!"

She felt the impact of those words like daggers
against her bare skin. She should have realized that
he thought her frigid, but it had never really registered
before.

"Maybe Tom Wheelor got more!" she threw at him.

His black eyes splintered with rage. He actually
started toward her before he checked himself with the
iron control that he kept on his temper.

Shelby saw that movement, and thanked God that
he stopped when he did. She lifted her chin. "Good
night, Justin. Thank you for a roof over my head and
a place to live."

His eyelids flickered as she started up the staircase.
Looking at her he recalled years of dreams, of remembered delight in just being with her, frustration at having to hold back only to lose her anyway. He still cared.
He'd lied to protect his pride, but he cared so much. And
he was losing her, all over again.

He wanted to tell her that he hadn't meant to accuse
her of being frigid. He'd wanted her to distraction, and
she hadn't wanted him. That had hurt far more than
having her break their engagement, especially when
he'd found out that Tom Wheelor was her lover. It had
damned near killed him. And here she was throwing
it in his teeth, hitting him in his most vulnerable spot.
He'd always wondered if she found him revolting physically. That was what made him believe that she'd meant
what she told him about not wanting him, about wanting Tom Wheelor instead—that reluctance in her to let
him get close to her.

And she was different now. She wasn't the shy, introverted young woman he'd known six years ago. She was oddly reckless; high-spirited and uninhibited when she forgot herself. But he couldn't bend. He couldn't make himself bend enough to tell her what was in his heart, how much he still wanted her, because he didn't dare trust her again. She'd hurt him too badly. He watched her go up the staircase, his eyes black and soft and full of hunger. He didn't move until she was out of sight.

CHAPTER FOUR

SHELBY HAD HOPED beyond hope that Justin might still love her. That he might have married her not so much out of pity as out of love. But her wedding day had convinced her that what little emotion had been left in him after years of bitterness was all gone. He still blamed her for what he thought she'd done with Tom Wheelor, and he thought she was frigid.

She didn't know how to deal with her own fears and his anger. Her marriage was going to be as empty as her life had been. There would be no black-headed little babies to nurse, no soft, sweet loving in the darkness, no shared delight in making a life together. There would be only separate bedrooms and separate lives and Justin's hunger for vengeance.

The black depression that she'd taken to bed on her wedding night got worse. Justin tolerated her presence, but he was away more often than not. At meals, he spoke to her only when it was necessary, and he never touched her. He was like a polite host instead of a husband. And day by miserable day, Shelby began to feel a new recklessness. While Justin was away one weekend, she went on a white-water rafting race with Abby's friend Misty Davies. She tried her hand at skydiving. She joined a fencing class. She went back to the old, more reckless days of her adolescence. Justin had never really known

her, she thought sometimes. He seemed surprised by
the things she enjoyed and a time or two he acted as if
her lifestyle bothered him. Well, what had he expected
her to do, she fumed, stay at home and arrange flowers?
Perhaps that was the image he had of her, that she was
a pretty socialite with beauty and no brains.

She'd kept working after the wedding, but Barry Holman insisted that she take a few days off. It wasn't right,
he said, for her to work through her honeymoon. She
wanted to laugh at that, and tell him that her husband
didn't want a honeymoon. Justin had come home from
his latest trip and had gone straight to the feedlot office with an abrupt and coolly polite greeting. After a
few bored hours, Shelby phoned the office, just to see
how things were going. She liked her job. She missed
working terribly. It was something to do; it helped keep
her mind off her marriage and her own inadequacies.

When she called, the poor temporary secretary,
Tammy Lester, answered the phone, obviously half out
of her mind trying to cope with an impatient, frustrated
Barry Holman. So Shelby dressed in a cool white and
red summery dress and white high heels and went to
work.

The old sedan she drove broke down halfway there
and she had to have it towed in to the dealer car lot
where she had her mechanical work done.

Once Shelby was at the dealership, as fate would
have it, she noticed Abby's little sports car was there and
up for sale. The sight of the car brought back memories.
Shelby had driven one like it during six of the blackest
months in her life, the time she'd spent in Switzerland
after she'd given back Justin's ring. She'd loved that
car, but she'd wrecked it accidentally. The wreck hadn't

dampened her enthusiasm for fast cars, though. Now she wanted one—it appealed to the wild streak in her that had never totally disappeared. It wasn't a suicidal streak; she just loved a challenge. She liked sports cars and the exhilaration of driving in the fast lane.

Justin didn't know that Shelby had a wild streak, because he'd accepted the illusion of what she appeared to be rather than wondering what was beneath the surface. Well, he was in for a few shocks, she decided, starting now.

Because the dealer knew that Shelby had just married Justin, he didn't even ask for a cosigner on the note. He sold her the car outright, with payments she could afford on her own salary.

She parked the vehicle right outside the office, delighting in its new paint job. Abby had had it painted red with white racing stripes just before she traded it for something more sedate. The new colors suited Shelby very well. She sighed over it, delighted that she could afford it and even manage the payments by herself. All her life she'd depended on her father's money. There was something challenging and very satisfying about taking care of herself financially. She was sorry now that she'd panicked at being on her own and rushed into marrying Justin. She'd hoped for something more than a roof over her head, but that wasn't going to happen. Justin was taking care of her, just as he'd taken care of Abby, and if he had any lingering desire for her, it didn't show. After he'd accused her of being frigid, she'd kept out of his way altogether. If only she wasn't so repressed, she could have told him what the problem was and how frightened she was of intimacy. But it was hopeless. Justin would probably be as embarrassed as she was to talk about it, anyway. So things would just have to rock along as they had been, until one of them broke the silence.

When she got to the office, Barry Holman was pacing the floor while the temporary secretary cried. They both turned as Shelby put her purse in the top drawer of the desk and smiled.

"Can I help?" she asked.

The woman at her desk cried even harder. "He yells," she wailed, pointing at Barry Holman, who looked furiously angry from his blond head to his big feet.

"Only at incompetents!" he flashed back.

"Now, now," Shelby soothed. "I'm here. I'll take care of everything. Tammy, why don't you make Mr. Holman a cup of coffee while I straighten out whatever's fouled up, then I'll show you how to update the files and you can keep busy with that. Okay?"

Tammy smiled, her soft brown eyes quiet. "Okay."

She got up and Shelby sat down. Her dark brows lifted as Barry Holman glanced at her uncomfortably.

"It's your vacation," he said. "You shouldn't be here."

"Why not? Justin is working, why shouldn't I?"

He frowned. "Well…"

"Tell me what needs to be done, and then I'll show you my new car." She grinned. "It was Abby's, and they let me buy it without even a cosigner."

"Naturally, considering your husband's credit line," he mused. She gave him a strange look, but he ignored it, delighting in his good fortune. "Here, this is what's giving Tammy fits."

He produced two scribbled pages of notes on a legal pad that he wanted transcribed and put into English instead of abbreviations and scrawls, and fifty copies run off with different salutations on each.

"Simple, isn't it?" he said. He glared toward the back of the office. "She cried."

Shelby wanted to. It was an hour's work just to translate his handwriting. But she knew how to use the computer's word-processing program, and Tammy had three simplified tutorials spread out on the desk, none of which would explain the program to a person who'd never used a computer.

"She asked me what these were for." Barry Holman sighed, picking up one of the diskettes in its jacket. He looked up. "She thought they were negatives."

Shelby had to bite her lower lip. "She's never had any computer training," she reminded him.

"That's no excuse for not having a brain," he returned hotly.

"Mr. Holman!" Tammy exclaimed, glaring at him as she came back with three cups of black coffee on a tray. "That was unkind and unfair."

"Didn't they tell you at the temporary-services agency that computer experience was necessary to do this job?" he grumbled.

"I have computer experience," Tammy replied with hauteur. "I play games on my brother's Atari all the time."

Mr. Holman looked as if *he* wanted to cry. He ground his teeth together, went back into his office and closed the door.

"I guess I told him." Tammy grinned wickedly.

There was a loud, feverish, furious, *"Damn!"* from the vicinity of Mr. Holman's office. Shelby and Tammy exchanged amused glances.

"They didn't tell me about the computer," Tammy confided. "They asked if I had office skills, and I do. I type over a hundred words a minute and take dictation at ninety. But I don't read Sanskrit," she whispered, pointing at the scribbling on the legal sheets.

Shelby burst out laughing. It felt so good to laugh, and she thanked God for this job, which was going to save her sanity. She shook her head and, putting the books aside, she began to explain the computer's operation to Tammy.

After work, she took the long route home. Mr. Holman had relaxed after lunch, and he was tolerating Tammy much better now. In fact, he hadn't even growled when Shelby had mentioned that it might be economical to have two secretaries in the office because of the backlog of filing and updating the computer's entries. He'd talked about taking on an associate, and if he hired Tammy full time, he could do it.

Shelby turned the small sports car onto the highway sharply, delighting in its rack-and-pinion steering and easy handling. She gunned it up and up and up, loving the speed, loving the freedom and the wind tearing through her long hair. She felt reckless. As she'd told Justin, she had nothing left to lose. She was going to enjoy her life from now on. Justin could just do his worst.

There was a slow car in front, and she didn't even brake. She surged around it and barely got back into her lane as a white car sped in the opposite direction. She thought it looked familiar, but she didn't look in the rearview mirror. It was going toward the feedlot. She passed the turnoff, increasing her speed. She wasn't ready to go home to her cell just yet.

Calhoun was muttering a prayer as he pulled up in front of the feedlot. That was Abby's old car, and it had been Shelby at the wheel. He'd barely recognized her in that split second, her face laughing with pleasure at the speed, her hair flying in the wind. She made Abby's friend Misty Davies look like a safe driver by comparison.

Justin looked up from his desk as Calhoun came in and closed the door behind him. "It's almost time to go home," he remarked, glancing at his Rolex. "I didn't think you were coming back today from Montana."

Calhoun grinned. "I missed Abby. Speaking of Abby," he added, perching himself lazily on the edge of his brother's desk, "a wild woman driving her sports car just came within an inch of running me down."

"Didn't Abby sell it?" Justin remarked.

"She certainly did. I insisted."

"I see." Justin smiled faintly. He leaned back with his cigarette smoking in his lean fingers. "I gather that some other fool's wife is driving it?"

"You could put it that way. She was doing eighty if she was doing a mile." His dark eyes narrowed. "Are you sure you want Shelby to have it?"

There was a shocked silence. "What do you mean, do I want Shelby to have it?" Justin sat up abruptly. "Are you telling me Shelby was driving that sports car?"

"I'm afraid so," Calhoun said quietly. "You didn't know?"

Justin's expression became grim. Shelby wasn't happy and he knew it. Her most recent behavior was already worrying him, although he was careful to keep his misgivings from Shelby. But purchasing a sports car was going too far. He was going to have to talk to her. He'd avoided confrontations, letting her settle in, keeping his distance while he tried to cope with the anguish of having Shelby in his house when she backed away the minute he came into the room. But this was too much.

He couldn't let her kill herself. He got up from the desk without even looking at Calhoun, plucked his hat off the hat rack and started for the door. "Was she going toward the house?" he asked curtly.

"The opposite direction," Calhoun told him. His eyes narrowed. "Justin, what's going on between the two of you?"

The older man looked at him, black eyes glittering. "My private life is none of your business."

Calhoun folded his arms. "Abby says Shelby is running wild, and that you're apparently doing nothing to stop her. Are you that hell-bent on revenge?"

"You make it sound as if she's suicidal," Justin said coldly. "She's not."

"If she was happy, she wouldn't be like this," the younger man persisted. "You've got to stop trying to live in the past. It's time to forget what happened."

"That's damned easy for you to say." Justin's black eyes flashed. "She threw me over and slept with another man!"

Calhoun stared at him. "You don't have my track record, but you're no more a saint than I am, big brother. Suppose Shelby couldn't accept the women in your past?"

"It's different with men," the older man said irritably. "Is it?"

"She was mine. I was so damned careful never to put a foot wrong with her. I held back and gritted my teeth to keep from scaring her, and she flinched away from me every time I touched her. And all the while she was sleeping with that pasty-faced boy millionaire. How do you think I felt?" he blazed. "And then she told me that I was too poor to suit her expensive tastes, she wanted somebody rich."

"She didn't marry him, did she?" Calhoun returned. "She left for Europe and went wild, just as she's going wild now. She was in a wreck in Switzerland, Justin. In a sports car," he added, watching the horror grow in his brother's eyes, "just like the one she's driving now. She was grieving for you. Even her father realized that, at last."

Justin fumbled a cigarette into his mouth and lit it. "Nobody ever told me that."

"When would you ever listen to anything about her?" Calhoun replied. "It's only in the past few months that you've calmed down enough to talk about anything connected with the Jacobses."

"I wanted her," Justin ground out. "You can't imagine how I felt when she broke it off."

"Yes, I can," Calhoun replied. "I was there. I know what it was like for you. But you never even considered that Shelby might have had a reason. She tried to explain it once, to tell you why she broke off the engagement. You wouldn't even listen."

"What was there to listen to?" Justin asked impatiently. "She'd already told me the truth, in the beginning."

"I never believed it," Calhoun replied. "And neither would you have, if you hadn't been in love for the first time in your life and so damned uncertain about your own ability to keep Shelby. You were always worried about losing her to another man. Even to me. Remember?"

It was hard to argue with the truth. Justin knew he'd been possessive about Shelby. Hell, he still was. But how could he help it? She was a beautiful woman, and he was a plain, unworldly man. He'd never been able to understand why Shelby had stayed with him as long as she had.

"Even now," Calhoun continued quietly, "it seems to me that you're trying your best to make her leave you."

Justin smiled mockingly. "What do you expect me to do, tie her in the cellar?" he asked reasonably. "I can't make her stay if she doesn't want to. Hell——" he laughed coldly "——I can't even touch her. She flinched away from me the one time I tried to make love to her," he said bluntly, remembering. His eyes went blacker and he looked away. "I can't get near her. She's afraid of me that way."

"How interesting," Calhoun said, choosing his words, "that such an experienced woman of the world could be afraid of sex. Isn't it?"

Justin frowned. "What do you mean?"

Calhoun didn't answer him. He was smiling a little when he started out the door, but Justin couldn't see the smile. "I've got to get home. See you, big brother." And before Justin could reply, he was gone.

Justin took a minute to get his temper under control. He went out the door behind Calhoun without a word to his secretary, his eyes narrow with concern. Calhoun had delayed him too long. Suppose Shelby wrecked that little car?

He went up and down the road, but he didn't see any sign of the sports car. Later, he went to the house, and almost went down on his knees with relief when he found it parked at the steps.

He had to force himself to behave normally when his hands were almost shaking from fear that he might find her in a ditch somewhere. He walked into the house, tossing his hat onto the hat rack, and went into the dining room, where Shelby was sitting in a chair halfway down the long cherry-wood table, talking to Maria about some new recipe.

She looked toward the doorway, but when she saw him, all the laughter and animation went out of her like a light that was suddenly turned off. She was wearing a red and white dress and her hair was down around her shoulders in a pretty, dark, waving tangle. The wind, he thought absently, tearing through her hair in the convertible.

"I've traded cars," she said defiantly. "How do you like it? It was Abby's. You don't even have to cosign with me, I can make the payments from my salary."

Justin glanced at Maria, who knew the look and made herself scarce. He sat down at the head of the table, lit a cigarette and leaned back in the chair to stare intently at Shelby. "The last thing in the world you need is a sports car. You already drive too damned fast."

She searched his dark eyes, reading the thinly veiled concern. "Somebody saw me in the car this afternoon," she guessed.

He nodded. "Calhoun."

"I thought it was him." She studied her hands in her lap, turning the thin gold band on her wedding finger. "I like speed," she said hotly.

"I don't like funerals," he shot back. "I don't intend having to go to yours. You'll take that sports car back tomorrow or I'll take it back for you."

"It's mine!" she cried. Her green eyes flashed angrily. "And I won't take it back!"

He took a long draw from his cigarette. In his reclining position, his white silk shirt was drawn taut over tanned muscles. His chest was thick with hair that peeked out through the unfastened top buttons of his shirt. His jacket was off, his sleeves rolled up. He looked devastatingly masculine, from his disheveled black hair to his sensuous mouth.

"I'm not going to argue about it, honey," he replied. Through a veil of smoke, his black eyes searched hers. "Calhoun told me you wrecked a car overseas."

She flushed. "That was an accident."

"You aren't going to have any accidents here," he said. "I won't let you kill yourself."

"For heaven's sake, Justin, I'm not suicidal!" she protested. She lifted her coffee cup to her lips and took a fortifying sip of the black liquid.

"I didn't say you were," he agreed. He moved his ashtray on the tablecloth, watching it spin around. "But you need a firmer hand than you've been getting."

"I'm not Abby," she said. Her finely etched features grew hard as she looked at him. "I don't need a guardian."

He looked back, black eyes searching, quiet. "And while we're on the subject, I don't like you working for Barry Holman."

She blinked. She felt suddenly as if control of her own life was being taken away from her. "Justin, I didn't ask how you liked it," she reminded him. "I told you before we married that I wanted to keep on working."

"There's more than enough to do around here," he said. He tapped an ash into the ashtray. "You can manage the house."

"Maria and Lopez do that very nicely, thank you," she replied. She stiffened. "I don't want to stay home and swirl around the house in silk lounge pajamas and throw parties, Justin, in case you wondered. I've had my fill of charity work and flower arranging and social warfare."

He was looking at the cigarette, not at her. "I thought

you might miss those things. In the old days, you never had to lift a finger."

She studied her neat hands in her lap, pleating the thin silky fabric of the red and white dress. "My father saw me as a parlor decoration," she said tautly. "He would have been outraged if I'd tried to change my image."

He frowned slightly. "Were you afraid of him?"

"I was *owned* by him," she replied. She sighed, raising her eyes to Justin's. The curiosity there puzzled her, but at least they were talking for a change instead of arguing. "He wasn't the easiest man to live with, and he had terrible ways of getting even when Ty and I disobeyed."

"He kept you pretty close to home," he recalled. "Although he trusted you with me."

"Did he really?" she laughed hollowly. "Justin, you were the second man I ever dated and the first I ever went out with alone. You look shocked. Did you think my father let me live the life of a playgirl? He was terrified that some fortune hunter might seduce me. I lived like a recluse while he was alive."

Justin wasn't sure he understood what he was hearing. His head tilted a little and his eyes narrowed. "Would you like to run that by me again?" he asked. "You hadn't been out with a man alone until you went with me?"

"That's it," she agreed. "I didn't get out of my father's sight until after I broke the engagement and went to Switzerland." She smiled sadly. "I guess the freedom was too much, because I ran wild. The sports car was just an outlet, a way of celebrating. I never meant to wreck it."

"How badly were you hurt?" he asked.

"I broke my leg and cracked two ribs," she said. "They said I was lucky."

He finished his cigarette and crushed it out. "I didn't realize you were that sheltered," he said quietly. He was only beginning to understand how innocent she'd been in those days. If she'd only dated one other man, then very likely her first taste of intimacy had been with him. He thought about that, and felt himself go taut. He'd expected her to have a little experience, even though he'd known she was virginal. But if she'd had none, it was easy to understand why his ardor would have frightened her so.

"I couldn't talk about things like that with you," she confessed. "I was young and hopelessly naive."

He stared at her narrowly, his black eyes glittering "I frightened you the night we got engaged, didn't I?" he asked suddenly. "That was why you pulled back—not because I disgusted you."

She caught her breath audibly. "You never disgusted me!" she burst out, hurting for him. "Oh, Justin, no! You didn't think that?"

"We didn't know very much about each other, Shelby," he said, his voice deep and measured. "I suppose we both had false ideas. I saw you as a sophisticated, elegant society woman. And while I knew you were innocent, I thought you'd had some experience with men. If I'd had any idea of what you've just told me, I damned sure wouldn't have been that demanding with you."

She went red and averted her eyes. She couldn't find the right words. Amazing, that they were married and she was twenty-seven years old, and this kind of talk could still embarrass her.

"I was afraid you couldn't stop," she murmured evasively.

He sighed heavily and lifted his coffee cup to his lips, draining it. "So was I," he said unexpectedly. "It was touch and go for a few seconds, at that. I'd gone hungry for a long time."

"I didn't think men had to, these days," she said softly. "I mean, society is so permissive and all."

"Society may be permissive. I'm not," he said flatly. His black eyes flashed at her. "I never was, in the way you mean. A gentleman doesn't seduce virgins—or take advantage of women who don't know the score. That leaves party girls." He held the cup in his big, lean hands, smoothing over it with his thumb. "And just to be frank, honey, the type never appealed very much to me."

Her soft eyes searched over his hard features, lingering on his chiseled mouth.

"I guess you never lacked offers, all the same," she said, letting her gaze fall to her lap again.

"I'm rich." There was cool cynicism in the words. "Sure, I get offers." He studied her face calculatingly. "In fact, Shelby, I had one while I was in New Mexico last week, wedding ring and all."

Her teeth clenched. She didn't want him to see that it bothered her, but it was hard to hide. "Did you?"

He put the cup down. "You're as possessive about me as I am about you," he said then, surprising her gaze up to lock with his in a slow, electric exchange. "You don't like the thought of other women making eyes at me, do you, Shelby?"

She crossed her legs. "No," she said honestly.

He smiled mockingly as he lit another cigarette. "Well,

if it's any comfort, I froze her out. I won't cheat on you, honey."

"I never thought you would," she replied. "Any more than I'd cheat on you."

"That would be the eighth wonder of the world," he remarked with deceptive softness, "considering your hang-ups. We've been married for almost two weeks, and you still look like a sacrificial lamb every time I come near you."

She drew in a slow, steadying breath. "Yes, I know," she said miserably. She smiled bitterly. "I'm aware of my own failings, Justin. I guess you won't believe it, but you can't possibly blame me any more than I blame myself for what I am."

He scowled. He hadn't meant to put her on the defensive. His pride was stung and he was striking out. But he didn't want to hurt her anymore. He'd done enough of that already.

"I didn't mean it like that," he said on a weary breath. "It's the way things happened, that's all." He looked his age for a minute, his expression bleak, his dark eyes haunted. "You savaged my pride, Shelby. It's taken a long time to put it behind me. I guess I haven't, just yet."

"I didn't get off scot-free, either," she murmured. Her thin shoulders slumped. "I've had my share of grief over what I did."

"Why?" he asked shortly.

She closed her eyes and winced. "I did it for your sake," she whispered.

He let out an angry breath. "Well, that's a new tack, at least." He ground out the half-finished cigarette and got to his feet. "I've got some paperwork to do before Maria gets supper on the table." He paused beside her chair, watching the way she stiffened as he got close to her. He reached down and caught a handful of her long hair, dragging her head back so that he could see her eyes. "Fear," he ground out, searching them. "That's all I ever see in your eyes when I come near you. Well, don't sweat it, honey. You won't be called on to make the supreme sacrifice. I'm not desperate!"

He let her go and moved past her with anger in every line of his powerful body, without another word or a backward glance.

Shelby felt the tears come and she didn't stop them. He didn't know why she was afraid, and she couldn't tell him. He just assumed that she withdrew because she didn't want him. Nothing was further from the truth. She did, desperately. But she wanted him controlled and gentle, and she remembered how it had been when he wasn't.

She got up from the table and went up to her room to spend a few quiet minutes before they ate, getting herself back together again. It was so hard to talk to him, to get around his growing impatience. Her rejection was doing terrible things to him, and even now she felt protective. She wanted to give him what he wanted, to erase those hard lines from his face. But she was so frightened of the demands he might make on her.

If only she could tell him. But her sheltered background made it too embarrassing to explain why she was the way she was. Until she could find a way to make him understand, it was going to put an even worse strain on their marriage.

CHAPTER FIVE

IF SHELBY HAD hoped to find Justin less angry over dinner, she was doomed to disappointment. He sat at the head of the table like a stone man, barely speaking through the meal. She couldn't talk to him. She didn't know what to say.

Afterward, he went out the door without a word and Shelby felt a sense of utter desperation. If only she could go to him and put her arms around him, explain how she felt, why she was the way she was. But would he believe her, with their past?

Misery wrapped around her like a blanket. She got her purse and went out to her car. If Justin thought she was going to sit around by herself for what was left of the evening, he could just think again.

She started the sports car, revved the engine, backed out and roared away. The wonderful thing about the little car was the delicious feel of its controlled speed. She loved the straight road, the sense of freedom she felt with the wind in her long hair, the exhilaration of being alone with her thoughts.

Justin hated her, but that was nothing new. He always had. She'd hurt him and he was never going to forgive her. She didn't know why she'd agreed to marry him; it was never going to work out. She'd been a fool to go through with it in the first place, so she had only herself to blame for her present misery.

She was so deep in thought that she didn't notice the stop sign until she was on it, and the loud baritone of a truck's horn made her blood freeze.

A huge transfer-trailer truck was barreling down the highway. Shelby's little car wasn't going to be fast enough to beat that mammoth vehicle across the intersection, and it was touch and go if she'd be able to stop at all.

With her heart in her throat, and the numb certainty of death stiffening her body, she hit the brake. The car went into a spin, the squeal of tires terrible in the late afternoon stillness, her face frozen with terror as she lost control and the sky went around and around and around…

The car spun into the deep ditch and leaned drunkenly sideways, but amazingly it didn't turn over. Shelby sat, shaken but unhurt, nausea bitter in her throat and the world spinning around her. There was the sound of another car screeching to a halt. A door opened. There was the sound of running feet and then, suddenly, a man's anguished shout.

"Shelby!" The man's face was familiar, but somehow unfamiliar. It was hoarse and choked and blackly furious. "Answer me, damn it, are you all right?"

She felt her seat belt being forced away from her with hands that were lean and brown and shaking. She felt those same hands running over her body, searching for blood or broken bones, exquisitely gentle.

"Are you all right?" Justin asked huskily. "Do you hurt anywhere? For God's sake, sweetheart, answer me!"

"I… I'm fine," she whispered numbly. "The door…?"

"It won't open, the frame's sprung. Easy does it, now." He carefully reached down to get her under the armpits and with formidable strength he lifted her clear of the car. When she was on the ground, swaying, he picked her up with exquisite tenderness and carried her up from the ditch. The truck driver had stopped down the road and was coming toward them, but Justin didn't seem to see him. His expression was rigid with control, but he couldn't stop his arms from trembling under her slender body.

That fact finally registered in Shelby's dazed mind. She looked up then and saw his face, and her breath fluttered. He was flour-white, only his eyes alive and glittering blackly in that set, haunted face. He looked down at her, his arms convulsively dragging her against his chest.

"You little fool…!" he choked.

As long as she lived, she knew she'd never forget the horror she saw in his eyes. She reached up to hold him, her only thought to remove that look from his eyes.

"It's all right, Justin," she murmured softly. His reaction fascinated her. She'd never seen him shaken before. It made her feel protective, that tiny chink in his cool armor.

"I'm fine, Justin," she whispered. Her eyes searched his, amazed at the vulnerability there. She touched his mouth, her soft fingers caressing as they slid up into his thick, dark hair. "Darling, I'm all right, really I am!" She pulled his mouth down and put hers softly against it, loving the way he let her kiss him, even if it was only out of shock—which, in fact, it was. For several seconds she savored the newness of it, then something stirred in her slender body, and her mouth pushed upward, hungry for a harder, deeper contact than this. It had been years since they'd kissed, since they'd really kissed. She moaned softly and he seemed to come out of his trance. His arm contracted, and his hard mouth opened hungrily against hers on a wild, shattered groan.

His mouth hurt as it dragged against hers while he muttered something violent and unintelligible against her soft lips. He pulled back with evident reluctance as the truck driver came running down the highway toward them.

"Is she all right?" the man asked, panting from the long run he'd had. "My God, I was sure I'd hit her...!"

"She's all right," Justin answered tersely. "But that damned car won't be when I can lay my hands on my rifle."

The truck driver sighed with pure relief. "Damn, lady, you can sure handle yourself," he said with admiration. "If you'd lost your nerve and thrown up your hands, you'd be dead and I'd be a mental patient."

"I'm sorry." Shelby wept, her nerve broken from the combination of the near miss and the exquisite ardor of Justin's hard mouth. "I'm so sorry. I didn't even see you coming!"

The truck driver, a young man with red hair, just shook his head, barely able to get his breath. "Are you sure you're all right?"

"I'm fine," she said, forcing a trembling smile. "Thank you for stopping. It wasn't your fault."

"That wouldn't have made me feel any better," she was told. "Well, if you're sure, I'll be on my way." He looked at Justin, and almost offered to help, but the glitter in those black eyes wasn't encouraging.

"As my wife said, thanks for stopping," Justin said.

The younger man nodded, smiled and walked away with patent relief, wondering why a woman that pretty would marry such a desperado. He was glad she wasn't hurt. He wouldn't have relished having to face that wild-eyed husband unarmed.

Justin didn't say another word. He turned, carrying Shelby to the Thunderbird. He balanced her on his knee, opened the passenger door and put her inside very gently.

"What about my car?" she asked.

His black eyes met hers. "Damn your car," he said huskily. He slammed the door and went around to get in under the wheel. But he didn't start the car. He sat with his hands, white-knuckled, gripping the steering wheel for a long moment while Shelby waited for the explosion that she knew was about to come. Justin had been badly shaken and somebody was going to pay for it. Now that he was sure she was all right, she could imagine that he was loading both verbal barrels.

"Go ahead, give me hell," she said tearfully, searching in the glove compartment for a tissue. "I was driving too fast, and I wasn't watching. I deserve every lecture I get." She blew her nose. "How did you get here so fast?"

He still didn't speak. After a minute, he sat back in the bucket seat and fumbled a cigarette out of his pocket. He lit it with still-trembling hands, staring straight ahead.

"I followed you," he said curtly. "When I heard you gun the car out of the driveway, I was afraid you might try to take out your temper on the highway, so I tagged along." His head turned and his black eyes flashed at her. "My God, I paid for sins I haven't even committed when I saw you spin out."

She could imagine how it had been for him, having to watch. Even though he didn't love her, it would have been terrible.

"I'm sorry," she said inadequately, folding her arms across her breasts shakily.

His chest rose and fell with a huge, angry breath. "Are you, really?" he said. He was back in control now, and the cool smile on his face infuriated her. "Well, you can say goodbye to that damned sports car. Tomorrow, I'll go downtown with you and steer you toward something safe."

"What did you have in mind, a Sherman tank?" she asked with ice in her tone.

"A bicycle, if you keep this up," he corrected angrily. "I told you once before, Shelby, your reckless days are over."

"You're not going to order me around!" she shot at him through trembling lips and clenched teeth. "I'm not your ward!"

"No," he agreed with a mocking smile. "You're my wife, aren't you? My saintly, untouched wife who can bear anyone's hands except mine."

It was too much. She burst into tears again, turning her face to the window, burying her eyes in the soggy tissue.

"Don't," he groaned. "For God's sake, stop it. I can't stand tears!"

"Then don't look, damn you," she whispered, stomping her foot.

He swore roughly, digging into his pocket for his freshly laundered linen handkerchief. He thrust it into her trembling hands, feeling as if someone had kicked him.

"You'll make yourself sick. Stop it. You're all right.

A miss is as good as a mile, isn't it?" he asked, his voice softer now, deeper. He touched her hair hesitantly. It was all coming back into focus, little by little. He frowned, because now he remembered something that panic had knocked out of his mind. She'd touched his face and whispered something, and she'd put her mouth against his to comfort him. What had she said…?

"You called me darling," he said aloud.

She moved jerkily. "Did I? I must have been out of my mind, mustn't I?" She sniffed and mopped herself up. "Can we go home, Justin? I need something to drink."

"I could use a neat whiskey myself," he said heavily. His eyes searched over her wan, sad little face. "Are you sure you're all right?"

"I'm tough," she murmured.

"Tough," he agreed. "And reckless, stupid, impulsive—"

"You stop that!" she protested. Her pale green eyes glared at him, red-rimmed.

"You kissed me."

She went from white to rose red and averted her eyes. "You were upset."

"I've been upset before, but you never kissed me, Shelby." His dark eyes narrowed as he reached for the ignition switch. "Come to think of it, in all the years we've known each other, that's the very first move toward me you've ever made."

She leaned back against the seat, her arms folded. "Justin, my purse is still in the car," she murmured evasively.

He reached down to the floor, picked it up and put it in her lap. "You grabbed it before I lifted you clear," he said. "It came along for the ride."

"You aren't really going to shoot Abby's old car, are you?"

He reversed the car and then pulled in a perfect circle back the way he'd come. "It might get that gentle a treatment if it's lucky," he muttered.

"Justin! It wasn't the car's fault!"

"Sit back and relax now, Shelby. I'll have you home in a minute."

She ground her teeth together as he sped down the road at no less a speed than she'd been driving. "Pot," she muttered.

"Pardon?"

"Pot! The one that calls the kettle black! You're doing sixty!"

"It's a big car."

"What has that got to do with it?"

"Never mind." He smoked his cigarette, frowning thoughtfully. Things had been pretty clear in his mind until ten minutes ago. Now he began to wonder if he hadn't got things twisted. He'd assumed that Shelby found him repulsive all those years ago, that she still did. But her soft lips had been warm and eager, and for those few seconds she'd been absolutely ardent. Of course, she was frightened, he had to admit, and reaction did funny things to people. But if she was that concerned when he was upset, there had to be a little caring left in her.

He pulled up in front of the house and, despite her protests, carried her up to the door where he balanced her long enough to open it.

"No need to worry Maria…" he began, but no sooner had he got the words out than Maria came running down the hall. When she saw Shelby's white face, a stream of Spanish broke from her.

"I'm all right," Shelby told her. "The car went into the ditch, that's all."

Maria looked at Justin. That wasn't all, but she knew better than to make a fuss. "What do you want me to do, Señor Justin?" Maria asked.

"I'll get her upstairs. How about pouring me a neat whiskey and bringing up a brandy for Shelby?"

"Sí, señor."

"Why can't I have a neat whiskey?" Shelby asked.

Justin's dark eyes searched hers and he pulled her just a little closer as he went easily up the staircase with his soft burden cradled against his chest. "You're just a baby."

"I'm twenty-seven," she reminded him.

He smiled gently. "I'm thirty-seven," he reminded her. "And that's a pretty formidable ten-year jump I've got on you, honey."

The careless endearment made her flush. She lowered her eyes to his shirt. He'd changed earlier, before they ate. This one was Western cut and blue plaid. It suited him. It smelled of detergent and starch, smoke and cologne. She loved being in his arms. If only she could tell him that, and explain why she was afraid of him. But she couldn't.

He carried her into her room and put her on the bed, his eyes going hungrily over the way that damned red and white dress clung in all the right places. It wasn't low-cut, but it displayed her high breasts in the best possible way, and looking at them made him ache.

Shelby frowned at the expression on his face. "What's wrong?" she asked, fatigue in her soft voice.

He straightened. "Nothing. I'll have Maria bring up the brandy. You'd better have a hot bath and then I'll take you to the doctor. I want you examined, to make sure you haven't done any damage."

She sat up, her eyes like saucers. "Justin, I'm all right!"

"You're not a doctor and neither am I. You took a hell of a jolt and you were damned near in shock when I pulled you out of that car." His jaw set stubbornly. "You're going. Hurry up and get changed. Wear something—" he hesitated "—less sexy."

Her eyebrows arched. "I beg your pardon?"

He turned toward the door. "I'll phone the doctor while you take a bath."

She stared after him blankly. "I don't want to go to the doctor."

He just closed the door, ignoring what she did or didn't want. Taking control, as usual, she fumed. She wanted to throw things. She was all right, couldn't he see that? She burst into tears of frustrated temper and went into the bathroom. She felt as if her knees had been knocked out from under her.

After her bath, she dried her hair and put on a neat white blouse and gray skirt and brightened it with a gray and red scarf at her throat. She wondered why he wanted her to wear something less sexy, and then felt her heart skip at the realization that *he* must have found the red and white dress sexy. She smiled demurely. That was the first time since their marriage that he'd admitted to finding her attractive. If only she could be sure that he wouldn't lose control, it might have given her enough courage to do more than just kiss him.

She picked up the brandy snifter Maria had left with

a teaspoon of brandy in it and sipped it quietly. She had kissed him, all right. He was going to worry that to death. But he'd been upset and she'd wanted so desperately to comfort him that her usual inhibitions hadn't built a wall between them. And the kiss had been delicious. Her mouth still tingled from the rough sweetness of his. And then she remembered why it had been so sweet. He'd let her make all the moves. He hadn't taken control away from her. She frowned.

A knock on the door interrupted her brooding. She opened it. Justin was already looking impatient.

"How do you feel?" he asked.

"I'm sore…" she began.

"The doctor's waiting. Let's go." He took the brandy snifter from her, put it on her dresser and escorted her out of the room.

The doctor he'd found was at the hospital emergency room. Shelby felt nervous and edgy, because she'd hardly been near a hospital since her wreck in Switzerland, except to Dr. Sims for her premarital examination. But this wasn't Dr. Sims. This was a nice young doctor named Hays, very personable and kindhearted, and obviously a little amused by Justin's irritated concern.

"You'll be stiff for a couple of days, but I'm sure your husband will be relieved to know that you've done no lasting damage," Dr. Hays said after he'd finished his examination and she'd answered the necessary questions. "Just one more thing—there's no possibility that you might be pregnant?" he asked quietly, made more curious by her blush and Justin's averted face. "An experience like this could be risky…"

"I'm not pregnant," she said huskily.

"Then you'll be fine. I'm going to give you some muscle relaxants in case you need them. You can take a non-aspirin analgesic for pain, and a little extra rest tomorrow might be beneficial. Of course, if you have any further problems, let me know."

Shelby thanked him and Justin muttered something before he escorted her out of the examination room and down the hall to pay the bill. By the time they were through and on their way back to the house, it was almost eight o'clock and dark outside.

Justin was quiet all the way home. Shelby knew why. It was the doctor's very natural question about pregnancy. It had embarrassed Justin and probably enraged him as well, because intimacy was such a bone of contention between them.

"You should have told him that we could get you in the *Guinness Book of World Records* if you got pregnant," he said through his teeth as he parked the car in the driveway and cut off the engine.

She turned her purse in her lap. Now that the tension was lifting, she only felt tired and sore. "What did you do with my car? It wasn't on the highway when we came past the intersection."

His black eyes shifted toward her and then away. "You don't want to talk about it, do you?"

"I'm frigid," she said dully. "Let's just leave it at that, unless you want a divorce."

"I want a wife," he said harshly. "I want kids." His jaw tautened as he lifted his cigarette to his mouth. "Oh, God, I want kids, Shelby," he said in a faintly vulnerable tone.

That was something they'd never talked about, except in the very early days of their association. She leaned her head back against her seat, nibbling her lower lip and stared down at her lap. "You probably won't believe it, but so do I, Justin."

He turned in his seat to look at her downcast face, his eyes dark and quiet. "How did you plan to get any without help?"

Her hands contracted on her purse. "I'm afraid," she said softly, because for once she was too tired to lie, to find excuses.

There was a long pause. "Well, childbirth isn't really the terror it used to be, from all I've heard," he said, getting the wrong end of the stick. "And there are drugs they can give you for pain."

She looked up at him, shocked. "What?"

It was incredible that he believed she was afraid to have a child. She just stared at him without moving.

"It doesn't have to be right away, either," he said dog gedly, averting his gaze out the window, as if the subject embarrassed him. It probably did. Shelby remembered that he'd always found it difficult to talk about things like pregnancy and that he never did discuss intimate matters in mixed company. In his own way, he was as reticent as she was. It was one of the things she'd always loved about him.

She was trying to understand what he meant when he took another draw from the cigarette and put it out. There was a dull flush across his cheekbones and he wouldn't look at her.

"You could talk to the doctor about something to take," he said tersely. "Or I could use something. You don't have to get pregnant if you don't want to. I won't force you to have a child."

She went beet red and stared out her window, her

hands trembling and cold as the intimacy of what he was saying finally got through to her. She cleared her throat. "I…could we go inside now?" she whispered. "I'm tired and I ache all over."

"It's hard for me to talk about it, too," he said quietly. "But I wanted you to know. To think it over. If that's why you won't let me touch you…"

"Oh, don't!" She buried her face in her hands.

He sighed roughly. "I'm sorry. I shouldn't have said anything." He got out and came around the car to help her out. "Did he give you any muscle relaxants or do I need to go to the drugstore for you?" he asked.

"He gave me some samples," she said. She walked alongside him up the steps, ashamed of the way she'd changed the subject and shied away from the discussion. She wanted to tell him what was wrong. But talking to Justin that way was so embarrassing.

"You go on up and have an early night," he said, as remote as if he'd been talking to a total stranger. "I'll have Maria bring you up some hot chocolate. Do you want anything to eat?"

"No, thank you." She paused at the foot of the staircase and smoothed her hand over the banister. She didn't want to go. Her eyes lifted to his across the hall and she looked at him with hopeless longing and anguished shame. "I shouldn't have married you," she whispered huskily. "I never meant to make you unhappy."

His jaw went taut. "I never meant to make you unhappy, either, but that's what I've done."

She hesitated. "You never told me what you did with the sports car," she said after a minute. "Can't I have it back?"

"Sure," he said, lifting his chin and pursing his lips.

"We can have it made into an ashtray or a piece of modern art."

Her eyebrows shot up. "What do you mean?"

He shrugged. "It's about five inches thick and four feet long by now. A bit big for an ashtray, I guess, but framed, it would make one hell of a wall decoration."

"What are you talking about? What did you do with it?"

"I gave it to Old Man Doyle."

She turned her head slightly as the words registered. "He owns a junkyard."

He smiled faintly. "Sure does. He has a brand-new crusher. You know, one of those big machines that you use to push old cars into scrap metal..."

She flushed. "You did that on purpose!"

"You're damned right I did," he said with a glittery challenge in his eyes. "If I'd taken it back to the car lot, I couldn't be sure that you wouldn't rush right down there and buy it again. This way," he added, pulling his hat low over his eyes, "I'm sure."

"I still owe for it! It was a lot of money!"

He smiled pleasantly. "I'm sure you can explain it to the insurance company. Atmospheric pressure? Termites...?"

She was stuck for a reply when he turned and went into the kitchen.

She went up the staircase, smoldering. It had been an upsetting day all around, and it wasn't improving. Her mind whirled with questions and problems.

AT FIRST, SHE HADN'T wanted to take the muscle relaxants, but she got sore as the night wore on. Finally she gave in, downing them with a sip of cooling hot chocolate. She put on her gray satin pajamas and climbed under the covers. Minutes later, she was asleep.

But then the dreams started. Over and over again, she could see herself in the sports car, but in Switzerland. She'd been speeding around the Alps with skill and ease until she was almost at the bottom of a mountain. She'd hit a patch of ice and all her experience at the wheel hadn't been able to save her. The car, that time, had rolled. And rolled. And rolled.

She was pitching down the side of the white mountain, sky and snow combining in a terrible descent. She waited for the impact, waited, screaming...

Hands lifted her from the pillow, gently shaking her.

"It's all right," someone said. "It's all right. Wake up, Shelby, you're dreaming."

She snapped awake as if a switch had been thrown in her brain. Justin was holding her, his black eyes narrow with concern.

"The car..." she whispered. "It was pitching down the mountain."

"You were dreaming, little one," he said. He smoothed the dark tangle of her hair away from her flushed cheeks and her shoulders. "Only dreaming. You're safe now."

"I always was, with you," she said involuntarily, leaning her head on his shoulder. She sighed heavily, relaxed now, secure. Her cheek moved and he stiffened, and she realized that she was resting on bare skin, not a pajama top.

The light was on and he was sitting beside her on the bed, his dark hair tousled. She almost lost her nerve when she lifted her cheek away from his muscular upper arm, but she breathed easily when she saw that he was only bare from the waist up. He was wearing dark silk pajama

trousers, but his muscular chest was completely bare.
Thick black hair curled down to the low waistband of
the pajamas, and the very sight of him was breathtaking.

Shelby felt her breath catch at all that masculinity so
close to her. She knew without being told that he wasn't
wearing anything under those trousers, and it made her
feel threatened.

"Did you take those pills the doctor gave you?" he
asked quietly.

"Yes. They made the aching stop, but now I'm having nightmares." She laughed jerkily. She pushed back
her thick cloud of hair, glancing up at him apprehen-
sively. "Did I wake you?"

"Not really." He sighed. "I don't sleep well these days.
It doesn't take much to wake me. I heard you scream"

She didn't sleep well, either, and probably for the
same reason. She locked her arms around her knees,
curling up to rest her forehead there. "Today's accident
brought back the wreck I had in Switzerland," she murmured drowsily. "I was concussed and I kept drifting in
and out." She moved her forehead against the soft satin.
"They told me I called for you night and day after they
brought me to the hospital," she said without meaning to.

"Me, and not your lover?" he asked coldly.

"I've never had a lover, Justin," she said shyly.

"Sure. And I'm the king of Siam." He got to his feet,
looking down at her half angrily. She was lovely in those
satin pajamas. He'd never thought about what she wore
to sleep in, but now he was sure he'd think of nothing
else. The jacket was low-cut and he'd had a deliciously
tempting glimpse of her firm breasts when she'd first
come awake. They were small, he thought speculatively,
but perfectly formed if their outline under that jacket

was anything to go by. His eyes narrowed and he had to pull his gaze away, because he wanted to look at them with a hunger that made him go rigid.

He turned away. "If you're all right, I'll go back and try to sleep. I've got an early appointment in town at the bank."

She watched him go with a deep sadness. The distance between them grew all the time, and she was making him unhappier by the day. "Thank you for coming to see about me," she said dully.

He paused with his hand on the doorknob, his gaze concerned. "You'd die before you'd do it, I know," he said slowly. "But if you get frightened again, you can double up with me." He laughed coldly. "It's safe enough, in case you're worried. I won't risk my ego again with you."

He was gone before she could contradict him. She winced at the pain those words had revealed. She felt worse than ever, knowing how she'd hurt him.

And it was so unnecessary. All she had to do was tell him. For God's sake, she was twenty-seven years old! Yes, and sheltered to the point of obsession by her money-hungry father, who'd been afraid to lose her to a poor man. She'd never even been kissed intimately until the night they got engaged. She wondered if he knew that.

He probably didn't, she decided. She got out of bed and turned on the light, heading for the door. Maybe it was time she told him.

CHAPTER SIX

IT DIDN'T OCCUR to her until she was out in the hall, bare-footed, at Justin's door, that three o'clock in the morning wasn't the best time to share intimate secrets with a man who'd gone starving for physical satisfaction since his marriage. She hesitated, nibbling her lower lip. The light was still on in his room, but it was pretty quiet in there.

She frowned, wondering what to do, and brushed back her unruly hair with a sigh.

"He's not in there," came a soft, deeply amused voice at her back.

She whirled to find Justin behind her, holding a jigger of whiskey. "What are you doing out here?" she asked.

"Watching you prowl the halls. What were you planning to do, go in there and rape me?"

She burst out laughing. It bubbled up from some unknown place, and her eyes twinkled up at him. "I don't know how," she confessed.

He actually smiled. She was pretty when she laughed. She was pretty any way at all. He lifted the whiskey ruefully. "I thought it might help me sleep," he said.

"I'm afraid nothing's going to help me," she murmured. She shifted from one bare foot to the other, aware of his curious scrutiny and her own loud heartbeat.

"Do you want to sleep with me?" he asked.

She flushed. "That wasn't the only reason I came."

She glanced up and then down again at his own bare, very big feet. "Did you know that nobody had ever kissed me intimately until you did?"

He blinked. "You came down the hall at three o'clock in the morning to tell me that?"

She shrugged. "It seemed pretty important at the time," she said. She looked up at him sadly, her pale green eyes searching his lean, craggy face, his sensuous mouth, the firm, hair-roughened muscles of his chest and stomach. "It's amazing," she murmured, her eyes fascinated by the bare expanse of brown muscle.

"What is?" He frowned, watching the way her eyes went over him. It was disturbing. Surely she knew that.

"That you don't have to chase women out of your room with a broom handle," she murmured absently.

His eyebrows arched. "Have you been into my brandy snifter?"

"I guess it sounds that way, doesn't it?" She raised her eyes to his. "Can I sleep with you, Justin? I'm still pretty shaky. If..." She cleared her throat and looked away. "If it won't bother you too much, I mean. I don't want to make things any worse for you than they already are."

"I'm not sure they could get worse," he said quietly. He searched her wide, soft eyes. "All right. Come on."

She followed him inside. She'd never been in his room before, although she'd been by it a number of times and had peeked in curiously.

The furniture was old. Antique, like that in the house she'd grown up in. She wondered if it went far back in his family, if he'd inherited it from his parents. She smoothed her hand over a long bedpost, admiring the slickly polished wood of the four-poster and the beige and brown striped sheets on the bed.

"I didn't think you liked colored sheets," she said conversationally. "Maria said you didn't."

"I don't," he said curtly. "Maria does. She swears that she lost all the white sheets and had to replace them."

"Well, these are nice," she murmured.

"Climb in."

He held the top sheet back and let her slide under it. "I'll adjust the air-conditioning if it's too cool in here to suit you," he offered.

"No, it's fine," she said. "I hate a hot bedroom, even in winter."

He smiled faintly. "So do I." He turned off the light and came back to the bed. The mattress lowered as he sat down, obviously finishing off his whiskey.

"You, uh, you do sleep in pajama bottoms?" she asked, grateful for the darkness that spared her blushes.

He actually laughed. "Oh, my God."

"Well, you don't have to make fun of me," she muttered, fluffing the pillow before she laid her head on it.

"I always thought you were a sophisticated girl," he said pleasantly. "You know, the liberated sort with a string of men on your sleeve and the kind of sophistication that goes with champagne and diamonds."

"Boy, were you in for a shock," she murmured. "Until you came along, I'd only dated one man, and the most he did was to make a grab for me and get himself slapped. My father was obsessed with keeping me innocent until he could sell me to someone who'd make him even richer. But you don't know that, of course. You think he's a saint."

He switched on the light. His eyes were black and steady on hers, noticing the flush that covered her cheeks.

"Will you turn that off, please?" she asked tightly.

"If I'm going to talk about such things, I can't look at you and do it."

"Prude," he accused.

She glared at him. "Look who's talking."

He smiled ruefully. He cut off the lights, too. She felt the mattress shift as he lay back on it and pulled the sheet up over his hips.

"All right. If you want to talk, go ahead."

"My father never wanted you to marry me, Justin, despite the show he put on for you," she said shortly. "He wanted me to marry Tom Wheelor's racing stables so that he could merge them with his and get out of debt."

"That's a hard pill to swallow, considering what I know about your father," he said, remembering that it was her father's money that had helped his family's feedlot. He wondered if she'd ever found that out, and almost said so when he heard her sigh.

She shifted. "Nevertheless, it's true. He was all set to ruin you if I hadn't gone along with him when he cooked up that story about my marrying Tom."

"You admitted that you'd slept with Tom," he reminded her. His tone darkened. "And I know how little you wanted to sleep with me."

"It wasn't because I found you repulsive," she said.

"Wasn't it?"

Before she could say another word, he'd rolled over. One lean arm went across her body, dragging her against him. In the darkness, he sought her mouth with his and kissed her with rough abandon. Her hands went up against his hair-roughened chest, pushing at solid warm muscle, while his mouth demanded things that frightened her. His knee insinuated itself between both of hers, and she stiffened and pushed harder, fighting him.

He let her go without another word and got up. His hand flicked the light switch. When he turned toward her, his eyes were blazing like forest fires, his face livid with barely controlled rage.

"Get out!" he said in a biting fury.

She knew that she couldn't say anything now that would calm him. If she tried to argue or smooth it over, she might unleash something physical that would scar her even more than his ardor had six years before.

She got out of the bed, her eyes apologetic and tearful, and did as he'd told her. She didn't look back. She closed the door gently and, still crying, made her way down the long staircase.

Justin's study was quiet. She turned on the light, went to the liquor cabinet, and with hands that shook, found a brandy snifter. She poured brandy into it and swished it around. She wanted to jump off the roof, but perhaps this would do instead.

The house was so quiet. So peaceful. But her mind was in turmoil. Why couldn't he understand that violent lovemaking frightened her? Why wouldn't he listen?

She'd pushed him away, that was why. She'd fought him. But if she hadn't, and he'd lost control... Her eyes closed on a shudder. She couldn't even bear the thought.

Her legs shook as she made her way to the sofa and sat down, her body bowed, her forehead resting on the rim of the glass. Tears blurred it. She sipped and sipped, until finally the sting of the liquor began to soothe her nerves.

When she realized that she was no longer alone, she didn't even look up.

"I know you hate me," she said numbly. "You didn't have to come all the way down here to say it."

Justin winced at the tears on her face, at the anguish in her soft voice. His pride was shattered all over again. But it hurt him to see her cry.

He poured himself another whiskey and sat down on the edge of the heavy coffee table in front of her. "I've been up there calling you names," he said after a minute. "Until it suddenly got through to me what you'd said, about never letting another man kiss you intimately."

"I'm a scarlet woman, though," she said bitterly. "I slept with Tom. I even told you so."

"You've just told me that your father lied about it." His black eyes narrowed. He took a sip of the whiskey and put the glass down. He knelt just in front of her, not touching her, his eyes on a level with hers. "I remembered something else, too. Just after you wrecked the car, you kissed me. You weren't afraid of me, and you weren't repulsed, either, Shelby. But you were making all the moves, weren't you?"

Her eyes lifted to his. So he'd made the connection. She sighed worriedly. "Yes," she said finally. "I wasn't afraid, you see."

"But up until then," he added, his shrewd eyes making lightning assessments, "I'd been pretty rough with you when we made love."

She flushed, avoiding his gaze. "Yes."

"And it wasn't revulsion at all. It was fear. Not of getting pregnant. But of intimacy itself."

"Give that man a cigar," she murmured with forced humor.

He sighed, watching her fondle the brandy snifter. He took it out of her hands and put it on the coffee table. "Get up."

Startled, she felt him lift her from the sofa. He put

her to one side and stretched out on the cushions, moving toward the back. "Now sit down."

She did, hesitantly, because she didn't understand this approach.

He took one of her hands and drew it to his chest. "Think of me as a human sacrifice," he murmured drily. "A stepping stone in the educational process."

Her lips parted on a sudden gasp as she realized what he was doing. Her eyes darted up to his, curious, shy. "But you...you don't like that," she said perceptively, because in the past he'd always made the moves, he'd never encouraged her to.

"I'm going to learn to like it," he said frankly. "If it takes this to get you close to me, I'm more than willing to give you the advantage, Shelby."

Tears stung her eyes. She bit her lower lip to stop its trembling. "Oh, Justin," she whispered shakily.

"Can you do it this way?" he asked softly, his eyes black and alive with tenderness. "If I let you, can you make love to me?"

The tears broke from her eyes and ran down her cheeks. "I wanted to tell you," she wept. "But I was too embarrassed."

"It's all right." He put his big hand over hers and traced the tiny blue veins in it. "I should have realized it a long time ago. I won't hurt you. I'll never hurt you."

She laughed through the tears. Amazing that he should puzzle it out for himself. She smiled and bent hesitantly to his warm mouth and touched it with her lips.

Justin felt as if his heart were about to burst. God only knew why he'd never understood before. Obviously Wheelor had hurt her, and she'd drawn away from any further intimacy. He hated knowing that the other man had been her first lover, but he couldn't stand by any longer and watch Shelby beat herself to death emotionally over it. They had to start someplace to build a life together, and this was the very best way.

He felt her soft, shy mouth with a sense of wonder. She still didn't know a lot about kissing, and he smiled under her searching lips. He'd been celibate for a long time, but in his younger days, his lack of looks hadn't kept him from getting some experience. He knew what to do with a woman, even if discussing such things in public made him uncomfortable.

He didn't touch her. As he'd promised, he lay there with his body keeping him on the rack and let her soft mouth toy with his.

"Come closer," he breathed against her lips. "You're as safe as you want to be."

"It isn't hurting you?" she asked worriedly.

"When it gets that bad, I'll tell you," he promised, lying through his teeth, because it was already that bad.

She smiled, moving so that her soft breasts rested fully on his chest, her legs chastely beside his and not over them. There was a fine tremor in his lips when she bent again, but he still hadn't tried to pull her down or to make the kiss more intimate.

Her hands moved into his thick hair, ruffling it, and her lips traced patterns on his face, loving its strength. He was so sweet to kiss. She laughed with pure delight at the new freedom to touch him as she'd wanted to for so many lonely years.

His eyes opened and he studied her curiously. "What was that all about?"

"If you knew," she said, "how long I've wanted to do this…"

His jaw clenched. "You might have told me."

"I couldn't." She touched his broad chest. "It's so intimate a thing to talk about." Impulsively, she leaned down and brushed her mouth over the hard muscle of his breastbone. "Justin, I've missed you so much."

His chest rose heavily under the tiny caress. "I've missed you, too," he said huskily. "God, Shelby, I can't…!" He clenched his teeth.

She looked up. "It isn't enough for you, is it?" she asked hesitantly. "I guess I seem pretty green."

His eyes darkened. "I want to touch you," he breathed. "I want to put you on your back and slide that jacket out of my way."

Her body trembled over his. "If you lost control, it would be just the way it was upstairs," she ground out. "I got scared!"

"I swear to God I won't lose it," he said curtly. "Not if I have to run out into the night screaming."

She believed him. It was the most difficult thing she'd ever done, to trust him now. But she swallowed hard and moved gently alongside him and onto her back, watching him shift so that he was poised over her.

"Trust comes hard, doesn't it?" he asked softly.

"Yes." She searched his face quietly. "I could have died this afternoon. I keep thinking about it, and how insignificant things seem at the point of death. All I thought about was you, and what a sad memory I'd left you with."

"Is that what this is all about?" he asked with a smile.

"Not really." She studied his hard mouth. "I was hungry for you when you let me kiss you. I wanted to know if I could stop being afraid. But upstairs, when you grabbed me, I just went to pieces."

"I'm not going to grab you this time." He bent, barely touching her mouth with his. He brushed it, bit at it, until her lips began slowly to follow his. He felt her breath quicken. And then his fingers began to trace patterns on the pajama jacket.

At first she stiffened, but his movements were very slow and undemanding, and his mouth was gentle. He lifted his head, feeling her begin to relax, and he smiled reassuringly. "Okay?" he whispered.

The tenderness was new. Her eyes smiled up at him. "Okay."

He looked down at her breasts and saw hard peaks forming where his fingers teased. He put his thumb over a hard tip and heard her gasp and felt her body shudder. He liked that reaction, so he did it again, and this time she arched a little.

"I like that," he said softly, holding her eyes. "Do it again."

She did, but only because she couldn't help it. "I feel...strange," she whispered. "Shuddery."

"So do I," he whispered back, and brushed his mouth lazily over her lips until they parted. "Do you want me to tell you what I'm going to do now?"

Her heartbeat went wild. "Yes," she said against his mouth.

He smiled. "I'm going to unbutton your jacket."

Her breath sighed out quickly against his lips as she felt his hard fingers flicking buttons out of buttonholes. Then the fabric was open down the middle and he was slowly easing it away. He drew it just to the curve of her breasts and looked into her eyes, registering the faint shyness there and the excitement that she couldn't hide.

"You're small," he whispered. His fingers drew along one smooth curve. "I like my women small."

She trembled at the way he said it, at the knowledge in his black eyes, at the experience in the fingers that traced up and over and then stopped short of that hard, aching peak. She shuddered when he did that. He did it again, and she gasped.

His nose brushed against hers. His breath mingled with her own, tasting smoky and warm. "Yes, you want it, don't you?" he mused softly. He traced her again and this time he didn't stop. His hand smoothed over her and down, taking the hard tip into his moist palm and pressing down over it.

She cried out. The sound seemed to shock her because she swallowed, moistening her lips with her tongue.

"You act," he whispered, moving the fabric aside sensually, "just like a virgin with her first man." He peeled the satin away from her breasts and looked down. His breath caught, because the creamy mounds and their hard mauve tips were shaped so exquisitely that they took his breath.

"Do you really not mind...that I'm small?" she heard herself whisper.

"Oh, God, no," he returned. His eyes held hers and his fingers traced her soft skin. "Will it shock you if I put my mouth on them?"

"Yes," she said, smiling.

He smiled back and bent his head toward her body. She arched up at the first touch of his lips on her breasts, thinking that in all her life, she'd never dreamed there could be such pleasure in being touched. Her hands tangled in his thick hair and held him against her while his light, brushing caresses made her tremble. She moaned and tears sprung to her eyes.

He felt her body tremble and understood why. It was the advantage he'd been waiting for. His lean, callused hands smoothed down her hips, over her flat belly. They caressed the satin away so expertly that she didn't mind, didn't care. His hands touched her as if she'd always belonged to him, and she loved the touch, the slow tenderness of his rough hands on her skin.

His mouth opened, moist, the suction on her breast making her draw up with pleasure. She felt her hands helplessly gripping his muscular arms, pulling at him. She was whispering something that she didn't understand, pleading with him for something she didn't even know about. She needed…something.

Her mouth bit at his shoulder. When he lifted his head and looked down at her, she could barely see him through a red haze. She thought he smiled as his mouth fastened on hers. Then she felt his tongue go into her mouth in slow, exquisite thrusts and her body went wild under his.

She pulled at him, her arms around his neck. She felt him against her, felt the hard, warm contours of his body and the heat of his rough skin against her soft skin. She realized dimly that his pajama trousers were gone, but the touch of him against her was so exquisite that she didn't really want him to stop.

"It's going to happen now," he whispered into her mouth as his knee eased between her long, trembling legs. "I won't hurt you. I won't rush you. You can still stop me in time, if you want to. We're going to do this with such tenderness that you won't be afraid of me. Now just lie still and trust me for another few…seconds…"

She was trembling and so was he, but she'd never wanted anything in her life the way she wanted to belong to him. This was Justin. He was her husband and she loved him more than her life. He'd been so patient, so tender, that she wanted to give him her body along with her heart.

"Justin," she whispered achingly, watching his face harden. She felt the first touch of him and jerked a little.

"Shh," he whispered back. He smiled at her, forcing himself to hold back. "I'm going to watch you," he breathed huskily. "I'll know the instant it happens if there's the first hint of pain."

It was incredibly intimate. The lights were on. But all she could see was his face. She could feel his breath, quick and hard on her face, she could see the pulse beating in his throat. But she wasn't afraid, not even of his weight on her body, crushing her down into the cushions. He was hers, and she was going to take him…

She felt the pain like a hot knife. She clutched at him and her eyes got as big as saucers. She cried out and tears ran down her face.

Justin's eyes darkened and the pupils grew and grew and she realized then that he was frozen like a statue over her. His lips parted. His breath blew out. He looked down at her incredulously. He moved again, and watched her clench her teeth even as he knew for certain why she was doing it.

"I'm sorry," she whispered. Her hands reached up. "Don't stop," she said. "It's all right, I think I can… bear it…!"

"My God!"

He drew back, struggling away from her to sit up with his back to her, bowed, his body shuddering wildly. "My God, Shelby!"

"Justin, you didn't...you didn't have to stop," she whispered, biting her lip. "It would have been all right."

He wasn't listening. His head was in his hands and he shivered. He reached for the whiskey glass that still had a swallow of liquid in it, and his hands shook so badly that he almost spilled it before he got it to his mouth.

He stood up and Shelby flushed and averted her shocked eyes from his blatant masculinity.

"I'm sorry," he said curtly. He reached for his pajama bottoms and got into them distractedly. Then he stood looking down at her until she went bloodred and tried to curl up.

But he wouldn't let her. He reached down unsteadily to pick her up. He cradled her in his arms and sat down in his armchair, holding her with marvelous tenderness, whispering endearments into her dark hair, holding her while the tears came.

When she stopped, he mopped her eyes with a tissue. Her cheek was against his broad, shuddering chest, nestled against the thick hair, and her breasts were lying soft against his stomach. She shivered at the intimacy of it because she didn't have a stitch on.

"You're my wife," he whispered when he saw her embarrassment. "It's all right if I see you without your clothes."

She curled closer. "Yes, I guess it is. It's just...new."

"My God, yes, I know."

There was an unmistakable note in his voice. She

looked up, giving him a sudden and total view of her pretty breasts. He had to drag his eyes back up to hers.

"My virgin bride," he whispered huskily. His fingers touched her breasts hesitantly, with something like reverence. "Oh, Shelby. Shelby!"

"I... Dr. Sims made me have some minor surgery, but he muttered about it when I wouldn't let him do a proper job," she said, hiding her eyes from him. "I guess it wasn't quite enough..." Her face went red.

"Why wouldn't you let him do it properly?"

"So that I could prove that I hadn't slept with Tom," she said simply.

"You little fool!" He tilted her eyes up to his. "If I hadn't stopped upstairs, or if I'd ever lost my head with you... God, it doesn't even bear thinking about!"

She bit her lip, staring at his broad chest with its thick pelt of hair. "Justin   it would have stopped hurting," she began shyly.

"Like hell it would." He leaned back with a rough sigh. "I hate to be the bearer of bad tidings, honey, but you're going to have to go back and have the rest of that surgery."

"But..."

He tilted her eyes up to his. "A little pain is one thing, but you've got one hell of a lot of proof there," he said curtly. He shifted restlessly, noting her embarrassment and feeling just a little of his own at trying to explain things to her. He drew her head against his chest and bent to brush his mouth softly over hers. "Put your clothes back on while I top off your brandy snifter. The feel of you is making me hurt."

He got up and put her down on the sofa with only a cursory glance. While she fumbled her way back into her pajamas, he poured brandy into her glass and whiskey into his, and then went searching for a cigarette.

She knew her face was flaming. She'd never imagined that intimacy was so…intimate. But along with the shyness was a kind of excitement that went along with her new discoveries of Justin. He didn't lose control and go wild and hurt her. He was slow and patient and considerate. That made her blush even more.

"Who told you that men go nuts and hurt women when they make love?" he asked conversationally. "Because you seemed to think that's what was going to happen upstairs."

She took the brandy snifter and watched him go back to the armchair, where he sat and pulled up an ashtray. "You did," she said hesitantly. "The night we got engaged, and you lost control."

His eyebrows shot up. "Did I lose it that badly?"

"I thought so." She studied the snifter. "I knew I had this problem, you see, and I'd already been told about the surgery I'd have to have before my first time." She shrugged. "I've been terrified of it ever since my fifteenth birthday, when the doctor examined me for a female dysfunction. Some girls have a little discomfort, but he told me it would be unbearable if I didn't have the surgery. Then when you came on so strong, and I didn't think I could stop you…"

"You didn't tell me any of this," he said quietly.

"How could I?" She sighed miserably. "Oh, Justin, I'm twenty-seven and as green as a preadolescent! I can't even talk about it now without blushing!"

"I thought you were repulsed by me," he said, his voice deep with remembered pain. "I never dreamed… And then you told me what you did about Wheelor, and my ego shattered." His broad shoulders rose and fell. "I've been a lot rougher with you than I ever would have been if I'd known the truth. It hurt so damned bad to think that you'd been with someone else, and when you flinched away, it made me sick."

"At least now you know why I flinched away," she said with a sigh.

He took a draw from the cigarette. "I want you damned bad," he said without preamble.

She lowered her eyes to the carpet. "I want you, too."

"Then let's do something about it. Go see Dr. Sims. Have the surgery. Let's have a real marriage. The kind where two people sleep together, share together, make babies together."

Her face flamed, but she looked up. "You really do want children, don't you?"

"I want them with you," he said simply. "I never wanted them with any other woman."

"Then I won't need to…to take anything."

He smiled slowly. "No."

She got up, nervous and shy all over again. "I guess it wouldn't be a good idea for us to sleep together?" she asked without realizing how wistful she sounded.

He got up, drawing her eyes as he towered over her. "Maybe it wouldn't, but we're going to. Even if we can't make love, I can hold you."

Her breath sighed out. "Justin, I'm sorry for so many things."

"So am I, but we can't go back." He bent and brushed a gentle kiss across her mouth. "We'll take it one day at a time. I won't rush you again."

She smiled at him. "Thank you."

He smiled back, but he didn't say anything. She

watched him put everything away before he came back to her, turning out the light. He still had his cigarette in hand as they went upstairs together.

"Are you all right?" he asked her when they were in bed, and she was curled up beside him. "I didn't hurt you badly?"

"No," she whispered in the concealing darkness.

"I didn't frighten you, either?" he persisted, as if it mattered.

"Not at all," she assured him, going closer. He was warm and muscular and she loved the feel of him against her. "Not once." She nuzzled her cheek against him. "You're very tender."

"That's how lovemaking should be," he said quietly. "But I'm rusty, Mrs. Ballenger. I've been celibate for quite a while."

She held her breath. "A few months, you mean?"

"Um, not quite." He brushed his mouth over her forehead. "For about six years, Shelby."

She caught her breath. "My gosh! I didn't dream…!"

"It's a good thing," he murmured. "I guess you'd have run from me screaming if you'd known, thinking that a man who'd gone hungry that long would be ravenous and uncontrollable."

"But you weren't."

"You needed tenderness, so that's what you got. You won't always get it after we've had each other a few times," he said flatly. "I don't like it that way all the time."

The mind boggled at what he did like and she realized that he'd been curbing his instincts, holding back to make things easier for her. "Justin…"

"Shhh." He kissed her mouth softly. "Go to sleep. You're arousing me."

"I'm sorry."

He kissed her again and rolled over onto his stomach with a long sigh. "Good night, baby doll."

"Good night, Justin."

But she didn't sleep for a long time. There were a thousand questions buzzing around in her mind, and only a few answers. At least she'd gotten one big hurdle out of the way, and Justin still wanted her. That was something. Even if he couldn't love her, he might grow to have some kind of affection for her again. He couldn't blame her totally about the past, since he knew she was still innocent. Or could he? It occurred to her then that he might still want vengeance for the bitterness and humiliation he'd suffered. That was a sobering thought, and it kept her awake for a very long time.

CHAPTER SEVEN

JUSTIN COULD HARDLY believe what he saw when he woke up the next morning. He was so used to the dreams of Shelby ending at dawn. But here she was, with her long, dark hair on his pillow, her soft, elfin features relaxed in sleep, her mouth full and sweet and tempting.

He lay there, just watching her, for a long time. He'd been lonely without her. More lonely than he'd realized until they were speaking again. When they were dating, he'd dreamed of having Shelby in his bed, relaxed in sleep, and doing just this—watching her sleep. She couldn't know how precious she was to him, or that last night had been a revelation, a culmination of every longing he'd ever had, even though he hadn't been able to finish what he'd started. Just finding her virginal was a shock of pure delight.

He didn't even start to think about why she'd deceived him. He was too enraptured by the sight of her lovely face in sleep, by her dark head lying so trustingly on his pillow.

When she didn't stir, he smiled gently and bent to brush her lips with his.

He saw her long black eyelashes flutter and then lift. She sighed, saw him and smiled, a new softness in her pale green eyes.

"Good morning," she whispered.

"Good morning." He kissed her again. "Did you sleep well?"

"I've never slept so well in all my life. And you?"

"I could say the same." He pulled the sheet back over her, tucking it in. "You don't have to get up yet."

"Are you going to work this early?" she murmured with a sleepy glance at the clock.

"I have to fly up to Dallas, honey," he said, rising. "A new customer. I'll be home by dark."

"I don't have to be at work until nine," she said with a smug smile.

"I wish you'd give up that job," he said, frowning down at her.

"Justin, I like it," she protested, but not vehemently.

"I don't like having you so handy to Barry Holman," he murmured.

She stared at him. "Maybe he is a womanizer, but not with me," she told him. "He's a very nice man and he's good to me."

Justin turned away. It wouldn't do to have her know how jealous he was of her handsome boss. "I've got to get a shower."

She watched him rummage in his drawer for underwear and head toward the bathroom, her eyes hungry on his bare torso. It seemed so unreal, the intimacy that they'd shared the night before. She blushed just remembering it, but he was gone before he saw the scarlet flush on her cheeks.

She wondered if she should have told him about Tammy Lester and the way Mr. Holman seemed so interested in her. She might do that later.

But she dozed off while he was in the shower, and when she woke up again, he was dressed in a pale gray suit that clung lovingly to the powerful lines of his tall body, and he was straightening his red-and-gray-striped tie in the mirror.

"Is Maria up this early to feed you?" she murmured sleepily.

"I'll have breakfast on the plane." He turned, digging into his pockets, and tossed a set of car keys on the bed beside her. "Take the T-bird to work. Your transportation problem will have to wait until tomorrow."

She sat up, holding the keys. "But how will you get to the airport?"

He cocked an eyebrow. "I wonder if my heart will take all this concern?" he asked.

Her soft eyes ran over him and then the night before came back with alarming clarity. She saw him the way he'd been downstairs with her, felt again the intimacy...

"My God, what a scarlet blush," he murmured, loving her reactions. "I suppose you'd get under the bed if I started reminiscing?"

"You bet I would," she said with her last bit of pride. Then she ruined it all by smiling and hiding her face in her hands. "Oh, Justin," she whispered, remembering.

He sat down on the bed beside her, drawing her forehead against his chest. He smelled of cologne, and just being close to him made her weak and giddy.

"Do you feel like going to work?" he asked then, tilting her eyes up to his. "You don't have to."

"I know." She sighed gently. "But I'm only sore. I was more scared than hurt in the first place."

"You weren't the only one," he murmured. "I've got five new gray hairs this morning thanks to you."

She reached up and touched his neatly combed hair at the temple, where silver hairs were threaded through the black ones. "I'm sorry. I was running away, I guess. You seem to hate me from time to time."

"Sometimes I thought I did," he confessed, and he didn't smile. "Six years is a long time to brood. I believed you, about Wheelor." He slid his hand under her nape. The fingers contracted suddenly, not hard enough to hurt, but hard enough to pin her forehead to his jacket. "Why?" he asked in a deceptively soft voice. "Why lie to me about it? Wasn't breaking the engagement enough, without ripping my pride to shreds, as well?"

And there it was, she thought, the bitterness seeping through. He was never going to get over what she'd done, and the fact of her innocence physically didn't seem to make much difference. It certainly wasn't going to stop him from blaming her for the past, even if he wanted her desperately. He'd always wanted her, but that wasn't enough anymore. Her eyes went misty with sadness. He'd told her last night that he'd been six years without a woman. That showed how bitter he was, that he didn't even want women anymore. But he wanted her, and she could imagine that it made him forget the past when he was close to her. Years of celibacy would probably make a man forget a lot when he was in the throes of passion.

Her world crumbled. She closed her eyes with a small sigh.

"I told you why last night," she said. "It was Dad's idea."

"And I told you before, your father liked me. He did everything in the world to help me. That night he and Wheelor came to see me, he even cried, Shelby."

Her eyes lifted to his. "It all goes back to trust, and I know how little of that you have for me," she said.

"Not that it's all your fault, Justin. I didn't help things by deliberately lying to you in the beginning. But you don't trust me at all."

His jaw tautened. "I can't," he said. He let go of her all at once and got to his feet, moving away. "I want you, you know that. But I can't let you close. A woman who'll betray a man once will do it twice."

"I'm still a virgin," she reminded him uncomfortably.

"That isn't what I meant. You lied to me. You sold me out." He took a deep breath and pulled out a cigarette. "I'm not even sure you wouldn't do it now with that slick boss of yours." He glanced at her set face, his eyes glittering. "It's easy to see how little encouragement he'd need from you, and he's good-looking, isn't he, honey? There's nothing plain about him."

"You aren't plain," she muttered.

"How perceptive of you to know I was talking about myself," he snapped. "Stay out of trouble while I'm gone, and don't put your foot down on my accelerator."

"I won't touch your precious car, if you'd rather," she shot back, her green eyes flashing. "I'll take a cab, and let all of Jacobsville see me do it!"

He glared at her and she glared back. And all at once, he started to grin, then to smile, and finally laughter burst from his set lips and glittered in his black eyes.

"Hellcat," he murmured.

"Savage," she threw right back.

He tossed the cigarette into the big ashtray on his dresser and moved toward her purposefully. She threw off the covers and headed for the other side of the bed, but he was too quick. Before she was halfway over, he had her flat on her back and had pinned her with the length of his big, hard-muscled body.

"That's it, struggle," he encouraged with a groan. "My God, can you feel what's happening to me?"

She could. She stopped, her cheeks like red flags.

"Well, the world won't end," he said with soft amusement. "You know how I feel when I'm aroused, and last night we didn't have several layers of clothes between us."

"Stop!" She buried her face in his throat, clinging, trembling with embarrassment and excitement.

"You baby," he chided, but the words were tender. He rolled over onto his back, pulling her over with him, his dark eyes searching her pale ones as she poised over his chest. He looked down at the deep cleavage of her pajama jacket and the faint swell of her breasts above it where they were pressed against him. "Is this better?" he murmured.

"You're a horrible man, and I don't think I want to live with you anymore," she said, pouting.

"Yes, you do." He coaxed her mouth down to his by pulling a strand of her long, silky hair. "Kiss me."

"You'll rumple your suit," she said.

"I've got a lot of other suits, but I want to be kissed. Come on, I've got a plane to catch."

She gave in to the gentle teasing. All the arguing was forgotten the minute her soft mouth touched his hard one. She felt his hand sliding into her hair, pulling gently, and her lips parted to the soft, intense searching of his warm mouth.

"After you see the doctor, we'll have to wait a couple of days before we can finish what we started last night," he whispered into her mouth. "So don't start worrying about that and getting nervous all over again, okay?"

His dark eyes searched hers. "I won't rush you, Shelby. This time, it's going to be exactly the way you want it."

She kissed his eyes, gently closing the eyelids, lingering on the thick lashes in a rage of tenderness. She wanted to whisper that she loved him more than her own life, that everything she'd done that had hurt him had been, in the beginning, only to protect him. But he didn't trust her yet, and she was going to have to bring him around before she could share her deepest secrets with him.

"Will you believe me when I say that I'm not afraid of you anymore?" she whispered against his lips.

"Honey, that's pretty hard to miss, considering the position we're in," he whispered back.

"What positi… Justin!"

He laughed as he flipped her onto her back and slid over her, nibbling warmly at her lips. "This position," he whispered. "Kiss me goodbye and I'll go."

"I've already done…that…several times," she whispered, the words punctuated with soft, clinging kisses.

"Do it several more and I'll work on getting my legs to support me," he murmured drily. "My knees are pretty weak right now."

"So are mine." She linked her arms around his neck and bit his lower lip. "You're mine now," she said quietly, her eyes holding his. "Don't you go off and flirt with other women."

Her possessiveness made him ache. He slid his hands under her back and lifted her up, taking his time as he bent hungrily to her open mouth. He kissed her with growing insistence until his own body forced him to either stop or go on.

He rolled away reluctantly and got to his feet, taut

with pride as he looked down at his handiwork. She was sprawled in delicious abandon on the sheets, her hair like a halo around her, her mouth soft and red and swollen from his kisses, her eyes dreamy with desire.

"If I had a photograph of you that looked the way you look now," he said huskily, "I'd walk around bent double every time I looked at it. I've never seen a woman as beautiful as you are."

"I'm not even pretty," she chided, smiling. "But I'm glad you like me the way I am. I like you, too."

He drew in a slow breath. "I'd better get out of here while I can. It helps to remember your condition."

She averted her eyes to the sheets, feeling nervous.

"You'd really have let me go on, wouldn't you?" he asked, his voice deep with feeling. "Even knowing how bad it was going to hurt you, you wouldn't have stopped me."

"I wanted you to know," she whispered.

"It took a lot of courage." He frowned, watching her. "Did it hurt you when I accused you of being frigid?"

"A little," she said, trying to spare him.

He sighed angrily. "A lot, I imagine. Try to remember that I didn't know the truth, and don't hate me for it. There are a lot of things you don't know about me, either, Shelby." He turned then, retrieving his cigarette from the ashtray. "I'd better get a move on," he said after a cursory glance at the thin gold watch on his wrist. "No speeding," he cautioned from the door.

The remark intrigued her, but she knew he wasn't going to tell her any more than he wanted her to know. "All right. Have a good trip."

"I'll do my best."

He didn't say goodbye. He gave her one last glance

and closed the door behind him. Shelby watched him leave with mixed emotions. Sometimes she wished she could read his mind, because that was the only way she was ever going to know how he really felt about her. She wondered if he knew himself.

She got up and dressed and drove the Thunderbird to the office, taking a minute to make an appointment that afternoon with Dr. Sims. By the time she got home, she was worn out from the combination of an unexpectedly long day trying to keep peace between an irritable Mr. Holman and a venomous Tammy Lester, and having the rest of the surgery done—which was embarrassing as well as uncomfortable, because she had to tell Dr. Sims why she needed it.

But a cup of fresh coffee and a nice supper soothed her. She went upstairs to her own room, wishing she had the right to go straight to Justin's. But he hadn't said anything about the sleeping arrangements, so apparently he'd thought of last night as a temporary thing because of what had happened.

She went to sleep early. She didn't hear the car come in, or Justin's footsteps heading toward his own bedroom expectantly. She didn't hear the muffled curse when he found his bed empty, or the shocked silence when he found Shelby asleep in her own.

He closed the door firmly and went to his room, dreams going black in his eyes. He'd expected her to be waiting up, or at least sleeping in his bed. But she hadn't, and he didn't know if she'd just been uncertain about what to do or if she was putting a wall between them because of the argument they'd had that morning.

Shelby, blissfully unaware of what had happened after she was asleep, went down to breakfast the next morning full of hope. Only to find a cold, taciturn Justin at the table looking at her as if she'd just tried to shoot him.

She stopped suddenly in the doorway. Her long denim skirt swung around her calves, her hands going nervously to the blue cotton blouse and scarf she was wearing with it.

"Good morning," she said, faltering.

"Hell, no, it isn't," he said.

Her eyebrows arched. "It isn't?"

He lifted his coffee cup and sipped the rich black liquid. "I'll have one of the boys drive you to work," he said. "May I have the keys to the Thunderbird?"

She reached into her skirt pocket and put them beside him on the table, but he caught her hand before she could move away.

He looked up, his expression brooding. "Why did you go back to your own room?"

She sighed and then smiled. "Because I didn't know if you still wanted me to sleep with you," she said sadly. "You were half-mad when you left, and you didn't say anything." Her shoulders lifted and fell. "I didn't want to impose."

"My God, honey, we're married," he said huskily. "You couldn't impose on me if you tried."

She stared down at the big, lean hand holding hers. Its warm strength made her tingle. "You've been very remote since we've been married."

"I think you're beginning to understand why, though, aren't you?" he asked softly.

She looked down into his dark, quiet eyes. She nodded. "You…want me."

"That's part of it," he agreed without elaborating. "Did you see Dr. Sims?"

Her blush gave him the answer even before she nodded.

He drew her down in the chair beside him. "I'll drive you to work," he said and pushed a platter of eggs toward her.

She smiled, but she didn't let him see her do it.

Justin had calmed down by the time they got to Jacobsville, but Barry Holman set him off again immediately when they reached the office. The handsome blond lawyer was outside on the street, looking all around, and to an onlooker, it might have appeared as if he was waiting impatiently for Shelby. To Justin, unfortunately, that's exactly what it looked like.

Holman's head lifted when Justin pulled the Thunderbird up at the curb, and his face lit up. He smiled with exaggerated pleasure and rushed to meet Shelby with a cursory nod to Justin, whose expression turned murderous.

"Thank God you're here," Barry enthused, opening the door for her. "I was afraid you were going to be late. How pretty you look this morning!" He knew about day-before-yesterday's mishap, of course, but Shelby was shocked by his attentiveness and was already beginning to wonder what ailed him as he helped her onto the sidewalk. "I'll take good care of her, Justin," he said, adding fuel to the fire, grinning at her smoldering husband.

Justin didn't answer him or speak to Shelby. He slammed the car door, his eyes glittering in Shelby's direction, and roared away down the street.

"What's wrong?" Shelby asked, mentally nervous about Justin's unexpected anger. Mr. Holman had certainly given Justin a bad impression of their working relationship.

"That woman has got to go," he said without preamble, waving his hands. "She's locked herself in my office and she won't let me in. I've called the fire department, though," he added with a smug glitter in his eyes. "They'll break the door down and get her out, and then she can leave. Permanently."

Shelby put a hand to her head. "Mr. Holman, why is Tammy locked in your office?"

He cleared his throat. "It was the book."

"What book?"

"The book I threw at her," he said irritably.

"You threw a book at Tammy!" she gasped.

"Well, it was a dictionary." He shifted with his hands in his pockets. "We had a slight disagreement over the spelling of a legal term, which I should know, Shelby," he added angrily, "after all, I'm a lawyer. I know how to spell legal terms; they teach us that in law school."

Shelby, who'd sampled some of Mr. Holman's expertise at spelling legal terms, didn't say a word.

He shifted again. "Well, I said some things. Then she said some things. Then I sort of tossed the book her way. That was when she locked herself in my office."

"Just because of the book," she probed.

He stared down at the pavement. "Uh, yes. That. And the broken glass."

Her eyes gaped. "Broken glass?"

"The window, you know." He moved sheepishly toward the curb, having spotted what he was searching for earlier. He picked up the torn dictionary with a faint grin. "Here it is! I knew it had to be out here somewhere."

Shelby was torn between laughter and tears when the fire truck came blaring down the street with its siren going and pulled to a screeching halt at the curb.

"You didn't tell them why you needed them to come here, by any chance?" Shelby asked as she watched the firemen, because they'd come in a pumper truck and were very obviously unwinding a long, flat hose.

"No, come to think of it, I didn't. Hi, Jake!" Mr. Holman called to the fire chief with a big grin. "Good of you to come. Uh, there's not exactly a fire, though. I'm more in need of a different kind of help."

Jake, a big, burly man with a red face, came closer. "No fire? Well, what do you need us to do, Barry?" he asked, gesturing to the men to roll up the hose again.

"I need you to break down my office door with an ax," Mr. Holman said.

"Why?"

"I lost my key," Mr. Holman improvised.

"Then wouldn't a locksmith do you more good?" Jake continued. He was beginning to give Shelby's boss a strange kind of look.

Mr. Holman frowned thoughtfully. "Oh, no, I don't think so. It wouldn't make nearly the impression that an ax would."

Jake was looking puzzled.

"One of our…employees…has locked herself in the office and won't come out," Shelby explained.

"Well, my gosh, Barry, an ax banging the door down would scare her half to death!" Jake said.

"Yes." Mr. Holman smiled thoughtfully. "It sure as hell would."

Just as Jake started to speak, Tammy Lester came

out of the building, looking explosive, and went right up to Barry Holman and hit him as hard as she could.

"I quit," she said furiously, almost trembling with rage. "Sorry, Shelby, but you're back to being a one-woman office. I can't take one more day of Mr. God's Gift to Womanhood! And you can't spell, Mr. Big-Shot Attorney!"

"I can spell better than you can, you escapee from a high-school remedial spelling course!" he yelled after her. "And don't expect that I'll come running, begging you to come back! There must be hundreds of stupid women who can't spell in this town who need work!"

Jake was gaping at the normally calm attorney. So was Shelby. She was having a hard time trying not to laugh. That would only complicate things, of course. She eased past the fire chief and quickly went into the office to escape what was about to happen.

And sure enough, she'd barely gotten inside the carpeted office when Jake let Mr. Holman have it with both barrels. There was something about false alarms and potential arrests…at that point, Shelby closed the door and went to her computer.

She worried about the way Justin had reacted to Mr. Holman waiting on the street for her. It didn't look good, and Justin was already wildly jealous of the man. That didn't make a lot of sense, but then Shelby didn't know a lot about men. She assumed that it was only a surface jealousy, because Barry Holman was handsome and a womanizer and Justin was possessive and very territorial. She never once thought that it might be anything more than that.

Because it disturbed her, she phoned the house to explain to Justin what had happened. But Maria told her that he hadn't come back yet. She tried again at lunch, but he was out with a client. So she went back to work and forgot all about it, while Mr. Holman sputtered and muttered about Tammy for the rest of the day and finally closed the office an hour early because he wasn't getting any work done.

"Don't worry about making up the time," he told Shelby quietly. "We've got court next month, and you may have to put in some overtime getting out briefs and helping me with research." He glowered at the door. "I was going to let Miss Lester help with that, since she does seem to have a feel for legwork. But now that she's quit for such a stupid reason, you'll have to do it."

"Most secretaries would get nervous if their bosses threw books at them," Shelby pointed out.

"I didn't hit her, did I?" he asked mockingly. "I hit the window. That reminds me, you'd better call Jack Harper and get him over here tomorrow to put in another windowpane." He looked uncomfortable. "And, uh, you don't need to go into details about how it got broken. Do you?"

"I'll tell him an eagle flew through it," she agreed.

He glared and stomped off toward his car.

Shelby started toward where she usually parked her car when it dawned on her that she didn't have a car.

"Oh, Mr. Holman," she called without thinking, "could you drop me off at the feedlot? I haven't been able to get Justin, and he won't be here for another hour to pick me up."

"Sure. Come on."

He helped her into the black Mercedes and shot off down the road toward the Ballenger feedlot. "What happened to your new car?" he asked. "Engine trouble?"

She smiled wistfully. She hadn't told him about the sports car, even though he knew she had been driving Justin's car the day before. "Justin gave it to Mr. Doyle."

"He runs a junkyard," Mr. Holman reminded her.

"That's right, he does, and he has a brand-new car crusher." She sighed. "Justin said if I liked, he could have my sports car made into a nice wall decoration. It's about five inches thick..."

"What did he do that for?" the lawyer asked.

"He thinks I'm reckless," Shelby said. "I think he's planning to buy me something sedate. Like a Sherman tank."

Mr. Holman smiled. "I hope I didn't get you into any trouble this morning," he said belatedly as he turned off on the long road that led to the feedlot. "I wasn't thinking. I was glad to see you because I knew that you could talk her out of the office if the firemen didn't work."

"Tammy's really a nice woman," she said.

He glowered. "She's a pain."

"If you'd give her half a chance, she might surprise you. She's very efficient."

He shifted against the seat. "I did notice that you're pretty rushed. I didn't mean to rob you of her help."

She glanced at him. "You might consider asking Tammy to come back. Maybe she's sorry, too."

He pursed his lips. "Maybe she is. I suppose I could drop by her dad's house and just mention that she could come to work tomorrow."

"It might be a better idea to call first," Shelby said, remembering Tammy's temper.

"I'll do that." He pulled up at the feedlot office and grinned. "Thanks for being so understanding."

"My pleasure. No, don't get out. I can open the door

all by myself." She laughed. She got out, smiling at him, and waved him away.

Behind her, Justin stood watching, a cigarette smoking in his lean fingers, his height emphasized by the jeans and chambray shirt and boots he wore around the feedlot. His hat was pulled low over his black eyes and he looked dangerous.

Shelby turned and saw him and stopped suddenly. "Uh, hi."

He lifted the cigarette to his mouth. "You're an hour early."

"We had a problem at the office." She flushed, and that made it worse. "I need a ride to the house."

"Calhoun's going that way," he returned. "He can drop you off."

He went inside the building, leaving her standing in the sun with the sound of the cattle lowing and moving in the sprawling complex ringing in her ears.

Calhoun came out in a beige suit, scowling. "Justin is sitting behind his desk with his feet crossed, not doing a damned thing, and he dragged me out of a meeting to run you home," he said, stunned. "Not that I mind, Shelby. I'm just curious. Is he at you again?"

"When isn't he?" she said curtly. "Mr. Holman brought me out here. I guess Justin thinks I seduced him on the highway!"

"Shhh!" Calhoun put his finger to his lips and pulled her toward his white Jaguar. "Don't make him any worse than he already is. His secretary's already threatened to walk out!"

"He has that effect on so many people," she said with venom in her tone. "Overbearing, unfeeling, insensitive, insufferable...!"

"Now, now," he soothed. "You'll just work yourself into a lather, and it won't solve anything. He's only jealous. You're a woman. You ought to know exactly what to do about that."

She flushed and averted her face as he helped her into the front seat and got in beside her.

He glanced in her direction curiously, noting her scarlet blush. It amazed him how much alike Justin and Shelby were; both old-fashioned and full of hang-ups.

He started the car and cleared his throat. "Do you mind if I say something pretty personal, Shelby? Since we're related these days and all?"

She couldn't look at him. "That depends on what it is."

"Yes, I can imagine. You react just like Justin does," he mused. He pulled out onto the road and pressed down on the accelerator. "Well, it's this. My brother isn't exactly a lily, but in recent years he's been a hermit. He hasn't dated anybody. He's sort of rusty with women, is what I'm driving at."

"I could tell you what he is, if you weren't his brother," she muttered, clutching her purse.

"Shelby," he said patiently, "the best way to get a man's attention and knock the fire off his temper is just to hug him as hard as you can and let nature take care of the details."

She went scarlet. She knew that Calhoun was pretty much like her boss, a man who knew women well. But if she couldn't talk to Justin about intimacy, she certainly couldn't talk to Calhoun about it.

"He wouldn't like it," she said in a husky voice.

"He'd like it," he returned. He reached over and patted her shoulder gently. "He's so crazy about you that he can't see straight. You take my word for it, honey, he'll fold up like an accordion if you use the right approach. And that's all I'll say. How are you and the sports car getting along?"

She gaped at him. He didn't know? "Justin didn't tell you?"

"Justin doesn't talk much when he's at the office," he said pleasantly. "Mostly he works, and when he doesn't, he broods."

"I had a near-miss in the car, actually," she mumbled. "I spun out and almost hit a truck." She felt his stunned glance. "Justin took the car away and had it crushed."

"Good for Justin," he said unexpectedly. "That car was dangerous." He stared at her. "And you know better than most how dangerous."

She cleared her throat. "Switzerland was years ago."

"All the same, Justin was right. He wouldn't want to have to bury you so shortly after your wedding, you know."

"Wouldn't he?" she asked bitterly. "I think he hates me."

"I wish I could convince you what a joke that statement is." He pulled up in front of the house and smiled at her. "I dare you. Play up to him and see what happens. He's as unknowledgeable about women as you are about men, so keep that in mind. And don't, for God's sake, mention that I said so," he said under his breath. "The one time Justin and I really got into it, we both had to have stitches. Okay?"

"Okay." She opened the door and glanced back shyly. "You're a nice man."

"Of course I am," he said. "Ask Abby if you don't believe it." He grinned with the smugness of a man who knows how much he's loved. "See you."

"Tell Abby hello and give her my love."

He laughed and waved as he went down the road. Shelby thought about what he'd said and wondered if she might be able to get up enough nerve to take his advice.

If Calhoun was right, and Justin was as backward as she was, it might really be interesting to see what would happen. Then she remembered his ardor and wondered if Calhoun actually knew his brother at all. The Justin Shelby experienced on the sofa wasn't a man who didn't know what to do with women. Justin was pretty tight-lipped with everyone, and Calhoun might not know exactly how well informed his big brother was.

But the thought of tempting Justin was delicious, and now she had no more reason to be afraid of him. She knew that he could be tender and that he wouldn't lose control too soon. And now, thank goodness, there would be no more painful barrier to inhibit her. She smiled thoughtfully as she went up the steps, already making exciting plans for the night ahead.

CHAPTER EIGHT

IT WAS WELL after dark when Justin finally came home from the feedlot, looking worn and in a black temper. He spared a glance at the dining room, where Shelby was eating her lonely meal, and went upstairs without even a hello.

She sighed, wondering if there was worse to come. She finished her dessert and was sipping coffee when he came back downstairs. He'd obviously just showered, because his hair was still damp around the temples. He was wearing a clean gray-and-blue-plaid Western shirt with gray denim slacks, and his temper hadn't improved.

He sat at the head of the table and began to fill a plate with lukewarm beef and gravy and buttered new potatoes.

"Maria could warm it up for you in the microwave," Shelby ventured.

"If I want Maria to do anything, I'll ask her," he said.

So it was going to be that kind of evening. She put her napkin aside and straightened the skirt of the red-and-white dress she'd worn deliberately because Justin had thought it sexy.

She wasn't quite sure how to reach him. He looked so unapproachable, just as he had in the earliest days of their relationship. She studied his hard face quietly. "Justin, if you're still angry about this afternoon, Mr. Holman closed the office an hour early, and I was already on the street when I realized I didn't have a car," she said. "He was kind enough to drop me off at the feed-lot on his way home. He comes right by it, you know."

He looked up, black eyes glittering. "And you know how I feel about your damned boss."

She glowered at him. "Yes, I know, but I didn't think that you'd mind him giving me a ride home. He's a per-fect gentleman when he's around me," she said shortly. "I've told you that until I'm blue in the face, Justin!"

"You might have phoned me," he returned. "I'd have come after you."

"I didn't even know if you were at the feedlot," she said. She put her fork down gently. "I didn't know if you'd come, either, after the way you roared off this morning without even saying goodbye."

He pushed his plate away, hardly touched. "He was waiting for you, pacing back and forth," he replied icily. "And then he practically carried you to the sidewalk. I damned near got out of the car and went for him then, Shelby. I don't like other men touching you."

If he expected her to be irritated by that flat state-ment, he was disappointed. The admission made her pulse skip. She stared at him, wondering if he even re-alized what he was admitting. She sighed wistfully, and smiled at him. "I'm glad."

He frowned. "What?"

"I'm glad you don't like other men touching me." She picked up her coffee and sipped it. "I don't like other women touching you, either."

He shifted in the chair. "We weren't talking about that."

She smiled, because he seemed to have forgotten

what they *had* been talking about. She pushed back her long, dark hair and her eyes sparkled as they searched his. "Calhoun said you dragged him out of a meeting and made him drive me to the house."

He reached for a cigarette and looked uncomfortable. "I was pretty hot."

She wondered if it was his jealousy of her boss, or frustration. Calhoun had intrigued her by what he'd said about the way Justin would react if she made advances. She wanted to find out herself.

But thinking about it and doing it were entirely different things. Sitting there, looking at the taciturn, stern man across from her, she couldn't really imagine going over to him and sitting in his lap. It would have been lovely, though, to feel welcome if she reached out to him.

She colored delicately from her own thoughts and put her coffee cup down. "What about a car for me?" she asked.

"I forgot," he murmured. "We'll go tomorrow."

"All right."

He ignored the fresh apple pie in a saucer beside him and finished his coffee. "I got a new movie in the mail today," he remarked. "A black-and-white war movie, made in the early forties. I thought I might watch it."

"You'll enjoy that, I know."

He eyed her warily. "You could watch it with me. If you wanted to," he added carelessly, so she wouldn't know how badly he wanted her to.

But she sensed it. She smiled. "If I wouldn't be in your way, I'd like to. I like war movies."

"Do you?" He smiled slowly. "How about science-fiction?"

Her eyes lit up. "Oh, yes!"

He actually laughed. "I've got quite a collection of old ones, and a good many new releases."

"All we need now is some popcorn," she remarked.

"Maria!" he called.

The housekeeper came to the doorway. "*Sí,* Señor Justin?"

He threw a request at her in rapid-fire Spanish, and Maria grinned and answered in kind. She laughed, made another remark, which caused Justin's cheeks to go a ruddy shade, and went back to the kitchen with a wink in Shelby's direction.

"What did she say?" Shelby asked, because her Spanish was sketchy at best and she didn't have Justin's facility for languages.

"That she'd make the popcorn and bring it in," he replied shortly. "Well, come on, if you're coming."

He got up and went out of the room, leaving her to follow.

The living room was cozy with only the end table lamp on. Shelby curled up on the sofa, barefooted, with the bowl of popcorn between herself and Justin. Maria stuck her head in long enough to say that she and Lopez were going to her sister's for the evening, and then the house was quiet except for the loud excitement of bombs going off and machine-gun fire as the Allies and the Axis fought it out all over again on the screen.

When they got down to the inevitable unpopped kernels in the bottom of the bowl, Justin moved it and took off his boots before he lit a cigarette, propping his long legs on the coffee table. As the movie ran on, Shelby found herself moving helplessly closer to him. Her hand slid hesitantly across to his free one, where it lay on the sofa. She started to touch it and then stopped, shy and uncertain.

He glimpsed the movement and turned his head. "Do you have to have permission to touch me, Shelby?" he asked, his tone deep and slow and gentle.

"I don't know," she replied. "Do I?"

"No." He watched her with patient amusement until she moved her hand toward his again and touched it, tingling at the warm strength of his fingers as they wound through hers and contracted.

She smiled shyly and turned her attention back to the movie again. She didn't see it or hear it, though, because Justin's thumb was rubbing gently against her moist palm. She felt the movement like a brand, burning her blood, making her hungry. Her lips parted as she remembered the last time they'd been on this sofa together, and what they'd done. She remembered the leather cool against her back, the weight of Justin's body over hers in an intimacy that could still color her cheeks scarlet.

"Do you like mysteries?" she asked, for something to say during a lull in the battle scene.

"Sure," he said easily. "I've got a few Hitchcock thrillers, and a copy of *Arsenic and Old Lace* with Cary Grant."

"I love that one," she mused. "I laughed myself sick the first time I saw it."

"How about John Wayne Westerns?" he asked with a sly glance.

She laughed. "I've seen *Hondo* so many times, I can even growl along with the character's dog."

"So have I." He studied her for a long moment, admiring the way she looked in the red-and-white dress, liking the length of her dark hair. "We always did have a lot in common, Shelby. Especially guitar." He rubbed his thumb over the tips of her fingers. "Do you ever play?"

She shook her head. "Not anymore. I...lost the taste for it."

"So did I," he confessed, because after they'd broken it off, he couldn't bear the memories the guitar brought back. "Maybe we could practice together again sometime."

"That would be nice." She smiled at him. He smiled back. And the television set seemed a long way off as the smiles faded and the look became long and intensely arousing.

His fingers contracted roughly on hers and he drew in a steadying breath. "Come here, sweetheart," he said softly.

She tingled all over at the way he said the endearment, because he hardly ever used one at all. He made her feel young and vulnerable. She slid closer with subdued eagerness and curled up against him with her head going to rest naturally on his hard shoulder.

"Don't go to sleep," he murmured drily.

"I'm not sleepy," she said with a sigh. She smiled and nuzzled her cheek closer. "You smell spicy."

"You smell like a gardenia," he murmured. "It's a scent I never connected with anyone but you."

"It's the perfume I used," she said.

He took his hand away from hers and paused to put out his cigarette. Then he lifted her and turned her across him so that she was lying in his lap with her head on his chest.

"If you'd rather watch something else, I don't mind,"

he said softly, knowing full well that the movie was the last thing on both their minds.

She couldn't have cared less what was on the screen, because all she'd seen since the beginning of the movie was Justin's hard profile. But she didn't say that.

"This is fine," she assured him.

"Okay."

He smoothed her long hair, holding her slender hand to his broad chest while he tried to pretend an interest in the movie. He was aware of Shelby now, of the scent of her, of the softness of her breasts pressed against his hard chest, of her warm hand touching him.

Her caressing fingers made his heartbeat quicken. He felt the first stirrings of desire in his powerful body and when he looked down and saw the hunger echoing in her soft eyes, he lost all efforts at pretence. Unhurriedly, he unsnapped the pearly buttons of his shirt and slowly drew Shelby's hand against thick hair and hard, warm muscle, coaxing her to touch him. While her fingers worked on his body, his mouth began to trace patterns on her forehead, her closed eyelids, her nose, her cheeks, her chin and throat.

She felt her breathing quicken as he drew her closer. His nose brushed against hers. His mouth began to search for her lips, and when he found them, the touch was explosive.

She heard his breath sigh out heavily as his mouth became demanding, intimate. His fingers slid into the thick fall of hair at her nape and arched her throat so that her mouth pushed against his, answering his hungry ardor.

Her heart went wild. Her quick, unsteady breathing

suddenly matched his. She dug her nails helplessly into his hard chest, and he groaned against her lips.

"Sorry," she faltered.

He took her lower lip between his teeth and traced it with his tongue. "I liked it," he whispered, and his mouth opened hers, very slowly, while he stretched his length alongside hers. He sighed, and she felt the touch of his body from head to toe while the kiss grew warmer and slower and more intense. "Kiss me hard, Shelby," he breathed huskily.

She reached up, her inhibitions wearing away under the deep caresses. Her fingers slid into his thick, black hair and savored its coolness as her mouth began to answer his.

The movie blared away, the battle scenes loud in the stillness, but neither of them heard. The kisses grew longer, drugging, aching as Justin's hands worked at buttons and snaps. Shelby felt his bare chest against her breasts without a protest. It was delicious, the touch of skin against skin, just as it had been a few nights earlier. But this time, the old fears were greatly diminished, because now she knew that what he did wasn't going to hurt her. She knew how gentle he could be, how patient.

She felt his hands sliding the dress away, tenderly smoothing it down her long, trembling limbs. She caught her breath and in the dim light of the lamp, he smiled at her softly.

"It's all right," he whispered. "I won't go too fast. You can still stop me if you want to."

That gave her back the choice and made everything all right. She began to relax, letting her hands slide hungrily over his hard, hair-roughened muscles. It was heaven to touch him this way, to be given the freedom to learn him with her hands. She looked up into his dark eyes with the discoveries lying vulnerable in her soft eyes, and he smiled down at her.

"Oh, Justin," she whispered huskily. "It's so sweet!"

He bent and lowered his mouth onto hers, feeling the words sigh against his lips. He slid his hands gently over her, feeling the ripple of her skin under them. She was like satin to the touch, and he'd gone hungry for what seemed forever.

In the back of his mind, he knew there was no chance that he was going to be able to stop, but she didn't seem to be worried about that. She pulled him down to her and her mouth was suddenly as ardent as his, as uninhibited.

Still kissing her, he managed to get out of his own clothes, and then she was against him, trembling, while he slowed his pace and began to arouse her all over again with exquisite patience until he felt the passion shaking her slender body.

"Now," he whispered when she was crying with her need. He eased down, turning her face up to his with a caressing hand. "No. Don't turn away. I want to see."

She colored feverishly, but she looked up at him the instant his body took possession of hers.

His lips parted. It was the most profound experience of his life. All the long years of loving her, needing her, and it was finally going to happen. She was his. There were no more barriers. He felt her accept him totally and his breath caught.

She stiffened just a little at the newness, the stark intimacy, but he slowed and hesitated.

"It's all right," he whispered tenderly, and bent to kiss her, coaxing her to relax, to let it happen. "Yes.

Like that." He laughed jerkily at the ease of it, at the exquisite sense of oneness. "Oh, Shelby!"

Her face was bloodred, but she didn't look away. His face was taut with victory, his eyes glittering blackly with it. She reached up, her trembling hands going to his cheeks to bring his head down so that she could reach his mouth.

"Love…me," she whispered, her voice breaking as he moved and she felt the first sweet piercing pleasure. "Justin…love me!"

The words broke his control. He couldn't believe what he was hearing, much less what he was feeling. He went under in a wave of white heat, crying out as the force of the pleasure took his restraint and left him helpless in the drive for fulfillment.

Somewhere in the back of her mind, Shelby knew that she should be frightened by his lack of control. But his movements were causing a kind of silvery tension that made her body sing with pleasure. Ecstasy was just out of her reach, and she stretched toward it with her last thread of strength just as Justin caught her hips and pulled.

She felt the world go spinning down under her, and she cried out his name again and again and again…

He laughed. She felt his lips at her temples, on her cheeks, her mouth, in kisses that were as tender as they were comforting.

"The first time," he breathed, laughing again as his mouth covered hers, trembling. "My God, the first time!"

She opened her eyes, still shaking from the sudden descent from a kind of pleasure she'd never dreamed existed. She gazed up at him, fascinated by the way he looked. He seemed years younger. His hair was damp, his face sweaty, his eyes glittering with exultant pleasure. He was shuddering, his body heavy over hers, damp.

"Justin?" she whispered, disoriented.

"Are you all right, sweetheart?" he asked softly. "I didn't hurt you?"

"No." She blushed and lowered her eyes to the pulse in his throat.

"Look at me, you coward."

She forced her gaze up to his, and he bent and brushed his mouth over her closed eyes.

"I… I never realized…" She couldn't find the words. She clung to him, hiding her face against his damp throat.

He turned, holding her warmly against him on the long leather sofa, sighing with exquisite pleasure at the way she held him. "So many lonely nights, Shelby," he whispered. "So many dreams. But even the dreams weren't this sweet." He pulled her closer. "Kiss me, honey."

She lifted her face to his, obediently putting her swollen lips against his. He trembled and eased her gently onto her back, so that they were completely joined. He looked into her eyes with a dark, soft question in his. She didn't answer him. She lifted her body against him, and he saw the words in her eyes. He bent, sighing unsteadily, and his mouth opened over her parted lips. He moved down, and she clung, and the world went again into shared oblivion.

He carried her upstairs a long time later, cradling her in his arms like the most precious kind of treasure. He put her into his bed and climbed in beside her, turning off the lights. He curled her against his tired body and sighed with haunted pleasure. She was asleep only seconds before he was.

SHELBY FELT A kiss brush her lips. "Justin," she whispered softly and opened her eyes.

He was sitting on the bed beside her, dressed in jeans and a chambray shirt, smiling. "I have to go to work," he whispered.

"No," she moaned, reaching up.

He eased the covers away and brought her across him, touching her soft breasts with exquisite tenderness while he kissed her. "We made love," he whispered.

"Several times," she whispered back, and then spoiled her new image by flushing furiously.

He nibbled her lips. "I didn't use anything," he said quietly, searching her eyes.

The blush got worse. "Neither did I."

He touched her lips with one lean finger. "I know. Is it going to matter if you get pregnant?" he whispered.

"No," she moaned. "I want a child with you."

He caught his breath and bent to kiss her with aching tenderness, pleased beyond words at the way she said it, at the need he felt in himself, in her. "Did you sleep?"

"I'm still asleep," she whispered at his lips. "I dreamed it all, and I don't want to wake up."

"It wasn't a dream." He kissed her. "Have I hurt you?"

"Oh, no," she whispered quickly. "Not at all!"

His dark eyes sketched her face adoringly. "You'll sleep with me from now on," he said. "No more walls, no more looking back. We start here, now, together."

"Yes," she whispered, sighing, her heart in her eyes. "Don't go to work."

"I have to. So do you." He glowered down at her. "But no more rides with the boss, got that?"

"I'll call you. I promise." She reached up and kissed

his cheek. "You can't possibly be jealous after last night."

His lean hand smoothed her breast. "Don't kid yourself," he said softly. "I'll be ten times as possessive now that I've made love to you. You're mine."

"I always have been, Justin," she said quietly, wondering at the way he was looking at her, at the heat of possession in his black eyes. Surely he was sure of her now?

He searched her eyes and then let his gaze run hungrily over her slender body. "Exquisite," he breathed. "All of you. I've never felt anything half as profound in my life as what I felt with you. I feel…whole."

Her heart skipped a beat, because that was how she felt. But she loved him, and he only wanted her. Or was it possible that he was finally beginning to feel something for her?

"I feel that way, too," she said.

He smiled. "But you were a virgin, honey," he mused, brushing his mouth over her nose. "I wasn't."

She glared at him. "So I noticed."

That glare made him feel all man and a yard wide. He bent and nipped her mouth with his teeth, softly arousing. "It was a long time ago, and it has nothing to do with you. For the past six years, I haven't even kissed another woman, and that's gospel. You don't have a damned thing to be jealous of."

She hugged him fiercely, her head against his bare chest. "I'm sorry."

"There's nothing to apologize for," he replied. He kissed her forehead with breathless tenderness. "I've got to go," he groaned. "I don't want to, but Calhoun's going to be out of the office all day, and I have to be there."

"I know." She rubbed her cheek against him. "Will you drop me off at work?"

"Of course. What do you fancy for breakfast?"

She looked up at him with the answer sparkling in her eyes. He laughed with pure delight, stood up with her in his arms and tossed her into the center of the bed, watching her scramble under the sheet with indulgent amusement.

"Not now," he murmured drily at the blatant invitation in her eyes, even through her shyness. "Get dressed before all this stoic control melts."

"Spoilsport," she said, sighing.

"I don't want to overdo it," he said with sudden seriousness. "You're still new to this. I don't want to hurt you."

Her eyes softened. "And I was afraid of you." She shook her head.

"I can understand why. But you won't need to be ever again." He turned away, stretching hugely. "God knows how I'll keep my mind on work, but there's always tonight," he added from the doorway with a slow grin. "What do you want for breakfast?" he repeated.

She smiled shyly. "Eggs and bacon."

"It'll be waiting."

He went out, and she got up and got dressed, feeling as if her feet weren't even touching the floor when she walked.

He was at the table waiting when she got there. She'd put on a simple gray skirt with a pale blue blouse for work, and her hair was in a neat French twist. It was a sedate outfit, which was what she'd meant it to be. Since she knew how possessive Justin was, she didn't want to spoil their delicate new relationship by making it look as if she was taking special pains with her appearance to go to work.

He looked up when she came into the dining room, and he smiled at the image she projected.

"Very businesslike," he said with approval. He leaned back in his chair, the action pulling the shirt taut over his hard-muscled chest. He looked devastating that way, with the light shining on his black hair and emphasizing his deep tan. He wasn't a handsome man, but Shelby thought he was the most attractive man she'd ever seen.

"I'm glad you approve," she said, smiling at him.

He got up and seated her next to him, pausing to drop a warm, slow kiss on her mouth. His eyes searched hers, warm and soft and darkly glowing. "Pretty creature," he whispered. "Eat your eggs before I make a meal out of you."

She laughed with pure delight and dragged her eyes down to her plate. She could hardly believe the way things had changed in the past few days. Her eyes adored him. He was hers, now. For the first time, she felt really married. Finally they were on their way to a lasting relationship.

The following days emphasized it. She thought about Justin all day at work, and when they got home at night, there were no more arguments, no more barriers. He kissed her coming and going, and every night he made love to her, and she slept in his arms. It was as close to heaven as she'd ever been, like a waking dream that never seemed to sour or end. They spent time together, riding, playing the guitar, watching movies on the VCR. It was a new beginning, and Shelby could almost believe that what they had was perfect.

But even as they drew close physically, even as they

spent more time together, Shelby could still feel the emotional distance between them. Justin shared none of his deepest feelings with her. He never spoke of love, even when they were the most intimate. He didn't talk about the past or the future. It seemed to her as if he was doing his best to take it one day at a time, without bothering about tomorrow.

His reticence worried her. She was as much in love with him now as she had been in the very beginning, but Justin was adept at hiding what he felt. He had a poker face that she'd never been able to see through. He wanted her. That was obvious and delightful. But if there was more than desire in him, Shelby never saw it.

She kept on with her job, even though she knew that Justin wanted her to give it up. He was only fractionally less jealous of her boss, but he didn't make any more harsh remarks. Meanwhile, Barry Holman had talked Tammy Lester into coming back to work, and things were developing very nicely between them. Shelby expected a breakthrough any day, because they were already exchanging heated looks.

And there was another development at home, too. Over four weeks had passed since Shelby and Justin had been intimate for the first time, and there were growing signs that their intimacy might bear fruit. She hadn't mentioned her suspicions to him, but she was almost sure that she was pregnant. The thought made her delightfully happy. Having a child with Justin would make her happiness complete, and he'd said himself that he wanted children. It would be the final balm, to heal the breach that existed between them. And when the baby came, Justin might begin to care about her as well as the child.

She was curled up on the sofa when he came into the room, scowling. He'd just been on the phone and he looked preoccupied.

"Is something wrong?" she asked gently, sitting up straight. He looked very somber for a change.

He glanced at her and grimaced. "I've got to fly up to Wyoming for a few days. I've been asked to appear in court as a character witness for a friend of mine who's being sued." He sighed. "I don't want to go, but he'd do it for me. I think he's getting a raw deal."

He sat down beside her, drawing her close, while he smoked his cigarette and explained that the rancher was being accused of selling contaminated beef to a packing plant.

"You're sure he didn't do it?"

"I'm sure," he replied. He kissed her absently. "I wish I could take you with me, but I'm going to stay with Quinn Sutton. He's not much of a woman's man."

"I see. He's a grizzled old hermit," she teased.

He chuckled. "Actually, he's about my age and jaded. He lost his wife to another man about ten years ago and he never got over it. She had a child, a little boy. She left the boy behind and Quinn's raised him. I don't know what the boy will do if his dad goes to jail." He shook his head. "Hell of a mess."

"I hope he doesn't have to go to jail," she said. Her pale green eyes searched his face. "I'll miss you, Justin."

He wrapped her up tight and kissed her hungrily. "No less than I'll miss you, honey," he whispered. "I'll phone you every night. Maybe it won't take too long."

"It had better not. If you leave me alone at night too long, I'll run away with some sexy man," she teased, knowing there wasn't a sexier man alive than her husband.

But Justin, still unsure of her even after the weeks of exquisite pleasure, didn't realize what she meant. He held her, his chin on her hair, and stared quietly over her head, wondering if she was already beginning to tire of him. She was a beautiful woman, and he wasn't a handsome man. She seemed to enjoy sleeping with him, but he wanted much more than her slender body in the darkness. He wanted her to love him.

"Don't speed while I'm gone," he cautioned quietly.

She laughed softly. The small American car he'd bought her wasn't a speeding kind of automobile. He'd made sure of that first, but apparently he wasn't going to trust her completely.

"I won't," she promised. "And Maria and Lopez will be here at night, so you don't have to worry about me. I'll be fine. I'll just be lonely," she added, sitting up. Her eyes searched his. "Justin, you're worried. What about?"

He shifted. "Just business, honey," he said evasively. His eyes narrowed as they searched hers. "You aren't getting tired of marriage already, are you?"

She actually gasped. "What?"

"You heard me. I can't give you all that your father could. I just hope it's enough."

She reached up, bringing his face down to hers. "Oh, Justin, you're all I want!"

She kissed him, feeling the ripple run through his powerful body at the touch of her mouth against his. It still amazed her, that wild reaction she got when she kissed or touched him. He never said anything about it, but he seemed to love having her make the first move, having her reach out to him. She didn't do it often, because she was still the least bit shy with him. But it was getting easier. His response was encouraging.

He lifted her, turned her, and his mouth grew hungry. The passion between them never seemed to wane. If anything, it was even stronger now than it had been at the beginning. She held nothing back, and her lack of inhibition keyed a similar lack in him. He was still tender, but occasionally his ardor grew demanding and fierce, and at those times she knew a fulfillment that surpassed her wildest dreams.

"When do you have to go?" she whispered, trembling because his hands were under her soft blouse, touching her.

"Tomorrow."

"So soon?"

He lifted her, getting to his feet in one smooth, graceful motion. "We've got all night," he whispered over her mouth before he took it. "God, I want you! I want you all the time…"

She moaned under his hard mouth, loving his touch, needing the ardent sweetness of his arms. She clung to him as he opened the door and carried her slowly upstairs. If only she could tell him how much she loved him, share the delightful secret that she was hoarding. She wanted to. In fact, she started to. But as she opened her mouth to tell him, his lips began to probe hers tenderly. And as always, the spark of desire knocked every thought out of her mind except Justin, and the exquisite pleasure of loving him in the darkness.

He was gone when she woke up the next morning. She barely remembered feeling his mouth brush hers, hearing his whispered goodbye. But she'd been so tired, and she hadn't fully awakened. When she did, she wished then that she'd made him listen. She had an odd feeling that she should have tried harder, a premonition that their harmony was about to be disrupted. But perhaps it was only her condition and her uncertainty about Justin's feelings for her. Surely they were so close now that nothing could rebuild the old wall that had kept them apart for six years.

CHAPTER NINE

COURT WAS IN SESSION, and there was more work than ever in the small office for Shelby and Tammy. Mr. Holman was working on two divorce cases, a land settlement, a suit for damages resulting from a highway car crash, and he was defending a local man who'd been charged with manslaughter. No sooner did Tammy get through researching one case than she had to start on the next. The land settlement involved complicated research in the county clerk's office, looking up plats and deeds. One of the divorces involved allegations of child abuse, and that required a deposition from an emergency-room physician who'd treated the child—Mr. Holman did that, of course, with the court stenographer. But Tammy had to get the medical records and take down potential testimony from a psychologist and check into the husband's criminal record. The car crash meant more delving into police records and interviewing potential witnesses, and the manslaughter charge looked like a full-time job in itself.

Shelby didn't envy the young woman her paralegal status. Tammy had been taking courses at night at a nearby junior college, and now it was paying off. Mr. Holman had already raised her salary and she was coping with things Shelby couldn't begin to understand. It was a good thing, Shelby thought, that she hadn't wanted that training herself. With her almost positive pregnancy, she wouldn't be able to work for many more months. She knew Justin was going to insist that she stay home the last month or so of her pregnancy. Secretly, she wanted that, too. She wanted the time to plan things for the baby, to get furniture and fix up a room for a nursery. She smiled, thinking about the look on Justin's face when she told him the news.

"I said," Mr. Holman interrupted her thoughts gently, "I'm afraid you're going to have to put in some overtime this week—you and Tammy. Civil court's in full swing, and superior court convenes next week. We don't have a lot of time to get our cases in order."

"I don't mind," Shelby assured him. "Justin's out of town, so I've got nothing to do in the evenings."

"His loss, my gain." The blond lawyer grinned. "Thanks, Shelby. I don't know what I'd do without you. I've got to run to the courthouse and then I'll be at Carson's Café for lunch. Back about one."

"Okay, boss."

He started out the door and collided with Tammy, who was rushing in. He caught her upper arms to steady her and she rested her hands on his chest to support herself. They looked at each other and froze there, a tableau that Shelby found oddly touching.

"You okay?" Barry Holman asked the young woman.

Tammy's full lips parted. "Yes," she breathed. She didn't look up, and she was blushing.

His hands contracted for a minute, then he let her go. "Be careful," he said softly, and smiled. "I don't want to lose you."

"Yes, sir," Tammy murmured huskily.

He let his glance drop to her mouth for one long instant, then he was gone, frowning and impatient all over again.

Shelby had to smother a grin. From fighting tooth and nail, the two of them had become shy and reserved and uncomfortable with each other. Tammy actually seemed to vibrate when the boss came into a room, and her face lit up like a neon sign.

"I, uh, have some notes to type," Tammy said, faltering.

Shelby smiled. "I'll go out and get us some lunch. What would you like?"

"Tuna-fish salad and crackers, and iced tea. Here. And thanks a million! I'll go tomorrow." Tammy grinned.

"That's a deal. I won't be long. Hold the fort."

Shelby went around the corner to the drugstore and found Abby bent over a greeting-card display.

"What are you looking for?" she asked her sister-in-law conspiratorially.

Abby chuckled, her blue-gray eyes lighting up. "A card for my gorgeous husband. His birthday is week after next," she reminded Shelby.

"How could I forget, when we're having the party for him?" Shelby replied. "Which reminds me, I was supposed to call you two days ago to go over the arrangements. I got busy..." She flushed. What had happened was that Justin had wrestled her down on the carpet when she'd picked up the phone to call Abby, and nothing had gotten done for the rest of the night.

"I gather that things are going well over at your place," Abby mused, watching the scarlet blush. "Calhoun says Justin sits around dreaming at the feedlot instead of working, and that he's got a photograph of you on his desk that he just stares at all the time."

Shelby laughed delightedly. "Does he, really?"

"You newlyweds." Abby smiled. "I'm glad it's working out for you. I knew it would. You two were always equal halves of a whole—even Tyler mentioned it that night you and Justin danced together at the square dance."

Shelby blushed. "I never dreamed it would work out like this, though," she confessed. "I've never been so happy."

"I imagine Justin feels the same." She studied Shelby's face curiously. "Why are you still working? Don't you want to stay at home?"

"Well, I didn't think it would be right to just walk off and leave Mr. Holman," Shelby confessed. "Tammy Lester's working out very well and sooner or later I'll go home. It's just that I wanted to try my wings. I've never been independent before. It's fun."

"So is marriage." Abby grinned. "I'm having a ball just being a housewife, as traitorous as that sounds coming from a modern woman. Was that Tammy I saw in the window this morning?" she added. "The shade was pulled down, but it was dark and there was a light behind her. She was leaning over Mr. Holman. She sure does look like you," she added. "Maybe not in person, but your silhouettes are really similar."

"It's probably because we both have long hair and we're tall and slender," Shelby said. "But she's stuck on the boss, and just between us, I think it's mutual. They started out hating each other. Now they're at the throat-clearing, foot-shuffling stage."

"Guess what comes next," Abby said wickedly.

Shelby laughed softly, averting her eyes. "Well, they'll get to that stage before much longer, I suppose. Calhoun doesn't know about the surprise party, does he?" she asked to divert the younger woman.

"Heavens, no, and he wouldn't drag it out of me at gunpoint, I promise. Justin phoned the other night and said he'd invited a couple of people who wouldn't be on my list. I don't guess he mentioned that to you?"

Shelby frowned. "Well…no. Who do you suppose he's invited?" Her green eyes flashed. "Surely he wouldn't invite any of his old flames…?" she mused to herself.

"I wouldn't worry too much about that," Abby murmured, because Justin had once confessed to her that he'd never been in Calhoun's league as a ladykiller. But Shelby didn't need to know that, and it was Justin's place to tell her when and if he wanted to.

"Then who?" she persisted.

"We'll have to wait and see. You might ask him when he gets back. Pity about Mr. Sutton, isn't it?" Abby sighed. "I met him and his son at one of those cattle conventions Calhoun and I went to month before last. He's not much to look at, very reserved, but bristling with masculinity, if you know what I mean. He looked right through me, and there was a woman who came on to him…" Abby shivered. "I used to think Justin was kind of remote when I first went to live with the Ballengers, but Mr. Sutton makes Justin look like an extrovert. He hates women."

"His loss," Shelby said with a faint grin. "Of course, he obviously has never encountered women of our caliber."

Abby burst out laughing. "Shame on you."

Shelby laughed, too. "Call me when you have time

and we'll get those arrangements for the party finished. I've got to run. Tammy's at the office by herself."

"Okay. I'll just go through these cards again. Have a nice lunch."

"See you."

Shelby puzzled over what Abby had said all the way back to the office. She couldn't help but wonder whom Justin had invited that he hadn't told her about. She'd have to ask him.

He'd flown to Wyoming on Wednesday, and although he'd hoped to be back two days later, there had been complications and the hearing had been held over until Monday. He wasn't going to get back for the weekend.

"Oh, Justin," she moaned. "And I have to work late next week. We've got court."

"Quit that damned job," he said shortly. "A woman's place is at home, having children and keeping things straight."

A cold, deep voice in the background laughed and made a curt remark that Justin replied to.

"What was that?" Shelby asked curiously.

"Mr. Sutton thinks women are best when floured and salted and fried in lard," he mused.

"You can tell Mr. Sutton that men have to be marinated first," she shot back.

There was a murmur of voices and a deeply appealing laugh in the background. "Shame on you," Justin murmured. "I've got to go. This turkey goes to bed at nine, so I'll be left up in the dark if I don't hang up. Be good, sweetheart. I'll see you Monday evening."

"You can pick me up at work if I'm not here, okay?" she asked softly.

"Okay. Good night."

"Good night, Justin," she said softly and kissed the receiver before she put it back in the cradle. She missed him already until it was almost unbearable. She wanted him to come home so badly.

The next two days passed all too slowly, but Monday was hectic and she didn't have time to look forward to seeing her husband. It was one tangle after another. The phone never stopped and Tammy had to run to the courthouse twice to take information to Mr. Holman in court.

By the end of the day, Shelby wondered if she was ever going to get to go home. Mr. Holman came in needing letters typed and a new brief prepared. It was pages long, and even with the computer, it took Shelby a long time.

Meanwhile, Tammy was flitting around the office following orders while Mr. Holman got more and more impatient. Shelby knew there was going to be trouble from the way Tammy began gnawing on her lower lip and glaring toward the boss's office. At nine o'clock, he came to the doorway and made a sarcastic remark about a property-line measurement that Tammy had written incorrectly and the younger girl exploded.

"You expect miracles!" she told the angry blond man. "I'm working overtime, I haven't had supper, I've had to get down on my hands and knees to get some of this stuff for you, and you're yelling at me! I hate you!"

"You cream puff!" he threw back. "If you think this is hard work, try practicing law, honey!"

He gave her a smug smile and went back into his office.

"Oh, no, you don't, big shot," Tammy muttered. She followed him in, slamming the door.

There were raised voices. A chair scraped and some-

thing fell. Then there was a long, poignant silence that
grew and grew. Shelby, sitting at her computer, smiled
to herself. It looked as if that next step in the boss's
courtship had just been taken.

But to the man sitting across the street in the black
Thunderbird, the two figures so closely silhouetted in
the window, against the thin shade, didn't look like
Barry Holman and Tammy. They looked to him like
Barry Holman and Shelby. From her height to her long
hair, it looked like Shelby in that man's arms.

Justin felt his heart stop dead in his chest. He'd come
straight from the airport into town, desperate to see
Shelby again, so hungry for the sight of her that he'd
taken a chance on her still being in the office. Only to
find…this.

He thought the wounding would never stop. It was
killing him to see Shelby in that man's arms. It couldn't
be— but, then, it had to be. She'd teased him about finding another man if he stayed away too long. She wasn't
a virgin anymore; she was a sensual woman now. Perhaps the hunger had gotten to her. It wasn't rational, but
then, neither was jealousy, and he was eaten up with it.
He wanted to go in there and kill that man. He wanted
to throw Shelby out of his house, out of his life. He'd
trusted her, and she'd betrayed him, again.

He didn't want to believe it, but what else could he
believe? That was Shelby in that window, Shelby with
her boss. He knew the sight of her too well to mistake her for anybody else, and who else could there be,
because there was only one woman at the office and
Shelby was the woman!

He started the car and pulled out onto the street, his
dark eyes black with hurt, seeing the end of his dreams.

She'd been fire in his arms, loving him, holding him, giving him everything he'd ever wanted. But she'd betrayed him in the past, and he'd forgotten that in their new closeness. He'd forgotten what she'd done to him before. She hadn't slept with Wheelor, but she'd still betrayed him—she'd thrown him over. And now history was repeating itself, and he didn't know what he was going to do. He drove home without even knowing how to get there, sick at heart and already grieving for Shelby all over again. How could she do that to him? How could she!

At the office, Shelby finally finished her chores and wondered whether or not to knock on Barry Holman's door. She decided against it. If they were in a clinch, it would be cruel to interrupt them.

She phoned the house and asked if Justin was there, but Maria said that he hadn't arrived yet. So she went out, leaving a note on her desk, got into her car and drove home. So much for Justin's promise to come and pick her up. But maybe he hadn't gotten home yet. She smiled, comforting herself with that thought.

She pulled into the driveway and left the car at the front steps, eager to see if he'd come in. She darted down the hall to his study, and there he was.

"Hello!" She laughed.

But the man whose black, cold eyes sought hers across the room didn't remotely resemble the tender lover who'd left for Wyoming last Wednesday. He was smoking a cigarette, and he looked as indifferent to her as a stranger might.

"You're late," he remarked.

"I…we had court," she said, faltering. "I told you I'd be working late."

"So you did." He took another draw from the cigarette. "You look worried. Is anything wrong?"

"I thought you might be glad to see me," she said with a hesitant smile.

He smiled back, but it wasn't pleasant. He was dying inside, but he wasn't about to let her see it. "Did you?" he asked carelessly. "I suppose you don't remember what you did to me six years ago. I'm sorry to disappoint you if you expected me to have fallen under your spell again. I haven't. What we had those few weeks was a small recompense for the anguish you gave me in the past. But I didn't realize you expected to build a future on it." He laughed coldly. "Sorry, honey. Once was enough. But don't think I can't live without you. You're like wine—I don't need to get drunk on you to enjoy the occasional sip."

She couldn't believe what she was hearing. She knew her face had gone quite pale. She was almost surely pregnant and Justin was telling her that he didn't want her anymore.

"I thought...you realized that I hadn't slept with Tom."

"Sure I did," he admitted. "But you broke the engagement all the same, didn't you, and told the whole damned world that I wasn't rich enough to suit you." His eyes glittered coldly. "Now it's my turn. I'm rich and I don't want you anymore, honey. Try that on for size."

She turned and ran, a sob breaking in her throat as she went helter-skelter up the staircase and into her old room. She locked the door and threw herself on the bed, crying helplessly. It was like a nightmare.

Several minutes passed. She'd thought, hoped, that Justin hadn't meant it. She'd listened and waited, hoping against hope that he might come after her, that he might reconsider what he'd said. But there were no footsteps on the staircase and she was finally forced to the conclusion that he wasn't going to follow her.

It didn't seem to bother him, either, that she'd gone to bed in her old room. She heard his footsteps much later going down the hall toward the bedroom they'd shared. The door closed and stayed closed.

Shelby didn't know what had gone wrong. When Justin had left for Wyoming, everything had been perfect for them. His emotional distance had disturbed her, but she'd been sure that he was beginning to feel something for her. Now, he was a stranger. The revenge she hadn't thought he wanted was now evident. He looked at her as if he couldn't care less about her, and what he'd said had cut her to the bone.

She finally slept, wondering how she was going to manage to go on. Exhausted, tears streaking her pale cheeks, she faced the loss of everything she'd ever loved. And Justin was first on that list.

Down the hall, the man who'd just returned from Wyoming was lying awake, too, missing the familiar sound of Shelby's breathing, the feel of her soft body against his in the darkness. He felt guilty and sick at the way he'd spoken to her, at the tears and hurt he'd caused. But he was hurting, too. He'd thought that Shelby loved him, and all along she'd only married him because she'd lost her home and security. She was playing him for a fool all over again, keeping a man in the background. The fact that it was her handsome boss only made it worse. Now he knew why she'd fought him about giving up her job. She was in love with her playboy boss, that was why she'd refused to come home. And now he'd seen proof of her disloyalty. He could hardly bear the pain.

He didn't know how he was going to go on living with her after what he'd seen.

Just for a minute, he considered the possibility of confronting her with the truth. But what good would that do? He'd confronted her with Tom Wheelor, and she'd lied. She'd lied at the time, and she'd lied since. He'd been lured into a false sense of security. He'd really begun to trust her again. What a good thing that he'd gone into town unannounced tonight to bring her home. Now she couldn't fool him again. He'd seen the real Shelby, and he was disgusted with her. He knew she'd been a virgin when she'd married him, but now that he'd gotten her over the hurdle of her first time, probably she was enjoying a totally new relationship with her boss.

That was the last straw. With an angry sigh, he closed his eyes and forced himself to put her out of his mind.

The next morning, he went downstairs with a carefully schooled expression, determined not to let Shelby know that he was cut to the bone emotionally. He'd die before he'd show it.

Shelby was up early, too, drinking black coffee and nibbling halfheartedly at toast. She looked up when he came into the dining room, her eyes swollen from crying all night, her expression one of hopeful uncertainty.

"You didn't mean what you said last night, did you?" she asked. Her green eyes searched his. "Did you, Justin?"

He moved past her and sat down casually at the head of the table, pouring coffee into his cup from the carafe before he answered her. "I meant every word of it, Shelby," he replied. He helped himself to bacon, eggs and biscuits, as nonchalantly as if she were a business associate. "Have some eggs."

She couldn't bear the sight of them, much less the taste. Her appetite had long since gone, and she was already in danger of losing the tiny bites of toast she'd taken. She shook her head.

His dark eyes narrowed as he studied her. She looked worn. Her long hair was luxurious, but her face was pale and pinched, even with makeup.

"I'm not very hungry," she added.

"Suit yourself." He didn't show his own lack of appetite. He was quiet long enough to clean his plate, but he could feel Shelby's eyes and they made him uncomfortable.

"What kind of relationship do you have in mind for us now?" she asked with the shreds of her pride drawn around her.

He pushed his plate aside and sipped his coffee. "You're my wife," he said coolly. "You'll live in my house and I'll take care of you. But we'll have separate rooms, and separate lives, from now on."

Her eyes closed on a wave of sorrow and shame. *And what about the baby I'm carrying,* she wanted to ask. *What about our child?*

"Surely sleeping alone won't bother you now," he chided. "Since you've already satisfied your curiosity."

"It won't bother me," she said huskily. She couldn't finish her coffee. The smell of it made her stomach churn. She got to her feet very slowly. "I'll be late if I don't leave now."

His eyes flashed. "God forbid that you should be late for…work," he said.

She was too sick to notice the hesitation or the venom

in his tone. She got out while she could, forcing herself not to show weakness. That was the one thing she couldn't afford at the moment.

She went to work and was violently sick in the bathroom the minute she got there. She mopped her face with wet paper towels and sat quietly at her desk until she got the nausea under control. It was going to take time to reconcile herself to Justin's new coldness. It was like having a glimpse of heaven and then being forced back to reality again. She didn't know why he'd taken this way to get back at her. It was going to be almost impossible for her to stay with him, but she had nowhere else to go. Not yet, at any rate. And certainly not until she was over the first phases of morning sickness and able to move around better than this.

When the boss and Tammy got to the office, she had the nausea under control temporarily. But the late hours were difficult for her, and her appetite was well and truly gone. As the days dragged by, just to put one foot in front of the other was an ordeal.

Abby came over one evening and they worked out the details for Calhoun's birthday party. Abby noticed the atmosphere and almost said something, but Shelby looked so bad that she bit her tongue and kept quiet. Obviously, something had gone wrong.

"You haven't forgotten Calhoun's party?" Shelby asked Justin as they had an increasingly rare meal together before the party.

He looked up from food he didn't even taste, his eyes quiet and somehow haunted for an instant before he blinked and removed the expression. She looked bad. Her color was terrible and she seemed weak and lackluster. He knew it was because of his coldness, but he couldn't help it any more than he could help his feelings of betrayal and hurt.

"I haven't forgotten," he replied. He leaned back in his chair and studied her. "You don't look well."

"It's been a long week, Justin," she said dully. "And a little unexpected. You don't need to worry," she said with a faint laugh. "I'm all right. I'm just fine, in fact. I've got a roof over my head and food to eat, and a job. I've got everything you promised me when we got married. I don't have a complaint."

She put her fork down and got up, swaying a little. She caught the back of the chair, praying that the sudden blackness would relent before she went down. It did, and she turned away from Justin's quick movement toward her.

"Are you all right?" The words were torn from him. He hated the way she looked. She made him feel cold with guilt. Amazing, when she'd hurt him, not the reverse.

"I told you. I'm fine." She left the room with her head high, and went upstairs without another word. They spent no time at all together now. If they had a meal at the same time, it was unusual. Afterward, he always went to his study and she went to her room. Maria noticed, but she and Lopez kept silent. With Justin in his present mood, it was safer that way.

The night of the party, Shelby rested before she dressed. She'd found a dark emerald velvet dress that she'd worn the year before. It had been a little too small when she and Justin married, but the weight loss made it just the right size. It was floor length, sleeveless, with an A-line skirt and a rounded neckline. She pinned up her hair and complemented the dress with a dainty emerald necklace that had been her grandmother's. She looked frail even with makeup, and she wished that things were different between her and Justin. Abby would surely have mentioned her brief happiness to Calhoun. When Calhoun came tonight and was able to see the distance between his brother and sister-in-law, he was bound to mention it to Justin. Shelby didn't think she could bear another confrontation.

She touched her stomach, wondering how much longer she should wait before she saw the doctor. They could tell at six weeks, she knew, and it was almost that. But the problem was going to be how to keep it from Justin in a small community like Jacobsville. Perhaps she could go up to Houston and have herself tested at a clinic.

Music was playing downstairs. She dabbed on a tiny bit of perfume and went downstairs, carefully holding onto the banister. She felt wobbly. The past week had been a terrible strain, due to overwork and Justin's unexplained cold attitude.

She spotted Abby and Calhoun when she got to the first landing. They were arm in arm, looking so happy that they broke her heart. Calhoun was big and blond and Abby was slender and dark. They made a handsome contrast, Calhoun in dark evening clothes and Abby in a pale blue silk that matched her eyes.

Shelby didn't see Justin until she got downstairs. He was dressed in a dinner jacket, and he looked very elegant. Shelby wondered if he planned to put on an act for their guests, or if he was going to be himself. She didn't dare look at him too closely. He might see the hurt and longing in her eyes.

She turned toward the door, where Lopez in his white

jacket was just opening it to admit the newest guest.
Shelby stopped dead at the sight of the man who stood
nervously just inside the hall, shifting his feet as he
searched the room for a familiar face.

Shelby's eyes flashed. She couldn't believe that Justin had had the audacity to invite him. It was Calhoun's
birthday, and she knew Justin wouldn't expect her to
make a scene.

But that didn't even register as she moved out into
the hall, ignoring Justin, and picked up a very expensive antique vase on the way.

"Hello, Tom," she greeted Tom Wheelor with icy
politeness. "How nice to see you again."

And without a break in her stride, she lifted the vase
and threw it straight at Wheelor's balding head.

CHAPTER TEN

SHELBY WATCHED, FASCINATED, as the antique vase whizzed past Tom's left ear and crashed into the hat stand in the corner, knocking Justin's battered black Stetson to the floor.

"Shelby?" Tom asked, moving back a step.

She reached out for the flower arrangement Maria had painstakingly created for the hall table.

"Shelby, don't!" Tom whirled, his hands over his head, and ran out the front door.

Shelby took off after him, blind to the shocked looks from the other guests, including her wide-eyed husband.

"Insect," she raged. "Weak-kneed money man!" She let him get halfway down the stairs before she heaved the flower arrangement in its delft bowl. It connected. Tom almost lost his balance as he caught onto the balustrade with shards of pottery shattering around him.

He struggled the rest of the way down the steps and ran for his car. Shelby watched him go with fury in her eyes. He'd been responsible, indirectly, for all her heartaches. How could he have the gall to come tonight, of all nights, and at Justin's invitation? Did Tom really think she'd forgotten his part in her anguish? She'd even told him at the time just what she thought of him.

She turned and went back up the steps. She didn't even look at Justin.

"Good evening," she greeted the guests, as if nothing at all had happened. "Happy birthday, Calhoun! We're so glad Abby let us throw this party for you." She went close and kissed his tanned cheek.

"Thanks, Shelby," Calhoun murmured.

"Shall we go in to dinner?" Shelby nodded to the others, mostly friends of Justin's and Calhoun's whom she barely knew. She took Justin's arm as if she feared his touch would burn her. She didn't look at him or speak to him.

"What the hell was that all about?" he asked when they were temporarily out of earshot of the others, heading into the elegantly arranged dining room.

She ignored his question. "How dare you invite that man here?" she asked instead. "How dare you bring him into our home, after the way he let my father use him to break us up?"

"I wanted to see if there were any embers left from the fire," he said with a cool smile.

"Embers?" She took a sharp breath. "You're lucky I didn't kill him. I'm sorry I didn't!"

"Temper, temper."

"You can go to hell, Justin, dear," she said with a smile as icy as his. "And take your moods and your taste for revenge and your cold heart with you."

His black eyes narrowed. "Still sticking to your story that your father made you break it off with me?"

"Why can't you believe me?"

"Very simple," he replied as the others filed into the room. "It was your father's money that pulled the feedlot out of bankruptcy. He footed the whole damned bill." His eyes registered her shock. "Surprised? It's hardly the act of a man who wanted to break us up, wouldn't you agree?"

Shelby knew her heart was going to beat her to death. She grabbed the back of a chair and almost went down, to Justin's surprise.

"Here, sit down, for God's sake," he muttered, easing her into her place. "Are you all right?"

"No, I'm not." She laughed shakily.

Abby, noticing Shelby's sudden pallor, sat quickly across from her. "Can I get you anything?" she whispered, glancing at the others.

"I'll be fine, if Justin will get away from me," she breathed, looking up at him with quiet rage.

He straightened, searching her furious eyes for a long moment. "My pleasure, Mrs. Ballenger," he said coldly, and turned his attention to their guests.

Shelby never knew afterward how she got through that dinner. She sat like a statue, answering questions, smiling, being the perfect hostess. But when she escaped upstairs to repair her makeup, Abby was two steps behind.

"What's happened?" her sister-in-law asked without preamble.

"For one thing, I'm pregnant," Shelby said stiffly.

Abby's breath sighed out, and her eyes softened. "Oh, Shelby! Does Justin know?"

"He doesn't, and you're not to tell him." Shelby sat down in her wing chair, easing her head back. "He's on the rampage again about the past. Just for a little while, things were going so well. Then he came back from Wyoming a stranger. He's been ice-cold ever since. How can I possibly tell him about the baby when he's acting like that?"

"It might soften his mood," Abby suggested.

"I don't need pity." She put her face in her hands with a tiny shudder. "It's never going to work, Abby.

He can't leave the past alone. I don't know what to do. I can't live like this anymore."

The tears slid past her hands and Abby bent, hugging her, saying all the right things, while she wanted nothing more than to go downstairs and hit Justin in the knee with a stick.

"What are you going to do?" Abby asked when the tears diminished and Shelby was wiping her red-rimmed green eyes with a tissue.

"I'm going to cut my losses, of course," Shelby said wearily. "I'm going to Houston tomorrow. I have a cousin there who'll let me stay with her until I can figure out where I'm going. I'll phone her later. I just need a little time to think. I can't do it here."

"What about your job?" Abby persisted, grasping at straws to keep Shelby from doing something stupid.

"Tammy and Mr. Holman are getting along very well," Shelby said. "As a matter of fact, I think they're very likely going to get married in the not-too-distant future. Tammy will take care of everything. I'll phone her tonight, too."

"You can't walk out on Justin like this, without trying to talk to him," Abby said softly, choosing her words. "I don't know what's gone wrong, but I do know how Justin feels about you. Shelby, you didn't see him that night Calhoun took you home from the square dance. But he was heartbroken that he'd made you cry. He cares deeply about you."

"He has a wonderful way of expressing affection," Shelby said. "First he tells me that we'll live separate lives, then he brings that…that *man* here!"

"I think he got the idea that you weren't carrying a torch for dear Tom." Abby chuckled.

"Tom and my father were two of a kind, both out to increase their already substantial fortunes," Shelby said. She stared down at the crumpled wet tissue. "But what hurts the most is that my father funded Justin and Calhoun's feedlot, and I didn't know it until Justin told me tonight." She sighed. "No wonder he wouldn't believe what I said about Dad trying to break us up. My father surely fixed things for me. Justin will never believe me again."

"He might listen if he knew about the baby."

"He's not going to," Shelby said doggedly. "It's my baby, not his. He can go to hell."

Abby's breath sighed out. Shelby looked bad, and talking wasn't going to solve anything. "Let's not discuss this now. You need to get some sleep and give this more thought when you're not so tired. Why don't you go to bed? I'll play hostess for you. I'll tell Justin you've got an upset stomach or a headache."

"He's the only headache I've got," Shelby said wearily.

Abby stood up, about to leave, when the door opened and Justin came in. He looked odd. Drawn and quiet and frankly puzzled.

"There's a woman here. A Miss Lester," he added. "She says she works with you."

"She's our paralegal," Shelby said dully. She wouldn't look at him. "What does she want?"

"She's coming up the staircase now. You can ask her." He shifted uncomfortably. "How long has she worked with you?"

"Several weeks," Shelby said. She looked up as Tammy came sheepishly into the room, looking bright-eyed and radiant. "Hi," she said with a smile. "What are you doing here?"

"I couldn't wait until tomorrow to show you my ring. Look!" She extended her left hand, where a huge diamond sparkled. "He gave it to me tonight."

Shelby laughed and got to her feet unsteadily to hug the younger woman. "I'm so happy for you. I had a feeling this was coming the other night, when the two of you went into his office and there was such silence!"

Tammy grinned. "Yes. Well, we seem to have started a good deal of gossip in town, outlined as we were against the window shade." She flushed. "Neither of us were thinking about being observed. But since we're engaged, it will be all right."

Justin had gone white. Abby saw his face and frowned but Shelby hadn't noticed. She was still talking to Tammy.

"Where's the boss?" she asked.

"Outside in the car, waiting impatiently. We're on our way to his parents' house to break the news. He wouldn't come in because of the party, but I just had to tell you! Isn't it great?" Tammy laughed.

"It certainly is. Congratulations!"

"Thank you. I'd better run." She hugged Shelby again. "See you bright and early tomorrow, okay?"

Shelby wanted to tell her that she wasn't going to be there Monday, but she couldn't, in front of Justin. Her plans to leave had to be kept secret.

"Yes," she agreed. "See you tomorrow. Tell the boss how happy I am for him, too," she added with a laugh.

"Okay. And I'm sorry for interrupting," Tammy added with a shy glance at Justin and Abby. "But I couldn't help it! Good night."

She left. Shelby sat down heavily. "Thank goodness," she told Abby with a breathless laugh. "Now the office can get back to normal again. It's been incredible working there for the past few weeks."

"She looks like you," Justin said curtly.

"Yes, she does," Abby agreed. She looked at Justin. Suddenly she knew that Justin had seen Barry Holman and Tammy in that window shade, silhouetted, and he'd thought it was Shelby. Maybe if she got out, they could talk about it and settle their differences.

"I'd better get back downstairs. Sure you're okay now?" she asked Shelby.

"I'm fine," Shelby assured her. "Thanks, Abby."

"I'll make your excuses."

Justin watched her go, searching for the right words to undo the damage he'd done. Shelby looked so wounded, so fragile. He could have shot himself for that frailty. He'd caused it by jumping to conclusions, by not listening to her. He hadn't trusted her, and now he wondered if he could ever repair the damage.

"Shelby…" he began slowly.

"I don't feel well," she said without preamble. "I'd like to lie down."

"You've lost weight," he remarked.

"Have I really?" She laughed, and it had a hollow sound. "Please go away, Justin. I don't have a single thing to say to you. I don't even want to have to look at you after what you did to me. Inviting that man here…!"

"I had to know!"

She looked up at him as she got to her feet. Her eyes blazed angrily. "I told you the truth. You wouldn't listen. You never have. You prefer your own interpretation, so go ahead and enjoy it. I don't care what you think anymore."

He stiffened. His pride was going to take a few knocks

before this was over, and he knew he deserved it, after the way he'd treated her.

"Why did your father break us up?"

"He wanted me to marry Tom," she said, turning away from him. "He didn't want a poor son-in-law. On the other hand, he didn't like to make enemies, not in a small community, so he let me be the scapegoat. You played right into his hands when you went into business for yourself. That gave him leverage, and he used it."

"Then why did he lend me the money?" he asked curtly. "For God's sake, it was that loan that eventually caused his downfall. It took me years to pay it back, but it wasn't in time to do him any good."

She stared at the bed, with her back to Justin. "It was a long time ago. You may find the past comforting, but I don't. I had great hopes for the present until you decided to start evening old scores. Now I just feel tired and I want to go to bed."

He opened his mouth, but the words wouldn't come. He didn't know what to say. "I...saw you. At least, I thought it was you. In the window of your office when I came to pick you up the night I got home from Wyoming," he confessed hesitantly.

She turned. Her eyes widened. "You thought you saw me kissing him?"

His broad shoulders lifted and fell. "You and Tammy have similar profiles, and you'd never told me there was anyone in the office with you."

Her chin lifted. "Thank you," she choked huskily, "for your sterling opinion of my character and morals. Thank you for believing that I could never betray you with another man."

His cheeks went ruddy. "You'd betrayed me once!" he shot at her. "You left me for another man."

"I never did," she said firmly. "Never! My father threatened to ruin you and made me say what I did. He promised to save you, but I never realized that he did it with his own money."

"You dated Tom Wheelor," he added.

"No; it broke my father's heart that I refused to marry Tom," she said with a cold laugh. "Life without you was the purest hell I ever knew. I tried to tell you, but you wouldn't listen. You *still* won't listen." Tears clouded her eyes. "Well, I'm tired of talking to you, Justin. You're too bitter and too much in love with the past to ever give up your grudges. I can't live like this anymore. You've hurt me more than you'll ever know, even though I have to admit that my own cowardice helped things along. But what I did, I did to protect you, because I loved you too much to let you lose everything. All I ever wanted was you. But you only ever wanted me one way, and now that you've —how did you put it?—satisfied your desire for me, even that's gone, isn't it?"

His teeth ground together on a wave of pain. "Oh, God, Shelby," he whispered huskily.

"Well, don't lose any sleep over it, Justin. Maybe we were doomed from the beginning. Without trust, we don't have anything." She brushed the loose strands of hair away from her face. "I thought there was a chance for us, before you went to Wyoming. But if you still can't trust me, then we don't even have a common ground to build on. I'm so tired, Justin," she said then, sitting on the edge of her bed. "I'm so tired of fighting. I just want to go to sleep."

He ran his hand through his thick black hair, watching her. "Of course," he said quietly. "Tomorrow we'll talk."

She wasn't going to be here tomorrow, but she wasn't about to tell him that. "Yes. Tomorrow."

He wanted to hold her. To talk to her. To confess that his coldness had been out of jealousy, because he didn't think such a lovely woman could ever really love him. He'd never thought it, and his own uncertainty about his attraction for a woman like Shelby was the biggest part of the problem. But she did look worn, and it would be cruel to make her evening any harder than he already had.

"Get some rest. If you need me, just sing out."

"You're the last person on earth I need, Justin," she said quietly.

He drew in a slow breath. "My God, I know that. I always was." His black eyes slid over her hungrily. "It never seemed to make any difference, though. I couldn't stop wanting you. I never will."

He went out the door without looking back, and Shelby lay down on the coverlet and cried for all the happy years she'd never have with him, for the child she was carrying that he didn't even know about. She cried for all of them, and fell asleep in her evening gown, lying on top of the covers.

Justin found her that way the next morning. He didn't wake her. She looked so fragile, with her black hair haloed around her sleeping face. She was pale and he felt the guilt all the way to his soul. He'd hurt her. She was the most precious thing in his world, and he'd done nothing but hurt her.

He took off her shoes and pulled the quilted coverlet over her, his black eyes adoring on her face. "I'd fight the world for you, little one," he said softly, "What an irony it is that I can't seem to stop hurting you."

She didn't hear him. He reached down and touched her cheek gently, tracing it up to her eyebrows. His dark eyes softened, became tender.

"I love you," he breathed huskily. "Oh, God, I love you so! Why can't I tell you?" He bent and brushed his mouth with exquisite tenderness over her lips, a light touch that wouldn't awaken her. He stood up again, sighing heavily as he studied her sleeping face. "You said that I didn't trust you. Maybe the truth is more that I don't trust myself. You need someone gentler than I am. Someone less abrasive and set in his ways. I always knew it, but I couldn't find the strength to give you up." He lifted her slender hand in his and savored its softness. He smiled wistfully. "It would serve me right if I lost you. But I don't think I could stay alive if I did."

He put her hand on the coverlet and after one last glance at her sleeping face, he turned and went out of the room. Perhaps later they could talk, and he would tell her all these things when she was awake and listening. If he kept holding back, he stood a very real chance of losing her.

Shelby woke an hour after he left and her mind registered her evening-gown-clad person along with the coverlet that had been put over her. She wondered if she'd done that, or if Maria had covered her. Well, it didn't matter. She had things to do and not much time to do them in.

She tried to phone Tammy, but Tammy must have left for the office. Well, she'd call her from Cousin Carey's house in Houston. She did phone Cousin Carey and ask if she could visit for a day or two, and an invitation was extended with flattering immediacy. She and

Carey had known each other since grammar school and were friends as well as relatives. She promised to see her cousin later in the day, hung up and got a reservation on the midday flight out of the Jacobsville airport that was Houston-bound.

She packed a suitcase, taking only what she had to have, and prayed that her morning sickness would hold off until she could get away.

She sneaked downstairs, called a cab and was almost out the door when Maria came into the hall to announce breakfast and found Shelby with a suitcase and a cab waiting.

"Señora!" Maria exclaimed helplessly.

"I'm only going away for a couple of days," Shelby said, faltering. "Abby knows where I'll be. You mustn't tell Justin. Promise me!"

Maria grimaced, but she finally agreed. She watched Shelby climb into the cab and drive away. She'd promised not to tell Justin. She hadn't promised not to call Abby. She picked up the phone and quickly dialed Abby's number.

JUSTIN WAS ON the telephone when Abby came into his office, dressed in jeans and a plaid shirt, her hair uncombed and no makeup on. She closed the door and sat down in the visitor's chair, watching the expressions that crossed her former guardian's face as he abruptly ended the telephone conversation and hung up.

"What's wrong?" he asked, because she looked worried.

"Everything!" she muttered, frowning. "I was half asleep when Maria called. Shelby made her promise not to call you, so she called me instead. I've broken speed records getting here. And now that I have—" she sighed "—I don't know how to say this to you."

He'd stiffened at the mention of Shelby's name. He'd had a premonition about her. He knew how badly he'd hurt her, and she'd mentioned last night that she couldn't take any more.

"She's left me, hasn't she, Abby?" he asked quietly.

"Yes, she has. The question is, what are you going to do about it?"

He lit a cigarette with steady hands while his world collapsed around his ears. He stared at the desk. "I'm going to let her go," he said after a minute. "I've hurt her enough."

Abby's breath stuck in her throat. "Justin!"

He looked up, the pain in his eyes making them even blacker. "You don't know how I've treated her," he said. "I was jealous and scared to death of losing her..." He broke off to run his hand roughly through his hair. "What have I got to offer her? How do I keep her?"

"You might try telling her that you love her," Abby said simply. "That's all she ever wanted."

His jaw clenched. "She wouldn't listen, after last night."

"You saw Barry Holman and Tammy, didn't you?" Abby asked.

He stared at her blankly. "Yes."

"And instead of telling Shelby, and letting her explain, you went off the deep end."

He smiled faintly. "Bingo."

"Oh, Justin." She shook her head. "She's on her way to Houston."

"Maybe she'll find someone there who can give her what she needs," he said, feeling bitter that he'd ruined all his chances.

Abby was getting nowhere and if Justin didn't go after Shelby, things were going to fall apart. She bit her lower lip. She didn't want to steal Shelby's thunder, but Justin was being difficult.

"Justin…how do you feel about babies?" she asked.

He was only half listening, his heart lying like lead in his chest. "I like babies," he said absently.

"Good. Then why don't you go after Shelby and get yours back?"

At first Abby didn't think he'd heard her. His eyes swung around and he stared at her. "I beg your pardon?" he asked.

"I said, Shelby's pregnant. If you really want a baby, you'd better get to the airport before she carries yours off to Houston with her."

"What the hell are you talking about?" he exploded.

"Now, Justin…!"

But he was on his feet and the chair was on the floor. He grabbed onto the desk for support. His eyes were wild and there was a tremor in the lean hand holding his cigarette. "A baby? Shelby's pregnant, and she didn't tell me?"

Abby was uncertain about what to do, so she rushed out of the office and found Calhoun.

"Come on." She pulled at his big hand. "I need you."

He grinned. "Now, honey, this isn't the place…"

"Justin's in shock."

That wiped the smile off his face. He followed her into Justin's office. The older man was right where Abby had left him, still white in the face and looking as if he'd been stabbed.

"You need to take him to the airport," Abby instructed.

"Airport, hell, he needs a doctor. What did you do to him?" he asked in a half whisper.

"I told him Shelby was pregnant."

Calhoun whistled through his teeth.

"And that she was on her way to Houston."

"I can drive," Justin said unsteadily. He started toward the door, but his eyes were dilated and his hand shook as he tried to put out the cigarette, knocking the glowing tip onto the desk.

Calhoun got it into the ashtray and took his brother firmly by the arm. "Don't you worry, big brother, I'll get you there on time." He glanced at Abby. "Which terminal?"

She grimaced. "Jacobsville airport only has one terminal."

"You're a big help," Calhoun muttered. "Anyway, I think there are only a couple of flights to Houston during off-peak hours."

"She's pregnant," Justin said huskily. "She didn't tell me. She knew and she couldn't tell me. It's all my fault. I failed her."

"Everything will be all right," Abby said reassuringly.

"God, I hope so." Justin glanced at her. "Thanks, honey."

"Don't tell Shelby I told you," Abby returned. "It's her place to tell you, but I was afraid you'd let her go if I didn't."

He only nodded, and finally he moved away from Calhoun and went out the door. But he didn't argue when Calhoun gestured toward the Jaguar and got in under the wheel.

"What if the plane's already gone?" Justin asked, smoking like a furnace all the way to the airport.

"Then we'll get you a ticket to Houston." He grinned. "I'm going to be an uncle. Imagine that." He glanced at his taciturn brother. "And here I thought you and Shelby were living chastely."

"Shut up," Justin said, hiding embarrassment in bad temper.

"Whatever you say, big brother." He whistled to himself as he swung the car onto the highway and gunned the accelerator.

They reached the airport in record time. Justin was out the door almost before Calhoun stopped the car, half running to get into the terminal. They found the flight to Houston and Justin went to the ticket counter only to be told that the plane was scheduled to take off in less than five minutes.

Justin outdistanced Calhoun on his way to the concourse, his eyes fixed on the distant gate, his heart bursting with fear that she was going to get away before he got there. He broke into a run as the gate numbers got bigger, determined to make it in time.

Only another minute, he told himself, and he'd have her in sight. Then he could talk to her, he could make her understand how much he loved her.

He pushed past a group of departing passengers from the concourse and made it to the empty ticket counter just in time to watch the clerk pull down the Houston sign and replace it with one for another city.

"The Houston flight," Justin asked curtly. "Where is it?"

"It left about two minutes ago," the clerk said pleasantly. "It's taxiing out to the runway now."

Justin felt his heart stop. He moved around the desk to the window and looked out. Planes were taking off, and one of them had Shelby on it. Shelby and his baby.

He stood there, frozen, his heart shattering. It was his own fault. He'd driven her to this. But he didn't know how in hell he was going to live with it. He could only imagine the anguish that had caused her to run away.

Calhoun touched his shoulder gently. "How about something to eat? Then we'll get you a seat on the next plane."

"I don't even know where to look for her, do you realize that?" he asked huskily. "My God, Cal, I don't know where she's gone!"

"It will be all right," Calhoun said firmly. "We'll find her. I swear we will."

Justin turned away from the window. "Food be damned, I want a drink." He strode off toward the flashing Restaurant and Lounge sign down the concourse.

Calhoun followed, wondering how he was going to keep his big brother sober after his devastating letdown. Justin was shattered and Calhoun didn't quite know what to do for him. He'd said that they'd find Shelby, but he had no better idea of how to go about it than Justin did. It wasn't going to be easy to find one lone pregnant woman in a city the size of Houston. Especially if she didn't want to be found.

He stood out in the corridor, watching Justin go into the lounge and sit at a window table. He gave the waitress an order, and Calhoun sighed heavily. Well, maybe it would be a good idea if he went to the ticket desk and found out when the next plane left for Houston so he could get Justin a seat.

He was on his way down the concourse when a familiar face caught his eye. He stopped in the middle of the aisle and stared. He wasn't dreaming. That gray-clad woman with the small suitcase was Shelby, and she was coming straight toward him.

CHAPTER ELEVEN

SHELBY FELT THE ground shake under her at the sight of Calhoun barring her path. She'd been certain Maria wouldn't say anything, but now she wasn't sure. Unless, of course, Calhoun was here to meet a client.

"Uh, hi, Calhoun," she said with a shaky smile.

He sighed. "Hi, yourself, Shelby." He noted the small suitcase she was carrying. "Going somewhere?"

She shifted restlessly. "Yes," she murmured. She stared at his suit instead of his face. "I'm leaving your brother."

"I know. Maria called Abby. Justin knows, too."

Shelby felt her face going pale, but a quick look around didn't produce Justin, and she sighed with relief. "He isn't with you, then?"

He took her arm gently. "I think it might help things along if you had a look at him. Come on, now, he won't bite."

"That's what you think," she muttered. "Where is he?"

"In there." He pulled her just inside the lounge entrance and nodded toward the corner, where Justin sat bareheaded and stooped with a bottle of whiskey and a shot glass in front of him. He was staring at the bottle obliviously while a forgotten cigarette sent up spirals of smoke from his free hand.

Shelby frowned. Justin didn't drink, as a rule. She remembered Abby saying something about him getting drunk the night of the square dance, but she knew it was a rare thing for him. He liked to be in control all the time. He didn't like having his mind fogged.

"What's he doing?" Shelby asked.

"Getting drunk, I imagine." Calhoun took the suitcase from her and looked down at her pale, fragile features. "Now, Shelby, would you say that he looks like a happy man?"

She grimaced. "No."

"Does he look like a man who's overjoyed that his wife has gone off and left him?"

She shook her head. In fact, he looked exactly the opposite. He looked defeated. Her pale green eyes ran over him lovingly, a soft sadness in their depths.

"I had to drive him here because he was shaking too bad to handle a car," he said quietly, nodding at her shocked expression. "He won't like remembering that, and when he's back together, I'm going to catch hell for having seen him in this condition. But I wanted you to know just how upset he is. That man loves you, honey. For years, you've been the only star in his sky. He's been alone all that time, and despite the fact that he's given you hell, I know he'd die for you. If you don't love him, the kindest thing you can do is to get out. But if you care about him, don't run away. Get in there and talk to him."

"I love him," she said simply. "But he believes bad things about me. He won't listen..."

"If you tell him how you feel, he'll listen. Believe it."

She looked up at him, weakening. "It's so hard..."

"Isn't life?" He bent and kissed her cheek gently. "Go on. Get it over. I'll sit in the concourse over there and look like a passenger and drink coffee. I'll look after your suitcase, too."

She smiled softly. "Thanks, Calhoun."

"My pleasure. Now go on."

She hesitated, but only for a minute. Calhoun was right. She was going to have to face Justin.

She walked nervously toward the table where he was sitting. As she got closer, she could see the paleness of his skin, the new lines that cut into his face.

"Justin?" she said hesitantly when she reached him.

He glanced up. Something flashed in his eyes as they went over her, tracing her body reverently. "You aren't here," he said quietly. "You left."

She bit her lip. He sounded as if he was talking to a ghost. "Not yet," she said gently. She eased into the chair beside his and stared at his lean hands. "I'm sorry to just run out like that. But I'd had all I could take."

"I know that," he said, his voice soft, tender. "I'm not blaming you. I never gave you a chance." He lifted the shot glass to his lips, but her fingers touched the back of his hand, coaxing him to put it down. He laughed hollowly. "I hate liquor, did I ever tell you? But it isn't every day a man loses everything he loves."

Tears moistened her eyes. She caught his hand and held it in both of hers, her face lifted, her expression open, loving. "You never said that you loved me, Justin," she whispered. "But I never stopped loving you. I never will. All I ever wanted was you."

His fingers contracted convulsively around hers. His black eyes glittered over his face. "Didn't you know, even without the words?" He breathed roughly. "My God, I'd have walked through fire if you'd asked me to. You were my world. I loved you…"

Her head nuzzled against his shoulder and she hated the crowded room, because she wanted nothing more

in life than to throw her arms around him and hold him
and kiss him and tell him all the things she'd never
said before.

His arm went around her, holding her, and he drew
in a shaky breath. "My God," he whispered at her forehead. "I thought you married me because you were
alone and frightened."

"And I thought you married me because you felt
sorry for me," she replied, letting the tears run freely
down her face. "And all along, I loved you so."

His lean fingers brushed away the tears. He searched
her misty eyes. "We've got to get out of here," he whispered. "I have to make you understand what I feel. I can't
lose you now. Oh, God, Shelby, I'll die without you," he
said huskily, and it was in his eyes, blazing out of them
like black fire.

The tears came again. She got up, taking his hand.
He went with her, holding her against him, even while
he settled the tab, as if he couldn't bear to release her
even that long.

Calhoun saw them come out of the lounge. He grinned
knowingly and picked up Shelby's suitcase. "I'll drop you
two off at the house," he offered. "Then I've got a meeting to get to."

They barely heard him. Justin looked completely obliv-
ious, and Shelby was so close to him that she seemed a
part of him.

He put them in the backseat and drove off, smiling
smugly at his role in this reunion. Not that they seemed
to notice him. They were too busy looking at each other.

He let them out at the front steps of the Ballenger
house, setting the bag on the steps beside them. "I phoned
Abby while you two were in the lounge. She said how

about coming over to our place for supper? Maria's going to her sister's tonight, and Shelby sure isn't up to cooking."

"That would be nice," Justin said quietly. He clapped his brother on the shoulder. "Thanks."

"You'd do the same for me," Calhoun replied. He grinned. "In fact, you did, or have you already forgotten? See you at six. Goodbye, Shelby."

"Thanks, Calhoun," she said, smiling at him.

Justin picked up the suitcase and helped her into the house. Maria came running, a stream of Spanish echoing from her lips. Justin abruptly swung her up by the waist and planted a heartfelt kiss on her tanned cheek. She giggled when he put her down.

"Señor!" she chided. She was dressed up. "Lopez and I are leaving now, but I had to wait and make sure everything was all right. *Señor,* what about a meal this evening?"

"Calhoun's invited us over to eat with him and Abby," Shelby told her, and hugged her. "Thank you for calling Abby. I'll never forget what you did for us."

Maria grinned. "You would have found a way, *señora.*" She laughed. "I only helped a little bit. Lopez and I must hurry. We will be back tomorrow, *señor.* I will cook you a magnificent breakfast!"

"We'll look forward to that. Godspeed."

Maria smiled and went down the hall into the kitchen, where Lopez was waiting.

Justin led Shelby into the living room, where Maria had a tray of coffee and small cakes waiting for them. After she sat down, he poured the coffee. But before he handed her the cup, he bent and kissed her with exquisite tenderness.

"I love you," he whispered softly, searching her eyes. "I always did, even if I couldn't find the right way to tell you."

She kissed him back. "That was all you ever had to say," she replied. "I loved you, too, Justin. But you never seemed to believe that I could."

He gave her coffee to her and sat down close beside her to sip his. "I was a poor man in those days, and I've never been much to look at," he confessed. "You came from a wealthy background, you were beautiful and pursued." He laughed. "I never felt like serious competition for men like Wheelor."

"Money and looks never counted for much with me," she said firmly. "You had qualities much more important." Her eyes searched his quietly. "But the important thing was that I loved you," she said. "Love doesn't depend on surface things or possessions."

He looked at her with undisguised hunger. "No. I don't suppose it does. I was unsure of you."

She smiled. "And now?"

"And now." He laughed softly. His free hand touched her face. The smile faded. "I've made you unhappy. I've hurt you and scorned you, all because I didn't trust you. But if I'd known how you felt, there wouldn't have been any doubts. None. Can you believe that, and forgive me for the way I've treated you?"

"I love you," she said simply. "Nothing else matters." She reached up and kissed him hungrily. "I understand why you thought what you did, Justin. It was my father's mischief-making, not anything either of us did that caused such heartache. But now it's enough that you love me. It's everything."

He put down his cup and hers and drew her across

his lap, holding her hungrily. "I'd take back the whole six years, if I could," he whispered huskily. "I'd do anything to make it up to you."

"Justin...you've already made it up to me," she said with soft hesitation. She took his lean hand and pressed it slowly, gently, to her still-flat abdomen. She held it there and searched his eyes. "I'm carrying your baby."

He knew. But hearing it from her made it profound and infinitely touching. He caressed the softness gently and, bending, brought her mouth under his to kiss her with exquisite caring.

"Shelby," he whispered. He kissed her again. "Shelby. You and a baby..."

"You aren't sorry?" she whispered, softly teasing.

He smiled at her with pride and love in his dark eyes. "I'm not sorry about anything. Are we having a son or a daughter?"

"I don't care, as long as we have a healthy baby." She reached up to hold him. "And I'm quitting my job, in case I haven't mentioned it. I think Tammy and the boss are going to be very happy without me."

"I'm going to be very happy with you, if this is what you really want," he said. He traced her lips with a long finger. "I won't cheat you of outside interests, if you want them. I won't insist that you be only a wife and mother."

"I won't be," she assured him, "although that's going to be my most important job for a little while. Then I may take courses or do some volunteer work. But right now, the baby is my main concern."

He laughed softly. "How long?" he whispered.

"I think I'm just at six weeks," she whispered back. "I'm going to the doctor next week to make sure."

"The first time we made love," he breathed, holding her eyes. "Wasn't it?"

She hid her face against him, laughing with shy embarrassment. "Yes."

"I'm good," he murmured dryly.

She pressed closer. "You're very good," she whispered and lifted her face.

He bent, easing his mouth down onto hers, caressing it. She relaxed against him, loving his touch, loving the strength of his body so close to hers. She sighed, and the sound went into his mouth, kindling a new and overwhelming desire.

Her hands slid around to the back of his head and he drew her hips against his, turning her, while his mouth became more and more demanding.

He wanted her. She knew the signs now, in ways she hadn't before. And she moaned, because he loved her and she loved him, and this time would be different than the other times. It would be the most poignant time of their lives.

"Do you want me?" he whispered against her lips. "Because I want you. Right here."

"The first time…was right here," she breathed, jerking a little when his hand eased between them to work at the pearly buttons down the front of her gray dress.

"It's handy." He chuckled, the sound rich and deep with love. "But there's always the carpet."

Her eyes searched his. "How kinky."

"Not at all. It's thick and soft…and there's no one to see us. And just to make sure…"

He got up, still smiling, and went to close and lock the door. He took off his shirt, watching the way her eyes went to the thick curling hair that arrowed down to the belt of his jeans. He liked the way she looked at him. Her eyes grew dark and soft and faintly sensuous.

He drew her up from the sofa, putting her hands on his chest, smoothing them over the warm, pulsating muscle. "Is it dangerous for the baby?" he asked softly.

She shook her head and pressed her lips against him. "Not if you're gentle. And when have you ever hurt me?"

"No regrets, Shelby?" he asked, hesitating.

She reached up to put her mouth against his. "Not even one."

His hands caught her hips and pulled them into his, moving her body with his so that she felt the force of his need. Her body reacted to it in a now familiar way and she reached up to get closer, signaling her hunger in subtle ways.

She kissed him until her lips grew swollen and tender, until her body began to feel the familiar hot shakiness that he aroused so easily in her.

He eased her down onto the carpet, sliding alongside her easily. He had her dress unbuttoned and her undergarments out of the way with lazy skill, and then she felt his mouth, and all her inhibitions went out the window.

She held his mouth against her, drowning in its moist caresses, loving the way he was with her. There had never been any fear of intimacy since their first time. Her body knew what kind of pleasure lay ahead, and now it reacted with delight, not apprehension.

For long, lazy minutes, he aroused her, not satisfied until she was trembling from head to toe and completely at his mercy. Only then did he undress himself, feasting on her soft curves and creamy skin while he discarded the rest of his clothing and lay back down beside her.

She looked up with misty eyes as he arched above her, catching his weight on his powerful arms, and she felt the exquisite tracing of his skin on hers as he eased down over her.

Her breath jerked at the first touch of him, and he laughed wickedly.

"It shouldn't shock you anymore," he whispered at her lips as he moved even closer. "You're an old married woman now."

"It isn't shock, it's…pleasure!" She clutched at him as he began to move. She buried her mouth against his shoulder, moaning again as his body merged so gently with hers. "Justin!"

"I love you," he whispered softly. "I've never really shown you how much, but now I'm going to. Lie still for me, little one. Let me take you straight into the sun." He eased his mouth over hers, and began to speak to her in husky whispers, in fluent Spanish. Love words. Descriptive words that he punctuated with slow caresses and tender tracings that made her weep with new pleasure. There was no holding back this time, no hidden worry, no barrier. He adjusted his movements to the needs of her body, taking his time, treating her with exquisite tenderness. And somewhere in the slow fire of it, she heard her voice cry out as she followed him into the whirlwind of fulfillment.

She couldn't stop trembling afterward. She clung to his shoulders, trying to keep her breathing steady, her heartbeat from shaking her. But he seemed just as affected, which made it less inhibiting.

"It's all right." He soothed her with his hands, kissing her face gently with lips that adored her. "It's all right.

It's just the shock of coming down from such a height, sweetheart," he breathed. "I feel it, too."

"It's never been like this before," she whispered brokenly.

"But we never made love like this before," he whispered back. He lifted his head to search her dazed eyes. "Not this completely."

She touched his mouth with trembling fingers, lost in him, totally his. "I don't want to stop."

"Neither do I," he whispered softly. "We don't have to. We're alone in the house, with nothing else to do. We'll go upstairs and see if we can top what we've just had together."

He got up slowly, picked her up and started for the door.

"Justin, our clothes," she whispered, glancing back at the very evident turmoil of their garments leaving a visible trail.

He balanced her on his leg and unlocked the door. He opened it and started up the long staircase with her cradled against his damp, hair-roughened chest. "They'll still be there when we get back," he promised.

"But we don't have any clothes on," she protested.

He looked down at the pretty pink body in his arms with pure pride of possession. "I noticed."

"But Maria and Lopez…"

"…won't be back tonight." He put his mouth over hers. After a few seconds of it, she began to cling to him, loving the feel of him against her soft bareness. Loving, she thought while she could, was the most incredible pleasure. She kissed him back, all thought of arguing gone from her whirling mind.

It was longer the second time. He drew it out, his

voice soft and slow, speaking partly in Spanish as he taught her new words and coached her in their enunciation. And all the while, he touched her, adored her with his hands and his eyes, whispered all she meant to him, how pleased he was about the baby they'd made. They reached heights they'd never scaled, and it was almost dark when they awoke in each other's arms.

"We slept," she murmured.

"No wonder." He grinned down at her, laughing when she blushed.

"I'm thirsty," she whispered.

"So am I." He got up, stretching lazily while her eyes adored his blatant nudity. "How about something cold and icy? And something to nibble on?"

"That would be lovely." She moved against the sheets, her eyes sultry. "Don't be long."

He chuckled. "I'll be back before you miss me."

He looked around for something to put on. His clothes were downstairs. Finally he went into the bathroom and came out with a huge colored beach towel with a giant frog on it. It was her bedroom he'd carried her to, and there was a noticeable shortage of male clothing.

"Damned flashy thing," he muttered, glaring playfully at her as he wrapped it around his hips. "You couldn't buy a plain one, I don't suppose?"

"I like frogs," she murmured.

He arched an eyebrow and, ignoring Shelby's giggles, went downstairs.

He filled two glasses with ice and sweetened tea from the refrigerator, made ham sandwiches, and put it all on a tray. He went out of the kitchen into the hall and paused at the foot of the staircase to adjust his slip-

ping towel when the front door suddenly opened and
Calhoun walked in.

He stopped dead, staring at his taciturn, very digni-
fied brother standing in the hall with a giant frog towel
wrapped around his lean hips. Justin was carrying a tray
full of food and drink and he looked...strange.

"I thought you and Shelby were coming to supper,"
Calhoun began.

"Supper?" Justin echoed.

"Supper. It's almost seven. You didn't call and your
phone seems to be off the hook. We were afraid something might have happened, so I came over to see about
you."

Justin blinked. He'd taken the phone off the hook
when he'd carried Shelby upstairs. He looked down at his
towel. "Nothing's wrong. I was, uh, just taking a bath,"
he improvised, a little embarrassed at being caught in
such a compromising situation even in his own home.

Calhoun noticed the open door of the living room
and the trail of clothing. "In the living room?" he asked.
"And since when do you wear dresses?"

Justin glared at him, his lips in a thin line. "I was
sorting clothes at the same time. Then I got hungry."

"You were invited to supper."

"I got hungry first. I was going to have a bite to eat
before I started getting ready." His complexion had gone
ruddy by now.

Calhoun was grinning from ear to ear. "In the shower?"

"I was going to eat first," Justin said stubbornly.

"Where's Shelby?" Calhoun asked curiously.

Justin cleared his throat. "Upstairs. She was tired."

Just then, a plaintive voice came from upstairs. "Justin, are you ever coming back?" Shelby moaned. "I'm lonely."

Justin's face went scarlet. "I'll be right there!" he called tersely. He glared harder at Calhoun. "She's taking a shower, too."

Calhoun had to stifle laughter. He grinned knowingly at his older brother and turned on his heel. "When you finish your snack in the shower and get through sorting clothes, come on over and we'll feed you." He glanced at the towel. "Better put on some pants first, though, we wouldn't want to shock Abby. Honest to God, Justin, a frog?"

"It was the only damned thing I could find, and what's it to you?" Justin demanded hotly.

"Oh, I think it suits you," Calhoun replied. "I like frogs."

"We forgot the time," Justin said stiffly. "We'll be there in about thirty minutes, if it's convenient."

"No rush." Calhoun grinned wickedly. "If you think the living-room carpet is a good place, you ought to try it in a whirlpool bath," he murmured, and got out quick, because Justin looked torn between shock and homicide.

Justin carried the tray upstairs, his dignity bruised, and put it on the bedside table.

"Iced tea! I'm parched." Shelby laughed and picked up her glass to drink thirstily. "I heard voices."

"Calhoun came to see where we were," Justin muttered. "We were invited to supper, remember?"

"I didn't think about it," Shelby confessed.

"Neither did I. We can go in a half hour. Still want a snack first?"

"Maybe we'd better wait. We can always have them for a bedtime snack. I'll wrap them up and put them in the refrigerator when I've dressed." She looked at her husband lovingly. "Calhoun and Abby are married, too," she reminded him. "It's not so shocking to be caught spending the afternoon in bed with your wife, is it?"

He shifted. "No. But it's uncomfortable," he confessed with a wry glance. "Six years of celibacy makes a man secretive, I guess."

"Six years." She reached up and kissed him very tenderly. "I thought I'd made you too bitter to sleep with anyone else. But it wasn't that at all, was it, Justin?" she asked quietly.

He touched her fingers to his lips. "I didn't want anyone else," he said with a sigh. "I loved you too much. It was you or nobody."

She had to bite her lip to stem the tears. "That's how I felt. I tried so hard to protect you," she whispered.

"I was doing the same thing for you, when we got married. I suppose both of us went overboard, though."

"But no more." She smiled. "Now we'll use our protective instincts on our baby."

"That sounds like a good idea." He bent and kissed her. "We'd better get dressed and go see the in-laws, little mama," he murmured. "Before they come back."

"It was nice of Abby to invite us."

"Yes. I hope you feel up to what's coming," he added. "Knowing Calhoun, it's going to be a trying supper."

She laughed, hiding her face against him. "I love you."

"I love you, too, honey." He got up, frog and all. "Shelby, would you have told me about the baby if Calhoun hadn't gotten me to the airport on time?"

She nodded. "It was your right. I wasn't really leaving you, Justin, I just needed a little time to think things through. I'd have come back. I'm not equipped to live without you any more." She stared at him hungrily. "Were you coming after me?"

"Of course." He chuckled. "I figured I'd spend several months searching the city for you, but that wouldn't have stopped me. I felt bad about what I'd said and done. But it was because I loved you that I'd have gone looking for you, honey, not out of guilt."

"Yes. Now I know." She sighed lazily, so much in love with him that she felt near to bursting with it. "I could eat a horse."

"I'll phone Abby to cook one. Get up and get your clothes on, woman. I'm starving."

"Don't look at me. Not eating was your idea."

She got out of bed and he swung her up against him, his eyes full of tenderness. "It sure was. I take these spells from time to time." He bent and kissed her. "Will you mind?"

She linked her arms around his neck and held him closer. "I won't mind at all."

Outside the night sky grew even darker, and a few miles down the road, Abby was starting to reheat the meat and vegetables in her Irish stew one last time. She'd tried to tell Calhoun that champagne didn't really go with such a simple dish, but he was too busy chilling it to listen. So Abby just laughed, and got down her best champagne flutes. Maybe he was right at that. It did seem like a good night for a celebration.

* * * * *

QUINN

To Barry Call of Charbons in Gainesville, GA.
Many thanks.

CHAPTER ONE

THE NOISE OUTSIDE the cabin was there again, and Amanda shifted restlessly with the novel in her lap, curled up in a big armchair by the open fireplace in an Indian rug. Until now, the cabin had been paradise. There was three feet of new snow outside, she had all the supplies she needed to get her through the next few wintery weeks of Wyoming weather, and there wasn't a telephone in the place. Best of all, there wasn't a neighbor.

Well, there was, actually. But nobody in their right mind would refer to that man on the mountain as a neighbor. Amanda had only seen him once and once was enough.

She'd met him, if their head-on encounter could be referred to as a meeting, on a snowy Saturday last week. Quinn Sutton's majestic ranch house overlooked this cabin nestled against the mountainside. He'd been out in the snow on a horse-drawn sled that contained huge square bales of hay, and he was heaving them like feather pillows to a small herd of red-and-white cattle. The sight had touched Amanda, because it indicated concern. The tall, wiry rancher out in a blizzard feeding his starving cattle. She'd even smiled at the tender picture it made.

And then she'd stopped her four-wheel-drive vehicle and stuck her blond head out the window to ask directions to the Blalock Durning place, which was the cabin one of her aunt's friends was loaning her. And the tender picture dissolved into stark hostility.

The tall rancher turned toward her with the coldest black eyes and the hardest face she'd ever seen in her life. He had a day's growth of stubble, but the stubble didn't begin to cover up the frank homeliness of his lean face. He had amazingly high cheekbones, a broad forehead and a jutting chin, and he looked as if someone had taken a straight razor to one side of his face, which had a wide scratch. None of that bothered Amanda because Hank Shoeman and the other three men who made music with her group were even uglier than Quinn Sutton. But at least Hank and the boys could smile. This man looked as if he invented the black scowl.

"I said," she'd repeated with growing nervousness, "can you tell me how to get to Blalock Durning's cabin?"

Above the sheepskin coat, under the battered gray ranch hat, Quinn Sutton's tanned face didn't move a muscle. "Follow the road, turn left at the lodgepoles," he'd said tersely, his voice as deep as a rumble of thunder.

"Lodgepoles?" she'd faltered. "What do they look like?"

"Lady," he said with exaggerated patience, "a lodgepole is a pine tree. It's tall and piney, and there are a stand of them at the next fork in the road."

"You don't need to be rude, Mr....?"

"Sutton," he said tersely. "Quinn Sutton."

"Nice to meet you," she murmured politely. "I'm Amanda." She wondered if anyone might accidentally recognize her here in the back of beyond, and on the off chance, she gave her mother's maiden name instead of her own last name. "Amanda Corrie," she added un-truthfully. "I'm going to stay in the cabin for a few weeks."

"This isn't the tourist season," he'd said without the slightest pretense at friendliness. His black eyes cut her like swords.

"Good, because I'm not a tourist," she said.

"Don't look to me for help if you run out of wood or start hearing things in the dark," he added coldly. "Somebody will tell you eventually that I have no use whatsoever for women."

While she was thinking up a reply to that, a young boy of about twelve had come running up behind the sled.

"Dad!" he called, amazingly enough to Quinn Sutton. "There's a cow in calf down in the next pasture. I think it's a breech!"

"Okay, son, hop on," he told the boy, and his voice had become fleetingly soft, almost tender. He looked back at Amanda, though, and the softness left him. "Keep your door locked at night," he'd said. "Unless you're expecting Durning to join you," he added with a mocking smile.

She'd stared at him from eyes as black as his own and started to tell him that she didn't even know Mr. Durning, who was her aunt's friend, not hers. But she bit her tongue. It wouldn't do to give this man an opening. "I'll do that little thing," she agreed. She glanced at the boy, who was eyeing her curiously from his perch on the sled. "And it seems that you do have at least one use for women," she added with a vacant smile. "My condolences to your wife, Mr. Sutton."

She'd rolled up the window before he could speak

and she'd whipped the four-wheel-drive down the road with little regard for safety, sliding all over the place on the slick and rutted country road.

She glared into the flames, consigning Quinn Sutton to them with all her angry heart. She hoped and prayed that there wouldn't ever be an accident or a reason she'd have to seek out his company. She'd rather have asked help from a passing timber wolf. His son hadn't seemed at all like him, she recalled. Sutton was as dangerous looking as a timber wolf, with a face like the side of a bombed mountain and eyes that were coal-black and cruel. In the sheepskin coat he'd been wearing with that raunchy Stetson that day, he'd looked like one of the old mountain men might have back in Wyoming's early days. He'd given Amanda some bad moments and she'd hated him after that uncomfortable confrontation. But the boy had been kind. He was redheaded and blue-eyed, nothing like his father, not a bit of resemblance.

She knew the rancher's name only because her aunt had mentioned him, and cautioned Amanda about going near the Sutton ranch. The ranch was called Ricochet, and Amanda had immediately thought of a bullet going awry. Probably one of Sutton's ancestors had thrown some lead now and again. Mr. Sutton looked a lot more like a bandit than he did a rancher, with his face unshaven, that wide, awful scrape on his cheek and his crooked nose. It was an unforgettable face all around, especially those eyes....

She pulled the Indian rug closer and gave the book in her slender hand a careless glance. She wasn't really in the mood to read. Memories kept tearing her heart. She leaned her blond head back against the chair and her dark eyes studied the flames with idle appreciation of their beauty.

The nightmare of the past few weeks had finally caught up with her. She'd stood onstage, with the lights beating down on her long blond hair and outlining the beige leather dress that was her trademark, and her voice had simply refused to cooperate. The shock of being unable to produce a single note had caused her to faint, to the shock and horror of the audience.

She came to in a hospital, where she'd been given what seemed to be every test known to medical science. But nothing would produce her singing voice, even though she could talk. It was, the doctor told her, purely a psychological problem, caused by the trauma of what had happened. She needed rest.

So Hank, who was the leader of the group, had called her Aunt Bess and convinced her to arrange for Amanda to get away from it all. Her aunt's rich boyfriend had this holiday cabin in Wyoming's Grand Teton Mountains and was more than willing to let Amanda recuperate there. Amanda had protested, but Hank and the boys and her aunt had insisted. So here she was, in the middle of winter, in several feet of snow, with no television, no telephone and facilities that barely worked. Roughing it, the big, bearded bandleader had told her, would do her good.

She smiled when she remembered how caring and kind the guys had been. Her group was called Desperado, and her leather costume was its trademark. The four men who made up the rest of it were fine musicians, but they looked like the Hell's Angels on stage in denim and leather with thick black beards and mustaches and untrimmed hair. They were really pussycats under that rough exterior, but nobody had ever been game enough to try to find out if they were.

Hank and Deke and Jack and Johnson had been trying to get work at a Virginia night spot when they'd run into Amanda Corrie Callaway, who was also trying to get work there. The club needed a singer and a band, so it was a match made in heaven, although Amanda with her sheltered upbringing had been a little afraid of her new backup band. They, on the other hand, had been nervous around her because she was such a far cry from the usual singers they'd worked with. The shy, introverted young blonde made them self-conscious about their appearance. But their first performance together had been a phenomenal hit, and they'd been together four years now.

They were famous, now. Desperado had been on the music videos for two years, they'd done television shows and magazine interviews, and they were recognized everywhere they went. Especially Amanda, who went by the stage name of Mandy Callaway. It wasn't a bad life, and it was making them rich. But there wasn't much rest or time for a personal life. None of the group was married except Hank, and he was already getting a divorce. It was hard for a homebound spouse to accept the frequent absences that road tours required.

She still shivered from the look Quinn Sutton had given her, and now she was worried about her Aunt Bess, though the woman was more liberal minded and should know the score. But Sutton had convinced Amanda that she wasn't the first woman to be at Blalock's cabin. She should have told that arrogant rancher what her real relationship with Blalock Durning was, but he probably wouldn't have believed her.

Of course, she could have put him in touch with Jerry
and proved it. Jerry Allen, their road manager, was one
of the best in the business. He'd kept them from starving during the beginning, and they had an expert crew
of electricians and carpenters who made up the rest of
the retinue. It took a huge bus to carry the people and
equipment, appropriately called the "Outlaw Express."

Amanda had pleaded with Jerry to give them a few
weeks rest after the tragedy that had cost her her nerve,
but he'd refused. Get back on the horse, he'd advised.
And she'd tried. But the memories were just too horrible.

So finally he'd agreed to Hank's suggestion and she
was officially on hiatus, as were the other members of
the group, for a month. Maybe in that length of time
she could come to grips with it, face it.

It had been a week and she felt better already. Or she
would, if those strange noises outside the cabin would
just stop! She had horrible visions of wolves breaking
in and eating her.

"Hello?"

The small voice startled her. It sounded like a boy's.
She got up, clutching the fire poker in her hand and went
to the front door. "Who's there?" she called out tersely.

"It's just me. Elliot," he said. "Elliot Sutton."

She let out a breath between her teeth. Oh, no, she
thought miserably, what was he doing here? His father
would come looking for him, and she couldn't bear to
have that…that savage anywhere around!

"What do you want?" she groaned.

"I brought you something."

It would be discourteous to refuse the gift, she guessed,
especially since he'd apparently come through several feet

of snow to bring it. Which brought to mind a really interesting question: where was his father?

She opened the door. He grinned at her from under a thick cap that covered his red hair.

"Hi," he said. "I thought you might like to have some roasted peanuts. I did them myself. They're nice on a cold night."

Her eyes went past him to a sled hitched to a sturdy draft horse. "Did you come in that?" she asked, recognizing the sled he and his father had been riding the day she'd met them.

"Sure," he said. "That's how we get around in winter, what with the snow and all. We take hay out to the livestock on it. You remember, you saw us. Well, we usually take hay out on it, that is. When Dad's not laid up," he added pointedly, and his blue eyes said more than his voice did.

She knew she was going to regret asking the question before she opened her mouth. She didn't want to ask. But no young boy came to a stranger's house in the middle of a snowy night just to deliver a bag of roasted peanuts.

"What's wrong?" she asked with resigned perception.

He blinked. "What?"

"I said, what's wrong?" She made her tone gentler. He couldn't help it that his father was a savage, and he was worried under that false grin. "Come on, you might as well tell me."

He bit his lower lip and looked down at his snow-covered boots. "It's my dad," he said. "He's bad sick and he won't let me get the doctor."

So there it was. She knew she shouldn't have asked.

"Can't your mother do something?" she asked hope-fully.

"My mom ran off with Mr. Jackson from the live-stock association when I was just a little feller," he re-plied, registering Amanda's shocked expression. "She and Dad got divorced and she died some years ago, but Dad doesn't talk about her. Will you come, miss?"

"I'm not a doctor," she said, hesitating.

"Oh, sure, I know that," he agreed eagerly, "but you're a girl. And girls know how to take care of sick folks, don't they?" The confidence slid away and he looked like what he was—a terrified little boy with nobody to turn to. "Please, lady," he added. "I'm scared. He's hot and shaking all over and—!"

"I'll get my boots on," she said. She gathered them from beside the fireplace and tugged them on, and then she went for a coat and stuffed her long blond hair under a stocking cap. "Do you have cough syrup, aspirins, throat lozenges—that sort of thing?"

"Yes, ma'am," he said eagerly, then sighed. "Dad won't take them, but we have them."

"Is he suicidal?" Amanda asked angrily as she went out the door behind him and locked the cabin before she climbed on the sled with the boy.

"Well sometimes things get to him," he ventured. "But he doesn't ever get sick, and he won't admit that he is. But he's out of his head and I'm scared. He's all I got."

"We'll take care of him," she promised, and hoped she could deliver on the promise. "Let's go."

"Do you know Mr. Durning well?" he asked as he called to the draft horse and started him back down the road and up the mountain toward the Sutton house.

"He's sort of a friend of a relative of mine," she said evasively. The sled ride was fun, and she was enjoying the cold wind and snow in her face, the delicious mountain air. "I'm only staying at the cabin for a few weeks. Just time to…get over something."

"Have you been sick, too?" he asked curiously.

"In a way," she said noncommittally.

The sled went jerkily up the road, around the steep hill. She held on tight and hoped the big draft horse had steady feet. It was a harrowing ride at the last, and then they were up, and the huge redwood ranch house came into sight, blazing with light from its long, wide front porch to the gabled roof.

"It's a beautiful house," Amanda said.

"My dad added on to it for my mom, before they married," he told her. He shrugged. "I don't remember much about her, except she was redheaded. Dad sure hates women." He glanced at her apologetically. "He's not going to like me bringing you…."

"I can take care of myself," she returned, and smiled reassuringly. "Let's go see how bad it is."

"I'll get Harry to put up the horse and sled," he said, yelling toward the lighted barn until a grizzled old man appeared. After a brief introduction to Amanda, Harry left and took the horse away.

"Harry's been here since Dad was a boy," Elliot told her as he led her down a bare-wood hall and up a steep staircase to the second storey of the house. "He does most everything, even cooks for the men." He paused outside a closed door, and gave Amanda a worried look. "He'll yell for sure."

"Let's get it over with, then."

She let Elliot open the door and look in first, to make sure his father had something on.

"He's still in his jeans," he told her, smiling as she blushed. "It's okay."

She cleared her throat. So much for pretended sophistication, she thought, and here she was twenty-four years old. She avoided Elliot's grin and walked into the room.

Quinn Sutton was sprawled on his stomach, his bare muscular arms stretched toward the headboard. His back gleamed with sweat, and his thick, black hair was damp with moisture. Since it wasn't hot in the room, Amanda decided that he must have a high fever. He was moaning and talking unintelligibly.

"Elliot, can you get me a basin and some hot water?" she asked. She took off her coat and rolled up the sleeves of her cotton blouse.

"Sure thing," Elliot told her, and rushed out of the room.

"Mr. Sutton, can you hear me?" Amanda asked softly. She sat down beside him on the bed, and lightly touched his bare shoulder. He was hot, all right—burning up. "Mr. Sutton," she called again.

"No," he moaned. "No, you can't do it...!"

"Mr. Sutton..."

He rolled over and his black eyes opened, glazed with fever, but Amanda barely noticed. Her eyes were on the rest of him, male perfection from shoulder to narrow hips. He was darkly tanned, too, and thick, black hair wedged from his chest down his flat stomach to the wide belt at his hips. Amanda, who was remarkably innocent not only for her age, but for her profession as well, stared like a star-struck girl. He was beautiful, she thought, amazed at the elegant lines of his body, at the ripple of muscle and the smooth, glistening skin.

"What the hell do you want?" he rasped.

So much for hero worship, she thought dryly. She lifted her eyes back to his. "Elliot was worried," she said quietly. "He came and got me. Please don't fuss at him. You're raging with fever."

"Damn the fever, get out," he said in a tone that might have stopped a charging wolf.

"I can't do that," she said. She turned her head toward the door where Elliot appeared with a basin full of hot water and a towel and washcloth over one arm.

"Here you are, lady," he said. "Hi, Dad," he added with a wan smile at his furious father. "You can beat me when you're able again."

"Don't think I won't," Quinn growled.

"There, there, you're just feverish and sick, Mr. Sutton," Amanda soothed.

"Get Harry and have him throw her off my land," Quinn told Elliot in a furious voice.

"How about some aspirin, Elliot, and something for him to drink? A small whiskey and something hot—"

"I don't drink whiskey," Quinn said harshly.

"He has a glass of wine now and then," Elliot ventured.

"Wine, then." She soaked the cloth in the basin. "And you might turn up the heat. We don't want him to catch a chill when I sponge him down."

"You damned well aren't sponging me down!" Quinn raged.

She ignored him. "Go and get those things, please, Elliot, and the cough syrup, too."

"You bet, lady!" he said grinning.

"My name is Amanda," she said absently.

"Amanda," the boy repeated, and went back downstairs.

"God help you when I get back on my feet," Quinn said with fury. He laid back on the pillow, shivering when she touched him with the cloth. "Don't...!"

"I could fry an egg on you. I have to get the fever down. Elliot said you were delirious."

"Elliot's delirious to let you in here," he shuddered. Her fingers accidentally brushed his flat stomach and he arched, shivering. "For God's sake, don't," he groaned.

"Does your stomach hurt?" she asked, concerned. "I'm sorry." She soaked the cloth again and rubbed it against his shoulders, his arms, his face.

His black eyes opened. He was breathing roughly, and his face was taut. The fever, she imagined. She brushed back her long hair, and wished she'd tied it up. It kept flowing down onto his damp chest.

"Damn you," he growled.

"Damn you, too, Mr. Sutton." She smiled sweetly. She finished bathing his face and put the cloth and basin aside. "Do you have a long-sleeved shirt?"

"Get out!"

Elliot came back with the medicine and a small glass of wine. "Harry's making hot chocolate," he said with a smile. "He'll bring it up. Here's the other stuff."

"Good," she said. "Does your father have a pajama jacket or something long-sleeved?"

"Sure!"

"Traitor," Quinn groaned at his son.

"Here you go." Elliot handed her a flannel top, which she proceeded to put on the protesting and very angry Mr. Sutton.

"I hate you," Quinn snapped at her with his last ounce of venom.

"I hate you, too," she agreed. She had to reach around him to get the jacket on, and it brought her into much too close proximity to him. She could feel the hair on his chest rubbing against her soft cheek, she could feel her own hair smoothing over his bare shoulder and chest. Odd, that shivery feeling she got from contact with him. She ignored it forcibly and got his other arm into the pajama jacket. She fastened it, trying to keep her fingers from touching his chest any more than necessary because the feel of that pelt of hair disturbed her. He shivered violently at the touch of her hands and her long, silky hair, and she assumed it was because of his fever.

"Are you finished?" Quinn asked harshly.

"Almost." She pulled the covers over him, found the electric-blanket control and turned it on. Then she ladled cough syrup into him, gave him aspirin and had him take a sip of wine, hoping that she wasn't overdosing him in the process. But the caffeine in the hot chocolate would probably counteract the wine and keep it from doing any damage in combination with the medicine. A sip of wine wasn't likely to be that dangerous anyway, and it might help the sore throat she was sure he had.

"Here's the cocoa," Harry said, joining them with a tray of mugs filled with hot chocolate and topped with whipped cream.

"That looks delicious. Thank you so much," Amanda said, and smiled shyly at the old man.

He grinned back. "Nice to be appreciated." He glared at Quinn. "Nobody else ever says so much as a thank-you!"

"It's hard to thank a man for food poisoning," Quinn rejoined weakly.

"He ain't going to die," Harry said as he left. "He's too damned mean."

"That's a fact," Quinn said and closed his eyes.

He was asleep almost instantly. Amanda drew up a chair and sat down beside him. He'd still need looking after, and presumably the boy went to school. It was past the Christmas holidays.

"You go to school, don't you?" she asked Elliot.

He nodded. "I ride the horse out to catch the bus and then turn him loose. He comes to the barn by himself. You're staying?"

"I'd better, I guess," she said. "I'll sit with him. He may get worse in the night. He's got to see a doctor tomorrow. Is there one around here?"

"There's Dr. James in town, in Holman that is," he said. "He'll come out if Dad's bad enough. He has a cancer patient down the road and he comes to check on her every few days. He could stop by then."

"We'll see how your father is feeling. You'd better get to bed," she said and smiled at him.

"Thank you for coming, Miss... Amanda," Elliot said. He sighed. "I don't think I've ever been so scared."

"It's okay," she said. "I didn't mind. Good night, Elliot."

He smiled at her. "Good night."

He went out and closed the door. Amanda sat back in her chair and looked at the sleeping face of the wild man. He seemed vulnerable like this, with his black eyes closed. He had the thickest lashes she'd ever seen, and his eyebrows were thick and well shaped above his deep-set eyes. His mouth was rather thin, but it was perfectly shaped, and the full lower lip was sensuous. She liked that jutting chin, with its hint of stubbornness.

His nose was formidable and straight, and he wasn't that bad looking…asleep. Perhaps it was the coldness of his eyes that made him seem so much rougher when he was awake. Not that he looked that unintimidating even now. He had so many coarse edges.…

She waited a few minutes and touched his forehead. It was a little cooler, thank God, so maybe he was going to be better by morning. She went into the bathroom and washed her face and went back to sit by him. Somewhere in the night, she fell asleep with her blond head pillowed on the big arm of the chair. Voices woke her.

"Has she been there all night, Harry?" Quinn was asking.

"Looks like. Poor little critter, she's worn out."

"I'll shoot Elliot!"

"Now, boss, that's no way to treat the kid. He got scared, and I didn't know what to do. Women know things about illness. Why, my mama could doctor people and she never had no medical training. She used herbs and things."

Amanda blinked, feeling eyes on her. She found Quinn Sutton gazing steadily at her from a sitting position on the bed.

"How do you feel?" she asked without lifting her sleepy head.

"Like hell," he replied. "But I'm a bit better."

"Would you like some breakfast, ma'am?" Harry asked with a smile. "And some coffee?"

"Coffee. Heavenly. But no breakfast, thanks, I won't impose," she said drowsily, yawning and stretching uninhibitedly as she sat up, her full breasts beautifully outlined against the cotton blouse in the process.

Quinn felt his body tautening again, as it had the night before so unexpectedly and painfully when her hands had touched him. He could still feel them, and the brush of her long, silky soft hair against his skin. She smelled of gardenias and the whole outdoors, and he hated her more than ever because he'd been briefly vulnerable.

"Why did you come with Elliot?" Quinn asked her when Harry had gone.

She pushed back her disheveled hair and tried not to think how bad she must look without makeup and with her hair uncombed. She usually kept it in a tight braid on top of her head when she wasn't performing. It made her feel vulnerable to have its unusual length on display for a man like Quinn Sutton.

"Your son is only twelve," she answered him belatedly. "That's too much responsibility for a kid," she added. "I know. I had my dad to look after at that age, and no mother. My dad drank," she added with a bitter smile. "Excessively. When he drank he got into trouble. I can remember knowing how to call a bail bondsman at the age of thirteen. I never dated, I never took friends home with me. When I was eighteen, I ran away from home. I don't even know if he's still alive, and I don't care."

"That's one problem Elliot won't ever have," he replied quietly. "Tough girl, aren't you?" he added, and his black eyes were frankly curious.

She hadn't meant to tell him so much. It embarrassed her, so she gave him her most belligerent glare. "Tough enough, thanks," she said. She got out of the chair. "If you're well enough to argue, you ought to be able to take care of yourself. But if that fever goes up again, you'll need to see the doctor."

"I'll decide that," he said tersely. "Go home."

"Thanks, I'll do that little thing." She got her coat

and put it on without taking time to button it. She pushed her hair up under the stocking cap, aware of his eyes on her the whole time.

"You don't fit the image of a typical hanger-on," he said unexpectedly.

She glanced at him, blinking with surprise. "I beg your pardon?"

"A hanger-on," he repeated. He lifted his chin and studied her with mocking thoroughness. "You're Durning's latest lover, I gather. Well, if it's money you're after, he's the perfect choice. A pretty little tramp could go far with him... Damn!"

She stood over him with the remains of his cup of hot chocolate all over his chest, shivering with rage.

"I'm sorry," she said curtly. "That was a despicable thing to do to a sick man, but what you said to me was inexcusable."

She turned and went to the door, ignoring his muffled curses as he threw off the cover and sat up.

"I'd cuss, too," she said agreeably as she glanced back at him one last time, her eyes running helplessly over the broad expanse of hair-roughened skin. "All that sticky hot chocolate in that thicket on your chest," she mused. "It will probably take steam cleaning to remove it. Too bad you can't attract a 'hanger-on' to help you bathe it out. But, then, you aren't as rich as Mr. Durning, are you?" And she walked out, her nose in the air. As she went toward the stairs, she imagined that she heard laughter. But of course, that couldn't have been possible.

CHAPTER TWO

AMANDA REGRETTED THE hot-chocolate incident once she was back in the cabin, even though Quinn Sutton had deserved every drop of it. How dare he call her such a name!

Amanda was old-fashioned in her ideas. A real country girl from Mississippi who'd had no example to follow except a liberated aunt and an alcoholic parent, and she was like neither of them. She hardly even dated these days. Her working gear wasn't the kind of clothing that told men how conventional her ideals were. They saw the glitter and sexy outfit and figured that Amanda, or just "Mandy" as she was known onstage, lived like her alter ego looked. There were times when she rued the day she'd ever signed on with Desperado, but she was too famous and making too much money to quit now.

She put her hair in its usual braid and kept it there for the rest of the week, wondering from time to time about Quinn Sutton and whether or not he'd survived his illness. Not that she cared, she kept telling herself. It didn't matter to her if he turned up his toes.

There was no phone in the cabin, and no piano. She couldn't play solitaire, she didn't have a television. There was only the radio and the cassette player for company, and Mr. Durning's taste in music was really extreme.

He liked opera and nothing else. She'd have died for some soft rock, or just an instrument to practice on. She could play drums as well as the synthesizer and piano, and she wound up in the kitchen banging on the counter with two stainless-steel knives out of sheer boredom.

When the electricity went haywire in the wake of two inches of freezing rain on Sunday night, it was almost a relief. She sat in the darkness laughing. She was trapped in a house without heat, without light, and the only thing she knew about fireplaces was that they required wood. The logs that were cut outside were frozen solid under the sleet and there were none in the house. There wasn't even a pack of matches.

She wrapped up in her coat and shivered, hating the solitude and the weather and feeling the nightmares coming back in the icy night. She didn't want to think about the reason her voice had quit on her, but if she spent enough time alone, she was surely going to go crazy reliving that night onstage.

Lost in thought, in nightmarish memories of screams and her own loss of consciousness, she didn't hear the first knock on the door until it came again.

"Miss Corrie!" a familiar angry voice shouted above the wind.

She got up, feeling her way to the door. "Keep your shirt on," she muttered as she threw it open.

Quinn Sutton glared down at her. "Get whatever you'll need for a couple of days and come on. The power's out. If you stay here you'll freeze to death. It's going below zero tonight. My ranch has an extra generator, so we've still got the power going."

She glared back. "I'd rather freeze to death than go anywhere with you, thanks just the same."

He took a slow breath. "Look, your morals are your own business. I just thought—"

She slammed the door in his face and turned, just in time to have him kick in the door and come after her.

"I said you're coming with me, lady," he said shortly. He bent and picked her up bodily and started out the door. "And to hell with what you'll need for a couple of days."

"Mr. . . . Sutton!" she gasped, stunned by the unexpected contact with his hard, fit body as he carried her easily out the door and closed it behind them.

"Hold on," he said tautly and without looking at her. "The snow's pretty heavy right through this drift."

In fact, it was almost waist deep. She hadn't been outside in two days, so she hadn't noticed how high it had gotten. Her hands clung to the old sheepskin coat he was wearing. It smelled of leather and tobacco and whatever soap he used, and the furry collar was warm against her cold cheek. He made her feel small and helpless, and she wasn't sure she liked it.

"I don't like your tactics," she said through her teeth as the wind howled around them and sleet bit into her face like tiny nails.

"They get results. Hop on." He put her up on the sled, climbed beside her, grasped the reins and turned the horse back toward the mountain.

She wanted to protest, to tell him to take his offer and go to hell. But it was bitterly cold and she was shivering too badly to argue. He was right, and that was the hell of it. She could freeze to death in that cabin easily enough, and nobody would have found her until spring came or until her aunt persuaded Mr. Durning to come and see about her.

"I don't want to impose," she said curtly.

"We're past that now," he replied. "It's either this or bury you."

"I'm sure I know which you'd prefer," she muttered, huddling in her heavy coat.

"Do you?" he asked, turning his head. In the daylight glare of snow and sleet, she saw an odd twinkle in his black eyes. "Try digging a hole out there."

She gave him a speaking glance and resigned herself to going with him.

He drove the sled right into the barn and left her to wander through the aisle, looking at the horses and the two new calves in the various stalls while he dealt with unhitching and stalling the horse.

"What's wrong with these little things?" she asked, her hands in her pockets and her ears freezing as she nodded toward the two calves.

"Their mamas starved out in the pasture," he said quietly. "I couldn't get to them in time."

He sounded as if that mattered to him. She looked up at his dark face, seeing new character in it. "I didn't think a cow or two would matter," she said absently.

"I lost everything I had a few months back," he said matter-of-factly. "I'm trying to pull out of bankruptcy, and right now it's a toss-up as to whether I'll even come close. Every cow counts." He looked down at her. "But it isn't just the money. It disturbs me to see anything die from lack of attention. Even a cow."

"Or a mere woman?" she said with a faint smile. "Don't worry, I know you don't want me here. I'm… grateful to you for coming to my rescue. Most of the firewood was frozen and Mr. Durning apparently doesn't smoke, because there weren't a lot of matches around."

He scowled faintly. "No, Durning doesn't smoke. Didn't you know?"

She shrugged. "I never had reason to ask," she said, without telling him that it was her aunt, not herself, who would know about Mr. Durning's habits. Let him enjoy his disgusting opinion of her.

"Elliot said you'd been sick."

She lifted a face carefully kept blank. "Sort of," she replied.

"Didn't Durning care enough to come with you?"

"Mr. Sutton, my personal life is none of your business," she said firmly. "You can think whatever you want to about me. I don't care. But for what it's worth, I hate men probably as much as you hate women, so you won't have to hold me off with a stick."

His face went hard at the remark, but he didn't say anything. He searched her eyes for one long moment and then turned toward the house, gesturing her to follow.

Elliot was overjoyed with their new house guest. Quinn Sutton had a television and all sorts of tapes, and there was, surprisingly enough, a brand-new keyboard on a living-room table.

She touched it lovingly, and Elliot grinned at her. "Like it?" he asked proudly. "Dad gave it to me for Christmas. It's not an expensive one, you know, but it's nice to practice on. Listen."

He turned it on and flipped switches, and gave a pretty decent rendition of a tune by Genesis.

Amanda, who was formally taught in piano, smiled at his efforts. "Very good," she praised. "But try a B-flat instead of a B at the end of that last measure and see if it doesn't give you a better sound."

Elliot cocked his head. "I play by ear," he faltered.

"Sorry." She reached over and touched the key she wanted. "That one." She fingered the whole chord. "You have a very good ear."

"But I can't read music," he sighed. His blue eyes searched her face. "You can, can't you?"

She nodded, smiling wistfully. "I used to long for piano lessons. I took them in spurts and then begged a... friend to let me use her piano to practice on. It took me a long time to learn just the basics, but I do all right."

"All right" meant that she and the boys had won a Grammy award for their last album and it had been one of her own songs that had headlined it. But she couldn't tell Elliot that. She was convinced that Quinn Sutton would have thrown her out the front door if he'd known what she did for a living. He didn't seem like a rock fan, and once he got a look at her stage costume and her group, he'd probably accuse her of a lot worse than being his neighbor's live-in lover. She shivered. Well, at least she didn't like Quinn Sutton, and that was a good thing. She might get out of here without having him find out who she really was, but just in case, it wouldn't do to let herself become interested in him.

"I don't suppose you'd consider teaching me how to read music?" Elliot asked. "For something to do, you know, since we're going to be snowed in for a while, the way it looks."

"Sure, I'll teach you," she murmured, smiling at him. "If you dad doesn't mind," she added with a quick glance at the doorway.

Quinn Sutton was standing there, in jeans and red-checked flannel shirt with a cup of black coffee in one hand, watching them.

"None of that rock stuff," he said shortly. "That's a bad influence on kids."

"Bad influence?" Amanda was almost shocked, despite the fact that she'd gauged his tastes very well.

"Those raucous lyrics and suggestive costumes, and satanism," he muttered. "I confiscated his tapes and put them away. It's indecent."

"Some of it is, yes," she agreed quietly. "But you can't lump it all into one category, Mr. Sutton. And these days, a lot of the groups are even encouraging chastity and going to war on drug use..."

"You don't really believe that bull, do you?" he asked coldly.

"It's true, Dad," Elliot piped up.

"You can shut up," he told his son. He turned. "I've got a lot of paperwork to get through. Don't turn that thing on high, will you? Harry will show you to your room when you're ready to bed down, Miss Corrie," he added, and looked as if he'd like to have shown her to a room underwater. "Or Elliot can."

"Thanks again," she said, but she didn't look up. He made her feel totally inadequate and guilty. In a small way, it was like going back to that night...

"Don't stay up past nine, Elliot," Quinn told his son.

"Okay, Dad."

Amanda looked after the tall man with her jaw hanging loose. "What did he say?" she asked.

"He said not to stay up past nine," Elliot replied. "We all go to bed at nine," he added with a grin at her expression. "There, there, you'll get used to it. Ranch life, you know. Here, now, what was that about a B-flat? What's a B-flat?"

She was obviously expected to go to bed with the chickens and probably get up with them, too. Absently she picked up the keyboard and began to explain the basics of music to Elliot.

"Did he really hide all your tapes?" she asked curiously.

"Yes, he did," Elliot chuckled, glancing toward the stairs. "But I know where he hid them." He studied her with pursed lips. "You know, you look awfully familiar somehow."

Amanda managed to keep a calm expression on her face, despite her twinge of fear. Her picture, along with that of the men in the group, was on all their albums and tapes. God forbid that Elliot should be a fan and have one of them, but they were popular with young people his age. "They say we all have a counterpart, don't they?" she asked and smiled. "Maybe you saw somebody who looked like me. Here, this is how you run a C scale...."

She successfully changed the subject and Elliot didn't bring it up again. They went upstairs a half hour later, and she breathed a sigh of relief. Since the autocratic Mr. Sutton hadn't given her time to pack, she wound up sleeping in her clothes under the spotless white sheets. She only hoped that she wasn't going to have the nightmares here. She couldn't bear the thought of having Quinn Sutton ask her about them. He'd probably say that she'd gotten just what she deserved.

But the nightmares didn't come. She slept with delicious abandon and didn't dream at all. She woke up the next morning oddly refreshed just as the sun was coming up, even before Elliot knocked on her door to tell her that Harry had breakfast ready downstairs.

She combed out her hair and rebraided it, wrapping it around the crown of her head and pinning it there as she'd had it last night. She tidied herself after she'd washed up, and went downstairs with a lively step.

Quinn Sutton and Elliot were already making great inroads into huge, fluffy pancakes smothered in syrup when she joined them.

Harry brought in a fresh pot of coffee and grinned at her. "How about some hotcakes and sausage?" he asked.

"Just a hotcake and a sausage, please," she said and grinned back. "I'm not much of a breakfast person."

"You'll learn if you stay in these mountains long," Quinn said, sparing her a speaking glance. "You need more meat on those bones. Fix her three, Harry."

"Now, listen…" she began.

"No, you listen," Quinn said imperturbably, sipping black coffee. "My house, my rules."

She sighed. It was just like old-times at the orphanage, during one of her father's binges when she'd had to live with Mrs. Brim's rules. "Yes, sir," she said absently.

He glared at her. "I'm thirty-four, and you aren't young enough to call me 'sir.'"

She lifted startled dark eyes to his. "I'm twenty-four," she said. "Are you really just thirty-four?" She flushed even as she said it. He did look so much older, but she hadn't meant to say anything. "I'm sorry. That sounded terrible."

"I look older than I am," he said easily. "I've got a friend down in Texas who thought I was in my late thirties, and he's known me for years. No need to apologize." He didn't add that he had a lot of mileage on him, thanks to his ex-wife. "You look younger than twenty-four," he did add.

He pushed away his empty plate and sipped coffee, staring at her through the steam rising from it. He was wearing a blue-checked flannel shirt this morning, buttoned up to his throat, with jeans that were well fitting but not overly tight. He didn't dress like the men in Amanda's world, but then, the men she knew weren't the same breed as this Teton man.

"Amanda taught me all about scales last night," Elliot said excitedly. "She really knows music."

"How did you manage to learn?" Quinn asked her, and she saw in his eyes that he was remembering what she'd told him about her alcoholic father.

She lifted her eyes from her plate. "During my dad's binges, I stayed at the local orphanage. There was a lady there who played for her church. She taught me."

"No sisters or brothers?" he asked quietly.

She shook her head. "Nobody in the world, except an aunt." She lifted her coffee cup. "She's an artist, and she's been living with her latest lover—"

"You'd better get to school, son," Quinn interrupted tersely, nodding at Elliot.

"I sure had, or I'll be late. See you!"

He grabbed his books and his coat and was gone in a flash, and Harry gathered the plates with a smile and vanished into the kitchen.

"Don't talk about things like that around Elliot," Quinn said shortly. "He understands more than you think. I don't want him corrupted."

"Don't you realize that most twelve-year-old boys know more about life than grown-ups these days?" she asked with a faint smile.

"In your world, maybe. Not in mine."

She could have told him that she was discussing the way things were, not the way she preferred them, but she knew it would be useless. He was so certain that she was wildly liberated. She sighed. "Maybe so," she murmured.

"I'm old-fashioned," he added. His dark eyes narrowed on her face. "I don't want Elliot exposed to the liberated outlook of the so-called modern world until he's old enough to understand that he has a choice. I don't like a society that ridicules honor and fidelity and innocence. So I fight back in the only way I can. I go to church on Sunday, Miss Corrie," he mused, smiling at her curious expression. "Elliot goes, too. You might not know it from watching television or going to movies, but there are still a few people in America who also go to church on Sunday, who work hard all week and find their relaxation in ways that don't involve drugs, booze or casual sex. How's that for a shocking revelation?"

"Nobody ever accused Hollywood of portraying real life," she replied with a smile. "But if you want my honest opinion, I'm pretty sick of gratuitous sex, filthy language and graphic violence in the newer movies. In fact, I'm so sick of it that I've gone back to watching the old-time movies from the 1940s." She laughed at his expression. "Let me tell you, these old movies had real handicaps—the actors all had to keep their clothes on and they couldn't swear. The writers were equally limited, so they created some of the most gripping dramas ever produced. I love them. And best of all, you can even watch them with kids."

He pursed his lips, his dark eyes holding hers. "I like George Brent, George Sanders, Humphrey Bogart,

Bette Davis and Cary Grant best," he confessed. "Yes, I watch them, too."

"I'm not really all that modern myself," she confessed, toying with the tablecloth. "I live in the city, but not in the fast lane." She put down her coffee cup. "I can understand why you feel the way you do, about taking Elliot to church and all. Elliot told me a little about his mother..."

He closed up like a plant. "I don't talk to outsiders about my personal life," he said without apology and got up, towering over her. "If you'd like to watch television or listen to music, you're welcome. I've got work to do."

"Can I help?" she asked.

His heavy eyebrows lifted. "This isn't the city."

"I know how to cut open a bale of hay," she said. "The orphanage was on a big farm. I grew up doing chores. I can even milk a cow."

"You won't milk the kind of cows I keep," he returned. His dark eyes narrowed. "You can feed those calves in the barn, if you like. Harry can show you where the bottle is."

Which meant that he wasn't going to waste his time on her. She nodded, trying not to feel like an unwanted guest. Just for a few minutes she'd managed to get under that hard reserve. Maybe that was good enough for a start. "Okay."

His black eyes glanced over her hair. "You haven't worn it down since the night Elliot brought you here," he said absently.

"I don't ever wear it down at home, as a rule," she said quietly. "It...gets in my way." It got recognized, too, she thought, which was why she didn't dare let it loose around Elliot too often.

His eyes narrowed for an instant before he turned and shouldered into his jacket.

"Don't leave the perimeter of the yard," he said as he stuck his weather-beaten Stetson on his dark, thick hair. "This is wild country. We have bears and wolves, and a neighbor who still sets traps."

"I know my limitations, thanks," she said. "Do you have help, besides yourself?"

He turned, thrusting his big, lean hands into work gloves. "Yes, I have four cowboys who work around the place. They're all married."

She blushed. "Thank you for your sterling assessment of my character."

"You may like old movies," he said with a penetrating stare. "But no woman with your kind of looks is a virgin at twenty-four," he said quietly, mindful of Harry's sharp ears. "And I'm a backcountry man, but I've been married and I'm not stupid about women. You won't play me for a fool."

She wondered what he'd say if he knew the whole truth about her. But it didn't make her smile to reflect on that. She lowered her eyes to the thick white mug. "Think what you like, Mr. Sutton. You will anyway."

"Damned straight."

He walked out without looking back, and Amanda felt a vicious chill even before he opened the door and went out into the cold white yard.

She waited for Harry to finish his chores and then went with him to the barn, where the little calves were curled up in their stalls of hay.

"They're only days old," Harry said, smiling as he brought the enormous bottles they were fed from. In fact, the nipples were stretched across the top of buckets and filled with warm mash and milk. "But they'll grow. Sit down, now. You may get a bit dirty…"

"Clothes wash," Amanda said easily, smiling. But this outfit was all she had. She was going to have to get the elusive Mr. Sutton to take her back to the cabin to get more clothes, or she'd be washing out her things in the sink tonight.

She knelt down in a clean patch of hay and coaxed the calf to take the nipple into its mouth. Once it got a taste of the warm liquid, it wasn't difficult to get it to drink. Amanda loved the feel of its silky red-and-white coat under her fingers as she stroked it. The animal was a Hereford, and its big eyes were pink rimmed and soulful. The calf watched her while it nursed.

"Poor little thing," she murmured softly, rubbing between its eyes. "Poor little orphan."

"They're tough critters, for all that," Harry said as he fed the other calf. "Like the boss."

"How did he lose everything, if you don't mind me asking?"

He glanced at her and read the sincerity in her expression. "I don't guess he'd mind if I told you. He was accused of selling contaminated beef."

"Contaminated.. how?"

"It's a long story. The herd came to us from down in the Southwest. They had measles. Not," he added when he saw her puzzled expression, "the kind humans get. Cattle don't break out in spots, but they do develop cysts in the muscle tissue and if it's bad enough, it means that the carcasses have to be destroyed." He shrugged. "You can't spot it, because there are no definite symptoms, and you can't treat it because there isn't a drug that cures it. These cattle had it and contaminated the rest of our herd. It was like the end of the world. Quinn had sold the beef cattle to the packing-plant operator. When the meat was ordered destroyed, he came back on Quinn to recover his money, but Quinn had already spent it to buy new cattle. We went to court... Anyway, to make a long story short, they cleared Quinn of any criminal charges and gave him the opportunity to make restitution. In turn, he sued the people who sold him the contaminated herd in the first place." He smiled ruefully. "We just about broke even, but it meant starting over from scratch. That was last year. Things are still rough, but Quinn's a tough customer and he's got a good business head. He'll get through it. I'd bet on him."

Amanda pondered that, thinking that Quinn's recent life had been as difficult as her own. At least he had Elliot. That must have been a comfort to him. She said as much to Harry.

He gave her a strange look. "Well, yes, Elliot's special to him," he said, as if there were things she didn't know. Probably there were.

"Will these little guys make it?" she asked when the calf had finished his bottle.

"I think so," Harry said. "Here, give me that bottle and I'll take care of it for you."

She sighed, petting the calf gently. She liked farms and ranches. They were so real, compared to the artificial life she'd known since she was old enough to leave home. She loved her work and she'd always enjoyed performing, but it seemed sometimes as if she lived in another world. Values were nebulous, if they even existed, in the world where she worked. Old-fashioned ideas like morality, honor, chastity were laughed at or ignored. Amanda kept hers to herself, just as she kept her privacy intact. She didn't discuss her inner feelings with anyone. Probably her friends and associates would have died laughing if they'd known just how many hang-ups she had, and how distant her outlook on life was from theirs.

"Here's another one," Quinn said from the front of the barn.

Amanda turned her head, surprised to see him because he'd ridden out minutes ago. He was carrying another small calf, but this one looked worse than the younger ones did.

"He's very thin," she commented.

"He's got scours." He laid the calf down next to her. "Harry, fix another bottle."

"Coming up, boss."

Amanda touched the wiry little head with its rough hide. "He's not in good shape," she murmured quietly.

Quinn saw the concern on her face and was surprised by it. He shouldn't have been, he reasoned. Why would she have come with Elliot in the middle of the night to nurse a man she didn't even like, if she wasn't a kind woman?

"He probably won't make it," he agreed, his dark eyes searching hers. "He'd been out there by himself for a long time. It's a big property, and he's a very small calf," he defended when she gave him a meaningful look. "It wouldn't be the first time we missed one, I'm sorry to say."

"I know." She looked up as Harry produced a third bottle, and her hand reached for it just as Quinn's did. She released it, feeling odd little tingles at the brief contact with his lean, sure hand.

"Here goes," he murmured curtly. He reached under the calf's chin and pulled its mouth up to slide the nip-

ple in. The calf could barely nurse, but after a minute
it seemed to rally and then it fed hungrily.

"Thank goodness," Amanda murmured. She smiled
at Quinn, and his eyes flashed as they met hers, searching, dark, full of secrets. They narrowed and then
abruptly fell to her soft mouth, where they lingered
with a kind of questioning irritation, as if he wanted
very much to kiss her and hated himself for it. Her
heart leaped at the knowledge. She seemed to have a
new, built-in insight about this standoffish man, and she
didn't understand either it or her attitude toward him.
He was domineering and hardheaded and unpredict-
able and she should have disliked him. But she sensed
a sensitivity in him that touched her heart. She wanted
to get to know him.

"I can do this," he said curtly. "Why don't you go
inside?"

She was getting to him, she thought with fascination. He was interested in her, but he didn't want to be.
She watched the way he avoided looking directly at her
again, the angry glance of his eyes.

Well, it certainly wouldn't do any good to make him
furious at her, especially when she was going to be his
unwanted houseguest for several more days, from the
look of the weather.

"Okay," she said, giving in. She got to her feet slowly.
"I'll see if I can find something to do."

"Harry might like some company while he works in
the kitchen. Wouldn't you, Harry?" he added, giving
the older man a look that said he'd damned sure better
like some company.

"Of course I would, boss," Harry agreed instantly.

Amanda pushed her hands into her pockets with a

last glance at the calves. She smiled down at them. "Can I help feed them while I'm here?" she asked gently.

"If you want to," Quinn said readily, but without looking up.

"Thanks." She hesitated, but he made her feel shy and tongue-tied. She turned away nervously and walked back to the house.

Since Harry had the kitchen well in hand, she volunteered to iron some of Quinn's cotton shirts. Harry had the ironing board set up, but not the iron, so she went into the closet and produced one. It looked old, but maybe it would do, except that it seemed to have a lot of something caked on it.

She'd just started to plug it in when Harry came into the room and gasped.

"Not that one!" he exclaimed, gently taking it away from her. "That's Quinn's!"

She opened her mouth to make a remark, when Harry started chuckling.

"It's for his skis," he explained patiently.

She nodded. "Right. He irons his skis. I can see that."

"He does. Don't you know anything about skiing?"

"Well, you get behind a speedboat with them on…"

"Not waterskiing. *Snow* skiing," he emphasized.

She shrugged. "I come from southern Mississippi." She grinned at him. "We don't do much business in snow, you see."

"Sorry. Well, Quinn was an Olympic contender in giant slalom when he was in his late teens and early twenties. He would have made the team, but he got married and Elliot was on the way, so he gave it up. He still gets in plenty of practice," he added, shuddering. "On old Ironside peak, too. Nobody, but nobody, skis it except Quinn and a couple of other experts from Larry's Lodge over in Jackson Hole."

"I haven't seen that one on a map…" she began, because she'd done plenty of map reading before she came here.

"Oh, that isn't its official name, it's what Quinn calls it." He grinned. "Anyway, Quinn uses this iron to put wax on the bottom of his skis. Don't feel bad, I didn't know any better, either, at first, and I waxed a couple of shirts. Here's the right iron."

He handed it to her, and she plugged it in and got started. The elusive Mr. Sutton had hidden qualities, it seemed. She'd watched the winter Olympics every four years on television, and downhill skiing fascinated her. But it seemed to Amanda that giant slalom called for a kind of reckless skill and speed that would require ruthlessness and single-minded determination. Considering that, it wasn't at all surprising to her that Quinn Sutton had been good at it.

CHAPTER THREE

AMANDA HELPED HARRY do dishes and start a load of clothes in the washer. But when she took them out of the dryer, she discovered that several of Quinn's shirts were missing buttons and had loose seams.

Harry produced a needle and some thread, and Amanda set to work mending them. It gave her something to do while she watched a years-old police drama on television.

Quinn came in with Elliot a few hours later.

"Boy, the snow's bad," Elliot remarked as he rubbed his hands in front of the fire Harry had lit in the big stone fireplace. "Dad had to bring the sled out to get me, because the bus couldn't get off the main highway."

"Speaking of the sled," Amanda said, glancing at Quinn, "I've got to have a few things from the cabin. I'm really sorry, but I'm limited to what I'm wearing…."

"I'll run you down right now, before I go out again."

She put the mending aside. "I'll get my coat."

"Elliot, you can come, too. Put your coat back on," Quinn said unexpectedly, ignoring his son's surprised glance.

Amanda didn't look at him, but she understood why he wanted Elliot along. She made Quinn nervous. He was attracted to her and he was going to fight it to the bitter end. She wondered why he considered her such a threat.

He paused to pick up the shirt she'd been working on, and his expression got even harder as he glared at her. "You don't need to do that kind of thing," he said curtly.

"I've got to earn my keep somehow." She sighed. "I can feed the calves and help with the housework, at least. I'm not used to sitting around doing nothing," she added. "It makes me nervous."

He hesitated. An odd look rippled over his face as he studied the neat stitches in his shirtsleeve where the rip had been. He held it for a minute before he laid it gently back on the sofa. He didn't look at Amanda as he led the way out the door.

It didn't take her long to get her things together. Elliot wandered around the cabin. "There are knives all over the counter," he remarked. "Want me to put them in the sink?"

"Go ahead. I was using them for drumsticks," she called as she closed her suitcase.

"They don't look like they'd taste very good." Elliot chuckled.

She came out of the bedroom and gave him an amused glance. "Not that kind of drumsticks, you turkey. Here." She put down the suitcase and took the blunt stainless-steel knives from him. She glanced around to make sure Quinn hadn't come into the house and then she broke into an impromptu drum routine that made Elliot grin even more.

"Say, you're pretty good," he said.

She bowed. "Just one of my minor talents," she said. "But I'm better with a keyboard. Ready to go?"

"Whenever you are."

She started to pick up her suitcase, but Elliot reached down and got it before she could, a big grin on his freckled face. She wondered again why he looked so little like his father. She knew that his mother had been a redhead, too, but it was odd that he didn't resemble Quinn in any way at all.

Quinn was waiting on the sled, his expression unreadable, impatiently smoking his cigarette. He let them get on and turned the draft horse back toward his own house. It was snowing lightly and the wind was blowing, not fiercely but with a nip in it. Amanda sighed, lifting her face to the snow, not caring that her hood had fallen back to reveal the coiled softness of her blond hair. She felt alive out here as she never had in the city, or even back East. There was something about the wilderness that made her feel at peace with herself for the first time since the tragedy that had sent her retreating here.

"Enjoying yourself?" Quinn asked unexpectedly.

"More than I can tell you," she replied. "It's like no other place on earth."

He nodded. His dark eyes slid over her face, her cheeks flushed with cold and excitement, and they lingered there for one long moment before he forced his gaze back to the trail. Amanda saw that look and it brought a sense of foreboding. He seemed almost angry.

In fact, he was. Before the day was out, it was pretty apparent that he'd withdrawn somewhere inside himself and had no intention of coming out again. He barely said two words to Amanda before bedtime.

"He's gone broody," Elliot mused before he and Amanda called it a night. "He doesn't do it often, and not for a long time, but when he's got something on his mind, it's best not to get on his nerves."

"Oh, I'll do my best," Amanda promised, and crossed her heart.

But that apparently didn't do much good, in her case, because he glared at her over breakfast the next morning and over lunch, and by the time she finished mending a window curtain in the kitchen and helped Harry bake a cake for dessert, she was feeling like a very unwelcome guest.

She went out to feed the calves, the nicest of her daily chores, just before Quinn was due home for supper. Elliot had lessons and he was holed up in his room trying to get them done in time for a science-fiction movie he wanted to watch after supper. Quinn insisted that homework came first.

She fed two of the three calves and Harry volunteered to feed the third, the little one that Quinn had brought home with scours, while she cut the cake and laid the table. She was just finishing the place settings when she heard the sled draw up outside the door.

Her heart quickened at the sound of Quinn's firm, measured stride on the porch. The door opened and he came in, along with a few snowflakes.

He stopped short at the sight of her in an old white apron with wisps of blond hair hanging around her flushed face, a bowl of whipped potatoes in her hands.

"Don't you look domestic?" he asked with sudden, bitter sarcasm.

The attack was unexpected, although it shouldn't have been. He'd been irritable ever since the day before, when he'd noticed her mending his shirt.

"I'm just helping Harry," she said. "He's feeding the calves while I do this."

"So I noticed."

She put down the potatoes, watching him hang up his hat and coat with eyes that approved his tall, fit physique, the way the red-checked flannel shirt clung to his muscular torso and long back. He was such a lonely man, she thought, watching him. So alone, even with Elliot and Harry here. He turned unexpectedly, catching her staring and his dark eyes glittered.

He went to the sink to wash his hands, almost vibrating with pent-up anger. She sensed it, but it only piqued her curiosity. He was reacting to her. She felt it, knew it, as she picked up a dish towel and went close to him to wrap it gently over his wet hands. Her big black eyes searched his, and she let her fingers linger on his while time seemed to end in the warm kitchen.

His dark eyes narrowed, and he seemed to have stopped breathing. He was aware of so many sensations. Hunger. Anger. Loneliness. Lust. His head spun with them, and the scent of her was pure, soft woman, drifting up into his nostrils, cocooning him in the smell of cologne and shampoo. His gaze fell helplessly to her soft bow of a mouth and he wondered how it would feel to bend those few inches and take it roughly under his own. It had been so long since he'd kissed a woman, held a woman. Amanda was particularly feminine, and she appealed to everything that was masculine in him. He almost vibrated with the need to reach out to her.

But that way lay disaster, he told himself firmly. She was just another treacherous woman, probably bored with confinement, just keeping her hand in with attracting men. He probably seemed like a push-over, and she was going to use her charms to make a fool of him. He took a deep, slow breath and the glitter in his eyes became even more pronounced as he jerked the towel out of her hands and moved away.

"Sorry," she mumbled. She felt her cheeks go hot,

because there had been a cold kind of violence in the action that warned her his emotions weren't quite under control. She moved away from him. Violence was the one thing she did expect from men. She'd lived with it for most of her life until she'd run away from home.

She went back to the stove, stirring the sauce she'd made to go with the boiled dumpling.

"Don't get too comfortable in the kitchen," he warned her. "This is Harry's private domain and he doesn't like trespassers. You're just passing through."

"I haven't forgotten that, Mr. Sutton," she replied, and her eyes kindled with dark fire as she looked at him. There was no reason to make her feel so unwelcome. "Just as soon as the thaw comes, I'll be out of your way for good."

"I can hardly wait," he said, biting off the words.

Amanda sighed wearily. It wasn't her idea of the perfect rest spot. She'd come away from the concert stage needing healing, and all she'd found was another battle to fight.

"You make me feel so at home, Mr. Sutton," she said wistfully. "Like part of the family. Thanks so much for your gracious hospitality, and do you happen to have a jar of rat poison...?"

Quinn had to bite hard to keep from laughing. He turned and went out of the kitchen as if he were being chased.

After supper, Amanda volunteered to wash dishes, but Harry shooed her off. Quinn apparently did book work every night, because he went into his study and closed the door, leaving Elliot with Amanda for company. They'd watched the science-fiction movie Elliot had been so eager to see and now they were working on the keyboard.

"I think I've got the hang of C major," Elliot announced, and ran the scale, complete with turned under thumb on the key of F.

"Very good," she enthused. "Okay, let's go on to G major."

She taught him the scale and watched him play it, her mind on Quinn Sutton's antagonism.

"Something bothering you?" Elliot asked suspiciously.

She shrugged. "Your dad doesn't want me here."

"He hates women," he said. "You knew that, didn't you?"

"Yes. But why?"

He shook his head. "It's because of my mother. She did something really terrible to him, and he never talks about her. He never has. I've got one picture of her, in my room."

"I guess you look like her," she said speculatively.

He handed her the keyboard. "I've got red hair and freckles like she had," he confessed. "I'm just sorry that I…well, that I don't look anything like Dad. I'm glad he cares about me, though, in spite of everything. Isn't it great that he likes me?"

What an odd way to talk about his father, Amanda thought as she studied him. She wanted to say something else, to ask about that wording, but it was too soon. She hid her curiosity in humor.

"'There are more things in heaven and earth, Horatio, than are dreamt of in your philosophy,'" she intoned deeply.

He chuckled. "Hamlet," he said. "Shakespeare. We did that in English class last month."

"Culture in the high country." She applauded. "Very good, Elliot."

"I like rock culture best," he said in a stage whisper. "Play something."

She glanced toward Quinn's closed study door with a grimace. "Something soft."

"No!" he protested, and grinned. "Come on, give him hell."

"Elliot!" she chided.

"He needs shaking up, I tell you, he's going to die an old maid. He gets all funny and red when unmarried ladies talk to him at church, and just look at how grumpy he's been since you've been around. We've got to save him, Amanda," he said solemnly.

She sighed. "Okay. It's your funeral." She flicked switches, turning on the auto rhythm, the auto chords, and moved the volume to maximum. With a mischievous glance at Elliot, she swung into one of the newest rock songs, by a rival group, instantly recognizable by the reggae rhythm and sweet harmony.

"Good God!" came a muffled roar from the study.

Amanda cut off the keyboard and handed it to Elliot.

"No!" Elliot gasped.

But it was too late. His father came out of the study and saw Elliot holding the keyboard and started smoldering.

"It was her!" Elliot accused, pointing his finger at her.

She peered at Quinn over her drawn-up knees. "Would I play a keyboard that loud in your house, after you warned me not to?" she asked in her best meek voice.

Quinn's eyes narrowed. They went back to Elliot.

"She's lying," Elliot said. "Just like the guy in those truck commercials on TV...!"

"Keep it down," Quinn said without cracking a smile. "Or I'll give that thing the decent burial it really needs. And no more damned rock music in my house! That thing has earphones. Use them!"

"Yes, sir," Elliot groaned.

Amanda saluted him. "We hear and obey, excellency!" she said with a deplorable Spanish accent. "Your wish is our command. We live only to serve…!"

The slamming of the study door cut her off. She burst into laughter while Elliot hit her with a sofa cushion.

"You animal," he accused mirthfully. "Lying to Dad, accusing me of doing something I never did! How could you?"

"Temporary insanity," she gasped for breath. "I couldn't help myself."

"We're both going to die," he assured her. "He'll lie awake all night thinking of ways to get even and when we least expect it, pow!"

"He's welcome. Here. Run that G major scale again."

He let her turn the keyboard back on, but he was careful to move the volume switch down as far as it would go.

It was almost nine when Quinn came out of the study and turned out the light.

"Time for bed," he said.

Amanda had wanted to watch a movie that was coming on, but she knew better than to ask. Presumably they did occasionally watch television at night. She'd have to ask one of these days.

"Good night, Dad. Amanda," Elliot said, grinning as he went upstairs with a bound.

"Did you do your homework?" Quinn called up after him.

"Almost."

"What the hell does that mean?" he demanded.

"It means I'll do it first thing in the morning! 'Night, Dad!"

A door closed.

Quinn glared at Amanda. "That won't do," he said tersely. "His homework comes first. Music is a nice hobby, but it's not going to make a living for him."

Why not, she almost retorted, it makes a six-figure annual income for me, but she kept her mouth shut.

"I'll make sure he's done his homework before I offer to show him anything else on the keyboard. Okay?"

He sighed angrily. "All right. Come on. Let's go to bed."

She put her hands over her chest and gasped, her eyes wide and astonished. "Together? Mr. Sutton, really!"

His dark eyes narrowed in a veiled threat. "Hell will freeze over before I wind up in bed with you," he said icily. "I told you, I don't want used goods."

"Your loss," she sighed, ignoring the impulse to lay a lamp across his thick skull. "Experience is a valuable commodity in my world." She deliberately smoothed her hands down her waist and over her hips, her eyes faintly coquettish as she watched him watching her movements. "And I'm very experienced," she drawled. In music, she was.

His jaw tautened. "Yes, it does show," he said. "Kindly keep your attitudes to yourself. I don't want my son corrupted."

"If you really meant that, you'd let him watch movies and listen to rock music and trust him to make up his own mind about things."

"He's only twelve."

"You aren't preparing him to live in the real world," she protested.

"This," he said, "is the real world for him. Not some fancy apartment in a city where women like you lounge around in bars picking up men."

"Now you wait just a minute," she said. "I don't lounge around in bars to pick up men." She shifted her stance. "I hang out in zoos and flash elderly men in my trench coat."

He threw up his hands. "I give up."

"Good! Your room or mine?"

He whirled, his dark eyes flashing. Her smile was purely provocative and she was deliberately baiting him, he could sense it. His jaw tautened and he wanted to pick her up and shake her for the effect her teasing was having on him.

"Okay, I quit," Amanda said, because she could see that he'd reached the limits of his control and she wasn't quite brave enough to test the other side of it. "Good night. Sweet dreams."

He didn't answer her. He followed her up the stairs and watched her go into her room and close the door. After a minute, he went into his own room and locked the door. He laughed mirthlessly at his own rash action, but he hoped she could hear the bolt being thrown.

She could. It shocked her, until she realized that he'd done it deliberately, probably trying to hurt her. She laid back on her bed with a long sigh. She didn't know what to do about Mr. Sutton. He was beginning to get to her in a very real way. She had to keep her perspective. This was only temporary. It would help to keep it in mind.

Quinn was thinking the same thing. But when he turned out the light and closed his eyes, he kept feeling Amanda's loosened hair brushing down his chest, over his flat stomach, his loins. He shuddered and woke up sweating in the middle of the night. It was the worst and longest night of his life.

The next morning, Quinn glared at Amanda across the breakfast table after Elliot had left for school.

"Leave my shirts alone," he said curtly. "If you find any more tears, Harry can mend them."

Her eyebrows lifted. "I don't have germs," she pointed out. "I couldn't contaminate them just by stitching them up."

"Leave them alone," he said harshly.

"Okay. Suit yourself." She sighed. "I'll just busy myself making lacy pillows for your bed."

He said something expressive and obscene; her lips fell open and she gaped at him. She'd never heard him use language like that.

It seemed to bother him that he had. He put down his fork, left his eggs and went out the door as if leopards were stalking him.

Amanda stirred her eggs around on the plate, feeling vaguely guilty that she'd given him such a hard time that he'd gone without half his breakfast. She didn't know why she needled him. It seemed to be a new habit, maybe to keep him at bay, to keep him from noticing how attracted she was to him.

"I'm going out to feed the calves, Harry," she said after a minute.

"Dress warm. It's snowing again," he called from upstairs.

"Okay."

She put on her coat and hat and wandered out to the barn through the path Quinn had made in the deep snow. She'd never again grumble at little two- and three-foot drifts in the city, she promised herself. Now that she knew what real snow was, she felt guilty for all her past complaints.

The barn was warmer than the great outdoors. She pushed snowflakes out of her eyes and face and went to fix the bottles as Harry had shown her, but Quinn was already there and had it done.

"No need to follow me around trying to get my attention," Amanda murmured with a wicked smile. "I've already noticed how sexy and handsome you are."

He drew in a furious breath, but just as he was about to speak she moved closer and put her fingers against his cold mouth.

"You'll break my heart if you use ungentlemanly language, Mr. Sutton," she told him firmly. "I'll just feed the calves and admire you from afar, if you don't mind. It seems safer than trying to throw myself at you."

He looked torn between shaking her and kissing her. She stood very still where he towered above her, even bigger than usual in that thick shepherd's coat and his tall, gray Stetson. He looked down at her quietly, his narrowed eyes lingering on her flushed cheeks and her soft, parted mouth.

Her hands were resting against the coat, and his were on her arms, pulling. She could hardly breathe as she realized that he'd actually touched her voluntarily. He jerked her face up under his, and she could see anger and something like bitterness in the dark eyes that held hers until she blushed.

"Just what are you after, city girl?" he asked coldly.

"A smile, a kind word and, dare I say it, a round of hearty laughter?" she essayed with wide eyes, trying not to let him see how powerfully he affected her.

His dark eyes fell to her mouth. "Is that right? And nothing more?"

Her breath came jerkily through her lips. "I...have to feed the calves."

His eyes narrowed. "Yes, you do." His fingers on her arms contracted, so that she could feel them even through the sleeves of her coat. "Be careful what you offer me," he said in a voice as light and cold as the snow outside the barn. "I've been without a woman for one hell of a long time, and I'm alone up here. If you're not what you're making yourself out to be, you could be letting yourself in for some trouble."

She stared up at him only half comprehending what he was saying. As his meaning began to filter into her consciousness, her cheeks heated and her breath caught in her throat.

"You...make it sound like a threat," she breathed.

"It is a threat, Amanda," he replied, using her name for the first time. "You could start something you might not want to finish with me, even with Elliot and Harry around."

She bit her lower lip nervously. She hadn't considered that. He looked more mature and formidable than he ever had before, and she could feel the banked-down fires in him kindling even as he held her.

"Okay," she said after a minute.

He let her go and moved away from her to get the bottles. He handed them to her with a long, speculative look.

"It's all right," she muttered, embarrassed. "I won't attack you while your back is turned. I almost never rape men."

He lifted an eyebrow, but he didn't smile. "You crazed female sex maniac," he murmured.

"Goody Two Shoes," she shot back.

A corner of his mouth actually turned up. "You've got that one right," he agreed. "Stay close to the house while it's snowing like this. We wouldn't want to lose you."

"I'll just bet we wouldn't," she muttered and stuck her tongue out at his retreating back.

She knelt down to feed the calves, still shaken by her confrontation with Quinn. He was an enigma. She was almost certain that he'd been joking with her at the end of the exchange, but it was hard to tell from his poker face. He didn't look like a man who'd laughed often or enough.

The littlest calf wasn't responding as well as he had earlier. She cuddled him and coaxed him to drink, but he did it without any spirit. She laid him back down with a sigh. He didn't look good at all. She worried about him for the rest of the evening, and she didn't argue when the television was cut off at nine o'clock. She went straight to bed, with Quinn and Elliot giving her odd looks.

CHAPTER FOUR

AMANDA WAS SUBDUED at the breakfast table, more so when Quinn started watching her with dark, accusing eyes. She knew she'd deliberately needled him for the past two days, and now she was sorry. He'd hinted that her behavior was about to start something, and she was anxious not to make things any worse than they already were.

The problem was that she was attracted to him. The more she saw of him, the more she liked him. He was different from the superficial, materialistic men in her own world. He was hardheaded and stubborn. He had values, and he spoke out for them. He lived by a rigid code of ethics, and *honor* was a word that had great meaning for him. Under all that, he was sensitive and caring. Amanda couldn't help the way she was beginning to feel about him. She only wished that she hadn't started off on the wrong foot with him.

She set out to win him over, acting more like her real self. She was polite and courteous and caring, but without the rough edges she'd had in the beginning. She still did the mending, despite his grumbling, and she made cushions for the sofa out of some cloth Harry had put away. But all her domestic actions only made things worse. Quinn glared at her openly now, and his lack of politeness raised even Harry's eyebrows.

Amanda had a sneaking hunch that it was attraction to her that was making him so ill humored. He didn't act at all like an experienced man, despite his marriage, and the way he looked at her was intense. If she could bring him out into the open, she thought, it might ease the tension a little.

She did her chores, including feeding the calves, worrying even more about the littlest one because he wasn't responding as well today as he had the day before. When Elliot came home, she refused to help him with the keyboard until he did his homework. With a rueful smile and a knowing glance at his dad, he went up to his room to get it over with.

Meanwhile, Harry went out to get more firewood and Amanda was left in the living room with Quinn watching an early newscast.

The news was, as usual, all bad. Quinn put out his cigarette half angrily, his dark eyes lingering on Amanda's soft face.

"Don't you miss the city?" he asked.

She smiled. "Sure. I miss the excitement and my friends. But it's nice here, too." She moved toward the big armchair he was sitting in, nervously contemplating her next move. "You don't mind all that much, do you? Having me around, I mean?"

He glared up at her. He was wearing a blue-checked flannel shirt, buttoned up to the throat, and the hard muscles of his chest strained against it. He looked twice as big as usual, his dark hair unruly on his broad forehead as he stared up into her eyes.

"I'm getting used to you, I guess," he said stiffly. "Just don't get too comfortable."

"You really don't want me here, do you?" she asked
quietly.

He sighed angrily. "I don't like women," he muttered.

"I know." She sat down on the arm of his chair, facing him. "Why not?" she asked gently.

His body went taut at the proximity. She was too
close. Too female. The scent of her got into his nostrils
and made him shift restlessly in the chair. "It's none
of your damned business why not," he said evasively.
"Will you get up from there?"

She warmed at the tone of his voice. So she did dis-
turb him! Amanda smiled gently as she leaned forward.
"Are you sure you want me to?" she asked and suddenly
threw caution to the wind and slid down into his lap,
putting her soft mouth hungrily on his.

He stiffened. He jerked. His big hands bit into her
arms so hard they bruised. But for just one long, sweet
moment, his hard mouth gave in to hers and he gave
her back the kiss, his lips rough and warm, the pressure bruising, and he groaned as if all his dreams had
come true at once.

He tasted of smoke for the brief second that he allowed the kiss. Then he was all bristling indignation
and cold fury. He slammed to his feet, taking her with
him, and literally threw her away, so hard that she fell
against and onto the sofa.

"Damn you," he ground out. His fists clenched at his
sides. His big body vibrated with outrage. "You cheap
little tart!"

She lay trembling, frightened of the violence in his
now white face and blazing dark eyes. "I'm not," she defended feebly.

"Can't you live without it for a few days, or are you

desperate enough to try to seduce me?" he hissed. His eyes slid over her with icy contempt. "It won't work. I've told you already, I don't want something that any man can have! I don't want any part of you, least of all your overused body!"

She got to her feet on legs that threatened to give way under her, backing away from his anger. She couldn't even speak. Her father had been like that when he drank too much, white-faced, icy hot, totally out of control. And when he got that way, he hit. She cringed away from Quinn as he moved toward her and suddenly, she whirled and ran out of the room.

He checked his instinctive move to go after her. So she was scared, was she? He frowned, trying to understand why. He'd only spoken the truth; did she not like hearing what she was? The possibility that he'd been wrong, that she wasn't a cheap little tart, he wouldn't admit even to himself.

He sat back down and concentrated on the television without any real interest. When Elliot came downstairs, Quinn barely looked up.

"Where's Amanda going?" he asked his father.

Quinn raised an eyebrow. "What?"

"Where's Amanda going in such a rush?" Elliot asked again. "I saw her out the window, tramping through waist-deep snow. Doesn't she remember what you told her about old McNaber's traps? She's headed straight for them if she keeps on the way she's headed... Where are you going?"

Quinn was already on his feet and headed for the back door. He got into his shepherd's coat and hat without speaking, his face pale, his eyes blazing with mingled fear and anger.

"She was crying," Harry muttered, sparing him a glance. "I don't know what you said to her, but—"

"Shut up," Quinn said coldly. He stared the older man down and went out the back door and around the house, following in the wake Amanda's body had made. She was already out of sight, and those traps would be buried under several feet of snow. Bear traps, and she wouldn't see them until she felt them. The thought of that merciless metal biting her soft flesh didn't bear thinking about, and it would be his fault because he'd hurt her.

Several meters ahead, into the woods now, Amanda was cursing silently as she plowed through the snowdrifts, her black eyes fierce even through the tears. Damn Quinn Sutton, she panted. She hoped he got eaten by moths during the winter, she hoped his horse stood on his foot, she hoped the sled ran over him and packed him into the snow and nobody found him until spring. It was only a kiss, after all, and he'd kissed her back just for a few seconds.

She felt the tears burning coldly down her cheeks as they started again. Damn him. He hadn't had to make her feel like such an animal, just because she'd kissed him. She cared about him. She'd only wanted to get on a friendlier footing with him. But now she'd done it. He hated her for sure, she'd seen it in his eyes, in his face, when he'd called her those names. Cheap little tart, indeed! Well, Goody Two Shoes Sutton could just hold his breath until she kissed him again, so there!

She stopped to catch her breath and then plowed on. The cabin was somewhere down here. She'd stay in it even if she did freeze to death. She'd shack up with a grizzly bear before she'd spend one more night under

Quinn Sutton's roof. She frowned. Were there grizzly bears in this part of the country?

"Amanda, stop!"

She paused, wondering if she'd heard someone call her name, or if it had just been the wind. She was in a break of lodgepole pines now, and a cabin was just below in the valley. But it wasn't Mr. Durning's cabin. Could that be McNaber's...?

"Amanda!"

That was definitely her name. She glanced over her shoulder and saw the familiar shepherd's coat and dark worn Stetson atop that arrogant head.

"Eat snow, Goody Two Shoes!" she yelled back. "I'm going home!"

She started ahead, pushing hard now. But he had the edge, because he was walking in the path she'd made. He was bigger and faster, and he had twice her stamina. Before she got five more feet, he had her by the waist.

She fought him, kicking and hitting, but he simply wrapped both arms around her and held on until she finally ran out of strength.

"I hate you," she panted, shivering as the cold and the exertion got to her. "I hate you!"

"You'd hate me more if I hadn't stopped you," he said, breathing hard. "McNaber lives down there. He's got bear traps all over the place. Just a few more steps, and you'd have been up to your knees in them, you little fool! You can't even see them in snow this deep!"

"What would you care?" she groaned. "You don't want me around. I don't want to stay with you anymore. I'll take my chances at the cabin!"

"No, you won't, Amanda," he said. His embrace didn't even loosen. He whipped her around, his big hands rough on her sleeves as he shook her. "You're coming back with me, if I have to carry you!"

She flinched, the violence in him frightening her. She swallowed, her lower lip trembling and pulled feebly against his hands.

"Let go of me," she whispered. Her voice shook, and she hated her own cowardice.

He scowled. She was paper white. Belatedly he realized what was wrong and his hands released her. She backed away as far as the snow would allow and stood like a young doe at bay, her eyes dark and frightened.

"Did he hit you?" he asked quietly.

She didn't have to ask who. She shivered. "Only when he drank," she said, her voice faltering. "But he always drank." She laughed bitterly. "Just…don't come any closer until you cool down, if you please."

He took a slow, steadying breath. "I'm sorry," he said, shocking her. "No, I mean it. I'm really sorry. I wouldn't have hit you, if that's what you're thinking. Only a coward would raise his hand to a woman," he said with cold conviction.

She wrapped her arms around herself and stood, just breathing, shivering in the cold.

"We'd better get back before you freeze," he said tautly. Her very defensiveness disarmed him. He felt guilty and protective all at once. He wanted to take her to his heart and comfort her, but even as he stepped toward her, she backed away. He hadn't imagined how much that would hurt until it happened. He stopped and stood where he was, raising his hands in an odd gesture of helplessness. "I won't touch you," he promised. "Come on, honey. You can go first."

Tears filmed her dark eyes. It was the first endearment she'd ever heard from him and it touched her deeply. But she knew it was only casual. Her behavior had shocked him and he didn't know what to do. She let out a long breath.

Without a quip or comeback, she eased past him warily and started back the way they'd come. He followed her, giving thanks that he'd been in time, that she hadn't run afoul of old McNaber's traps. But now he'd really done it. He'd managed to make her afraid of him.

She went ahead of him into the house. Elliot and Harry took one look at her face and Quinn's and didn't ask a single question.

She sat at the supper table like a statue. She didn't speak, even when Elliot tried to bring her into the conversation. And afterward, she curled up in a chair in the living room and sat like a mouse watching television.

Quinn couldn't know the memories he'd brought back, the searing fear of her childhood. Her father had been a big man, and he was always violent when he drank. He was sorry afterward, sometimes he even cried when he saw the bruises he'd put on her. But it never stopped him. She'd run away because it was more than she could bear, and fortunately there'd been a place for runaways that took her in. She'd learned volumes about human kindness from those people. But the memories were bitter and Quinn's bridled violence had brought them sweeping in like storm clouds.

Elliot didn't ask her about music lessons. He excused himself a half hour early and went up to bed. Harry had long since gone to his own room.

Quinn sat in his big chair, smoking his cigarette, but he started when Amanda put her feet on the floor and glanced warily at him.

"Don't go yet," he said quietly. "I want to talk to you."

"We don't have anything to say to each other," she said quietly. "I'm very sorry for what I did this afternoon. It was impulsive and stupid, and I promise I'll never do it again. If you can just put up with me until it thaws a little, you'll never have to see me again."

He sighed wearily. "Is that what you think I want?" he asked, searching her face.

"Of course it is," she replied simply. "You've hated having me here ever since I came."

"Maybe I have. I've got more reason to hate and distrust women than you'll ever know. But that isn't what I want to talk about," he said, averting his gaze from her wan face. He didn't like thinking about that kiss and how disturbing it had been. "I want to know why you thought I might hit you."

She dropped her eyes to her lap. "You're big, like my father," she said. "When he lost his temper, he always hit."

"I'm not your father," Quinn pointed out, his dark eyes narrowing. "And I've never hit anyone in a temper, except maybe another man from time to time when it was called for. I never raised my hand to Elliot's mother, although I felt like it a time or two, in all honesty. I never lifted a hand to her even when she told me she was pregnant with Elliot."

"Why should you have?" she asked absently. "He's your son."

He laughed coldly. "No, he isn't."

She stared at him openly. "Elliot isn't yours?" she asked softly.

He shook his head. "His mother was having an affair with a married man and she got caught out." He shrugged.

"I was twenty-two and grass green and she mounted a campaign to marry me. I guess I was pretty much a sitting duck. She was beautiful and stacked and she had me eating out of her hand in no time. We got married and right after the ceremony, she told me what she'd done. She laughed at how clumsy I'd been during the courtship, how she'd had to steel herself not to be sick when I'd kissed her. She told me about Elliot's father and how much she loved him, then she dared me to tell people the truth about how easy it had been to make me marry her." He blew out a cloud of smoke, his eyes cold with memory. "She had me over a barrel. I was twice as proud back then as I am now. I couldn't bear to have the whole community laughing at me. So I stuck it out. Until Elliot was born, and she and his father took off for parts unknown for a weekend of love. Unfortunately for them, he wrecked the car in his haste to get to a motel and killed both of them outright."

"Does Elliot know?" she asked, her voice quiet as she glanced toward the staircase.

"Sure," he said. "I couldn't lie to him about it. But I took care of him from the time he was a baby, and I raised him. That makes me his father just as surely as if I'd put the seed he grew from into his mother's body. He's my son, and I'm his father. I love him."

She studied his hard face, seeing behind it to the pain he must have suffered. "You loved her, didn't you?"

"Calf love," he said. "She came up on my blind side and I needed somebody to love. I'd always been shy and clumsy around girls. I couldn't even get a date when I was in school because I was so rough edged. She paid me a lot of attention. I was lonely." His big shoulders shrugged. "Like I said, a sitting duck. She taught me some hard lessons about your sex," he added, his narrowed eyes on her face. "I've never forgotten them. And nobody's had a second chance at me."

Her breath came out as a sigh. "That's what you thought this afternoon, when I kissed you," she murmured, reddening at her own forwardness. "I'm sorry. I didn't realize you might think I was playing you for a sucker."

He frowned. "Why did you kiss me, Amanda?"

"Would you believe, because I wanted to?" she asked with a quiet smile. "You're a very attractive man, and something about you makes me weak in the knees. But you don't have to worry about me coming on to you again," she added, getting to her feet. "You teach a pretty tough lesson yourself. Good night, Mr. Sutton. I appreciate your telling me about Elliot. You needn't worry that I'll say anything to him or to anybody else. I don't carry tales, and I don't gossip."

She turned toward the staircase, and Quinn's dark eyes followed her. She had an elegance of carriage that touched him, full of pride and grace. He was sorry now that he'd slapped her down so hard with cruel words. He really hadn't meant to. He'd been afraid that she was going to let him down, that she was playing. It hadn't occurred to him that she found him attractive or that she'd kissed him because she'd really wanted to.

He'd made a bad mistake with Amanda. He'd hurt her and sent her running, and now he wished he could take back the things he'd said. She wasn't like any woman he'd ever been exposed to. She actually seemed unaware of her beauty, as if she didn't think much of it. Maybe he'd gotten it all wrong and she wasn't much more experienced than he was. He wished he could ask her. She disturbed him very much, and now he wondered if it wasn't mutual.

Amanda was lying in bed, crying. The day had been

horrible, and she hated Quinn for the way he'd treated her. It wasn't until she remembered what he'd told her that she stopped crying and started thinking. He'd said that he'd never slept with Elliot's mother, and that he hadn't been able to get dates in high school. Presumably that meant that his only experience with women had been after Elliot's mother died. She frowned. There hadn't been many women, she was willing to bet. He seemed to know relatively nothing about her sex. She frowned. If he still hated women, how had he gotten any experience? Finally her mind grew tired of trying to work it out and she went to sleep.

AMANDA WAS UP helping Harry in the kitchen the next morning when Quinn came downstairs after a wild, erotic dream that left him sweating and swearing when he woke up. Amanda had figured largely in it, with her blond hair loose and down to her lower spine, his hands twined in it while he made love to her in the stillness of his own bedroom. The dream had been so vivid that he could almost see the pink perfection of her breasts through the bulky, white-knit sweater she was wearing, and he almost groaned as his eyes fell to the rise and fall of her chest under it.

She glanced at Quinn and actually flushed before she dragged her eyes back down to the pan of biscuits she was putting into the oven.

"I didn't know you could make biscuits," Quinn murmured.

"Harry taught me," she said evasively. Her eyes went back to him again and flitted away.

He frowned at that shy look until he realized why he was getting it. He usually kept his shirts buttoned up to his throat, but this morning he'd left it open halfway down his chest because he was still sweating from that dream. He pursed his lips and gave her a speculative stare. He wondered if it were possible that he disturbed her as much as she disturbed him. He was going to make it his business to find out before she left here. If for no other reason than to salve his bruised ego.

He went out behind Elliot, pausing in the doorway. "How's the calf?" he asked Amanda.

"He wasn't doing very well yesterday," she said with a sigh. "Maybe he's better this morning."

"I'll have a look at him before I go out." He glanced out at the snow. "Don't try to get back to the cabin again, will you? You can't get through McNaber's traps without knowing where they are."

He actually sounded worried. She studied his hard face quietly. That was nice. Unless, of course, he was only worried that she might get laid up and he'd have to put up with her for even longer.

"Is the snow ever going to stop?" she asked.

"Hard to say," he told her. "I've seen it worse than this even earlier in the year. But we'll manage, I suppose."

"I suppose." She glared at him.

He pulled on his coat and buttoned it, propping his hat over one eye. "In a temper this morning, are we?" he mused.

His eyes were actually twinkling. She shifted back against the counter, grateful that Harry had gone off to clean the bedrooms. "I'm not in a temper. Cheap little tarts don't have tempers."

One eyebrow went up. "I called you that, didn't I?" He let his eyes run slowly down her body. "You shouldn't have kissed me like that. I'm not used to aggressive women."

"Rest assured that I'll never attack you again, Goody Two Shoes."

He chuckled softly. "Won't you? Well, disappointment is a man's lot, I suppose."

Her eyes widened. She wasn't sure she'd even heard him. "You were horrible to me!"

"I guess I was." His dark eyes held hers, making little chills up and down her spine at the intensity of the gaze. "I thought you were playing games. You know, a little harmless fun at the hick's expense."

"I don't know how to play games with men," she said stiffly, "and nobody, anywhere, could call you a hick with a straight face. You're a very masculine man with a keen mind and an overworked sense of responsibility. I wouldn't make fun of you even if I could."

His dark eyes smiled into hers. "In that case, we might call a truce for the time being."

"Do you think you could stand being nice to me?" she asked sourly. "I mean, it would be a strain, I'm sure."

"I'm not a bad man," he pointed out. "I just don't know much about women, or hadn't that thought occurred?"

She searched his eyes. "No."

"We'll have to have a long talk about it one of these days." He pulled the hat down over his eyes. "I'll check on the calves for you."

"Thanks." She watched him go, her heart racing at the look in his eyes just before he closed the door. She was more nervous of him now than ever, but she didn't know what to do about it. She was hoping that the chinook would come before she had to start worrying too much. She was too confused to know what to do anymore.

CHAPTER FIVE

AMANDA FINISHED THE breakfast dishes before she went out to the barn. Quinn was still there, his dark eyes quiet on the smallest of the three calves. It didn't take a fortune teller to see that something was badly wrong. The small animal lay on its side, its dull, lackluster red-and-white coat showing its ribs, its eyes glazed and unseeing while it fought to breathe.

She knelt beside Quinn and he glanced at her with concern.

"You'd better go back in the house, honey," he said.

Her eyes slid over the small calf. She'd seen pets die over the years, and now she knew the signs. The calf was dying. Quinn knew it, too, and was trying to shield her.

That touched her, oddly, more than anything he'd said or done since she'd been on Ricochet. She looked up at him. "You're a nice man, Quinn Sutton," she said softly.

He drew in a slow breath. "When I'm not taking bites out of you, you mean?" he replied. "It hurts like hell when you back away from me. You'll never know how sorry I am for what happened yesterday."

One shock after another. At least it took her mind off the poor, laboring creature beside them. "I'm sorry, too," she said. "I shouldn't have been so…" She stopped, averting her eyes. "I don't know much about men,

Quinn," she said finally. "I've spent my whole adult life backing away from involvement, emotional or physical. I know how to flirt, but not much more." She risked a glance at him, and relaxed when she saw his face. "My aunt is Mr. Durning's lover, you know. She's an artist. A little flighty, but nice. I've...never had a lover."

He nodded quietly. "I've been getting that idea since we wound up near McNaber's cabin yesterday. You reacted pretty violently for an experienced woman." He looked away from her. That vulnerability in her pretty face was working on him again. "Go inside now. I can deal with this."

"I'm not afraid of death," she returned. "I saw my mother die. It wasn't scary at all. She just closed her eyes."

His dark eyes met hers and locked. "My father went the same way." He looked back down at the calf. "It won't be long now."

She sat down in the hay beside him and slid her small hand into his big one. He held it for a long moment. Finally his voice broke the silence. "It's over. Go have a cup of coffee. I'll take care of him."

She hadn't meant to cry, but the calf had been so little and helpless. Quinn pulled her close, holding her with quiet comfort, while she cried. Then he wiped the tears away with his thumbs and smiled gently. "You'll do," he murmured, thinking that sensitivity and courage was a nice combination in a woman.

She was thinking the exact same thing about him. She managed a watery smile and with one last, pitying look at the calf, she went into the house.

Elliot would miss it, as she would, she thought. Even Quinn had seemed to care about it, because she saw him occasionally sitting by it, petting it, talking to it.

He loved little things. It was evident in all the kittens and puppies around the place, and in the tender care he took of all his cattle and calves. And although Quinn cursed old man McNaber's traps, Elliot had told her that he stopped by every week to check on the dour old man and make sure he had enough chopped wood and supplies. For a taciturn iceman, he had a surprisingly warm center.

She told Harry what had happened and sniffed a little while she drank black coffee. "Is there anything I can do?" she asked.

He smiled. "You do enough," he murmured. "Nice to have some help around the place."

"Quinn hasn't exactly thought so," she said dryly.

"Oh, yes he has," he said firmly as he cleared away the dishes they'd eaten his homemade soup and corn bread in. "Quinn could have taken you to Mrs. Pearson down the mountain if he'd had a mind to. He doesn't have to let you stay here. Mrs. Pearson would be glad of the company." He glanced at her and grinned at her perplexed expression. "He's been watching you lately. Sees the way you sew up his shirts and make curtains and patch pillows. It's new to him, having a woman about. He has a hard time with change."

"Don't we all?" Amanda said softly, remembering how clear her own life had been until that tragic night. But it was nice to know that Quinn had been watching her. Certainly she'd been watching him. And this morning, everything seemed to have changed between them. "When will it thaw?" she asked, and now she was dreading it, not anticipating it. She didn't want to leave Ricochet. Or Quinn.

Harry shrugged. "Hard to tell. Days. Weeks. This is

raw mountain country. Can't predict a chinook. Plenty
think they can, though," he added, and proceeded to tell
her about a Blackfoot who predicted the weather with
jars of bear grease.

She was much calmer, but still sad when Quinn finally came back inside.

He spared her a glance before he shucked his coat,
washed his hands and brawny forearms and dried them
on a towel.

He didn't say anything to her, and Harry, sensing the
atmosphere, made himself scarce after he'd poured two
cups of coffee for them.

"Are you all right?" he asked her after a minute, staring down at her bent head.

"Sure." She forced a smile. "He was so little, Quinn."
She stopped when her voice broke and lowered her eyes
to the table. "I guess you think I'm a wimp."

"Not really." Without taking time to think about the
consequences, his lean hands pulled her up by the arms,
holding her in front of him so that her eyes were on a
level with his deep blue, plaid flannel shirt. The sleeves
were rolled up, and it was open at the throat, where
thick, dark hair curled out of it. He looked and smelled
fiercely masculine and Amanda's knees weakened at
the unexpected proximity. His big hands bit into her
soft flesh, and she wondered absently if he realized just
how strong he was.

The feel of him so close was new and terribly exciting, especially since he'd reached for her for the first
time. She didn't know what to expect, and her heart
was going wild. She lowered her eyes to his throat.
His pulse was jumping and she stared at it curiously,

only half aware of his hold and the sudden increase of his breathing.

He was having hell just getting a breath. The scent of her was in his nostrils, drowning him. Woman smell. Sweet and warm. His teeth clenched. It was bad enough having to look at her, but this close, she made his blood run hot and wild as it hadn't since he was a young man. He didn't know what he was doing, but the need for her had haunted him for days. He wanted so badly to kiss her, the way she'd kissed him the day before, but in a different way. He wasn't quite sure how to go about it.

"You smell of flowers," he said roughly.

That was an interesting comment from a nonpoetic man. She smiled a little to herself. "It's my shampoo," she murmured.

He drew in a steadying breath. "You don't wear your hair down at all, do you?"

"Just at night," she replied, aware that his face was closer than it had been, because she could feel his breath on her forehead. He was so tall and overwhelming this close. He made her feel tiny and very feminine.

"I'm sorry about the calf, Amanda," he said. "We lose a few every winter. It's part of ranching."

The shock of her name on his lips made her lift her head. She stared up at him curiously, searching his dark, quiet eyes. "I suppose so. I shouldn't have gotten so upset, though. I guess men don't react to things the way women do."

"You don't know what kind of man I am," he replied. His hands felt vaguely tremulous. He wondered if she knew the effect she had on him. "As it happens, I get attached to the damned things, too." He sighed heavily. "Little things don't have much choice in this world. They're at the mercy of everything and everybody."

Her eyes softened as they searched his. He sounded different when he spoke that way. Vulnerable. Almost tender. And so alone.

"You aren't really afraid of me, are you?" he asked, as if the thought was actually painful.

She grimaced. "No. Of course not. I was ashamed of what I'd done, and a little nervous of the way you reacted to it, that's all. I know you wouldn't hurt me." She drew in a soft breath. "I know you resent having me here," she confessed. "I resented having to depend on you for shelter. But the snow will melt soon, and I'll leave."

"I thought you'd had lovers," he confessed quietly. "The way you acted…well, it just made all those suspicions worse. I took you at face value."

Amanda smiled. "It was all put-on. I don't even know why I did it. I guess I was trying to live down to your image of me."

He loved the sensation her sultry black eyes aroused in him. Unconsciously his hands tightened on her arms. "You haven't had a man, ever?" he asked huskily.

The odd shadow of dusky color along his cheekbones fascinated her. She wondered about the embarrassment asking the question had caused. "No. Not ever," she stammered.

"The way you look?" he asked, his eyes eloquent.

"What do you mean, the way I look?" she said, bristling.

"You know you're beautiful," he returned. His eyes darkened. "A woman who looks like you do could have her pick of men."

"Maybe," she agreed without conceit. "But I've never wanted a man in my life, to be dominated by a man. I've made my own way in the world. I'm a musician," she told him, because that didn't give away very much. "I support myself by playing a keyboard."

"Yes, Elliot told me. I've heard you play for him. You're good." He felt his heartbeat increasing as he looked at her. She smelled so good. He looked down at her mouth and remembered how it had felt for those few seconds when he'd given in to her playful kiss. Would she let him do it? He knew so little about those subtle messages women were supposed to send out when they wanted a man's lovemaking. He couldn't read Amanda's eyes. But her lips were parted and her breath was coming rather fast from between them. Her face was flushed, but that could have been from the cold.

She gazed up into his eyes and couldn't look away. He wasn't handsome. His face really seemed as if it had been chipped away from the side of the Rockies, all craggy angles and hard lines. His mouth was thin and faintly cruel looking. She wondered if it would feel as hard as it looked if he was in control, dominating her lips. It had been different when she'd kissed him....

"What are you thinking?" he asked huskily, because her eyes were quite frankly on his mouth.

"I...was wondering," she whispered hesitantly, "how hard your mouth would be if you kissed me."

His heart stopped and then began to slam against his chest. "Don't you know already?" he asked, his voice deeper, harsher. "You kissed me."

"Not...properly."

He wondered what she meant by properly. His wife had only kissed him when she had to, and only in the very beginning of their courtship. She always pushed him away and murmured something about mussing her makeup. He couldn't remember one time when he'd kissed anyone with passion, or when he'd ever been kissed by anyone else like that.

His warm, rough hands let go of her arms and came up to frame her soft oval face. His breath shuddered out of his chest when she didn't protest as he bent his dark head.

"Show me what you mean…by properly," he whispered.

He had to know, she thought dizzily. But his lips touched hers and she tasted the wind and the sun on them. Her hands clenched the thick flannel shirt and she resisted searching for buttons, because she wanted very much to touch that thicket of black, curling hair that covered his broad chest. She went on her tiptoes and pushed her mouth against his, the force of the action parting his lips as well as her own, and she felt him stiffen and heard him groan as their open mouths met.

She dropped back onto her feet, her wide, curious eyes meeting his stormy ones.

"Like that?" he whispered gruffly, bending to repeat the action with his own mouth. "I've never done it…with my mouth open," he said, biting off the words against her open lips.

She couldn't believe he'd said that. She couldn't believe, either, the sensations rippling down to her toes when she gave in to the force of his ardor and let him kiss her that way, his mouth rough and demanding as one big hand slid to the back of her head to press her even closer.

A soft sound passed her lips, a faint moan, because she couldn't get close enough to him. Her breasts were flattened against his hard chest, and she felt his heartbeat against them. But she wanted to be closer than that, enveloped, crushed to him.

"Did I hurt you?" he asked in a shaky whisper that touched her lips.

"What?" she whispered back dizzily.

"You made a sound."

Her eyes searched his, her own misty and half closed and rapt. "I moaned," she whispered. Her nails stroked him through the shirt and she liked the faint tautness of his body as he reacted to it. "I like being kissed like that." She rubbed her forehead against him, smelling soap and detergent and pure man. "Could we take your shirt off?" she whispered.

Her hands were driving him nuts, and he was wondering the same thing himself. But somewhere in the back of his mind he remembered that Harry was around, and that it might look compromising if he let her touch him that way. In fact, it might get compromising, because he felt his body harden in a way it hadn't since his marriage. And because it made him vulnerable and he didn't want her to feel it, he took her gently by the arms and moved her away from him with a muffled curse.

"Harry," he said, his breath coming deep and rough.

She colored. "Oh, yes." She moved back, her eyes a little wild.

"You don't have to look so threatened. I won't do it again," he said, misunderstanding her retreat. Had he frightened her again?

"Oh, it's not that. You didn't frighten me." She lowered her eyes to the floor. "I'm just wondering if you'll think I'm easy...."

He scowled. "Easy?"

"I don't usually come on to men," she said softly.

"And I've never asked anybody to take his shirt off before." She glanced up at him, fascinated by the expression on his face. "Well, I haven't," she said belligerently. "And you don't have to worry; I won't throw myself at you anymore, either. I just got carried away in the heat of the moment...."

His eyebrows arched. None of what she was saying made sense. "Like you did yesterday?" he mused, liking the color that came and went in her face. "I did accuse you of throwing yourself at me," he said on a long sigh.

"Yes. You seem to think I'm some sort of liberated sex maniac."

His lips curled involuntarily. "Are you?" he asked, and sounded interested.

She stamped her foot. "Stop that. I don't want to stay here anymore!"

"I'm not sure it's a good idea myself," he mused, watching her eyes glitter with rage. God, she was pretty! "I mean, if you tried to seduce me, things could get sticky."

The red in her cheeks got darker. "I don't have any plans to seduce you."

"Well, if you get any, you'd better tell me in advance," he said, pulling a cigarette from his shirt pocket. "Just so I can be prepared to fight you off."

That dry drawl confused her. Suddenly he was a different man, full of male arrogance and amusement. Things had shifted between them during that long, hard kiss. The distance had shortened, and he was looking at her with an expression she couldn't quite understand.

"How did you get to the age you are without winding up in someone's bed?" Quinn asked then. He'd wondered at her shyness with him and then at the way she blushed all the time. He didn't know much about women, but he wanted to know everything about her.

Amanda wrapped her arms around herself and shrugged. When he lit his cigarette and still stood there waiting for an answer, she gave in and replied. "I couldn't give up control," she said simply. "All my life I'd been dominated and pushed around by my father. Giving in to a man seemed like throwing away my rights as a person. Especially giving in to a man in bed," she stammered, averting her gaze. "I don't think there's anyplace in the world where a man is more the master than in a bedroom, despite all the liberation and freedom of modern life."

"And you think that women should dominate there."

She looked up. "Well, not dominate." She hesitated. "But a woman shouldn't be used just because she's a woman."

His thin mouth curled slightly. "Neither should a man."

"I wasn't using you," she shot back.

"Did I accuse you?" he returned innocently.

She swallowed. "No, I guess not." She folded her arms over her breasts, wincing because the tips were hard and unexpectedly tender.

"That hardness means you feel desire," he said, grinning when she gaped and then glared at him. She made him feel about ten feet tall. "I read this book about sex," he continued. "It didn't make much sense to me at the time, but it's beginning to."

"I am not available as a living model for sex education!"

He shrugged. "Suit yourself. But it's a hell of a loss to my education."

"You don't need educating," she muttered. "You were married."

He nodded. "Sure I was." He pursed his lips and let his eyes run lazily over her body. "Except that she never wanted me, before or after I married her."

Amanda's lips parted. "Oh, Quinn," she said softly. "I'm sorry."

"So was I, at the time." He shook his head. "I used to wonder at first why she pulled back every time I kissed her. I guess she was suffering it until she could get me to put the ring on her finger. Up until then, I thought it was her scruples that kept me at arm's length. But she never had many morals." He stared at Amanda curiously, surprised at how easy it was to tell her things he'd never shared with another human being. "After I found out what she really was, I couldn't have cared less about sharing her bed."

"No, I don't suppose so," she agreed.

He lifted the cigarette to his lips and his eyes narrowed as he studied her. "Elliot's almost thirteen," he said. "He's been my whole life. I've taken care of him and done for him. He knows there's no blood tie between us, but I love him and he loves me. In all the important ways, I'm his father and he's my son."

"He loves you very much," she said with a smile. "He talks about you all the time."

"He's a good boy." He moved a little closer, noticing how she tensed when he came close. He liked that reaction a lot. It told him that she was aware of him, but shy and reticent. "You don't have men," he said softly. "Well, I don't have women."

"Not for…a few months?" she stammered, because she couldn't imagine that he was telling the truth.

He shrugged his powerful shoulders. "Well, not for a bit longer than that. Not much opportunity up here. And I can't go off and leave Elliot while I tomcat around town. It's been a bit longer than thirteen years."

"A bit?"

He looked down at her with a curious, mocking smile. "When I was a boy, I didn't know how to get girls. I was big and clumsy and shy, so it was the other boys who scored." He took another draw, a slightly jerky one, from his cigarette. "I still have the same problem around most women. It's not so much hatred as a lack of ability, and shyness. I don't know how to come on to a woman," he confessed with a faint smile.

Amanda felt as if the sun had just come out. She smiled back. "Don't you, really?" she asked softly. "I thought it was just that you found me lacking, or that I wasn't woman enough to interest you."

He could have laughed out loud at that assumption. "Is that why you called me Goody Two Shoes?" he asked pleasantly.

She laughed softly. "Well, that was sort of sour grapes." She lowered her eyes to his chest. "It hurt my feelings that you thought I didn't have any morals, when I'd never made one single move toward any other man in my whole life."

He felt warm all over from that shy confession. It took down the final brick in his wall of reserve. She wasn't like any woman he'd ever known. "I'm glad to know that. But you and I have more in common than a lack of technique," he said, hesitating.

"We do?" she asked. Her soft eyes held his. "What do you mean?"

He turned and deliberately put out his cigarette in the

ashtray on the table beside them. He straightened and looked down at her speculatively for a few seconds before he went for broke. "Well, what I mean, Amanda," he replied finally, "is that you aren't the only virgin on the place."

CHAPTER SIX

"I DIDN'T HEAR THAT," Amanda said, because she knew she hadn't. Quinn Sutton couldn't have told her that he was a virgin.

"Yes, you did," he replied. "And it's not all that far-fetched. Old McNaber down the hill's never had a woman, and he's in his seventies. There are all sorts of reasons why men don't get experience. Morals, scruples, isolation, or even plain shyness. Just like women," he added with a meaningful look at Amanda. "I couldn't go to bed with somebody just to say I'd had sex. I'd have to care about her, want her, and I'd want her to care about me. There are idealistic people all over the world who never find that particular combination, so they stay celibate. And really, I think that people who sleep around indiscriminately are in the minority even in these liberated times. Only a fool takes that sort of risk with the health dangers what they are."

"Yes, I know." She watched him with fascinated eyes. "Haven't you ever...wanted to?" she asked.

"Well, that's the problem, you see," he replied, his dark eyes steady on her face.

"What is?"

"I have...wanted to. With you."

She leaned back against the counter, just to make sure she didn't fall down. "With me?"

"That first night you came here, when I was so sick, and your hair drifted down over my naked chest. I shivered, and you thought it was with fever," he mused. "It was a fever, all right, but it didn't have anything to do with the virus."

Her fingers clenched the counter. She'd wondered about his violent reaction at the time, but it seemed so unlikely that a cold man like Quinn Sutton would feel that way about a woman. He was human, she thought absently, watching him.

"That's why I've given you such a hard time," he confessed with narrowed, quiet eyes. "I don't know how to handle desire. I can't throw you over my shoulder and carry you upstairs, not with Elliot and Harry around, even if you were the kind of woman I thought at first you were. The fact that you're as innocent as I am only makes it more complicated."

She looked at him with new understanding, as fascinated by him as he seemed to be by her. He wasn't that bad looking, she mused. And he was terribly strong, and sexy in an earthy kind of way. She especially liked his eyes. They were much more expressive than that poker face.

"Fortunately for you, I'm kind of shy, too," she murmured.

"Except when you're asking men to take their clothes off," Quinn said, nodding.

Harry froze in the doorway with one foot lifted while Amanda gaped at him and turned red.

"Put your foot down and get busy," Quinn muttered irritably. "Why were you standing there?"

"I was getting educated." Harry chuckled. "I didn't know Amanda asked people to take their clothes off!"

"Only me," Quinn said, defending her. "And just my shirt. She's not a bad girl."

"Will you stop!" Amanda buried her face in her hands. "Go away!"

"I can't. I live here," Quinn pointed out. "Did I smell brandy on your breath?" he asked suddenly.

Harry grimaced even as Amanda's eyes widened. "Well, yes you do," he confessed. "She was upset and crying and all…"

"How much did you give her?" Quinn persisted.

"Only a few drops," Harry promised. "In her coffee, to calm her."

"Harry, how could you!" Amanda laughed. The coffee had tasted funny, but she'd been too upset to wonder why.

"Sorry," Harry murmured dryly. "But it seemed the thing to do."

"It backfired," Quinn murmured and actually smiled.

"You stop that!" Amanda told him. She sat down at the table. "I'm not tipsy. Harry, I'll peel those apples for the pie if I can have a knife."

"Let me get out of the room first, if you please," Quinn said, glancing at her dryly. "I saw her measuring my back for a place to put it."

"I almost never stab men with knives," she promised impishly.

He chuckled. He reached for his hat and slanted it over his brow, buttoning his old shepherd's coat because it was snowing outside again.

Amanda looked past him, the reason for all the upset coming back now as she calmed down. Her expression became sad.

"If you stay busy, you won't think about it so much," Quinn said quietly. "It's part of life, you know."

"I know." She managed a smile. "I'm fine. Despite Harry," she added with a chuckle, watching Harry squirm before he grinned back.

Quinn's dark eyes met hers warmly for longer than he meant, so that she blushed. He tore his eyes away finally, and went outside.

Harry didn't say anything, but his smile was speculative.

Elliot came home from school and persuaded Amanda to get out the keyboard and give him some more pointers. He admitted that he'd been bragging about her to his classmates and that she was a professional musician.

"Where do you play, Amanda?" Elliot asked curiously, and he stared at her with open puzzlement. "You look so familiar somehow."

She sat very still on the sofa and tried to stay calm. Elliot had already told her that he liked rock music and she knew Quinn had hidden his tapes. If there was a tape in his collection by Desperado, it would have her picture on the cover along with that of her group.

"Do I really look familiar?" she asked with a smile. "Maybe I just have that kind of face."

"Have you played with orchestras?" he persisted.

"No. Just by myself, sort of. In nightclubs," she improvised. Well, she had once sang in a nightclub, to fill in for a friend. "Mostly I do backup. You know, I play with groups for people who make tapes and records."

"Wow!" he exclaimed. "I guess you know a lot of famous singers and musicians?"

"A few," she agreed.

"Where do you work?"

"In New York City, in Nashville," she told him. "All over. Wherever I can find work."

He ran his fingers up and down the keyboard. "How did you ever wind up here?"

"I needed a rest," she said. "My aunt is…a friend of Mr. Durning. She asked him if I could borrow the cabin, and he said it was all right. I had to get away from work for a while."

"This doesn't bother you, does it? Teaching me to play, I mean?" he asked and looked concerned.

"No, Elliot, it doesn't bother me. I'm enjoying it." She ran a scale and taught it to him, then showed him the cadences of the chords that went with it.

"It's so complicated," he moaned.

"Of course it is. Music is an art form, and it's complex. But once you learn these basics, you can do anything with a chord. For instance…"

She played a tonic chord, then made an impromptu song from its subdominant and seventh chords and the second inversion of them. Elliot watched, fascinated.

"I guess you've studied for years," he said with a sigh.

"Yes, I have, and I'm still learning," she said. "But I love it more than anything. Music has been my whole life."

"No wonder you're so good at it."

She smiled. "Thanks, Elliot."

"Well, I'd better get my chores done before supper," he said, sighing. He handed Amanda the keyboard. "See you later."

She nodded. He went out. Harry was feeding the two calves that were still alive, so presumably he'd tell

Elliot about the one that had died. Amanda hadn't had the heart to talk about it.

Her fingers ran over the keyboard lovingly and she began to play a song that her group had recorded two years back, a sad, dreamy ballad about hopeless love that had won them a Grammy. She sang it softly, her pure, sweet voice haunting in the silence of the room as she tried to sing for the first time in weeks.

"Elliot, for Pete's sake, turn that radio down, I'm on the telephone!" came a pleading voice from the back of the house.

She stopped immediately, flushing. She hadn't realized that Harry had come back inside. Thank God he hadn't seen her, or he might have asked some pertinent questions. She put the keyboard down and went to the kitchen, relieved that her singing voice was back to normal again.

Elliot was morose at the supper table. He'd heard about the calf and he'd been as depressed as Amanda had. Quinn didn't look all that happy himself. They all picked at the delicious chili Harry had whipped up; nobody had much of an appetite.

After they finished, Elliot did his homework while Amanda put the last stitches into a chair cover she was making for the living room. Quinn had gone off to do his paperwork and Harry was making bread for the next day.

It was a long, lazy night. Elliot went to bed at eight-thirty and not much later Harry went to his room.

Amanda wanted to wait for Quinn to come back, but something in her was afraid of the new way he looked at her. He was much more a threat now than he had been before, because she was looking at him with new and interested eyes. She was drawn to him more than ever. But he didn't know who she really was, and she couldn't tell him. If she were persuaded into any kind of close relationship with him, it could lead to disaster.

So when Elliot went to bed, so did Amanda. She sat at the dresser and let down her long hair, brushing it with slow, lazy strokes, when there was a knock at the door.

She was afraid that it might be Quinn, and she hesitated. But surely he wouldn't make any advances toward her unless she showed that she wanted them. Of course he wouldn't.

She opened the door, but it wasn't Quinn. It was Elliot. And as he stared at her, wheels moved and gears clicked in his young mind. She was wearing a long granny gown in a deep beige, a shade that was too much like the color of the leather dress she wore onstage. With her hair loose and the color of the gown, Elliot made the connection he hadn't made the first time he saw her hair down.

"Yes?" she prompted, puzzled by the way he was looking at her. "Is something wrong, Elliot?"

"Uh, no," he stammered. "Uh, I forgot to say goodnight. Good night!" He grinned.

He turned, red faced, and beat a hasty retreat, but not to his own room. He went to his father's and searched quickly through the hidden tapes until he found the one he wanted. He held it up, staring blankly at the cover. There were four men who looked like vicious bikers surrounding a beautiful woman in buckskin with long, elegant, blond hair. The group was one of his favorites—Desperado. And the woman was Mandy. Amanda. His Amanda. He caught his breath. Boy, would she be in for it if his dad found out who she was! He put the tape into his pocket, feeling guilty for taking it when Quinn had told him not to. But these were desperate circumstances. He had to protect Amanda until he could figure out how to tell her that he knew the truth. Meanwhile, having her in the same house with him was sheer undiluted heaven! Imagine, a singing star that famous in his house. If only he could tell the guys! But that was too risky, because it might get back to Dad. He sighed. Just his luck, to find a rare jewel and have to hide it to keep someone from stealing it. He closed the door to Quinn's bedroom and went quickly back to his own.

Amanda slept soundly, almost missing breakfast. Outside, the sky looked blue for the first time in days, and she noticed that the snow had stopped.

"Chinook's coming," Harry said with a grin. "I knew it would."

Quinn's dark eyes studied Amanda's face. "Well, it will be a few days before they get the power lines back up again," he muttered. "So don't get in an uproar about it."

"I'm not in an uproar," Harry returned with a frown. "I just thought it was nice that we'll be able to get off the mountain and lay in some more supplies. I'm getting tired of beef. I want a chicken."

"So do I!" Elliot said fervently. "Or bear, or beaver or moose, anything but beef!"

Quinn glared at both of them. "Beef pays the bills around here," he reminded them.

They looked so guilty that Amanda almost laughed out loud.

"I'm sorry, Dad," Elliot sighed. "I'll tell my stomach to shut up about it."

Quinn's hard face relaxed. "It's all right. I wouldn't mind a chicken stew, myself."

"That's the spirit," Elliot said. "What are we going to do today? It's Saturday," he pointed out. "No school."

"You could go out with me and help me feed cattle," Quinn said.

"I'll stay here and help Harry," Amanda said, too quickly.

Quinn's dark eyes searched hers. "Harry can manage by himself. You can come with me and Elliot."

"You'll enjoy it," Elliot assured her. "It's a lot of fun. The cattle see us and come running. Well, as well as they can run in several feet of snow," he amended.

It was fun, too. Amanda sat on the back of the sled with Elliot and helped push the bales of hay off. Quinn cut the strings so the cattle could get to the hay. They did come running, reminding Amanda so vividly of women at a sale that she laughed helplessly until the others had to be told why she was laughing.

They came back from the outing in a new kind of harmony, and for the first time, Amanda understood what it felt like to be part of a family. She looked at Quinn and wondered how it would be if she never had to leave here, if she could stay with him and Elliot and Harry forever.

But she couldn't, she told herself firmly. She had to remember that this was a vacation, with the real world just outside the door.

Elliot was allowed to stay up later on Saturday night, so they watched a science-fiction movie together while Quinn grumbled over paperwork. The next morning they went to church on the sled, Amanda in the one skirt and blouse she'd packed, trying not to look too conspicuous as Quinn's few neighbors carefully scrutinized her.

When they got back home, she was all but shaking. She felt uncomfortable living with him, as if she really was a fallen woman now. He cornered her in the kitchen while she was washing dishes to find out why she was so quiet.

"I didn't think about the way people would react if you went with us this morning," he said quietly. "I wouldn't have subjected you to that if I'd just thought."

"It's okay," she said, touched by his concern. "Really. It was just a little uncomfortable."

He sighed, searching her face with narrowed eyes. "Most people around here know how I feel about women," he said bluntly. "That was why you attracted so much attention. People get funny ideas about woman haters who take in beautiful blondes."

"I'm not beautiful," she stammered shyly.

He stepped toward her, towering over her in his dress slacks and good white shirt and sedate gray tie. He looked handsome and strong and very masculine. She liked the spicy cologne he wore. "You're beautiful, all right," he murmured. His big hand touched her cheek, sliding down it slowly, his thumb brushing with soft abrasion over her full mouth.

Her breath caught as she looked up into his dark, soft eyes. "Quinn?" she whispered.

He drew her hands out of the warm, soapy water, still holding her gaze, and dried them on a dishcloth. Then he guided them, first one, then the other, up to his shoulders.

"Hold me," he whispered as his hands smoothed over her waist and brought her gently to him. "I want to kiss you."

She shivered from the sensuality in that soft whisper, lifting her face willingly.

He bent, brushing his mouth lazily over hers. "Isn't this how we did it before?" he breathed, parting his lips as they touched hers. "I like the way it feels to kiss you like this. My spine tingles."

"So...does mine." She slid her hands hesitantly into the thick, cool strands of hair at his nape and she went on tiptoe to give him better access to her mouth.

He accepted the invitation with quiet satisfaction, his mouth growing slowly rougher and hungrier as it fed on hers. He made a sound under his breath and all at once he bent, lifting her clear off the floor in a bearish embrace. His mouth bit hers, parting her lips, and she clung to him, moaning as the fever burned in her, too.

He let her go at once when Elliot called, "What?" from the living room. "Amanda, did you say something?"

"No... No, Elliot," she managed in a tone pitched a little higher than normal. Her answer appeared to satisfy him, because he didn't ask again. Harry was outside, but he probably wouldn't stay there long.

She looked up at Quinn, surprised by the intent stare he was giving her. He liked the way she looked, her face flushed, her mouth swollen from his kisses, her eyes wide and soft and faintly misty with emotion.

"I'd better get out of here," he said hesitantly.

"Yes." She touched her lips with her fingers and he watched the movement closely.

"Did I hurt your mouth?" he asked quietly.

She shook her head. "No. Oh, no, not at all," she said huskily.

Quinn nodded and sighed heavily. He smiled faintly and then turned and went back into the living room without another word.

It was a long afternoon, made longer by the strain

Amanda felt being close to him. She found her eyes meeting his across the room and every time she flushed from the intensity of the look. Her body was hungry for him, and she imagined the reverse was equally true. He watched her openly now, with smoldering hunger in his eyes. They had a light supper and watched a little more television. But when Harry went to his room and Elliot called good-night and went up to bed, Amanda weakly stayed behind.

Quinn finished his cigarette with the air of a man who had all night, and then got up and reached for Amanda, lifting her into his arms.

"There's nothing to be afraid of," he said quietly, searching her wide, apprehensive eyes as he turned and carried her into his study and closed the door behind them.

It was a fiercely masculine room. The furniture was dark wood with leather seats, the remnants of more prosperous times. He sat down in a big leather armchair with Amanda in his lap.

"It's private here," he explained. His hand moved one of hers to his shirt and pressed it there, over the tie. "Even Elliot doesn't come in when the door's shut. Do you still want to take my shirt off?" he asked with a warm smile.

Amanda sighed. "Well, yes," she stammered. "I haven't done this sort of thing before...."

"Neither have I, honey," he murmured dryly. "I guess we'll learn it together, won't we?"

She smiled into his dark eyes. "That sounds nice." She lowered her eyes to the tie and frowned when she saw how it was knotted.

"Here, I'll do it." He whipped it off with the ease of

long practice and unlooped the collar button. "Now.
You do the rest," he said deeply, and looked like a man
anticipating heaven.

Her fingers, so adept on a keyboard, fumbled like
two left feet while she worried buttons out of buttonholes. He was heavily muscled, tanned skin under a
mass of thick, curling black hair. She remembered how
it had looked that first night she'd been here, and how
her hands had longed to touch it. Odd, because she'd
never cared what was under a man's shirt before.

She pressed her hands flat against him, fascinated
by the quick thunder of his heartbeat under them. She
looked up into dark, quiet eyes.

"Shy?" he murmured dryly.

"A little. I always used to run a mile when men got
this close."

The smile faded. His big hand covered hers, pressing them closer against him. "Wasn't there ever anyone you wanted?"

She shook her head. "The men I'm used to aren't like
you. They're mostly rounders with a line a mile long.
Everything is just casual to them, like eating mints."
She flushed a little. "Intimacy isn't a casual thing to
me."

"Or to me." His chest rose and fell heavily. He
touched her bright head. "Now will you take your hair
down, Amanda?" he asked gently. "I've dreamed about
it for days."

Amanda smiled softly. "Have you, really? It's something of a nuisance to wash and dry, but I've gotten
sort of used to it." She unbraided it and let it down,
enchanted by Quinn's rapt fascination with it. His big
hands tangled in it, as if he loved the feel of it. He

brought his face down and kissed her neck through it, drawing her against his bare chest.

"It smells like flowers," he whispered.

"I washed it before church this morning," she replied. "Elliot loaned me his blow-dryer but it still took all of thirty minutes to get the dampness out." She relaxed with a sigh, nuzzling against his shoulder while her fingers tugged at the thick hair on his chest. "You feel furry. Like a bear," she murmured.

"You feel silky," he said against her hair. With his hand, Quinn tilted her face up to his and slid his mouth onto hers in the silent room. He groaned softly as her lips parted under his. His arms lifted and turned her, wrapped her up, so that her breasts were lying on his chest and her cheek was pressed against his shoulder by the force of the kiss.

He tasted of smoke and coffee, and if his mouth wasn't expert, it was certainly ardent. She loved kissing him. She curled her arms around his neck and turned a little more, hesitating when she felt the sudden stark arousal of his body.

Her eyes opened, looking straight into his, and she colored.

"I'm sorry," he murmured, starting to shift her, as if his physical reaction to her embarrassed him.

"No, Quinn," she said, resisting gently, holding his gaze as she relaxed into him, shivering a little. "There's nothing to apologize for. I...like knowing you want me," she whispered, lowering her eyes to his mouth. "It just takes a little getting used to. I've never let anyone hold me like this."

His chest swelled with that confession. His cheek rested on her hair as he settled into the chair and relaxed himself, taking her weight easily. "I'm glad about that," he said. "But it isn't just physical with me. I wanted you to know."

She smiled against his shoulder. "It isn't just physical with me, either." She touched his hard face, her fingers moving over his mouth, loving the feel of it, the smell of his body, the warmth and strength of it. "Isn't it incredible?" She laughed softly. "I mean, at our ages, to be so green..."

He laughed, too. It would have stung to have heard that from any other woman, but Amanda was different. "I've never minded less being inexperienced," he murmured.

"Oh, neither have I." She sighed contentedly.

His big hand smoothed over her shoulder and down her back to her waist and onto her rib cage. He wanted very much to run it over her soft breast, but that might be too much too soon, so he hesitated.

Amanda smiled to herself. She caught his fingers and, lifting her face to his eyes, deliberately pulled them onto her breast, her lips parting at the sensation that steely warmth imparted. The nipple hardened and she caught her breath as Quinn's thumb rubbed against it.

"Have you ever seen a woman...without her top on?" she whispered, her long hair gloriously tangled around her face and shoulders.

"No," he replied softly. "Only in pictures." His dark eyes watched the softness his fingers were tracing. "I want to see you that way. I want to touch your skin... like this."

She drew his hand to the buttons of her blouse and lay quietly against him, watching his hard face as he loosened the buttons and pulled the fabric aside. The bra seemed to fascinate him. He frowned, trying to decide how it opened.

"It's a front catch," she whispered. She shifted a little, and found the catch. Her fingers trembled as she loosened it. Then, watching him, she carefully peeled it away from the high, taut throb of her breasts and watched him catch his breath.

"My God," he breathed reverently. He touched her with trembling fingers, his eyes on the deep mauve of her nipples against the soft pink thrust of flesh, his body taut with sudden aching longing. "My God, I've never seen anything so beautiful."

He made her feel incredibly feminine. She closed her eyes and arched back against his encircling arm, moaning softly.

"Kiss me...there," she whispered huskily, aching for his mouth.

"Amanda..." He bent, delighting in her femininity, the obvious rapt fascination of the first time in her actions so that even if he hadn't suspected her innocence he would have now. His lips brushed over the silky flesh, and his hands lifted her to him, arched her even more. She tasted of flower petals, softly trembling under his warm, ardent mouth, her breath jerking past her parted lips as she lay with her eyes closed, lost in him.

"It's so sweet, Quinn," she whispered brokenly.

His lips brushed up her body to her throat, her chin, and then they locked against her mouth. He turned her slowly, so that her soft breasts lay against the muted thunder of his hair-roughened chest. He felt her shiver before her arms slid around his neck and she deliberately pressed closer, drawing herself against him and moaning.

"Am I hurting you?" he asked huskily, his mouth poised just above hers, a faint tremor in his arms. "Amanda, am I hurting you?"

"No." She opened her eyes and they were like black pools, soft and deep and quiet. With her blond hair waving at her temples, her cheeks, her shoulders, she was so beautiful that Quinn's breath caught.

He sat just looking at her, indulging his hunger for the sight of her soft breasts, her lovely face. She lay quietly in his arms without a protest, barely breathing as the spell worked on them.

"I'll live on this the rest of my life," he said roughly, his voice deep and soft in the room, with only an occasional crackle from the burning fire in the potbellied stove to break the silence.

"So will I," she whispered. She reached up to his face, touching it in silence, adoring its strength. "We shouldn't have done this," she said miserably. "It will make it ..so much more difficult, when I have to leave. The thaw...!"

His fingers pressed against her lips. "One day at a time," he said. "Even if you leave, you aren't getting away from me completely. I won't let go. Not ever."

Tears stung her eyes. The surplus of emotion sent them streaming down her cheeks and Quinn caught his breath, brushing them away with his long fingers.

"Why?" he whispered.

"Nobody ever wanted to keep me before," she explained with a watery smile. "I've always felt like an extra person in the world."

He found that hard to imagine, as beautiful as she was. Perhaps her reticence made her of less value to sophisticated men, but not to him. He found her a pearl beyond price.

"You're not an extra person in my world," he replied. "You fit."

She sighed and nuzzled against him, closing her eyes as she drank in the exquisite pleasure of skin against skin, feeling his heart beat against her breasts. She shivered.

"Are you cold?" he asked.

"No. It's…so wonderful, feeling you like this," she whispered. "Quinn?"

He eased her back in his arm and watched her, understanding as she didn't seem to understand what was wrong.

His big, warm hand covered her breast, gently caressing it. "It's desire," he whispered softly. "You want me."

"Yes," she whispered.

"You can't have me. Not like this. Not in any honorable way." He sighed heavily and lifted her against him to hold her, very hard. "Now hold on, real tight. It will pass."

She shivered helplessly, drowning in the warmth of his body, in its heat against her breasts. But he was right. Slowly the ache began to ease away and her body stilled with a huge sigh.

"How do you know so much when you've…when you've never…?"

"I told you, I read a book. Several books." He chuckled, the laughter rippling over her sensitive breasts. "But, my God, reading was never like this!"

She laughed, too, and impishly bit his shoulder right through the cloth.

Then he shivered. "Don't," he said huskily.

She lifted her head, fascinated by the expression on his face. "Do you like it?" she asked hesitantly.

"Yes, I like it," he said with a rueful smile. "All too much." He gazed down at her bareness and his eyes darkened. "I like looking at your breasts, too, but I think we'd better stop this while we can."

He tugged the bra back around her with a grimace and hooked the complicated catch. He deftly buttoned her blouse up to her throat, his eyes twinkling as they met hers.

"Disappointed?" he murmured. "So am I. I have these dreams every night of pillowing you on your delicious hair while we make love until you cry out."

She could picture that, too, and her breath lodged in her throat as she searched his dark eyes. His body, bare and moving softly over hers on white sheets, his face above her...

She moaned.

"Oh, I want it, too," he whispered, touching his mouth with exquisite tenderness to hers. "You in my bed, your arms around me, the mattress moving under us." He lifted his head, breathing unsteadily. "I might have to hurt you a little at first," he said gruffly. "You understand?"

"Yes." She smoothed his shirt, absently drawing it back together and fastening the buttons with a sense of possession. "But only a little, and I could bear it for what would come afterward," she said, looking up. "Because you'd pleasure me then."

"My God, would I," he whispered. "Pleasure you until you were exhausted." He framed her face in his hands and kissed her gently. "Please go to bed, Amanda, before I double over and start screaming."

She smiled against his mouth and let him put her on her feet. She laughed when she swayed and he had to catch her.

"See what you do to me?" she mused. "Make me dizzy."

"Not half as dizzy as you make me." He smoothed down her long hair, his eyes adoring it. "Pretty little thing," he murmured.

"I'm glad you like me," she replied. "I'll do my best to stay this way for the next fifty years or so, with a few minor wrinkles."

"You'll be beautiful to me when you're an old lady. Good night."

She moved away from him with flattering reluctance, her dark eyes teasing his. "Are you sure you haven't done this before?" she asked with a narrow gaze. "You're awfully good at it for a beginner."

"That makes two of us," he returned dryly.

She liked the way he looked, with his hair mussed and his thin mouth swollen from her kisses, and his shirt disheveled. It made her feel a new kind of pride that she could disarrange him so nicely. After one long glance, she opened the door and went out.

"Lock your door," he whispered.

She laughed delightedly. "No, you lock yours the way you did the other night."

He shifted uncomfortably. "That was a low blow. I'm sorry."

"Oh, I was flattered," she corrected. "I've never felt so dangerous in all my life. I wish I had one of those long, black silk negligees…"

"Will you get out of here?" he asked pleasantly. "I think I did mention the urge to throw you on the floor and ravish you?"

"With Elliot right upstairs? Fie, sir, think of my reputation."

"I'm trying to, if you'll just go to bed!"

"Very well, if I must." She started up the staircase, her black eyes dancing as they met his. She tossed her hair back and smiled at him. "Good night, Quinn."

"Good night, Amanda. Sweet dreams."

"They'll be sweet from now on," she agreed. She turned reluctantly and went up the staircase. He watched her until she went into her room and closed the door.

It wasn't until she was in her own room that she realized just what she'd done.

She wasn't some nice domestic little thing who could fit into Quinn's world without any effort. She was Amanda Corrie Callaway, who belonged to a rock group with a worldwide reputation. On most streets in most cities, her face was instantly recognizable. How was Quinn going to take the knowledge of who she really was—and the fact that she'd deceived him by leading him to think she was just a vacationing keyboard player? She groaned as she put on her gown. It didn't bear thinking about. From sweet heaven to nightmare in one hour was too much.

CHAPTER SEVEN

AMANDA HARDLY SLEPT from the combined shock of Quinn's ardor and her own guilt. How could she tell him the truth now? What could she say that would take away the sting of her deceit?

She dressed in jeans and the same button-up pink blouse she'd worn the night before and went down to breakfast.

Quinn looked up as she entered the room, his eyes warm and quiet.

"Good morning," she said brightly.

"Good morning yourself," Quinn murmured with a smile. "Sleep well?"

"Barely a wink," she said, sighing, her own eyes holding his.

He chuckled, averting his gaze before Elliot became suspicious. "Harry's out feeding your calves," he said, "and I'm on my way over to Eagle Pass to help one of my neighbors feed some stranded cattle. You'll have to stay with Elliot—it's teacher workday."

"I forgot," Elliot wailed, head in hands. "Can you imagine that I actually forgot? I could have slept until noon!"

"There, there," Amanda said, patting his shoulder. "Don't you want to learn some more chords?"

"Is that what you do?" Quinn asked curiously, because now every scrap of information he learned about her was precious. "You said you played a keyboard for a living. Do you teach music?"

"Not really," she said gently. "I play backup for various groups," she explained. "That rock music you hate…" she began uneasily.

"That's all right," Quinn replied, his face open and kind. "I was just trying to get a rise out of you. I don't mind it all that much, I guess. And playing backup isn't the same thing as putting on those god-awful costumes and singing suggestive lyrics. Well, I'm gone. Stay out of trouble, you two," he said as he got to his feet in the middle of Amanda's instinctive move to speak, to correct his assumption that all she did was play backup. She wanted to tell him the truth, but he winked at her and Elliot and got into his outdoor clothes before she could find a way to break the news. By the time her mind was working again, he was gone.

She sat back down, sighing. "Oh, Elliot, what a mess," she murmured, her chin in her hands.

"Is that what you call it?" he asked with a wicked smile. "Dad's actually grinning, and when he looked at you, you blushed. I'm not blind, you know. Do you like him, even if he isn't Mr. America?"

"Yes, I like him," she said with a shy smile, lowering her eyes. "He's a pretty special guy."

"I think so, myself. Eat your breakfast. I want to ask you about some new chords."

"Okay."

They were working on the keyboard when the sound of an approaching vehicle caught Amanda's attention. Quinn hadn't driven anything motorized since the snow had gotten so high.

"That's odd," Elliot said, peering out the window curtain. "It's a four-wheel drive... Oh, boy." He glanced at Amanda. "You aren't gonna like this."

She lifted her eyebrows. "I'm not?" she asked, puzzled.

The knock at the back door had Harry moving toward it before Amanda and Elliot could. Harry opened it and looked up and up and up. He stood there staring while Elliot gaped at the grizzly-looking man who loomed over him in a black Western costume, complete with hat.

"I'm looking for Mandy Callaway," he boomed.

"Hank!"

Amanda ran to the big man without thinking, to be lifted high in the air while he chuckled and kissed her warmly on one cheek, his whiskers scratching.

"Hello, peanut!" he grinned. "What are you doing up here? The old trapper down the hill said you hadn't been in Durning's cabin since the heavy snow came."

"Mr. Sutton took me in and gave me a roof over my head. Put me down," she fussed, wiggling.

He put her back on her feet while Harry and Elliot still gaped.

"This is Hank," she said, holding his enormous hand as she turned to face the others. "He's a good friend, and a terrific musician, and I'd really appreciate it if you wouldn't tell Quinn he was here just yet. I'll tell him myself. Okay?"

"Sure," Harry murmured. He shook his head. "You for real, or do you have stilts in them boots?"

"I used to be a linebacker for the Dallas Cowboys." Hank grinned.

"That would explain it," Harry chuckled. "Your secret's safe with me, Amanda." He excused himself and went to do the washing.

"Me, too," Elliot said, grinning, "as long as I get Mr. Shoeman's autograph before he leaves."

Amanda let out a long breath, her eyes frightened as they met Elliot's.

"That's right," Elliot said. "I already knew you were Mandy Callaway. I've got a Desperado tape. I took it out of Dad's drawer and hid it as soon as I recognized you. You'll tell him when the time's right. Won't you?"

"Yes, I will, Elliot," she agreed. "I'd have done it already except that…well, things have gotten a little complicated."

"You can say that again." Elliot led the way into the living room, watching Hank sit gingerly on a sofa that he dwarfed. "I'll just go make sure that tape's hidden," he said, leaving them alone.

"Complicated, huh?" Hank said. "I hear this Sutton man's a real woman hater."

"He was until just recently." She folded her hands in her lap. "And he doesn't approve of rock music." She sighed and changed the subject. "What's up, Hank?"

"We've got a gig at Larry's Lodge," he said. "I know, you don't want to. Listen for a minute. It's to benefit cystic fibrosis, and a lot of other stars are going to be in town for it, including a few pretty well-known singers." He named some of them and Amanda whistled. "See what I mean? It's strictly charity, or I wouldn't have come up here bothering you. The boys and I want to do it." His dark eyes narrowed. "Are you up to it?"

"I don't know. I tried to sing here a couple of times, and my voice seems to be good enough. No more lapses.

But in front of a crowd…" She spread her hands. "I don't know, Hank."

"Here." He handed her three tickets to the benefit. "You think about it. If you can, come on up. Sutton might like the singers even if he doesn't care for our kind of music." He studied her. "You haven't told him, have you?"

She shook her head, smiling wistfully. "Haven't found the right way yet. If I leave it much longer, it may be too late."

"The girl's family sent you a letter," he said. "Thanking you for what you tried to do. They said you were her heroine…aw, now, Mandy, stop it!"

She collapsed in tears. He held her, rocking her, his face red with mingled embarrassment and guilt.

"Mandy, come on, stop that," he muttered. "It's all over and done with. You've got to get yourself together. You can't hide out here in the Tetons for the rest of your life."

"Can't I?" she wailed.

"No, you can't. Hiding isn't your style. You have to face the stage again, or you'll never get over it." He tilted her wet face. "Look, would you want somebody eating her guts out over you if you'd been Wendy that night? It wasn't your fault, damn it! It wasn't anybody's fault; it was an accident, pure and simple."

"If she hadn't been at the concert…"

"If, if, if," he said curtly. "You can't go back and change things to suit you. It was her time. At the concert, on a plane, in a car, however, it would still have been her time. Are you listening to me, Mandy?"

She dabbed her eyes with the hem of her blouse. "Yes, I'm listening."

"Come on, girl. Buck up. You can get over this if you set your mind to it. Me and the guys miss you, Mandy. It's not the same with just the four of us. People are scared of us when you aren't around."

That made her smile. "I guess they are. You do look scruffy, Hank," she murmured.

"You ought to see Johnson." He sighed. "He's let his beard go and he looks like a scrub brush. And Deke says he won't change clothes until you come back."

"Oh, my God," Amanda said, shuddering, "tell him I'll think hard about this concert, okay? You poor guys. Stay upwind of him."

"We're trying." He got up, smiling down at her. "Everything's okay. You can see the letter when you come to the lodge. It's real nice. Now stop beating yourself. Nobody else blames you. After all, babe, you risked your life trying to save her. Nobody's forgotten that, either."

She leaned against him for a minute, drawing on his strength. "Thanks, Hank."

"Anytime. Hey, kid, you still want that autograph?" he asked.

Elliot came back into the room with a pad and pen. "Do I!" he said, chuckling.

Hank scribbled his name and Desperado's curly-Q logo underneath. "There you go."

"He's a budding musician," Amanda said, putting an arm around Elliot. "I'm teaching him the keyboard. One of these days, if we can get around Quinn, we'll have him playing backup for me."

"You bet." Hank chuckled, and ruffled Elliot's red hair. "Keep at it. Mandy's the very best. If she teaches you, you're taught."

"Thanks, Mr. Shoeman."

"Just Hank. See you at the concert. So long, Mandy."

"So long, pal."

"What concert?" Elliot asked excitedly when Hank had driven away.

Amanda handed him the three tickets. "To a benefit in Jackson Hole. The group's going to play there. Maybe. If I can get up enough nerve to get back on-stage again."

"What happened, Amanda?" he asked gently.

She searched his face, seeing compassion along with the curiosity, so she told him, fighting tears all the way.

"Gosh, no wonder you came up here to get away," Elliot said with more than his twelve years worth of wisdom. He shrugged. "But like he said, you have to go back someday. The longer you wait, the harder it's going to be."

"I know that," she groaned. "But Elliot, I..." She took a deep breath and looked down at the floor. "I love your father," she said, admitting it at last. "I love him very much, and the minute he finds out who I am, my life is over."

"Maybe not," he said. "You've got another week until the concert. Surely in all that time you can manage to tell him the truth. Can't you?"

"I hope so," she said with a sad smile. "You don't mind who I am, do you?" she asked worriedly.

"Don't be silly." He hugged her warmly. "I think you're super, keyboard or not."

She laughed and hugged him back. "Well, that's half the battle."

"Just out of curiosity," Harry asked from the doorway, "who was the bearded giant?"

"That was Hank Shoeman," Elliot told him. "He's the drummer for Desperado. It's a rock group. And Amanda—"

"—plays backup for him," she volunteered, afraid to give too much away to Harry.

"Well, I'll be. He's a musician?" Harry shook his head. "Would have took him for a bank robber," he mumbled.

"Most people do, and you should see the rest of the group." She grinned. "Don't give me away, Harry, okay? I promise I'll tell Quinn, but I've got to do it the right way."

"I can see that," he agreed easily. "Be something of a shock to him to meet your friend after dark, I imagine."

"I imagine so," she said, chuckling. "Thanks, Harry."

"My pleasure. Desperado, huh? Suits it, if the rest of the group looks like he does."

"Worse," she said, and shuddered.

"Strains the mind, don't it?" Harry went off into the kitchen and Amanda got up after a minute to help him get lunch.

Quinn wasn't back until late that afternoon. Nobody mentioned Hank's visit, but Amanda was nervous and her manner was strained as she tried not to show her fears.

"What's wrong with you?" he asked gently during a lull in the evening while Elliot did homework and Harry washed up. "You don't seem like yourself tonight."

She moved close to him, her fingers idly touching the sleeve of his red flannel shirt. "It's thawing outside," she said, watching her fingers move on the fabric. "It won't be long before I'll be gone."

He sighed heavily. His fingers captured hers and

held them. "I've been thinking about that. Do you really have to get back?"

She felt her heart jump. Whatever he was offering, she wanted to say yes and let the future take care of itself. But she couldn't. She grimaced. "Yes, I have to get back," she said miserably. "I have commitments to people. Things I promised to do." Her fingers clenched his. "Quinn, I have to meet some people at Larry's Lodge in Jackson Hole next Friday night." She looked up. "It's at a concert and I have tickets. I know you don't like rock, but there's going to be all kinds of music." Her eyes searched his. "Would you go with me? Elliot can come, too. I...want you to see what I do for a living."

"You and your keyboard?" he mused gently.

"Sort of," she agreed, hoping she could find the nerve to tell him everything before next Friday night.

"Okay," he replied. "A friend of mine works there— I used to be with the Ski Patrol there, too. Sure, I'll go with you." The smile vanished, and his eyes glittered down at her. "I'll go damned near anywhere with you."

Amanda slid her arms around him and pressed close, shutting her eyes as she held on for dear life. "That goes double for me, mountain man," she said half under her breath.

He bent his head, searching for her soft mouth. She gave it to him without a protest, without a thought for the future, gave it to him with interest, with devotion, with ardor. Her lips opened invitingly, and she felt his hands on her hips with a sense of sweet inevitability, lifting her into intimate contact with the aroused contours of his body.

"Frightened?" he whispered unsteadily just over her mouth when he felt her stiffen involuntarily.

"Of you?" she whispered back. "Don't be absurd. Hold me any way you want. I adore you...!"

He actually groaned as his mouth pressed down hard on hers. His arms contracted hungrily and he gave in to the pleasure of possession for one long moment.

Her eyes opened and she watched him, feeding on the slight contortion of his features, his heavy brows drawn over his crooked nose, his long, thick lashes on his cheek as he kissed her. She did adore him, she thought dizzily. Adored him, loved him, worshiped him. If only she could stay with him forever like this.

Quinn lifted his head and paused as he saw her watching him. He frowned slightly, then bent again. This time his eyes stayed open, too, and she went under as he deepened the kiss. Her eyes closed in self-defense and she moaned, letting him see the same vulnerability she'd seen in him. It was breathlessly sweet.

"This is an education," he said, laughing huskily, when he drew slightly away from her.

"Isn't it, though?" she murmured, moving his hands from her hips up to her waist and moving back a step from the blatant urgency of his body. "Elliot and Harry might come in," she whispered.

"I wouldn't mind," he said unexpectedly, searching her flushed face. "I'm not ashamed of what I feel for you, or embarrassed by it."

"This from a confirmed woman hater?" she asked with twinkling eyes.

"Well, not exactly confirmed anymore," he confessed. He lifted her by the waist and searched her eyes at point-blank range until she trembled from the intensity of the look. "I couldn't hate you if I tried, Amanda," he said quietly.

"Oh, I hope not," she said fervently, thinking ahead to when she would have to tell him the truth about herself.

He brushed a lazy kiss across her lips. "I think I'm getting the hang of this," he murmured.

"I think you are, too," she whispered. She slid her arms around his neck and put her warm mouth hungrily against his, sighing when he caught fire and answered the kiss with feverish abandon.

A slight, deliberate cough brought them apart, both staring blankly at the small redheaded intruder.

"Not that I mind," Elliot said, grinning, "but you're blocking the pan of brownies Harry made."

"You can think of brownies at a time like this?" Amanda groaned. "Elliot!"

"Listen, he can think of brownies with a fever of a hundred and two," Quinn told her, still holding her on a level with his eyes. "I've seen him get out of a sickbed to pinch a brownie from the kitchen."

"I like brownies, too," Amanda confessed with a warm smile, delighted that Quinn didn't seem to mind at all that Elliot had seen them in a compromising position. That made her feel lighter than air.

"Do you?" Quinn smiled and brushed his mouth gently against hers, mindless of Elliot's blatant interest, before he put her back on her feet. "Harry makes his from scratch, with real baker's chocolate. They're something special."

"I'll bet they are. Here. I'll get the saucers," she volunteered, still catching her breath.

Elliot looked like the cat with the canary as she dished up brownies. It very obviously didn't bother him that Amanda and his dad were beginning to notice each other.

"Isn't this cozy?" he remarked as they went back into the living room and Amanda curled up on the sofa beside his dad, who never sat there.

"Cozy, indeed," Quinn murmured with a warm smile for Amanda.

She smiled back and laid her cheek against Quinn's broad chest while they watched television and ate brownies. She didn't move even when Harry joined them. And she knew she'd never been closer to heaven.

That night they were left discreetly alone, and she lay in Quinn's strong arms on the long leather couch in his office while wood burned with occasional hisses and sparks in the potbellied stove.

"I've had a raw deal with this place," he said eventually between kisses. "But it's good land, and I'm building a respectable herd of cattle. I can't offer you wealth or position, and we've got a ready-made family. But I can take care of you," he said solemnly, looking down into her soft eyes. "And you won't want for any of the essentials."

Her fingers touched his lean cheek hesitantly. "You don't know anything about me," she said. "When you know my background, you may not want me as much as you think you do." She put her fingers against his mouth. "You have to be sure."

"Damn it, I'm already sure," he muttered.

But was he? She was the first woman he'd ever been intimate with. Couldn't that blind him to her real suitability? What if it was just infatuation or desire? She was afraid to take a chance on his feelings, when she didn't really know what they were.

"Let's wait just a little while longer before we make any plans, Quinn. Okay?" she asked softly, turning in his hard arms so that her body was lying against his. "Make love to me," she whispered, moving her mouth up to his. "Please..."

He gave in with a rough groan, gathering her to him, crushing her against his aroused body. He wanted her beyond rational thought. Maybe she had cold feet, but he didn't. He knew what he wanted, and Amanda was it.

His hands smoothed the blouse and bra away with growing expertise and he fought out of his shirt so that he could feel her soft skin against his. But it wasn't enough. He felt her tremble and knew that it was reflected in his own arms and legs. He moved against her with a new kind of sensuousness, lifting his head to hold her eyes while he levered her onto her back and eased over her, his legs between both of hers in their first real intimacy.

She caught her breath, but she didn't push him to try to get away.

"It's just that new for you, isn't it?" he whispered huskily as his hips moved lazily over hers and he groaned. "God, it burns me to...feel you like this."

"I know." She arched her back, loving his weight, loving the fierce maleness of his body. Her arms slid closer around him and she felt his mouth open on hers, his tongue softly searching as it slid inside, into an intimacy that made her moan. She began to tremble.

His lean hand slid under her, getting a firm grip, and he brought her suddenly into a shocking, shattering position that made her mindless with sudden need. She clutched him desperately, shuddering, her nails digging into him as the contact racked her like a jolt of raw electricity.

He pulled away from her without a word, shuddering as he lay on his back, trying to get hold of himself.

"I'm sorry," he whispered. "I didn't mean to let it
go so far with us."

She was trembling, too, trying to breathe while great
hot tears rolled down her cheeks. "Gosh, I wanted you,"
she whispered tearfully. "Wanted you so badly, Quinn!"

"As badly as I wanted you, honey," he said heavily.
"We can't let things get that hot again. It was a close
call. Closer than you realize."

"Oh, Quinn, couldn't we make love?" she asked
softly, rolling over to look down into his tormented
face. "Just once…?"

He framed his face in his hands and brought her
closed eyes to his lips. "No. I won't compromise you."

She hit his big, hair-roughened chest. "Goody Two
Shoes…!"

"Thank your lucky stars that I am," he chuckled.
His eyes dropped to her bare breasts and lingered there
before he caught the edges of her blouse and tugged
them together. "You sex-crazed female, haven't you
ever heard about pregnancy?"

"That condition where I get to have little Quinns?"

"Stop it, you're making it impossible for me," he said
huskily. "Here, get up before I lose my mind."

She sat up with a grimace. "Spoilsport."

"Listen to you," he muttered, putting her back into
her clothes with a wry grin. "I'll give you ten to one
that you'd be yelling your head off if I started taking
off your jeans."

She went red. "My jeans…!"

His eyebrows arched. "Amanda, would you like me

to explain that book I read to you? The part about how men and women…"

She cleared her throat. "No, thanks, I think I've got the hang of it now," she murmured evasively.

"We might as well add a word about birth control," he added with a chuckle when he was buttoning up his own shirt. "You don't take the pill, I assume?"

She shook her head. The whole thing was getting to be really embarrassing!

"Well, that leaves prevention up to me," he explained. "And that would mean a trip into town to the drugstore, since I never indulged, I never needed to worry about prevention. *Now* do you get the picture?"

"Boy, do I get the picture." She grimaced, avoiding his knowing gaze.

"Good girl. That's why we aren't lying down anymore."

She sighed loudly. "I guess you don't want children."

"Sure I do. Elliot would love brothers and sisters, and I'm crazy about kids." He took her slender hands in his and smoothed them over with his thumbs. "But kids should be born inside marriage, not outside it. Don't you think so?"

She took a deep breath, and her dark eyes met his. "Yes."

"Then we'll spend a lot of time together until you have to meet your friends at this concert," he said softly. "And afterward, you and I will come in here again and I'll ask you a question."

"Oh, Quinn," she whispered with aching softness.

"Oh, Amanda," he murmured, smiling as his lips softly touched hers. "But right now, we go to bed. Separately. Quick!"

"Yes, sir, Mr. Sutton." She got up and let him lead her to the staircase.

"I'll get the lights," he said. "You go on up. In the morning after we get Elliot off to school you can come out with me, if you want to."

"I want to," she said simply. She could hardly bear to be parted from him even overnight. It was like an addiction, she thought as she went up the staircase. Now if only she could make it last until she had the nerve to tell Quinn the truth....

The next few days went by in a haze. The snow began to melt and the skies cleared as the long-awaited chinook blew in. In no time at all it was Friday night and Amanda was getting into what Elliot would recognize as her stage costume. She'd brought it, with her other things, from the Durning cabin. She put it on, staring at herself in the mirror. Her hair hung long and loose, in soft waves below her waist, in the beige leather dress with the buckskin boots that matched, she was the very picture of a sensuous woman. She left off the headband. There would be time for that if she could summon enough courage to get onstage. She still hadn't told Quinn. She hadn't had the heart to destroy the dream she'd been living. But tonight he'd know. And she'd know if they had a future. She took a deep breath and went downstairs.

CHAPTER EIGHT

AMANDA SAT IN the audience with Quinn and Elliot at a far table while the crowded hall rang with excited whispers. Elliot was tense, like Amanda, his eyes darting around nervously. Quinn was frowning. He hadn't been quite himself since Amanda came down the staircase in her leather dress and boots, looking expensive and faintly alien. He hadn't asked any questions, but he seemed as uptight as she felt.

Her eyes slid over him lovingly, taking in his dark suit. He looked out of place in fancy clothes. She missed the sight of him in denim and his old shepherd's coat, and wondered fleetingly if she'd ever get to see him that way again after tonight—if she'd ever lie in his arms on the big sofa and warm to his kisses while the fire burned in the stove. She almost groaned. Oh, Quinn, she thought, I love you.

Elliot looked uncomfortable in his blue suit. He was watching for the rest of Desperado while a well-known Las Vegas entertainer warmed up the crowd and sang his own famous theme song.

"What are you looking for, son?" Quinn asked.

Elliot shifted. "Nothing. I'm just seeing who I know."

Quinn's eyebrows arched. "How would you know anybody in this crowd?" he muttered, glancing around.

"My God, these are show people. Entertainers. Not people from our world."

That was a fact. But hearing it made Amanda heartsick. She reached out and put her hand over Quinn's.

"Your fingers are like ice," he said softly. He searched her worried eyes. "Are you okay, honey?"

The endearment made her warm all over. She smiled sadly and slid her fingers into his, looking down at the contrast between his callused, work-hardened hand and her soft, pale one. His was a strong hand, hers was artistic. But despite the differences, they fit together perfectly. She squeezed her fingers. "I'm fine," she said. "Quinn..."

"And now I want to introduce a familiar face," the Las Vegas performer's voice boomed. "Most of you know the genius of Desperado. The group has won countless awards for its topical, hard-hitting songs. Last year, Desperado was given a Grammy for 'Changes in the Wind,' and Hank Shoeman's song 'Outlaw Love' won him a country music award and a gold record. But their fame isn't the reason we're honoring them tonight."

To Amanda's surprise, he produced a gold plaque. "As some of you may remember, a little over a month ago, a teenage girl died at a Desperado concert. The group's lead singer leaped into the crowd, disregarding her own safety, and was very nearly trampled trying to protect the fan. Because of that tragedy, Desperado went into seclusion. We're proud to tell you tonight that they're back and they're in better form than ever. This plaque is a token of respect from the rest of us in the performing arts to a very special young woman whose compassion and selflessness have won the respect of all."

He looked out toward the audience where Amanda sat frozen. "This is for you—Amanda Corrie Callaway.

Will you come up and join the group, please? Come on, Mandy!"

She bit her lower lip. The plaque was a shock. The boys seemed to know about it, too, because they went to their instruments grinning and began to play the downbeat that Desperado was known for, the deep throbbing counter rhythm that was their trademark.

"Come on, babe!" Hank called out in his booming voice, he and Johnson and Deke and Jack looking much more like backwoods robbers than musicians with their huge bulk and outlaw gear.

Amanda glanced at Elliot's rapt, adoring face, and then looked at Quinn. He was frowning, his dark eyes searching the crowd. She said a silent goodbye as she got to her feet. She reached into her pocket for her headband and put it on her head. She couldn't look at him, but she felt his shocked stare as she walked down the room toward the stage, her steps bouncing as the rhythm got into her feet and her blood.

"Thank you," she said huskily, kissing the entertainer's cheek as she accepted the plaque. She moved in between Johnson and Deke, taking the microphone. She looked past Elliot's proud, adoring face to Quinn's. He seemed to be in a state of dark shock. "Thank you all. I've had a hard few weeks. But I'm okay now, and I'm looking forward to better times. God bless, people. This one is for a special man and a special boy, with all my love." She turned to Hank, nodded, and he began the throbbing drumbeat of "Love Singer."

It was a song that touched the heart, for all its mad beat. The words, in her soft, sultry, clear voice caught every ear in the room. She sang from the heart, with the heart, the words fierce with meaning as she sang them to Quinn.

"Love you, never loved anybody but you, never leave me lonely, love…singer."

But Quinn didn't seem to be listening to the words. He got to his feet and jerked Elliot to his. He walked out in the middle of the song and never looked back once.

Amanda managed to finish, with every ounce of willpower she had keeping her onstage. She let the last few notes hang in the air and then she bowed to a standing ovation. By the time she and the band did an encore and she got out of the hall, the truck they'd come in was long gone. There was no note, no message. Quinn had said it all with his eloquent back when he walked out of the hall. He knew who she was now, and he wanted no part of her. He couldn't have said it more clearly if he'd written it in blood.

She kept hoping that he might reconsider. Even after she went backstage with the boys, she kept hoping for a phone call or a glimpse of Quinn. But nothing happened.

"I guess I'm going to need a place to stay," Amanda said with a rueful smile, her expression telling her group all they needed to know.

"He couldn't handle it, huh?" Hank asked quietly. "I'm sorry, babe. We've got a suite, there's plenty of room for one more. I'll go up and get your gear tomorrow."

"Thanks, Hank." She took a deep breath and clutched the plaque to her chest. "Where's the next gig?"

"That's my girl," he said gently, sliding a protective arm around her. "San Francisco's our next stop. The boys and I are taking a late bus tomorrow." He grimaced at her knowing smile. "Well, you know how I feel about airplanes."

"Chicken Little," she accused. "Well, I'm not going to sit on a bus all day. I'll take the first charter out and meet you guys at the hotel."

"Whatever turns you on," Hank chuckled. "Come on. Let's get out of here and get some rest."

"You did good, Amanda," Johnson said from behind her. "We were proud."

"You bet," Deke and Jack seconded.

She smiled at them all. "Thanks, group. I shocked myself, but at least I didn't go dry the way I did last time." Her heart was breaking in two, but she managed to hide it. Quinn, she moaned inwardly. Oh, Quinn, was I just an interlude, an infatuation?

She didn't sleep very much. The next morning Amanda watched Hank start out for Ricochet then went down to a breakfast that she didn't even eat while she waited for him to return.

He came back three hours later, looking ruffled.

"Did you get my things?" she asked when he came into the suite.

"I got them." He put her suitcase down on the floor. "Part at Sutton's place, part at the Durning cabin. Elliot sent you a note." He produced it.

"And... Quinn?"

"I never saw him," he replied tersely. "The boy and the old man were there. They didn't mention Sutton and I didn't ask. I wasn't feeling too keen on him at the time."

"Thanks, Hank."

He shrugged. "That's the breaks, kid. It would have been a rough combination at best. You're a bright-lights girl."

"Am I?" she asked, thinking how easily she'd fit into

Quinn's world. But she didn't push it. She sat down on the couch and opened Elliot's scribbled note.

Amanda,
I thought you were great. Dad didn't say anything all the way home and last night he went into his study and didn't come out until this morning. He went hunting, he said, but he didn't take any bullets. I hope you are okay. Write me when you can. I love you.
Your friend, Elliot.

She bit her lip to keep from crying. Dear Elliot. At least he still cared about her. But her fall from grace in Quinn's eyes had been final, she thought bitterly. He'd never forgive her for deceiving him. Or maybe it was just that he'd gotten over his brief infatuation with her when he found out who she really was. She didn't know what to do. She couldn't remember ever feeling so miserable. To have discovered something that precious, only to lose it forever. She folded Elliot's letter and put it into her purse. At least it would be something to remember from her brief taste of heaven.

For the rest of the day, the band and Jerry, the road manager, got the arrangements made for the San Francisco concert, and final travel plans were laid. The boys were to board the San Francisco bus the next morning. Amanda was to fly out on a special air charter that specialized in flights for business executives. They'd managed to fit her in at the last minute when a computer-company executive had canceled his flight.

"I wish you'd come with us," Hank said hesitantly. "I guess I'm overreacting and all, but I hate airplanes."

"I'll be fine," she told him firmly. "You and the boys have a nice trip and stop worrying about me. I'll be fine."

"If you say so," Hank mumbled.

"I do say so." She patted him on the shoulder. "Trust me."

He shrugged and left, but he didn't look any less worried. Amanda, who'd gotten used to his morose predictions, didn't pay them any mind.

She went to the suite and into her bedroom early that night. Her fingers dialed the number at Ricochet. She had to try one last time, she told herself. There was at least the hope that Quinn might care enough to listen to her explanation. She had to try.

The phone rang once, twice, and she held her breath, but on the third ring the receiver was lifted.

"Sutton," came a deep weary-sounding voice.

Her heart lifted. "Oh, Quinn," she burst out. "Quinn, please let me try to explain—"

"You don't have to explain anything to me, Amanda," he said stiffly. "I saw it all on the stage."

"I know it looks bad," she began.

"You lied to me," he said. "You let me think you were just a shy little innocent who played a keyboard, when you were some fancy big-time entertainer with a countrywide following."

"I knew you wouldn't want me if you knew who I was," she said miserably.

"You knew I'd see right through you if I knew," he corrected, his voice growing angrier. "You played me for a fool."

"I didn't!"

"All of it was a lie. Nothing but a lie! Well, you can

go back to your public, Miss Callaway, and your outlaw buddies, and make some more records or tapes or
whatever the hell they are. I never wanted you in the
first place except in bed, so it's no great loss to me." He
was grimacing, and she couldn't see the agony in his
eyes as he forced the words out. Now that he knew who
and what she was, he didn't dare let himself weaken. He
had to make her go back to her own life, and stay out of
his. He had nothing to give her, nothing that could take
the place of fame and fortune and the world at her feet.
He'd never been more aware of his own inadequacies
as he had been when he'd seen Amanda on that stage
and heard the applause of the audience. It ranked as the
worst waking nightmare of his life, putting her forever
out of his reach.

"Quinn!" she moaned. "Quinn, you don't mean that!"

"I mean it," he said through his teeth. He closed his
eyes. "Every word. Don't call here again, don't come by,
don't write. You're a bad influence on Elliot now that
he knows who you are. I don't want you. You've worn
out your welcome at Ricochet." He hung up without another word.

Amanda stared at the telephone receiver as if it had
sprouted wings. Slowly she put it back in the cradle
just as the room splintered into wet crystal around her.

She put on her gown mechanically and got into bed,
turning out the bedside light. She lay in the dark and
Quinn's words echoed in her head with merciless coolness. *Bad influence. Don't want you. Worn out your welcome. Never wanted you anyway except in bed.*

She moaned and buried her face in her pillow. She
didn't know how she was going to go on, with Quinn's
cold contempt dogging her footsteps. He hated her now.

He thought she'd been playing a game, enjoying herself while she made a fool out of him. The tears burned her eyes. How quickly it had all ended, how finally. She'd hoped to keep in touch with Elliot, but that wouldn't be possible anymore. She was a bad influence on Elliot, so he wouldn't be allowed to contact her. She sobbed her hurt into the cool linen. Somehow, being denied contact with Elliot was the last straw. She'd grown so fond of the boy during those days she'd spent at Ricochet, and he cared about her, too. Quinn was being unnecessarily harsh. But perhaps he was right, and it was for the best. Maybe she could learn to think that way eventually. Right now she had a concert to get to, a sold-out one from what the boys and Jerry had said. She couldn't let the fans down.

Amanda got up the next morning, looking and feeling as if it were the end of the world. The boys took her suitcase downstairs, not looking too closely at her face without makeup, her long hair arranged in a thick, haphazard bun. She was wearing a dark pantsuit with a cream-colored blouse, and she looked miserable.

"We'll see you in San Francisco," Jerry told her with a smile. "I have to go nursemaid these big, tough guys, so you make sure the pilot of your plane has all his marbles, okay?"

"I'll check him out myself," she promised. "Take care of yourselves, guys. I'll see you in California."

"Okay. Be good, babe," Hank called. He and the others filed into the bus Jerry had chartered and Jerry hugged her impulsively and went in behind them.

She watched the bus pull away, feeling lost and alone, not for the first time. It was cold and snowy, but she hadn't wanted her coat. It was packed in her suitcase, and had already been put on the light aircraft. With a long sigh, she went back to the cab and sat disinterestedly in it as it wound over the snowy roads to the airport.

Fortunately the chinook had thawed the runways so that the planes were coming and going easily. She got out at the air charter service hangar and shook hands with the pilot.

"Don't worry, we're in great shape," he promised Amanda with a grin. "In fact, the mechanics just gave us another once-over to be sure. Nothing to worry about."

"Oh, I wasn't worried," she said absently and allowed herself to be shepherded inside. She slid into an empty aisle seat on the right side and buckled up. Usually she preferred to sit by the window, but today she wasn't in the mood for sight-seeing. One snow-covered mountain looked pretty much like another to her, and her heart wasn't in this flight or the gig that would follow it. She leaned back and closed her eyes.

It seemed to take forever for all the businessmen to get aboard. Fortunately there had been one more cancellation, so she had her seat and the window seat as well. She didn't feel like talking to anyone, and was hoping she wouldn't have to sit by some chatterbox all the way to California.

She listened to the engines rev up and made sure that her seat belt was properly fastened. They would be off as soon as the tower cleared them, the pilot announced. Amanda sighed. She called a silent goodbye to Quinn Sutton, and Elliot and Harry, knowing that once this plane lifted off, she'd never see any of them again. She winced at the thought. Oh, Quinn, she moaned inwardly, why wouldn't you *listen?*

The plane got clearance and a minute later, it shot

down the runway and lifted off. But it seemed oddly sluggish. Amanda was used to air travel, even to charter flights, and she opened her eyes and peered forward worriedly as she listened to the whine become a roar.

She was strapped in, but a groan from behind took her mind off the engine. The elderly man behind her was clutching his chest and groaning.

"What's wrong?" she asked the worried businessman in the seat beside the older man.

"Heart attack, I think." He grimaced. "What can we do?"

"I know a little CPR," she said. She unfastened her seat belt; so did the groaning man's seat companion. But just as they started to lay him on the floor, someone shouted something. Smoke began to pour out of the cockpit, and the pilot called for everyone to assume crash positions. Amanda turned, almost in slow motion. She could feel the force of gravity increase as the plane started down. The floor went out from under her and her last conscious thought was that she'd never see Quinn again....

Elliot was watching television without much interest, wishing that his father had listened when Amanda had phoned the night before. He couldn't believe that he was going to be forbidden to even speak to her again, but Quinn had insisted, his cold voice giving nothing away as he'd made Elliot promise to make no attempt to contact her.

It seemed so unfair, he thought. Amanda was no wild party girl, surely his father knew that? He sighed heavily and munched on another potato chip.

The movie he was watching was suddenly interrupted as the local station broke in with a news bulletin. Elliot listened for a minute, gasped and jumped up to get his father.

Quinn was in the office, not really concentrating on what he was doing, when Elliot burst in. The boy looked odd, his freckles standing out in an unnaturally pale face.

"Dad, you'd better come here," he said uneasily. "Quick!"

Quinn's first thought was that something had happened to Harry, but Elliot stopped in front of the television. Quinn frowned as his dark eyes watched the screen. They were showing the airport.

"What's this all—" he began, then stopped to listen.

"...plane went down about ten minutes ago, according to our best information," the man, probably the airport manager, was saying. "We've got helicopters flying in to look for the wreckage, but the wind is up, and the area the plane went down in is almost inaccessible by road."

"What plane?" Quinn asked absently.

"To repeat our earlier bulletin," the man on television seemed to oblige, "a private charter plane has been reported lost somewhere in the Grand Teton Mountains just out of Jackson Hole. One eyewitness interviewed by KWJC-TV newsman Bill Donovan stated that he saw flames shooting out of the cockpit of the twin-engine aircraft and that he watched it plummet into the mountains and vanish. Aboard the craft were prominent San Francisco businessmen Bob Doyle and Harry Brown, and the lead singer of the rock group Desperado, Mandy Callaway."

Quinn sat down in his chair hard enough to shake it.

He knew his face was as white as Elliot's. In his mind, he could hear his own voice telling Mandy he didn't want her anymore, daring her to ever contact him again. Now she was dead, and he felt her loss as surely as if one of his arms had been severed from his body.

That was when he realized how desperately he loved her. When it was too late to take back the harsh words, to go after her and bring her home where she belonged. He thought of her soft body lying in the cold snow, and a sound broke from his throat. He'd sent her away because he loved her, not because he'd wanted to hurt her, but she wouldn't have known that. Her last memory of him would have been a painful, hateful one. She'd have died thinking he didn't care.

"I don't believe it," Elliot said huskily. He was shaking his head. "I just don't believe it. She was onstage Friday night, singing again—" His voice broke and he put his face in his hands.

Quinn couldn't bear it. He got up and went past a startled Harry and out the back door in his shirtsleeves, so upset that he didn't even feel the cold. His eyes went to the barn, where he'd watched Amanda feed the calves, and around the back where she'd run from him that snowy afternoon and he'd had to save her from Mc-Naber's bear traps. His big fists clenched by his sides and he shuddered with the force of the grief he felt, his face contorting.

"Amanda!" He bit off the name.

A long time later, he was aware of someone standing nearby. He didn't turn because his face would have said too much.

"Elliot told me," Harry said hesitantly. He stuck his

hands into his pockets. "They say where she is, they may not be able to get her out."

Quinn's teeth clenched. "I'll get her out," he said huskily. "I won't leave her out there in the cold." He swallowed. "Get my skis and my boots out of the storeroom, and my insulated ski suit out of the closet. I'm going to call the lodge and talk to Terry Meade."

"He manages Larry's Lodge, doesn't he?" Harry recalled.

"Yes. He can get a chopper to take me up."

"Good thing you've kept up your practice," Harry muttered. "Never thought you'd need the skis for something this awful, though."

"Neither did I." He turned and went back inside. He might have to give up Amanda forever, but he wasn't giving her up to that damned mountain. He'd get her out somehow.

He grabbed the phone, ignoring Elliot's questions, and called the lodge, asking for Terry Meade in a tone that got instant action.

"Quinn!" Terry exclaimed. "Just the man I need. Look, we've got a crash—"

"I know," Quinn said tightly. "I know the singer. Can you get me a topo map of the area and a chopper? I'll need a first-aid kit, too, and some flares—"

"No sooner said than done," Terry replied tersely. "Although I don't think that first-aid kit will be needed, Quinn, I'm sorry."

"Well, pack it anyway, will you?" He fought down nausea. "I'll be up there in less than thirty minutes."

"We'll be waiting."

Quinn got into the ski suit under Elliot's fascinated gaze.

"You don't usually wear that suit when we ski together," he told his father.

"We don't stay out that long," Quinn explained. "This suit is a relatively new innovation. It's such a tight weave that it keeps out moisture, but it's made in such a way that it allows sweat to get out. It's like having your own heater along."

"I like the boots, too," Elliot remarked. They were blue, and they had a knob on the heel that allowed them to be tightened to fit the skier's foot exactly. Boots had to fit tight to work properly. And the skis themselves were equally fascinating. They had special brakes that unlocked when the skier fell, which stopped the ski from sliding down the hill.

"Those sure are long skis," Elliot remarked as his father took precious time to apply hot wax to them.

"Longer than yours, for sure. They fit my height," Quinn said tersely. "And they're short compared to jumping skis."

"Did you ever jump, Dad, or did you just do downhill?"

"Giant slalom," he replied. "Strictly Alpine skiing. That's going to come in handy today."

Elliot sighed. "I don't guess you'll let me come along?"

"No chance. This is no place for you." His eyes darkened. "God knows what I'll find when I get to the plane."

Elliot bit his lower lip. "She's dead, isn't she, Dad?" he asked in a choked tone.

Quinn's expression closed. "You stay here with Harry, and don't tie up the telephone. I'll call home as soon as I know anything."

"Take care of yourself up there, okay?" Elliot murmured as Quinn picked up the skis and the rest of his equipment, including gloves and ski cap. "I don't say it a lot, but I love you, Dad."

"I love you, too, son." Quinn pulled him close and gave him a quick, rough hug. "I know what I'm doing. I'll be okay."

"Good luck," Harry said as Quinn went out the back door to get into his pickup truck.

"I'll need it," Quinn muttered. He waved, started the truck, and pulled out into the driveway.

Terry Meade was waiting with the Ski Patrol, the helicopter pilot, assorted law enforcement officials and the civil defense director and trying to field the news media gathered at Larry's Lodge.

"This is the area where we think they are," Terry said grimly, showing Quinn the map. "What you call Ironside peak, right? It's not in our patrol area, so we don't have anything to do with it officially. The helicopter tried and failed to get into the valley below it because of the wind. The trees are dense down there and visibility is limited by blowing snow. Our teams are going to start here," he pointed at various places on the map. "But this hill is a killer." He grinned at Quinn. "You cut your teeth on it when you were practicing for the Olympics all those years ago, and you've kept up your practice there. If anyone can ski it, you can."

"I'll get in. What then?"

"Send up a flare. I'm packing a cellular phone in with the other stuff you asked for. It's got a better range than our walkie-talkies. Everybody know what to do? Right. Let's go."

He led them out of the lodge. Quinn put on his goggles, tugged his ski cap over his head and thrust his hands into his gloves. He didn't even want to think about what he might have to look at if he was lucky enough to find the downed plane. He was having enough trouble living with what he'd said to Amanda the last time he'd talked to her.

He could still hear her voice, hear the hurt in it when he'd told her he didn't want her. Remembering that was like cutting open his heart. For her sake, he'd sent her away. He was a poor man. He had so little to offer such a famous, beautiful woman. At first, at the lodge, his pride had been cut to ribbons when he discovered who she was, and how she'd fooled him, how she'd deceived him. But her adoration had been real, and when his mind was functioning again, he realized that. He'd almost phoned her back, he'd even dialed the number. But her world was so different from his. He couldn't let her give up everything she'd worked all her life for, just to live in the middle of nowhere. She deserved so much more. He sighed wearily. If she died, the last conversation would haunt him until the day he died. He didn't think he could live with it. He didn't want to have to try. She had to be alive. Oh, dear God, she had to be!

CHAPTER NINE

THE SUN WAS BRIGHT, and Quinn felt its warmth on his face as the helicopter set him down at the top of the mountain peak where the plane had last been sighted.

He was alone in the world when the chopper lifted off again. He checked his bindings one last time, adjusted the lightweight backpack and stared down the long mountainside with his ski poles restless in his hands. This particular slope wasn't skied as a rule. It wasn't even connected with the resort, which meant that the Ski Patrol didn't come here, and that the usual rescue toboggan posted on most slopes wouldn't be in evidence. He was totally on his own until he could find the downed plane. And he knew that while he was searching this untamed area, the Ski Patrol would be out in force on the regular slopes looking for the aircraft.

He sighed heavily as he stared down at the rugged, untouched terrain, which would be a beginning skier's nightmare. Well, it was now or never. Amanda was down there somewhere. He had to find her. He couldn't leave her there in the cold snow for all eternity.

He pulled down his goggles, suppressed his feelings and shoved the ski poles deep as he propelled himself down the slope. The first couple of minutes were tricky as he had to allow for the slight added weight of the

backpack. But it took scant time to adjust, to balance
his weight on the skis to compensate.

The wind bit his face, the snow flew over his dark
ski suit as he wound down the slopes, his skis throwing
up powdered snow in his wake. It brought back memories of the days when he'd maneuvered through the giant
slalom in Alpine skiing competition. He'd been in the
top one percent of his class, a daredevil skier with cold
nerve and expert control on the slopes. This mountain
was a killer, but it was one he knew like the back of his
hand. He'd trained on this peak back in his early days of
competition, loving the danger of skiing a slope where
no one else came. Even for the past ten years or so, he'd
honed his skill here every chance he got.

Quinn smiled to himself, his body leaning into the
turns, not too far, the cutting edge of his skis breaking his speed as he maneuvered over boulders, down
the fall line, around trees and broken branches or over
them, whichever seemed more expedient.

His dark eyes narrowed as he defeated the obstacles.
At least, thank God, he was able to do something instead of going through hell sitting at home waiting for
word. That in itself was a blessing, even if it ended in the
tragedy everyone seemed to think it would. He couldn't
bear to imagine Amanda dead. He had to think positively. There were people who walked away from airplane crashes. He had to believe that she could be one
of them. He had to keep thinking that or go mad.

He'd hoped against hope that when he got near the bottom of the hill, under those tall pines and the deadly updrafts and downdrafts that had defeated the helicopter's
reconnoitering, that he'd find the airplane. But it wasn't
there. He turned his skis sideways and skidded to a stop,

looking around him. Maybe the observer had gotten his sighting wrong. Maybe it was another peak, maybe it was miles away. He bit his lower lip raw, tasting the lip balm he'd applied before he came onto the slope. If anyone on that plane was alive, time was going to make the difference. He had to find it quickly, or Amanda wouldn't have a prayer if she'd managed to survive the initial impact.

He started downhill again, his heartbeat increasing as the worry began to eat at him. On an impulse, he shot across the fall line, parallel to it for a little while before he maneuvered back and went down again in lazy *S* patterns. Something caught his attention. A sound. Voices!

He stopped to listen, turning his head. There was wind, and the sound of pines touching. But beyond it was a voice, carrying in the silence of nature. Snow blanketed most sound, making graveyard peace out of the mountain's spring noises.

Quinn adjusted his weight on the skis and lifted his hands to his mouth, the ski poles dangling from his wrists. "Hello! Where are you?" he shouted, taking a chance that the vibration of his voice wouldn't dislodge snow above him and bring a sheet of it down on him.

"Help!" voices called back. "We're here! We're here!"

He followed the sound, praying that he wasn't following an echo. But no, there, below the trees, he saw a glint of metal in the lowering sun. The plane! Thank God, there were survivors! Now if only Amanda was one of them...

He went the rest of the way down. As he drew closer, he saw men standing near the almost intact wreckage of the aircraft. One had a bandage around his head, another was nursing what looked like a broken arm. He saw one woman, but she wasn't blond. On the ground were two still forms, covered with coats. Covered up.

Please, God, no, he thought blindly. He drew to a stop.

"I'm Sutton. How many dead?" he asked the man who'd called to him, a burly man in a gray suit and white shirt and tie.

"Two," the man replied. "I'm Jeff Coleman, and I sure am glad to see you." He shook hands with Quinn. "I'm the pilot. We had a fire in the cockpit and it was all I could do to set her down at all. God, I feel bad! For some reason, three of the passengers had their seat belts off when we hit." He shook his head. "No hope for two of them. The third's concussed and looks comatose."

Quinn felt himself shaking inside as he asked the question he had to ask. "There was a singer aboard," he said. "Amanda Callaway."

"Yeah." The pilot shook his head and Quinn wanted to die, he wanted to stop breathing right there… "She's the concussion."

Quinn knew his hand shook as he pushed his goggles up over the black ski cap. "Where is she?" he asked huskily.

The pilot didn't ask questions or argue. He led Quinn past the two bodies and the dazed businessmen who were standing or sitting on fabric they'd taken from the plane, trying to keep warm.

"She's here," the pilot told him, indicating a makeshift stretcher constructed of branches and pillows from the cabin, and coats that covered the still body.

"Amanda," Quinn managed unsteadily. He knelt beside her. Her hair was in a coiled bun on her head. Her face was alabaster white, her eyes closed, long black lashes lying still on her cheekbones. Her mouth was as pale as the rest of her face, and there was a bruise high on her forehead at the right temple. He stripped off his glove and felt the artery at her neck. Her heart was still beating, but slowly and not very firmly. Unconscious. Dying, perhaps. "Oh, God," he breathed.

He got to his feet and unloaded the backpack as the pilot and two of the other men gathered around him.

"I've got a modular phone," Quinn said, "which I hope to God will work." He punched buttons and waited, his dark eyes narrowed, holding his breath.

It seemed to take forever. Then a voice, a recognizable voice, came over the wire. "Hello."

"Terry!" Quinn called. "It's Sutton. I've found them."

"Thank God!" Terry replied. "Okay, give me your position."

Quinn did, spreading out his laminated map to verify it, and then gave the report on casualties.

"Only one unconscious?" Terry asked again.

"Only one," Quinn replied heavily.

"We'll have to airlift you out, but we can't do it until the wind dies down. You understand, Quinn, the same downdrafts and updrafts that kept the chopper out this morning are going to keep it out now."

"Yes, I know, damn it," Quinn yelled. "But I've got to get her to a hospital. She's failing already."

Terry sighed. "And there you are without a rescue toboggan. Listen, what if I get Larry Hale down there?" he asked excitedly. "You know Larry; he was national champ in downhill a few years back, and he's a senior member of the Ski Patrol now. We could airdrop you the toboggan and some supplies for the rest of the survivors by plane. The two of you could tow her to a point accessible by chopper. Do you want to risk it, Quinn?"

"I don't know if she'll be alive in the morning, Terry," Quinn said somberly. "I'm more afraid to risk doing nothing than I am of towing her out. It's fairly level, if I remember right, all the way to the pass that leads from Caraway Ridge into Jackson Hole. The chopper might be able to fly down Jackson Hole and come in that way, without having to navigate the peaks. What do you think?"

"I think it's a good idea," Terry said. "If I remember right, they cleared that pass from the Ridge into Jackson Hole in the fall. It should still be accessible."

"No problem," Quinn said, his jaw grim. "If it isn't cleared, I'll clear it, by hand if necessary."

Terry chuckled softly. "Hale says he's already on the way. We'll get the plane up—hell of a pity he can't land where you are, but it's just too tricky. How about the other survivors?"

Quinn told him their conditions, along with the two bodies that would have to be airlifted out.

"Too bad," he replied. He paused for a minute to talk to somebody. "Listen, Quinn, if you can get the woman to Caraway Ridge, the chopper pilot thinks he can safely put down there. About the others, can they manage until morning if we drop the supplies?"

Quinn looked at the pilot. "Can you?"

"I ate snakes in Nam and Bill over there served in Antarctica." He grinned. "Between us, we can keep these pilgrims warm and even feed them. Sure, we'll be okay. Get that little lady out if you can."

"Amen," the man named Bill added, glancing at Amanda's still form. "I've heard her sing. It would be a crime against art to let her die."

Quinn lifted the cellular phone to his ear. "They say

they can manage, Terry. Are you sure you can get them out in the morning?"

"If we have to send the snowplow in through the valley or send in a squad of snowmobiles and a horse-drawn sled, you'd better believe we'll get them out. The Ski Patrol is already working out the details."

"Okay."

Quinn unloaded his backpack. He had flares and matches, packets of high protein dehydrated food, the first-aid kit and some cans of sterno.

"Paradise," the pilot said, looking at the stores. "With that, I can prepare a seven-course meal, build a bonfire and make a house. But those supplies they're going to drop will come in handy, just the same."

Quinn smiled in spite of himself. "Okay."

"We can sure use this first-aid kit, but I've already set a broken arm and patched a few cuts. Before I became a pilot, I worked in the medical corps."

"I had rescue training when I was in the Ski Patrol," Quinn replied. He grinned at the pilot. "But if I ever come down in a plane, I hope you're on it."

"Thanks. I hope none of us ever come down again." He glanced at the two bodies. "God, I'm sorry about them." He glanced at Amanda. "I hope she makes it."

Quinn's jaw hardened. "She's a fighter," he said. "Let's hope she cares enough to try." He alone knew how defeated she'd probably felt when she left the lodge. He'd inflicted some terrible damage with his coldness. Pride had forced him to send her away, to deny his own happiness. Once he knew how famous and wealthy she was in her own right, he hadn't felt that he had the right to ask her to give it all up to live with him and Elliot in the wilds of Wyoming. He'd been doing what he thought was best for her. Now he only wanted her to live.

He took a deep breath. "Watch for the plane and Hale, will you? I'm going to sit with her."

"Sure." The pilot gave him a long look that he didn't see before he went back to talk to the other survivors.

Quinn sat down beside Amanda, reaching for one cold little hand under the coats that covered her. It was going to be a rough ride for her, and she didn't need any more jarring. But if they waited until morning, without medical help, she could die. It was much riskier to do nothing than it was to risk moving her. And down here in the valley, the snow was deep and fairly level. It would be like Nordic skiing; cross-country skiing. With luck, it would feel like a nice lazy sleigh ride to her.

"Listen to me, honey," he said softly. "We've got a long way to go before we get you out of here and to a hospital. You're going to have to hold on for a long time." His hand tightened around hers, warming it. "I'll be right with you every step of the way. I won't leave you for a second. But you have to do your part, Amanda. You have to fight to stay alive. I hope that you still want to live. If you don't, there's something I need to tell you. I sent you away not because I hated you, Amanda, but because I loved you so much. I loved you enough to let you go back to the life you needed. You've got to stay alive so that I can tell you that," he added, stopping because his voice broke.

He looked away, getting control back breath by breath. He thought he felt her fingers move, but he couldn't be sure. "I'm going to get you out of here, honey, one way or the other, even if I have to walk out with you in my arms. Try to hold on, for me." He brought her hand to his mouth and kissed the palm hungrily. "Try to hold on, because if you die, so do I. I can't keep going unless you're somewhere in the world, even if I never see you again. Even if you hate me forever."

He swallowed hard and put down her hand. The sound of an airplane in the distance indicated that supplies were on the way. Quinn put Amanda's hand back under the cover and bent to brush his mouth against her cold, still one.

"I love you," he whispered roughly. "You've got to hold on until I can get you out of here."

He stood, his face like the stony crags above them, his eyes glittering as he joined the others.

The plane circled and seconds later, a white parachute appeared. Quinn held his breath as it descended, hoping against hope that the chute wouldn't hang up in the tall trees and that the toboggan would soft-land so that it was usable. A drop in this kind of wind was risky at best.

But luck was with them. The supplies and the sled made it in one piece. Quinn and the pilot and a couple of the sturdier survivors unfastened the chute and brought the contents back to the wreckage of the commuter plane. The sled was even equipped with blankets and a pillow and straps to keep Amanda secured.

Minutes later, the drone of a helicopter whispered on the wind, and not long after that, Hale started down the mountainside.

It took several minutes. Quinn saw the flash of rust that denoted the distinctive jacket and white waist pack of the Ski Patrol above, and when Hale came closer, he could see the gold cross on the right pocket of the jacket—a duplicate of the big one stenciled on the jacket's back.

He smiled, remembering when he'd worn that same type of jacket during a brief stint as a ski patrolman. It was a special kind of occupation, and countless skiers owed their lives to those brave men and women. The National Ski Patrol had only existed since 1938. It was created by Charles Dole of Connecticut, after a skiing accident that took the life of one of his friends. Today, the Ski Patrol had over 10,000 members nationally, of whom ninety-eight percent were volunteers. They were the first on the slopes and the last off, patroling for dangerous areas and rescuing injured people. Quinn had once been part of that elite group and he still had the greatest respect for them.

Hale was the only color against the whiteness of the snow. The sun was out, and thank God it hadn't snowed all day. It had done enough of that last night.

Quinn's nerves were stretched. He hadn't had a cigarette since he'd arrived at the lodge, and he didn't dare have one now. Nicotine and caffeine tended to constrict blood vessels, and the cold was dangerous enough without giving it any help. Experienced skiers knew better than to stack the odds against themselves.

"Well, I made it." Hale grinned, getting his breath. "How are you, Quinn?" He extended a hand and Quinn shook it.

The man in the Ski Patrol jacket nodded to the others, accepted their thanks for the supplies he'd brought with him, which included a makeshift shelter and plenty of food and water and even a bottle of cognac. But he didn't waste time. "We'd better get moving if we hope to get Miss Callaway out of here by dark."

"She's over here," Quinn said. "God, I hate doing this," he added heavily when he and Hale were standing over the unconscious woman. "If there was any hope, any at all, that the chopper could get in here..."

"You can feel the wind for yourself," Hale replied, his eyes solemn. "We're the only chance she has. We'll get her to the chopper. Piece of cake," he added with a reassuring smile.

"I hope so," Quinn said somberly. He bent and nodded to Hale. They lifted her very gently onto the long sled containing the litter. It had handles on both ends, because it was designed to be towed. They attached the towlines, covered Amanda carefully and set out, with reassurances from the stranded survivors.

There was no time to talk. The track was fairly straightforward, but it worried Quinn, all the same, because there were crusts that jarred the woman on the litter. He towed, Hale guided, their rhythms matching perfectly as they made their way down the snow-covered valley. Around them, the wind sang through the tall firs and lodgepole pines, and Quinn thought about the old trappers and mountain men who must have come through this valley a hundred, two hundred years before. In those days of poor sanitation and even poorer medicine, Amanda wouldn't have stood a chance.

He forced himself not to look back. He had to concentrate on getting her to the Ridge. All that was important now, was that she get medical help while it could still do her some good. He hadn't come all this way to find her alive, only to lose her.

It seemed to take forever. Once Quinn was certain that they'd lost their way as they navigated through the narrow pass that led to the fifty-mile valley between the Grand Tetons and the Wind River Range, an area known as Jackson Hole. But he recognized landmarks as they went along, and eventually they wound their way around the trees and along the sparkling river until they reached the flats below Caraway Ridge.

Quinn and Hale were both breathing hard by now. They'd changed places several times, so that neither got too tired of towing the toboggan, and they were both in peak condition. But it was still a difficult thing to do.

They rested, and Quinn reached down to check Amanda's pulse. It was still there, and even seemed to be, incredibly, a little stronger than it had been. But she was pale and still and Quinn felt his spirits sink as he looked down at her.

"There it is," Hale called, sweeping his arm over the ridge. "The chopper."

"Now if only it can land," Quinn said quietly, and he began to pray.

The chopper came lower and lower, then it seemed to shoot up again and Quinn bit off a hard word. But the pilot corrected for the wind, which was dying down, and eased the helicopter toward the ground. It seemed to settle inch by inch until it landed safe. The pilot was out of it before the blades stopped.

"Let's get out of here," he called to the men. "If that wind catches up again, I wouldn't give us a chance in hell of getting out. It was a miracle that I even got in!"

Quinn released his bindings in a flash, leaving his skis and poles for Hale to carry, along with his own. He got one side of the stretcher while the pilot, fortunately no lightweight himself, got the other. They put the stretcher in the back of the broad helicopter, on the floor, and Quinn and Hale piled in—Hale in the passenger seat up front, Quinn behind with Amanda, carefully laying ski equipment beside her.

"Let's go!" the pilot called as he revved up the engine.

It was touch and go. The wind decided to play tag with them, and they almost went into a lodgepole pine on the way up. But the pilot was a tenacious man with good nerves. He eased down and then up, down and up until he caught the wind off guard and shot up out of the valley and over the mountain.

Quinn reached down and clasped Amanda's cold hand in his. Only a little longer, honey, he thought, watching her with his heart in his eyes. Only a little longer, for God's sake, hold on!

It was the longest ride of his entire life. He spared one thought for the people who'd stayed behind to give Amanda her chance and he prayed that they'd be rescued without any further injuries. Then his eyes settled on her pale face and stayed there until the helicopter landed on the hospital lawn.

The reporters, local, state and national, had gotten word of the rescue mission. They were waiting. Police kept them back just long enough for Amanda to be carried into the hospital, but Quinn and Hale were caught. Quinn volunteered Hale to give an account of the rescue and then he ducked out, leaving the other man to field the enthusiastic audience while he trailed quickly behind the men who'd taken Amanda into the emergency room.

He drank coffee and smoked cigarettes and glared at walls for over an hour until someone came out to talk to him. Hale had to go back to the lodge, to help plan the rescue of the rest of the survivors, but he promised to keep in touch. After he'd gone, Quinn felt even more alone. But at last a doctor came into the waiting room, and approached him.

"Are you related to Miss Callaway?" the doctor asked with narrowed eyes.

Quinn knew that if he said no, he'd have to wait for news of her condition until he could find somebody who was related to her, and he had no idea how to find her aunt.

"I'm her fiancé," he said without moving a muscle in his face. "How is she?"

"Not good," the doctor, a small wiry man, said bluntly. "But I believe in miracles. We have her in intensive care, where she'll stay until she regains consciousness. She's badly concussed. I gather she hasn't regained consciousness since the crash?" Quinn shook his head. "That sleigh ride and helicopter lift didn't do any good, either," he added firmly, adding when he saw the expression on Quinn's tormented face, "but I can understand the necessity for it. Go get some sleep. Come back in the morning. We won't know anything until then. Maybe not until much later. Concussion is tricky. We can't predict the outcome, as much as we'd like to."

"I can't rest," Quinn said quietly. "I'll sit out here and drink coffee, if you don't mind. If this is as close to her as I can get, it'll have to do."

The doctor took a slow breath. "We keep spare beds in cases like this," he said. "I'll have one made up for you when you can't stay awake any longer." He smiled faintly. "Try to think positively. It isn't medical, exactly, but sometimes it works wonders. Prayer doesn't hurt, either."

"Thank you," Quinn said.

The doctor shrugged. "Wait until she wakes up. Good night."

Quinn watched him go and sighed. He didn't know

what to do next. He phoned Terry at the lodge to see if Amanda's band had called. Someone named Jerry and a man called Hank had been phoning every few minutes, he was told. Quinn asked for a phone number and Terry gave it to him.

He dialed the area code. California, he figured as he waited for it to ring.

"Hello?"

"This is Quinn Sutton," he began.

"Yes, I recognize your voice. It's Hank here. How is she?"

"Concussion. Coma, I guess. She's in intensive care and she's still alive. That's about all I know."

There was a long pause. "I'd hoped for a little more than that."

"So had I," Quinn replied. He hesitated. "I'll phone you in the morning. The minute I know anything. Is there anybody we should notify...her aunt?"

"Her aunt is a scatterbrain and no help at all. Anyway, she's off with Blalock Durning in the Bahamas on one of those incommunicado islands. We couldn't reach her if we tried."

"Is there anybody else?" Quinn asked.

"Not that I know of." There was a brief pause. "I feel bad about the way things happened. I hate planes, you know. That's why the rest of us went by bus. We stopped here in some hick town to make sure Amanda got her plane, and Terry told us what happened. We got a motel room and we're waiting for a bus back to Jackson. It will probably be late tomorrow before we get there. We've already canceled the gig. We can't do it without Amanda."

"I'll book a room for you," Quinn said.

"Make it a suite," Hank replied, "and if you need anything, you know, anything, you just tell us."

"I've got plenty of cigarettes and the coffee machine's working. I'm fine."

"We'll see you when we get there. And Sutton—thanks. She really cares about you, you know?"

"I care about her," he said stiffly. "That's why I sent her away. My God, how could she give all that up to live on a mountain in Wyoming?"

"Amanda's not a city girl, though," Hank said slowly. "And she changed after those days she spent with you. Her heart wasn't with us anymore. She cried all last night..."

"Oh, God, don't," Quinn said.

"Sorry, man," Hank said quietly. "I'm really sorry, that's the last thing I should have said. Look, go smoke a cigarette. I think I'll tie one on royally and have the boys put me to bed. Tomorrow we'll talk. Take care."

"You, too."

Quinn hung up. He couldn't bear to think of Amanda crying because of what he'd done to her. He might lose her even yet, and he didn't know how he was going to go on living. He felt so alone.

He was out of change after he called the lodge and booked the suite for Hank and the others, but he still had to talk to Elliot and Harry. He dialed the operator and called collect. Elliot answered the phone immediately.

"How is she?" he asked quickly.

Quinn went over it again, feeling numb. "I wish I knew more," he concluded. "But that's all there is."

"She can't die," Elliot said miserably. "Dad, she just can't!"

"Say a prayer, son," he replied. "And don't let Harry teach you any bad habits while I'm gone."

"No, sir, I won't," Elliot said with a feeble attempt at humor. "You're going to stay, I guess?"

"I have to," Quinn said huskily. He hesitated. "I love her."

"So do I," Elliot said softly. "Bring her back when you come."

"If I can. If she'll even speak to me when she wakes up," Quinn said with a total lack of confidence.

"She will," Elliot told him. "You should have listened to some of those songs you thought were so horrible. One of hers won a Grammy. It was all about having to give up things we love to keep from hurting them. She always seemed to feel it when somebody was sad or hurt, you know. And she risked her own life trying to save that girl at the concert. She's not someone who thinks about getting even with people. She's got too much heart."

Quinn drew deeply from his cigarette. "I hope so, son," he said. "You get to bed. I'll call you tomorrow."

"Okay. Take care of yourself. Love you, Dad."

"Me, too, son," Quinn replied. He hung up. The waiting area was deserted now, and the hospital seemed to have gone to sleep. He sat down with his foam cup of black coffee and finished his cigarette. The room looked like he felt—empty.

CHAPTER TEN

IT WAS LATE morning when the nurse came to shake Quinn gently awake. Apparently around dawn he'd gone to sleep sitting up, with an empty coffee cup in his hand. He thought he'd never sleep at all.

He sat up, drowsy and disheveled. "How is Amanda?" he asked immediately.

The nurse, a young blonde, smiled at him. "She's awake and asking for you."

"Oh, thank God," he said heavily. He got quickly to his feet, still a little groggy, and followed her down to the intensive-care unit, where patients in tiny rooms were monitored from a central nurses' station and the hum and click and whir of life-supporting machinery filled the air. If she was asking for him, she must not hate him too much. That thought sustained him as he followed the nurse into one of the small cubicles where Amanda lay.

Amanda looked thinner than ever in the light, her face pinched, her eyes hollow, her lips chapped. They'd taken her hair down somewhere along the way and tied it back with a pink ribbon. She was propped up in bed, still with the IV in position, but she'd been taken off all the other machines.

She looked up and saw Quinn and all the weariness and pain went out of her face. She brightened, became beautiful despite her injuries, her eyes sparkling. Her last thought when she'd realized in the plane what was going to happen had been of Quinn. Her first thought when she'd regained consciousness had been of him. The pain, the grief of having him turn away from her was forgotten. He was here, now, and that meant he had to care about her.

"Oh, Quinn!" she whispered tearfully, and held out her arms.

He went to her without hesitation, ignoring the nurses, the aides, the whole world. His arms folded gently around her, careful of the tubes attached to her hand, and his head bent over hers, his cheek on her soft hair, his eyes closed as he shivered with reaction. She was alive. She was going to live. He felt as if he were going to choke to death on his own rush of feeling.

"My God," he whispered shakily. "I thought I'd lost you."

That was worth it all, she thought, dazed from the emotion in his voice, at the tremor in his powerful body as he held her. She clung to him, her slender arms around his neck, drowning in pleasure. She'd wondered if he hadn't sent her away in a misguided belief that it was for her own good. Now she was sure of it. He couldn't have looked that haggard, that terrible, unless she mattered very much to him. Her aching heart soared. "They said you brought me out."

"Hale and I did," he said huskily. He lifted his head, searching her bright eyes slowly. "It's been the longest night of my life. They said you might die."

"Oh, we Callaways are tough birds," she said, wiping away a tear. She was still weak and sore and her headache hadn't completely gone away. "You look terrible, my darling," she whispered on a choked laugh.

The endearment fired his blood. He had to take a deep breath before he could even speak. His fingers linked with hers. "I felt pretty terrible when we listened to the news report, especially when I remembered the things I said to you." He took a deep breath. "I didn't know if you'd hate me for the rest of your life, but even if you did, I couldn't just sit on my mountain and let other people look for you." His thumb gently stroked the back of her pale hand. "How do you feel, honey?"

"Pretty bad. But considering it all, I'll do. I'm sorry about the men who died. One of them was having a heart attack," she explained. "The other gentleman who was sitting with him alerted me. We both unfastened our seat belts to try and give CPR. Just after I got up, the plane started down," she said. "Quinn, do you believe in predestination?"

"You mean, that things happen the way they're meant to in spite of us?" He smiled. "I guess I do." His dark eyes slid over her face hungrily. "I'm so glad it wasn't your time, Amanda."

"So am I." She reached up and touched his thin mouth with just the tips of her fingers. "Where is it?" she asked with an impish smile as a sudden delicious thought occurred to her.

He frowned. "Where's what?"

"My engagement ring," she said. "And don't try to back out of it," she added firmly when he stood there looking shocked. "You told the doctor and the whole medical staff that I was your fiancée, and you're not ducking out of it now. You're going to marry me."

His eyebrows shot up. "I'm what?" he said blankly.

"You're going to marry me. Where's Hank? Has anybody phoned him?"

"I did. I was supposed to call him back." He checked his watch and grimaced. "I guess it's too late now. He and the band are on the way back here."

"Good. They're twice your size and at least as mean." Her eyes narrowed. "I'll tell them you seduced me. I could be pregnant." She nodded, thinking up lies fast while Quinn's face mirrored his stark astonishment. "That's right, I could."

"You could not," he said shortly. "I never...!"

"But you're going to," she said with a husky laugh. "Just wait until I get out of here and get you alone. I'll wrestle you down and start kissing you, and you'll never get away in time."

"Oh, God," he groaned, because he knew she was right. He couldn't resist her that way, it was part of the problem.

"So you'll have to marry me first," she continued. "Because I'm not that kind of girl. Not to mention that you aren't that kind of guy. Harry likes me and Elliot and I are already friends, and I could even get used to McNaber if he'll move those traps." She pursed her lips, thinking. "The concert tour is going to be a real drag, but once it's over, I'll retire from the stage and just make records and tapes and CDs with the guys. Maybe a video now and again. They'll like that, too. We're all basically shy and we don't like live shows. I'll compose songs. I can do that at the house, in between helping Harry with the cooking and looking after sick calves, and having babies," she added with a shy smile.

He wanted to sit down. He hadn't counted on this. All that had mattered at the time was getting her away from the wreckage and into a hospital where she could be cared for. He hadn't let himself think ahead. But she obviously had. His head spun with her plans.

"Listen, you're an entertainer," he began. His fingers curled around hers and he looked down at them with a hard, grim sigh. "Amanda, I'm a poor man. All I've got is a broken-down ranch in the middle of nowhere. You'd have a lot of hardships, because I won't live on your money. I've got a son, even if he isn't mine, and…"

She brought his hand to her cheek and held it there, nuzzling her cheek against it as she looked up at him with dark, soft, adoring eyes. "I love you," she whispered.

He faltered. His cheeks went ruddy as the words penetrated, touched him, excited him. Except for his mother and Elliot, nobody had ever said that to him before Amanda had. "Do you?" he asked huskily. "Still? Even after the way I walked off and left you there at the lodge that night? After what I said to you on the phone?" he added, because he'd had too much time to agonize over his behavior, even if it had been for what he thought was her own good.

"Even after that," she said gently. "With all my heart. I just want to live with you, Quinn. In the wilds of Wyoming, in a grass shack on some island, in a mansion in Beverly Hills—it would all be the same to me—as long as you loved me back and we could be together for the rest of our lives."

He felt a ripple of pure delight go through him. "Is that what you really want?" he asked, searching her dark eyes with his own.

"More than anything else in the world," she confessed. "That's why I couldn't tell you who and what

I really was. I loved you so much, and I knew you wouldn't want me..." Her voice trailed off.

"I want you, all right," he said curtly. "I never stopped. Damn it, woman, I was trying to do what was best for you!"

"By turning me out in the cold and leaving me to starve to death for love?" she asked icily. "Thanks a bunch!"

He looked away uncomfortably. "It wasn't that way and you know it. I thought maybe it was the novelty. You know, a lonely man in the backwoods," he began.

"You thought I was having the time of my life playing you for a fool," she said. Her head was beginning to hurt, but she had to wrap it all up before she gave in and asked for some more medication. "Well, you listen to me, Quinn Sutton, I'm not the type to go around deliberately trying to hurt people. All I ever wanted was somebody to care about me—just me, not the pretty girl on the stage."

"Yes, I know that now," he replied. He brought her hand to his mouth and softly kissed the palm. The look on his face weakened her. "So you want a ring, do you? It will have to be something sensible. No flashy diamonds, even if I could give you something you'd need sunglasses to look at."

"I'll settle for the paper band on a King Edward cigar if you'll just marry me," she replied.

"I think I can do a little better than that," he murmured dryly. He bent over her, his lips hovering just above hers. "And no long engagement," he whispered.

"It takes three days, doesn't it?" she whispered back. "That *is* a long engagement. Get busy!"

He stifled a laugh as he brushed his hard mouth gently over her dry one. "Get well," he whispered. "I'll read some books real fast."

She colored when she realized what kind of books he was referring to, and then smiled under his tender kiss. "You do that," she breathed. "Oh, Quinn, get me out of here!"

"At the earliest possible minute," he promised.

The band showed up later in the day while Quinn was out buying an engagement ring for Amanda. He'd already called and laughingly told Elliot and Harry what she'd done to him, and was delighted with Elliot's pleasure in the news and Harry's teasing. He did buy her a diamond, even if it was a moderate one, and a gold band for each of them. It gave him the greatest kind of thrill to know that he was finally marrying for all the right reasons.

When he got back to the hospital, the rest of the survivors had been airlifted out and all but one of them had been treated and released. The news media had tried to get to Amanda, but the band arrived shortly after Quinn left and ran interference. Hank gave out a statement and stopped them. The road manager, as Quinn found out, had gone on to San Francisco to make arrangements for canceling the concert.

The boys were gathered around Amanda, who'd been moved into a nice private room. She was sitting up in bed, looking much better, and her laughing dark eyes met Quinn's the minute he came in the door.

"Hank brought a shotgun," she informed him. "And Deke and Johnson and Jack are going to help you down the aisle. Jerry's found a minister, and Hank's already arranged a blood test for you right down the hall. The license—"

"Is already applied for," Quinn said with a chuckle. "I did that myself. Hello, boys," he greeted them, shaking hands as he was introduced to the rest of the band. "And you can unload the shotgun. I'd planned to hold it on Amanda, if she tried to back out."

"Me, back out? Heaven forbid!" she exclaimed, smiling as Quinn bent to kiss her. "Where's my ring?" she whispered against his hard mouth. "I want it on, so these nurses won't make eyes at you. There's this gorgeous redhead…"

"I can't see past you, pretty thing," he murmured, his eyes soft and quiet in a still-gaunt face. "Here it is." Quinn produced it and slid it on her finger. He'd measured the size with a small piece of paper he'd wrapped around her finger, and he hoped that the method worked. He needn't have worried, because the ring was a perfect fit, and she acted as if it were the three-carat monster he'd wanted to get her. Her face lit up, like her pretty eyes, and she beamed as she showed it to the band.

"Did you sleep at all?" Hank asked him while the others gathered around Amanda.

"About an hour, I think," Quinn murmured dryly. "You?"

"I couldn't even get properly drunk," Hank said, sighing, "so the boys and I played cards until we caught the bus. We slept most of the way in. It was a long ride. From what I hear," he added with a level look, "you and that Hale fellow had an even longer one, bringing Amanda out of the mountains."

"You'll never know." Quinn looked past him to Amanda, his dark eyes full of remembered pain. "I had to decide whether or not to move her. I thought it was riskier to leave her there until the next morning.

If we'd waited, we had no guarantee that the helicopter would have been able to land even then. She could have died. It's a miracle she didn't."

"Miracles come in all shapes and sizes," Hank mused, staring at her. "She's been ours. Without her, we'd never have gotten anywhere. But being on the road has worn her out. The boys and I were talking on the way back about cutting out personal appearances and concentrating on videos and albums. I think Amanda might like that. She'll have enough to do from now on, I imagine, taking care of you and your boy," he added with a grin. "Not to mention all those new brothers and sisters you'll be adding. I grew up on a ranch," he said surprisingly. "I have five brothers."

Quinn's eyebrows lifted. "Are they all runts like you?" he asked with a smile.

"I'm the runt," Hank corrected.

Quinn just shook his head.

AMANDA WAS RELEASED from the hospital two days later. Every conceivable test had been done, and fortunately there were no complications. The doctor had been cautiously optimistic at first, but her recovery was rapid— probably due, the doctor said with a smile, to her incentive. He gave Amanda away at the brief ceremony, held in the hospital's chapel just before she was discharged, and one of the nurses was her matron of honor. There were a record four best men; the band. But for all its brevity and informality, it was a ceremony that Amanda would never forget. The Methodist minister who performed it had a way with words, and Amanda and Quinn felt just as married as if they'd had the service performed in a huge church with a large crowd present.

The only mishap was that the press found out about the wedding, and Amanda and Quinn and the band were mobbed as they made their way out of the hospital afterward. The size of the band members made them keep well back. Hank gave them his best wild-man glare while Jack whispered something about the bandleader becoming homicidal if he was pushed too far. They escaped in two separate cars. The driver of the one taking Quinn and Amanda to the lodge managed to get them there over back roads, so that nobody knew where they were.

Terry had given them the bridal suite, on the top floor of the lodge, and the view of the snowcapped mountains was exquisite. Amanda, still a little shaky and very nervous, stared out at them with mixed feelings.

"I don't know if I'll ever think of them as postcards again," she remarked to Quinn, who was trying to find places to put everything from their suitcase. He'd had to go to Ricochet for his suit and a change of clothing.

"What, the mountains?" he asked, smiling at her. "Well, it's not a bad thing to respect them. But airplanes don't crash that often, and when you're well enough, I'm going to teach you to ski."

She turned and looked at him for a long time. Her wedding outfit was an off-white, very simple shirtwaist dress with a soft collar and no frills. But with her long hair around her shoulders and down to her waist, framed in the light coming through the window, she looked the picture of a bride. Quinn watched her back and sighed, his eyes lingering on the small sprig of lily of the valley she was wearing in her hair—a present from a member of the hospital staff.

"One of the nurses brought me a newspaper," Amanda said. "It told all about how you and Mr. Hale got me out." She hesitated. "They said that only a few men could ski that particular mountain without killing themselves."

"I've been skiing it for years," he said simply. He took off the dark jacket of his suit and loosened his tie with a long sigh. "I knew that the Ski Patrol would get you out, but they usually only work the lodge slopes— you know, the ones with normal ski runs. The peak the plane landed on was off the lodge property and out-of-the-way. It hadn't even been inspected. There are all sorts of dangers on slopes like that—fallen trees, boulders, stumps, debris, not to mention the threat of avalanche. The Ski Patrol marks dangerous runs where they work. They're the first out in the morning and the last off the slopes in the afternoon."

"You seem to know a lot about it," Amanda said.

"I used to be one of them," he replied with a grin. "In my younger days. It's pretty rewarding."

"There was a jacket Harry showed me," she frowned. "A rust-colored one with a big gold cross on the back…"

"My old patrol jacket." He chuckled. "I wouldn't part with it for the world. If I'd thought of it, I'd have worn it that day." His eyes darkened as he looked at her. "Thank God I knew that slope," he said huskily. "Because I'd bet money that you wouldn't have lasted on that mountain overnight."

"I was thinking about you when the plane went down," she confessed. "I wasn't sure that I'd ever see you again."

"Neither was I when I finally got to you." He took off his tie and threw it aside. His hand absently unfastened the top buttons of his white shirt as he moved toward her. "I was trying so hard to do the right thing," he murmured. "I didn't think I could give you what you needed, what you were used to."

"I'm used to you, Mr. Sutton," she murmured with a smile. Amanda slid her arms under his and around him, looking up at him with her whole heart in her dark eyes. "Bad temper, irritable scowl and all. Anything you can't give me, I don't want. Will that do?"

His broad chest rose and fell slowly. "I can't give you much. I've lost damned near everything."

"You have Elliot and Harry and me," she pointed out. "And some fat, healthy calves, and in a few years, Elliot will have a lot of little brothers and sisters to help him on the ranch."

A faint dusky color stained his high cheekbones. "Yes."

"Why, Mr. Sutton, honey, you aren't shy, are you?" she whispered dryly as she moved her hands back around to his shirt and finished unbuttoning it down his tanned, hair-roughened chest.

"Of course I'm shy," he muttered, heating up at the feel of her slender hands on his skin. He caught his breath and shuddered when she kissed him there. His big hands slid into her long, silky hair and brought her even closer. "I like that," he breathed roughly. "Oh, God, I love it!"

She drew back after a minute, her eyes sultry, drowsy. "Wouldn't you like to do that to me?" she whispered. "I like it, too."

He fumbled with buttons until he had the dress out of the way and she was standing in nothing except a satin teddy. He'd never seen one before, except in movies, and he stared at her with his breath stuck somewhere in his chest. It was such a sexy garment low on her lace-covered breasts, nipped at her slender waist, hugging her full hips. Below it were her elegant silk-clad legs, although he didn't see anything holding up her hose.

"It's a teddy," she whispered. "If you want to slide it down," she added shyly, lowering her eyes to his pulsating chest, "I could step out of it."

He didn't know if he could do that and stay on his feet. The thought of Amanda unclothed made his knees weak. But he slid the straps down her arms and slowly, slowly, peeled it away from her firm, hard-tipped breasts, over her flat stomach, and then over the panty hose she was wearing. He caught them as well and eased the whole silky mass down to the floor.

She stepped out of it, so much in love with him that all her earlier shyness was evaporating. It was as new for him as it was for her, and that made it beautiful. A true act of love.

She let him look at her, fascinated by the awe in his hard face, in the eyes that went over her like an artist's brush, capturing every line, every soft curve before he even touched her.

"Amanda, you're the most beautiful creature I've ever seen," he said finally. "You look like a drawing of a fairy I saw in an old-time storybook...all gold and ivory."

She reached up and leaned close against him, shivering a little when her breasts touched his bare chest. The hair was faintly abrasive and very arousing. She moved involuntarily and gasped at the sensation.

"Do you want to help me?" he whispered as he stripped off his shirt and his hands went to his belt.

"I..." She hesitated, her nerve retreating suddenly

at the intimacy of it. She grimaced. "Oh, Quinn, I'm such a coward!" She hid her face against his chest and felt his laughter.

"Well, you're not alone," he murmured. "I'm not exactly an exhibitionist myself. Look, why don't you get under the covers and close your eyes, and we'll pretend it's dark."

She looked up at him and laughed. "This is silly."

"Yes, I know." He sighed. "Well, honey, we're married. I guess it's time to face all the implications of sharing a bed."

He sat down, took off his boots and socks, stood to unbuckle his belt, holding her eyes, and slid the zip down. Everything came off, and seconds later, she saw for herself all the differences between men and women.

"You've gone scarlet, Mrs. Sutton," he observed.

"You aren't much whiter yourself, Mr. Sutton," she replied.

He laughed and reached for her and she felt him press against her. It was incredible, the feel of skin against skin, hair-rough flesh against silky softness. He bent and found her mouth and began to kiss her lazily, while his big, rough hands slid down her back and around to her hips. His mouth opened at the same time that his fingers pulled her thighs against his, and she felt for the first time the stark reality of arousal.

He felt her gasp and lifted his head, searching her flushed face. "That has to happen before anything else can," he whispered. "Don't be afraid. I think I know enough to make it easy for you."

"I love you, Quinn," she whispered back, forcing her taut muscles to relax, to give in to him. She leaned her body into his with a tiny shiver and lifted her mouth. "However it happens between us, it will be all right."

He searched her eyes and nodded. His mouth lowered to hers. He kissed her with exquisite tenderness while his hands found the softness of her breasts. Minutes later, his mouth traced them, covered the hard tips in a warm, moist suction that drew new sounds from her. He liked that, so he lifted her and put her on the big bed, and found other places to kiss her that made the sounds louder and more tormented.

The book had been very thorough and quite explicit, so he knew what to do in theory. Practice was very different. He hadn't known that women could lose control, too. That their bodies were so soft, or so strong. That their eyes grew wild and their faces contorted as the pleasure built in them, that they wept with it. Her pleasure became his only goal in the long, exquisite oblivion that followed.

By the time he moved over her, she was more than ready for him, she was desperate for him. He whispered to her, gently guided her body to his as he fought for control of his own raging need so that he could satisfy hers first.

There was one instant when she stiffened and tried to pull away, but he stopped then and looked down into her frightened eyes.

"It will only hurt for a few seconds," he whispered huskily. "Link your hands in mine and hold on. I'll do it quickly."

"All...all right." She felt the strength in his hands and her eyes met his. She swallowed.

He pushed, hard. She moaned a little, but her body

accepted him instantly and without any further difficulty.

Her eyes brightened. Her lips parted and she breathed quickly and began to smile. "It's gone," she whispered. "Quinn, I'm a woman now...."

"My woman," he whispered back. The darkness grew in his eyes. He bent to her mouth and captured it, held it as he began to move, his body dancing above hers, teaching it the rhythm. She followed where he led, gasping as the cadence increased, as the music began to grow in her mind and filtered through her arms and legs. She held on to him with the last of her strength, proud of his stamina, of the power in his body that was taking hers from reality and into a place she'd never dreamed existed.

She felt the first tremors begin, and work into her like fiery pins, holding her body in a painful arch as she felt the tension build. It grew to unbearable levels. Her head thrashed on the pillow and she wanted to push him away, to make him stop, because she didn't think she could live through what was happening to her. But just as she began to push him the tension broke and she fell, crying out, into a hot, wild satisfaction that convulsed her. Above her, Quinn saw it happen and finally gave in to the desperate fever of his own need. He drove for his own satisfaction and felt it take him, his voice breaking on Amanda's name as he went into the fiery depths with her.

Afterward, he started to draw away, but her arms went around him and refused to let go. He felt her tears against his hot throat.

"Are you all right?" he asked huskily.

"I died," she whispered brokenly. Her arms contracted. "Don't go away, please don't. I don't want to let you go," she moaned.

He let his body relax, giving her his full weight. "I'll crush you, honey," he whispered in her ear.

"No, you won't." She sighed, feeling his body pulse with every heartbeat, feeling the dampness of his skin on her own, the glory of his flesh touching hers. "This is nice."

He laughed despite his exhaustion. "There's a new word for it," he murmured. He growled and bit her shoulder gently. "Wildcat," he whispered proudly. "You bit me. Do you remember? You bit me and dug your nails into my hips and screamed."

"So did you," she accused, flushing. "I'll have bruises on my thighs…"

"Little ones," he agreed. He lifted his head and searched her dark, quiet eyes. "I couldn't help that, at the last. I lost it. Really lost it. Are you as sated as I am?" he mused. "I feel like I've been walking around like half a person all my life, and I've just become whole."

"So do I." Her eyes searched his, and she lifted a lazy hand to trace his hard, thin lips. After a few seconds, she lifted her hips where they were still joined to his and watched his eyes kindle. She drew in a shaky breath and did it again, delighting in the sudden helpless response of his body.

"That's impossible," he joked. "The book said so."

Amanda pulled his mouth down to hers. "Damn the book," she said and held on as he answered her hunger with his own.

They slept and finally woke just in time to go down to dinner. But since neither of them wanted to face having to get dressed, they had room service send up a tray.

They drank champagne and ate thick steaks and went back to bed. Eventually they even slept.

The next morning, they set out for Ricochet, holding hands all the way home.

CHAPTER ELEVEN

ELLIOT AND HARRY were waiting at the door when Quinn brought Amanda home. There was a big wedding cake on the table that Harry had made, and a special present that Elliot had made Harry drive him to town in the sleigh to get—a new Desperado album with a picture of Amanda on the cover.

"What a present," Quinn murmured, smiling at Amanda over the beautiful photograph. "I guess I'll have to listen to it now, won't I?"

"I even got Hank Shoeman's autograph," Elliot enthused. "Finally I can tell the guys at school! I've been going nuts ever since I realized who Amanda was...."

"You knew?" Quinn burst out. "And you didn't tell me? So that's why that tape disappeared."

"You were looking for it?" Elliot echoed.

"Sure, just after we got home from the lodge that night I deserted Amanda," Quinn said with a rueful glance at her. "I was feeling pretty low. I just wanted to hear her voice, but the tape was missing."

"Sorry, Dad," Elliot said gently. "I'll never do it again, but I was afraid you'd toss her out if you knew she was a rock singer. She's really terrific, you know, and that song that won a Grammy was one of hers."

"Stop, you'll make me blush," Amanda groaned.

"I can do that," Quinn murmured dryly and the

look he gave Amanda brought scarlet color into her hot cheeks.

"You were in the paper, Dad," Elliot continued excitedly. "And on the six o'clock news, too! They told all about your skiing days and the Olympic team. Dad, why didn't you keep going? They said you were one of the best giant slalom skiers this country ever produced, but that you quit with a place on the Olympic team in your pocket."

"It's a long story, Elliot," he replied.

"It was because of my mother, wasn't it?" the boy asked gravely.

"Well, you were on the way and I didn't feel right about deserting her at such a time."

"Even though she'd been so terrible to you?" he probed.

Quinn put his hands on his son's shoulders. "I'll tell you for a fact, Elliot, you were mine from the day I knew about your existence. I waited for you like a kid waiting for a Christmas present. I bought stuff and read books about babies and learned all the things I'd need to know to help your mother raise you. I'd figured, you see, that she might eventually decide that having you was pretty special. I'm sorry that she didn't."

"That's okay," Elliot said with a smile. "You did."

"You bet I did. And do."

"Since you like kids so much, you and Amanda might have a few of your own," Elliot decided. "I can help. Me and Harry can wash diapers and make formula…"

Amanda laughed delightedly. "Oh, you doll, you!" She hugged Elliot. "Would you really not mind other kids around?"

"Heck, no," Elliot said with genuine feeling. "All the other guys have little brothers and sisters. It gets sort of lonely, being the only one." He looked up at her admiringly. "And they'd be awful pretty, if some of them were girls."

She grinned. "Maybe we'll get lucky and have another redhead, too. My mother was redheaded. So was my grandmother. It runs in the family."

Elliot liked that, and said so.

"Hank Shoeman has a present for you, by the way," she told Elliot. "No, there's no use looking in the truck, he ordered it."

Elliot's eyes lit up. "What is it? An autographed photo of the group?"

"It's a keyboard," Amanda corrected gently, smiling at his awe. "A real one, a moog like I play when we do instrumentals."

"Oh, my gosh!" Elliot sat down. "I've died and gone to heaven. First I get a great new mother and now I get a moog. Maybe I'm real sick and have a high fever," he frowned, feeling his forehead.

"No, you're perfectly well," Quinn told him. "And I guess it's all right if you play some rock songs," he added with a grimace. "I got used to turnips, after all, that time when Harry refused to cook any more greens. I guess I can get used to loud music."

"I refused to cook greens because we had a blizzard and canned turnips was all I had," Harry reminded him, glowering. "Now that Amanda's here, we won't run out of beans and peas and such, because she'll remember to tell me we're out so I can get some more."

"I didn't forget to remind you," Quinn muttered.

"You did so," Elliot began. "I remember—"

"That's it, gang up on me." Quinn glowered at them.

"Don't you worry, sweet man, I'll protect you from ghastly turnips and peas and beans," she said with a quick glance at Harry and Elliot. "I like asparagus, so I'll make sure that's all we keep here. Don't you guys like asparagus?"

"Yes!" they chorused, having been the culprits who told Amanda once that Quinn hated asparagus above all food in the world.

Quinn groaned.

"And I'll make liver and onions every night," Amanda added. "We love that, don't we, gang?"

"We sure do!" they chorused again, because they knew it was the only meat Quinn wouldn't eat.

"I'll go live with McNaber," he threatened.

Amanda laughed and slid her arms around him. "Only if we get to come, too." She looked up at him. "It's all right. We all really hate asparagus and liver and onions."

"That's a fact, we do," Elliot replied. "Amanda, are you going to go on tour with the band?"

"No," she said quietly. "We'd all gotten tired of the pace. We're going to take a well-earned rest and concentrate on videos and albums."

"I've got this great idea for a video," Elliot volunteered.

She grinned. "Okay, tiger, you can share it with us when Hank and the others come for a visit."

His eyes lit up. "They're all coming? The whole group?"

"My aunt is marrying Mr. Durning," she told him, having found out that tidbit from Hank. "They're going to live in Hawaii, and the band has permission to use the cabin whenever they like. They've decided that if I like the mountains so much, there must be something special about them. Our next album is going to be built around a mountain theme."

"Wow." Elliot sighed. "Wait'll I tell the guys."

"You and the guys can be in the video," Amanda promised. "We'll find some way to fit you into a scene or two." She studied Harry. "We'll put Harry in, too."

"Oh, no, you won't!" he said. "I'll run away from home first."

"If you do, we'll starve to death." Amanda sighed. "I can't do cakes and roasts. We'll have to live on potatoes and fried eggs."

"Then you just make a movie star out of old Elliot and I'll stick around," he promised.

"Okay," Amanda said, "but what a loss to women everywhere. You'd have been super, Harry."

He grinned and went back to the kitchen to cook. Elliot eventually wandered off, too, and Quinn took Amanda into the study and closed the door.

They sat together in his big leather armchair, listening to the crackling of the fire in the potbellied stove.

"Remember the last time we were in here together?" he asked lazily between kisses.

"Indeed, I do," she murmured with a smile against his throat. "We almost didn't stop in time."

"I'm glad we did." He linked her fingers with his. "We had a very special first time. A real wedding night. That's marriage the way it was meant to be; a feast of first times."

She touched his cheek lightly and searched his dark eyes. "I'm glad we waited, too. I wanted so much to go to my husband untouched. I just want you to know that it was worth the wait. I love you, really love you, you know?" She sighed shakily. "That made it much more than my first intimate experience."

He brought his mouth down gently on hers. "I felt just that way about it," he breathed against her lips. "I never asked if you wanted me to use anything...?"

"So I wouldn't get pregnant?" She smiled gently. "I love kids."

"So do I." He eased back and pulled her cheek onto his chest, smoothing her long, soft hair as he smiled down into her eyes. "I never dreamed I'd find anyone like you. I'd given up on women. On life, too, I guess. I've been bitter and alone for such a long time, Amanda. I feel like I was just feverish and dreaming it all."

"You aren't dreaming." She pulled him closer to her and kissed him with warm, slow passion. "We're married and I'm going to love you for the rest of my life, body and soul. So don't get any ideas about trying to get away. I've caught you fair and square and you're all mine."

He chuckled. "Really? If you've caught me, what are you going to do with me?"

"Have I got an answer for that," she whispered with a sultry smile. "You did lock the door, didn't you?" she murmured, her voice husky as she lifted and turned so that she was facing him, her knees beside him on the chair. His heart began to race violently.

"Yes, I locked the door. What are you... Amanda!"

She smiled against his mouth while her hands worked at fastenings. "That's my name, all right," she whispered. She nipped his lower lip gently and laughed delightedly when she felt him helping her. "Life is short. We'd better start living it right now."

"I couldn't possibly agree more," he whispered back,

and his husky laugh mingled with hers in the tense silence of the room.

Beside them, the burning wood crackled and popped
in the stove while the snow began to fall again outside
the window. Amanda had started it, but almost immediately Quinn took control and she gave in with a warm
laugh. She knew already that things were done Sutton's
way around Ricochet. And this time, she didn't really
mind at all.

* * * * *